Praise for the **CONFLUENCE**

ANCIENTS OF DAYS

"A lusciously scenic quest for the past in an
artificial post-human world, resulting in
revelations 10 million years deep."
The Daily Telegraph (London)

"Exciting . . . colorful . . . highly entertaining and
beautifully written, full of exotic settings, unusual
characters, nuggets of scientific speculation and a healthy
dose of decadence. McAuley is one of the field's finest
practitioners and here he is writing at the top of his form."
Publishers Weekly (* Starred Review *)

CHILD OF THE RIVER

"A complex and ambitious book full
of mysteries and Really Big Ideas."
Pittsburgh Tribune-Review

"Powerful . . . a crafty and inventive writer . . .
a strikingly vivid world . . . a panoply of
strong characters and shifting alliances."
Locus

"The spectacle becomes colossal and the action reaches
fever pitch. I look forward to the next volume."
Washington Post Book World

Other Books by
Paul J. McAuley

PAUL J. McAULEY

ANCIENTS OF DAYS

THE SECOND BOOK OF CONFLUENCE

An Imprint of HarperCollins*Publishers*

First published in Great Britain by Victor Gollancz 1998.

Portions of this novel were first published in radically different form
as the novelette "Recording Angel" in *New Legends* (ed. Greg Bear),
Random Century (UK), 1995.

EOS
An Imprint of HarperCollins*Publishers*
10 East 53rd Street
New York, New York 10022-5299

Copyright © 1999 by Paul J. McAuley
Excerpt from *Shrine of Stars* copyright © 2000 by Paul J. McAuley
Library of Congress Catalog Card Number: 99-20951
ISBN: 0-380-79297-4

First Eos paperback printing: May 2000
First Eos hardcover printing: July 1999

Eos Trademark Reg. U.S. Pat. Off. and in Other Countries,
Marca Registrada, Hecho en U.S.A.
HarperCollins® is a trademark of HarperCollins Publishers Inc.

Printed in the U.S.A.

WCD 10 9 8 7 6 5 4 3 2 1

www.avonbooks.com/eos

For Kim Newman,
compañero

In books lies the soul of the whole Past Time; the articulate audible voice of the Past, when the body and material substance of it has altogether vanished like a dream.

Thomas Carlyle

THE WHISPERERS

PANDARAS ENTERED THE shadowy arena of the Basilica just as one half of the defense force charged at the other. Tamora led the point of the attacking wedge, screaming fearsomely; Yama ran up and down behind the double rank of the defending line and shouted at his thralls to stand firm.

The two sides met with a rattle of padded staves against round arm shields. Shadows shifted wildly as fireflies swooped overhead like a storm of sparks. For a moment it seemed that the attack must fail, but then one of the thralls in the defending line gave ground to Tamora's remorseless blows. Instead of closing the gap as the man went down in the press, the first rank wavered and broke, stumbling backward into the second. Yama shouted the order to regroup, but his thralls fell over each other or simply dropped their shields and staves and ran, and the wedge formation of the attacking force dissolved as thralls began to chase each other around the Basilica.

In the middle of the confusion, Tamora threw down her stave in disgust, and Yama blew and blew on his whistle until everyone stopped running. Pandaras came toward them, trotting over the pattern of chalked lines Tamora had carefully drawn on the marble floor that morning. His two fireflies spun above his small sleek head. He said cheerfully, "Did they do something wrong? I thought it was very energetic."

"You should be in the kitchen with the rest of the pan scourers," Tamora said, and went off to round up the thralls so that she could tell them exactly what they had done wrong. Her own fireflies seemed to have caught some of her anger; they flared with bright white light and whirled around her head like hornets sprung in defense of their nest. Her long queue of red hair gleamed like a rope of fresh blood. She wore a plastic corselet, much scratched and scored, and a short skirt of overlapping strips of scuffed leather that left her powerfully muscled legs mostly bare.

Pandaras said, "They are armed with sticks, master. Is that part of your plan?"

"We do not dare give them proper weapons yet," Yama told the boy. Like the thralls, he wore only a breechclout. The floor was cold and gritty under his bare feet, but he was sweating in the chill air, and his blood sang. He could feel it thrilling under his skin. His vigorous black hair was bushed up by the bandage around his forehead. A ceramic disc, of the kind believed to have been used as coins in the Age of Enlightenment, hung from his neck on a leather thong. At his back, his knife hung in its goatskin sheath from a leather harness that went over his shoulders and fastened across his chest.

He said, "We had them at drill most of the day. You should see how they keep in step!"

Pandaras looked up at his master, affecting concern. "How is your head, master? Is the wound making you feverish? You seem to think an army of polishers and floor sweepers, armed only with sticks, can frighten away the crack troops of the Department of Indigenous Affairs by putting on a marching display."

Yama smiled. "Why are you here, Pandaras? Do you really have something to tell me, or have you come expressly to annoy Tamora? I hope not. She is doing the best she can."

Pandaras looked to either side, then drew himself up until his sleek head was level with Yama's chest. He said, "I have learned something. You may have exiled me to the bowels of this broken-backed, bankrupt and debauched department, but I have still been working hard for you."

"You chose your place, as I remember."

Pandaras said, "And now you may thank me for my foresight. I have news which affects our whole scheme here, and I beg to be allowed to lay my prize at your feet. I don't think you'll be displeased."

"You have been spying, Pandaras. What did you find?"

"It was in the mausoleum they call the Hall of the Tranquil Mind," Pandaras said. "While you two have been playing soldiers with the hewers of wood and drawers of water, I've been risking my life in intrigue. A deadly game with the worst of penalties for losing, but I have had the good fortune to learn something that affects our whole scheme."

The Hall of the Tranquil Mind was a black, windowless edifice carved out of the basalt wall of the big cavern which housed the Department of Vatication. Yama had thought that it was locked up and derelict, like so much of the Department.

He said, "I suppose you went there to meet your sweetheart. Are you still chasing that scullion? You are dressed for the part."

Pandaras had washed and mended his ragged clothes and polished his boots. He had found or stolen a red silk scarf which was knotted around his long, flexible neck with such casual elegance that Yama suspected he had spent half the morning getting it just so. His two fireflies spun above his head like living jewels.

He winked and said, "Chased, caught, wooed, won. I didn't come to boast of my conquests, master. It's an old tale oft told, and there's not time. We're in mortal peril here, if I'm any judge of the situation."

Yama smiled. His self-appointed squire loved to conjure drama from the slightest of events.

Pandaras said, "There is a gallery that runs along one

side of the Hall of the Tranquil Mind, under the rim of the dome. If you happen to be standing at the top of the stairs to the gallery, and if you place your ear close to the wall, then you can hear anything said by those below. A device much favored by tyrants, I understand, who know that plotters often choose public buildings to meet, for any gathering in a public place can be easily explained away. But fortune favors the brave, master. Today I was placed in the role of tyrant, and I overheard the whispered plotting of a pair of schemers.''

Pandaras paused. Yama had turned away to look across the shadowy Basilica. Tamora was marshalling the reluctant thralls into three ranks. Her voice raised echoes under the shabby grandeur of the vaulted dome.

Pandaras said, "It is more important, master, than playing at soldiers."

"But this is important, too. It is why we are here, to begin with, and besides, it is useful to stay in practice."

Yama did not add that. it helped satisfy something in him that hungered for action. His sleep had been troubled by bloodthirsty dreams ever since he had entered the Palace of the Memory of the People, and sometimes an unfocused rage stirred up headaches that filled his sight with jagged red and black lightnings, and left him weak and ill. He had been hard-used since he had reached Ys and escaped Prefect Corin, and he had been wounded in an ambush when they had first arrived outside the gates of the Department of Vatication. He needed rest, but there was no time for it.

He said, "I must hear what Tamora has to say. Walk with me, Pandaras."

"The blow to the head has given you delusions, master. You believe yourself a soldier."

"And you believe that you are my squire, so we are equally deluded. Hush, now. We will speak of what you heard when Tamora has finished with our poor warriors."

Tamora had jumped on to a square stone plinth which had once supported a statue—only its feet remained, clad in daintily pointed slippers which still retained traces of yellow pigment. She looked at the six decads of thralls who had gathered around her, allowing scorn to darken her small, triangular face. It was a trick she had taught Yama. To be a teacher, she said, was to be an actor first. Unless delivered from the heart, no lesson could be convincing.

The thralls were all of the same bloodline, lean and long-armed and bowlegged, with loose gray skin that hung in heavy folds from bony joints. They had long, vulpine faces, untidy manes of coarse black or umber hair that tumbled down their bent backs and muddy yellow or green eyes that peered out from beneath heavy brows. They were a stupid and frustratingly obdurate bloodline. According to Syle, the Secretary of the Department of Vatication, their families had served here for more than twenty thousand years. But although they were naturally servile, the unaccustomed drill had made them sullen and mutinous, and they took every opportunity to make it clear that Tamora and Yama had no real authority over them. They glared at Tamora, sharp teeth pricking their thin black lips, as she told them how badly they had done.

She said, "You have all taken your turn at defense, and you have all taken your turn at attack. You should know that if you are to win through or stand firm, you must stay in formation. A defending rank is only as strong as its weakest member. If he falls, someone must immediately take his place. If an attacking formation breaks through a line, it must stay together."

One of the thralls said, "They ran and we chased 'em down, mistress. What's wrong with that?"

Tamora stared at the man until he lowered his gaze. She said, "There might be reserves waiting behind a turn in a corridor. If your disorganized rabble ran into them, then you'd be quickly slaughtered."

"But there wasn't anyone else," the thrall mumbled, and those around him muttered in agreement.

Tamora raised her voice. "This is an exercise. When you fight for real, you can't assume anything. That's why you must fight as you're told, not as you want. It's very easy to kill one man on his own, much harder to kill him when he's part of a formation. When you fight shoulder to shoulder, you defend those on either side of you, and they defend you. That way you don't have to worry about the enemy getting behind your back, because to do that they'd have to get around the line. And they won't, not in the corridors. Elsewhere, in the open, you fight in squares, as you tried yesterday.''

When Tamora paused for breath, a thrall stepped out of the front rank and said, ''We'd do better, mistress, if we had proper weapons.''

''I'll break open the armory when you've mastered those sticks,'' Tamora said. ''From what I've just seen, I've a mind to take the sticks away.''

The thrall did not back down. He was taller than the rest, if only because he was straight-backed. There were streaks of gray in his long mane. Most of the thralls possessed only one or two dim fireflies, but six hung in a neat cluster above his head, burning nearly as brightly as Tamora's. He said, ''We won't be fighting with these sticks, so why do we practice with them?''

The thralls muttered and nudged each other, and Pandaras told Yama, ''That's what they've been complaining about, down in the kitchens.''

Yama felt a sudden hot anger. He strode forward and confronted the gray-maned thrall. ''It is discipline, not weapons, that makes a fighting force,'' he said loudly. ''Between all of you, there is not the discipline to attack a nest of rats.''

The thrall returned Yama's glare. He said, ''Beg your pardon, dominie, but we do know a bit about rat-catching.''

Some of the other thralls laughed and Yama lost the last of his temper; it was easily lost these days. ''Come on,'' he said. ''Come on then, rat-catcher! Show me how well you fight!''

The thrall looked around at his fellows, but none were willing to support him. He said uneasily, ''It's not you I want to fight, dominie.''

"You cannot choose who to fight!" Yama asked Tamora to lend him her sword, and presented it hilt-first to the thrall. "Take this! Take it right now!"

The thrall dropped his stave and spread his empty hands. "Dominie . . ."

From above, Tamora said sharply, "Do as he commands or slink away like the cur you are."

Yama thrust the hilt of the sword at the thrall until he had to take it or have it fall on his feet. "Take it! Good. Now hold it up. It is not a broom. It is a weapon. You can kill with the point or with the cutting edge, and if you do not have the taste for blood, you can render your enemy insensible with a blow to the head with the flat of the blade. However, I do not recommend you try the last against anyone less skilled than you. The man who wounded me that way lost most of his fingers when I countered his stroke. Hold it up. Keep the tip of the blade level with your eyes."

Tamora said, "If you're any kind of man, you must know that the higher the angle the better the thrust. Obey your master! Show him you're a man!"

The other thralls had broken ranks and backed away, forming a rough circle around Yama and the gray-maned thrall. They laughed now, and Yama scowled at them and told them what Sergeant Rhodean had told him so many times.

"Do not mock an armed man unless you wish to fight him." He pointed at the gray-maned thrall and thumped himself just below the breastbone. "Now thrust at me. Aim here. If you miss the heart, you might get a lung. Either way you will have killed me. Come on!"

The thrall made a tentative jab that did not carry more than halfway. Yama batted the square point of the sword aside and leaned forward and shouted in the thrall's face.

"Come on! Kill me, or I will tear out your eyes as a lesson! Do it!"

The thrall yelled and sprang forward, swiping wildly. Yama stepped inside the swing and caught the thrall's arm at the elbow, pivoted in a neat half-turn and threw him from his hip. The thrall let go of the sword when he fell; Yama had it before it could ring on the marble floor and with a smooth swing laid the edge at the thrall's throat. For a moment, he struggled against the urge to complete the motion.

The thrall looked up at him, his yellow slitted eyes glaring behind the agitated orbits of his six fireflies. In the moment of shocked silence, Yama looked around. None of the other thralls would meet his gaze. He smiled and reversed the sword and presented it to Tamora.

She sheathed it, jumped down from the pedestal, and helped the thrall to his feet. "Bravely tried. Better than anything anyone else has done." She looked around at the others. "I don't mind if you hate us, but I do mind if you can't get angry. Without anger you'll have only fear when it comes to a fight. We can't teach you how to get angry, but if you can manage it we can teach you how to direct your anger. Tomorrow we begin again. Now get out of my sight. Go on! Run!"

Pandaras applauded languidly as the thralls dispersed around him, their claws clicking on marble. He said, "A bold display, master. I had not thought you could play-act so well."

Yama shrugged. Now it was over he felt self-conscious. His head wound throbbed. He said, "I was not play-acting. I lost my temper."

Tamora said, "Like I said, that's what's needed. You're getting an edge to you, Yama. That's good. We'll make you into something like one of the Fierce People, eh? The thralls have been servants for thousands of generations, and we've been treating them like volunteers. We have been too kind. They take up arms not because they want to, but because they have been told to. Grah, they will not do anything unless they are told, and then they do what they are told and no more. They can march in perfect formation all day long without losing step, but they haven't the heart to fight."

Tamora was angry with herself, and so all the more unforgiving. Nothing had gone right since they had been ambushed by hired ruffians when they had arrived at the Gate of Double Glory.

She added, "We're just a couple of caterans. We'll do our best with what we've been given, but in the end it won't matter. Indigenous Affairs will march right in and slaughter the thralls and take this place inside a day. This is a poor diversion in your search, Yama. I'm sorry for it."

"Without this subterfuge, I would not have been able to enter the Palace without being questioned. Besides," Yama said, "I enjoy these exercises."

It was true. The sound of padded staves thumping on shields and the smell of chalk and sweat had brought back happy memories of all the afternoons he had spent training with Telmon and Sergeant Rhodean in the gymnasium of the peel-house. The practice fights satisfied a fierceness he had not known he had possessed.

Tamora said, "I forget how young you are, and how hopeful. We might make these poor fools believe they have the heart for a fight, but it'll delay their deaths by no more than a minute. They know they're going to die, and they know that their wives and children will be killed too, or put into slavery. We'll be ransomed, but because our ransoms have already been paid into bond with the Department of Internal Harmony, we'll be freed and given our wages, and that'll be the end of that."

"I pray you are right. I think that Prefect Corin is still searching for me, and he is a high official in Indigenous Affairs."

They had talked about this before. Tamora said with exaggerated patience, "Of course I am right. It is how it has always been, since the world was made. If it were not for the ancient protocols, there would be constant civil war here. Your Prefect will not be able to interfere. I am sure the Indigenous Affairs sent those fools to ambush us, and perhaps Prefect Corin had a hand in it, but now we are inside the boundary of this Department he will dare do nothing else.

"Listen. Here is the problem. Not your Prefect, but the real problem. We fight because we're paid. Once captured no harm will come to us. But the thralls fight because they've been told to fight, and they've been told to fight because that fat fool who rules this place and claims to see into the future predicts victory. The thralls know in their guts that she is wrong. That is why they are so sullen.''

Yama said, "We do not know that Luria does not have the powers she claims.''

"Grah. *She* knows that she doesn't, and so does Syle, and so do the thralls. And the other pythoness is no more than a whey-faced wet-brained child stolen from her cradle. I have not heard her speak a single word since we came here.''

Pandaras said, "From what I hear, Daphoene might be young, but she does have power, and that's why she is forbidden to speak. Luria fears her because she thinks that one day innocent Daphoene will expose her fraud. Master, I must speak with you about what I heard.''

Yama said, "Daphoene is very young. She may appear to keep her own counsel, but perhaps she has none to offer.''

Tamora laughed. "Yama, you're so innocent that you're a danger to all around you. For once your pet rat has said something sensible. If Daphoene does have true foresight, then Luria has every reason to keep her quiet. Syle too, and that bloodless wife of his. For Daphoene will know how badly the defense of this place will go.''

Yama said, "Well, we will see her at work soon enough.''

In two days, the oracle would be opened for public inquisition, and the pythonesses would answer the questions of their petitioners. It might be the last time the ceremony was held, for ten days after that the deadline for challenging the quit claim would run out. The Department of Indigenous Affairs would be allowed to march on the crumbling glory of the High Morning Court of the Department of Vaticination, and occupy the place where once Hierarchs had swum amongst maps of the Galaxy's stars, ordering the voyages of ships that fell from star to star through holes in space and time.

Pandaras told Tamora, "My master has paid you to help him find his bloodline, and it is a better and more honorable task than this game of soldiers. As you will at once see, if you let me tell my tale."

"You run if you want," Tamora said. "I'd like to see you run, rat-boy. It would prove what I've always thought about you."

Pandaras said, with an air of affronted dignity, "I'll ignore the slights on my character, except to say that those who attribute base motives to all around them do so because they expect no better of themselves. But while you have been playing at soldiers, I have been risking my life. Master, please hear me out, I must tell you what I heard."

"If this is more kitchen gossip," Tamora said, "then hold your yap. You'd inflate the breaking of a glass into an epic tragedy."

"Neh, and why not? It's a painful death for the glass concerned, leaves its fellows bereft of a good companion, and makes them aware of their own mortality."

Yama said, "Pandaras claims to have overheard a conspiracy."

"Master, she will not believe me. It is not worth telling her."

"Out with it, Pandaras," Yama said. "Forget your injured dignity."

"There were two of them. They were whispering together, but I heard one say, 'Tomorrow, at dawn. Go straightaway, and come straight back.' This was a woman. The other may have been a servant, for he simply made a noise of assent, and the first said, 'Do this, and I see a great elevation. Fail, and she lives. And if she lives we all may die.' Then they both moved off, master, and I heard no more. But it is enough, don't you think?"

Tamora said, "We should expect nothing less. These old departments are rats' nests of poisonous intrigues and feuds over trifles."

Pandaras said, "If we can trust no one here, why must we stay? We should cut our losses and run."

Yama said, "You have not told us who these plotters were."

"Ah, as to that . . ."

Tamora scowled. "Grah. You were scared, and didn't dare look."

"Had I leaned out over the gallery rail, I might have been seen, and the game would have been up." Pandaras batted at the pair of fireflies which circled his head; they dipped away and circled back. "These cursed things we must use instead of candles would have given me away."

"As I said, you were scared."

Yama said, "It does not matter. The gate is closed at night, and opens again at sunrise. Whoever leaves when it opens tomorrow will be our man."

Tamora said, "And when we catch him we can cut the truth from him."

"No," Yama said. "I will follow him, and learn what I can. If there is a conspiracy, of course. There may be an innocent explanation."

Drilling the thralls was all very well, but Yama had done little else in the three days since they had arrived here. He was beginning to feel as if he was suffocating in the stale air of the Department of Vaticination, with its meaningless ceremonies and its constant reverent evocation of the dead days of its long-lost glory. He wanted to see more of the Palace. He wanted to find the records of his bloodline and move on. He wanted to go downriver and plunge into the war at the midpoint of the world.

"It's obviously some plot against the fat bitch," Tamora said thoughtfully. "It's because of Luria's refusal to bargain with the Department of Indigenous Affairs that we're here. Without her, there would be no dispute."

" 'Fail, and she lives. And if she lives we all may die,' " Pandaras said.

"When your rat-boy agrees with me," Tamora told Yama, "then you know I must be right. Perhaps the best thing to do would be to do nothing. In any case, you should not leave this place, Yama. We are protected by law and custom only as long as we stay within the boundaries of the Department of Vatication. I know that you want to begin your search for the records of your bloodline. But be patient. In a decad, the Department of Indigenous Affairs will take this place, no matter how well we train the thralls. Then we can search together, as we agreed. You're already wounded, and we have been misled about the kind of troops we were to command, and our employers plot against each other. It's clear someone here has allied themselves to Indigenous Affairs, and hopes to make a bargain after assassinating their rivals. It doesn't matter who is plotting against who, for there's no honor to be won here. The defense is simply a matter of form before the inevitable surrender. Like all of Gorgo's little jobs, this has nothing to commend it. Another reason to kill him, when we are done here."

Gorgo was the broker who had given Tamora this contract. He had tried to kill Yama because Yama had cost him the commission on a previous job and because he suspected that, with Yama's help, Tamora might free herself of her obligation to him. Yama had killed him instead, riddling him with a hundred tiny machines, but Tamora had not seen it and she did not or would not believe in what she called Yama's magic tricks.

"If we find out more," Yama said, "then we can end the plot before it begins."

"Grah! And if you leave here before the end of the contract, you'll be assassinated. You will stay here, for your own safety."

"I can take care of myself."

Tamora said sharply, "How is your wound? Does it trouble you?"

"A headache now and then," Yama admitted.

He had the beginning of a headache now. He felt as if his skull was too small to contain his thoughts, as if his brain was a bladder pumped up by a growing anger. Red and black sparks crawled at the edge of his vision. He had to stifle an impulse to draw his knife and do some harm.

He said, "I will not make the same mistake again. And I will do as I will."

Pandaras said, "Perhaps my master should leave now. Go and find the records of his bloodline, for that's why he is really here."

Tamora suddenly whirled, smashing her stave against the plinth with such force that it snapped in two. She glared at the splintered stub in her hand, then threw it hard and fast down the length of the Basilica. "Grah! Go then! Both of you! Go, and accept what falls out. Death, most likely. Even if you dodge the hirelings of the Department of Indigenous Affairs, you know nothing about the Palace, and it is a dangerous place."

"I will come back," Yama said. "I promised that I would help you and I was taught to keep my promises. Besides, I hope to learn something here. Is not one of the attributes of this Department the ability to find lost things?"

IT WAS THE custom of the Department of Vatication that everyone, from senior pythoness to lowliest collector of nightsoil, took their evening meal together in the refectory hall of the House of the Twelve Front Rooms. The pythonesses and their domestic staff—the secretary, the bursar, the chamberlain, the librarian, the sacristan, and a decad of holders of ancient offices which had dwindled to purely ceremonial functions or nothing more than empty titles—raised up on a platform at one end of the refectory; the thralls ranged around the other three sides. The refectory was not a convivial place. Yama supposed that there had once been tapestries muffling the bare stone walls—the hooks were still in place—and perhaps rugs on the flagstone floor, but now the gloomy high-ceilinged hall was undecorated, and lit only by the fireflies which danced attendance above the heads of every man and woman. The thralls ate in silence; only the chink and scrape of their knives underlay the high, clear voice of the praise-sayer, who, at a lectern raised in one corner of the refectory, recited suras from the Puranas. Alone amongst several hundred sullen servants, only Pandaras dared glance now and then at the people on the platform.

Although the refectory was bleak, Yama found the formal style of the meals, a decad of courses presented at intervals by liveried thralls, comfortingly familiar. It reminded him of suppers at the long banqueting table in the Great Hall of the peel-house. He sprawled in a nest of silk cushions (their delicate embroidery tattered, stained and musty) at a low square table he shared with Syle, the secretary of the Department of Vaticination, and Syle's pregnant wife, Rega. The rest of the domestic staff were grouped around other tables, and all were turned toward the couches on which the two pythonesses reclined.

The Department of Vaticination was one of the oldest in the Palace of the Memory of the People, and although it had fallen on hard times, it kept up its traditions. The food was poor, mostly rice and glutinous vegetable sauces eaten with wedges of unleavened bread (the thralls had it even worse, with only lentils and edible plastic), but it was served on fine, translucent porcelain, and accompanied by thin, bitter wine in fragile cups of blown glass veined with gold and silver.

Luria, the senior pythoness, overflowed her couch, looking, as Tamora liked to say, like a grampus stranded on a mudbank. Crowned by a tower of red and gold fireflies, she ate with surprising delicacy but ferocious appetite; usually, she had finished her portion and rung the bell to signal that the dishes should be taken away before the others on the platform were halfway done. Swags of flesh hung from her jowls and from her upper arms, and her eyes were half-hidden by the puffy ramparts of her cheeks. They were large, her eyes, and a lustrous brown, with long, delicate lashes. Her black hair was greased and tied in numerous plaits with colored silk ribbons, and she wore layers of colored gauze that floated and stirred on the faintest breeze. Whenever she chose to walk, she had to be supported by two thralls, but usually she was carried about on a chair. She had been pythoness for more than a century. She was the imperturbable center of such power that remained in the faded glory of the Department of Vaticination, like a bloated spider brooding in a tattered web in a locked, airless room. Yama knew that she did not miss a single nuance of the whispered conversations around her.

The junior pythoness, Daphoene, was Luria's starveling shadow. Only a single wan firefly flickered above her flat, pale face, as if she were no better than the least of the kitchen thralls. She wore a long white shift that, girdled with a belt of gold wires, covered her body from neck to ankles. Her head was shaven, and lumpy scars wormed across her scalp. She was blind. Her eyes, white as stones, were turned toward the ceiling while her fine-boned hands moved amongst the bowls and cups on the tray a servant held before her, questing independently like small restless animals. She never spoke, and did not appear to hear any of the conversations around her.

Yama suspected that Daphoene was inhabited by more than one person. Lately, he had begun to sense that everyone had folded within themselves a small irreducible kernel of self, the soul grown by the invisibly small machines which infected all of the changed bloodlines. But Daphoene was a vessel for an uncountable number of kernels, a constant ferment of flickering fragments.

The formal evening meals were a trial to Tamora, and she guyed her unease by playing up the part of an uncouth cateran. That evening, after the argument in the Basilica, she had chosen to sit alone at a table at the far end of the platform, and was more restless than ever. But the more she played the barbarian, the more she endeared herself to Syle, who would incline his head toward Yama and comment in an admiring, mock-scandalized whisper on the way Tamora tossed and caught her knife over and over, or yawned widely, or noisily spat a bit of gristle onto the floor, or drank from the fingerbowl, or, as now, scratched herself with a cat's lazy self-indulgence.

"Quite wonderfully untamed," Syle murmured to Yama. "Isn't she so thrillingly physical?"

"She comes from a people not much given to formalities," Yama whispered back.

"Fortunately, we didn't hire her for her manners,"

Syle's wife, Rega, said. Rega was older than Syle, with a pointed wit and a sharp gaze that measured everyone it fell upon and usually found them wanting. She was tremendously pregnant; as round as an egg, as her husband fondly put it, in a shift of purple satin that stretched like a drumhead over her distended belly. She had twisted her feathery hair into a tall cone that sat like a shell on top of her small head.

"She is tired, too," Yama said. "We have both been working hard."

The praise-sayer had been reciting from the sura which described how the Preservers had altered the orbits of every star in the Galaxy, as a feoffer might replant a forest as a formal garden. A monument, a game, a work of art—who could say? Who could understand the minds of those who had become gods, so powerful that they had escaped this Universe of things?

Yama knew these suras by heart, and had been paying little attention to the praise-singer. But now the man paused, and began to recite a sura from the last pages of the Puranas.

The world first showed itself as a golden embryo of sound. As soon as the thoughts of the Preservers turned to the creation of the world, the long vowel which described the form of the world vibrated in the pure realm of thought, and re-echoed on itself. From the knots in the play of vibrations, the crude matter of the world curdled. In the beginning, it was no more than a sphere of air and water with a little mud at the center.

And the Preservers raised up a man and set on his brow their mark, and raised up a woman of the same kind, and set on her brow the same mark. From the white clay of the middle region did they shape this race, and quickened them with their marks. And those of this race were the servants of the Preservers. And in their myriads this race shaped the world after the ideas of the Preservers.

Yama's blood quickened. It was a description of how the Preservers had created the first bloodline of Confluence: the Builders, his own bloodline, long thought to have vanished with their masters into the black hole at the heart of the Eye of the Preservers. He saw that Syle was watching him, and knew that Syle knew. Knew what he was. Knew why he was here. The sura had been chosen deliberately.

Luria rang her little bell. The attendants cleared away the bowls of rice and the dishes of sauces, and sprinkled the diners with water perfumed with rose petals.

"You will watch the exercises tomorrow," Luria told Syle. "I want to know how the training of our defense force is proceeding."

Without looking away from Yama, Syle said, "I am sure that it is in capable hands, pythoness." Yes, he knew. But what did he want?

Tamora said loudly, "Well, we didn't kill anyone today, and I believe my friend's wound is healing."

She had spoken out of turn. Luria took no more notice than if she had belched.

Syle said, "I watched the exercises yesterday, pythoness, but I will do so again tomorrow. It is very diverting. You should see how well the thralls march."

"It's a pity they can't fight," Tamora said.

"I have had a presentiment," Luria told Syle. "You will see to it that all is well."

Tamora said, "If you've seen something with your cards or dice, perhaps you could share it with us. It could help our plans."

There was a silence. Syle turned very pale. At last, Luria said in a soft croak, "Not dice, dear. Dice and cards are for street performers who take your money and promise anything they think will make you happy. I deal in the truth."

Syle said, "The pythoness entered a trance today. If she has said little to you, it is because she is exhausted. You will see how hard divination is in two days' time, at the public inquisition."

"Syle likes to explain things," Luria said. "You will show him the progress you have made. He will then explain it to me."

"Oh, pythoness, you should see how the thralls march!" Syle said again, and began to describe the precision of the martial drills at length, falling silent only when the last course, iced fruits and sweet yellow wine, was served.

Luria ate a token mouthful, then rang her bell. The praise-sayer fell silent. The meal was over. Luria's chair arrived and she was helped into it by two tall strong attendants and carried away. Another attendant took Daphoene's arm, and she rose and followed him with the childlike trust of a sleepwalker. Her mouth hung open and there was a slick of drool on her chin.

As the thralls began to move out of the hall, followed by flocks of faint fireflies, Rega told her husband, "You are kinder to Luria than she deserves. Certainly kinder to her than she is to you, who works so hard for her."

Syle said mildly, "She worries all the time about the quit claim, and of course about the public inquisition. We are all a little short of patience, these days."

Rega said, "Luria has her fine troops, who can march in formation all day long without missing a step. Why should she worry about the quit claim?" She smiled sweetly at Tamora and said, "You're doing your best, I'm sure, but you must wish for proper soldiers."

"We only have what we have," Syle said, again gazing at Yama. "I'm sure the thralls will fight to the death."

"I'm sure they will," Rega said. She held out her hand, and her husband helped her to her feet. Her round belly swayed, stretching the panels of her satin dress. She added, "A very quick death it will be, too. Yama, Tamora, I don't blame either of you. Our good pythoness has said that there will be victory, and so she does not trifle to provide the means to ensure it. Of course, it isn't possible to sell even one tenth of her jewels and trinkets. Although she does not wear or use any of them, they are heirlooms and cannot be sacrificed for anything as trivial as the defense of the Department. And so we must make do, with the fate of the Department in the balance.''

Tamora drew herself up. She was very angry. She showed her sharp white teeth and said, ''If you find anything I have done that does not satisfy you, then I will resign at once.''

Syle made fluttering motions with his hands. ''Please. Nothing of the sort is intended. I myself have seen how well you have drilled our thralls. A thrilling sight, to see them march!''

''Then perhaps your reports have been misunderstood,'' Tamora said. ''Excuse me. I have work to do.''

Syle caught Yama's arm and said quietly, ''Walk with me, if you will.''

Yama looked after Tamora, but she had leapt from the platform and was already halfway across the refectory, the crowd of thralls parting before her as rice parts before the scythe. He said, ''Of course.''

Syle's touch, its implication of familiarity, excited him. He felt the same quickening nervousness which had possessed him whenever he had attempted a dive off the end of the new quay into the strong river currents in which the children of the Amnan sported so easily. Not precisely fear, but an anticipation that heightened his senses. He liked Syle too much to be afraid of him, and not only because the tall, slightly built man, with his delicate bones, fine features, and white, feathery hair, reminded him of his sweetheart, Derev.

Syle had taught him much about the history of the Department of Vaticination and of its trade of prognostication. There were very many ways of gaining foresight, Syle said, but almost all of them were false, and those that remained could be divided into no more than three types. The least of these was sortilege, the drawing of lots, or astragalomancy, the use of dice or huckle-bones or sticks, neither of which, as Luria had pointed out, were practiced in the Department, although they were much abused by charlatans. Of more merit were those methods classed as divination, in which signs were scried in the client's physiogonomy, as in metascopy or chiromancy, or in the landscape, or in dust cast on a mirror (Syle said that gold was best, but the finings of any metal were better than ordinary dust or the husks of rice grains used by village witches). The form most often performed by the Department was rhabdomancy, or dowsing, used to find lost property or to find the best place for the site of a house or to locate a hidden spring. Finally, there was true foresight obtained through visions, either in dreams or in waking trances. It was the most difficult and most powerful method of all, and it was by custom what the pythonesses would attempt in two days' time at the public inquisition, although these days most clients wanted answers to trivial questions, to find things that were lost or hidden (wills were a perennial favorite, for many slighted by the wishes of rich, dead relatives came to believe that, hidden somewhere, there was a true will which would favor them), to speak with the dead, or to gain assurance of the success of a new business or a marriage.

The problem was that, as Syle put it, the business of the future was a thing of the past. The ordinary citizens of Ys would believe a roadside cartomancer as readily as the pythonesses of the Department of Vatication, and other departments no longer called upon its services when planning their business.

"Syle wants to ask you something," Rega told Yama. "Be good enough to humor him."

"This is not the place," her husband told her.

"We will be able to say anything we like soon enough. Don't do anything to ruin it." Rega gave her husband a cold look, but allowed him to kiss her on her forehead before she took her leave.

As Syle steered him toward the broad stair at the far end of the hall, Yama said, "Where are we going?" Thralls made way for them. Pandaras had disappeared, no doubt in pursuit of another amatory conquest.

"I have something to show you," Syle said. He had the tentative touch of an old man, although he was not much more than twice Yama's age, and much younger than his wife. "I promise not to keep you long. Is your wound healing? You should let brother Apothecary attend to it."

"Tamora said that the dressing should not be disturbed," Yama said. "Besides, it is mostly bruising."

He had been embarrassed in the brief fight. The ruffians had rushed up from behind as Tamora, Pandaras, and Yama had climbed toward the Gate of Double Glory. One had struck Yama with the flat of a blade; dazed and half-blinded by blood, Yama had saved himself with a lucky swipe that had hit his opponent's sword-hand, severing two fingers and causing the man to drop his weapon. By the time Yama had wiped blood from his eyes, Tamora had killed three of the ruffians and the two survivors had fled, with Pandaras chasing after them and screaming insults.

"We have lodged a protest with the Department of Internal Harmony over the incident," Syle said. "If it is successful, then we may move on to a formal hearing. Unfortunately, the petition of protest must be read and approved by a clerk of court in the first instance, and then a committee will be deputized to discuss it. That may take no more than fifty or sixty days if the business is rushed, but I do not suppose it will be rushed. Nothing ever is rushed in the Palace, but of course that is only proper. These are serious matters, and must be taken seriously. After that, well, the process of establishing a hearing usually takes at least two years."

"And in twelve days the ultimatum delivered by the Department of Indigenous Affairs will expire."

Syle said, "Yes, but I have faith in you, Yama."

Yama had learned a little of the art of diplomacy from his stepfather, the Aedile of Aeolis. Nothing must be said directly; to ask a question is to lose advantage. He said, "I have never been in this part of the Department before."

"This was the main entrance, once upon a time. Now no one uses it but me. It leads to the roof."

They reached the top of the stairway and went down a long corridor. Its walls were paneled in dark, heavily carved wood and hung with big square paintings whose pigments were so blackened by time that it was impossible to discern what scenes or persons they might once have depicted. A rat fled from their footsteps, pursued by a single wan firefly. It disappeared into a hole in the paneling, and rolled the end of a broken bottle across the hole to stop it. The feeble light of the firefly flickered behind the thick roundel of glass as the rat lay still and watched the two men pass.

The corridor ended at a pair of round metal doors, with a metal-walled antechamber sandwiched between them. The inner door was open, the outer dogged shut. Syle shut the inner door behind them and talked to the lock of the outer door—Yama felt its dim intelligence briefly waken—then instructed Yama to spin a wheel and pull the door open. It moved sweetly on its counterbalanced track, and Yama followed Syle over the high sill.

They were on the wide, flat roof of the House of the Twelve Front Rooms. It was lapped with metal plates that fitted together like the scales of a fish. Behind it was the cavern, dark except for a few tiny stars where people walked, attended by fireflies. The other buildings of the Department of Vatication—the Basilica, the Hall of the Tranquil Mind, the Hall of Great Achievements, and the Gate of Double Glory—were set symmetrically around the edge of this great hollow, dark shapes sunk deep in darkness. On the other side of the House of the Twelve Front Rooms, beyond the looming arch of the cavern's mouth, was the night sky. A cold wind blew past skeletal towers which jutted from the outer edge of the roof. Syle explained that in ancient times drugged pythonesses lashed to platforms on top of these towers had searched for intimations of the future in the patterns of clouds and the flight of birds. Beyond the towers, a narrow walkway projected from a corner of the roof into the windy darkness. It was along this walkway that Syle now led Yama, who clung to the single railing with sweating hands.

The House of the Twelve Front Rooms faced toward the Great River; even at noon, only a shallow curtain of light fell into the mouth of the cavern. Directly below the walkway, a long steep slope of scrub and bare rock fell to the spurs and spires and towers which had accreted around the ragged hem of the Palace, covering it as corals will cover a wreck in the warm lower reaches of the river. Beyond, the lights of Ys were spread along the edge of the broad river; Yama could see, across a hundred leagues of water, the flat edge of the world itself against the empty darkness of the night sky. Downriver, where the world narrowed to its vanishing point, was a dim red glow, as if a fire had been kindled beneath the horizon.

In the windy dark, his mild face illuminated by his crown of fireflies, Syle said, "In a few hours the Preservers will look upon us for the first time this year."

"I had forgotten. Will there be celebrations?"

"Amongst the rabble of the city, yes. If we stay out long enough we'll see their fireworks and bonfires. And later, perhaps, the fires of riots, and then the flashes of the weapons of the magistrates as they restore order."

"Ys is a strange and terrible city."

"It is a very large city, and there can only be order by suppressing any disorder at once, by whatever force is necessary. The Department of Indigenous Affairs has raised an army to fight the heretics; that is why they want new territory. But the magistrates are a greater army, one which constantly strives against a greater enemy. It is because we have fallen from grace that the people war against themselves with more hatred than against the heretics."

Yama remembered Pandaras's story of how his uncle had been trapped when magistrates had laid siege to a block of the city which had refused to pay an increase in taxes. He said, "In the city where I grew up, the people celebrate the setting of the Eye of the Preservers, not its rising. They sail across the river to the farside shore and hold a winter festival. They polish and repair the settings of the shrines, and renew the flags of the prayer strings. They light bonfires, and feast and dance, and lay flowers and other offerings at the shrines."

"The ordinary people of Ys celebrate the rising of the Eye because they think that once more they are beneath the beneficent gaze of the Preservers, and all evil must flee away. They bang gongs, rattle their pots and pans, and light firecrackers to drive evil into the open. I am not familiar with your city, Yama, but I wonder why its people are glad to believe that they are free of this gaze. Surely they must worship the Preservers, for else they would be unique amongst the ten thousand bloodlines of the Shaped."

"They celebrate the beginning of winter. They dislike the summer's heat."

"Ah. In any case, although the Eye is named because it has the appearance of the organ of sight, it does not share the function of its namesake. Anyone with a little learning knows that when the Preservers vanished beyond the horizon of the Universe, they left behind servants to watch over us, their poor creatures. Were not the shrines once the homes of countless avatars who guided and inspired us? Are not all of the changed bloodlines infected with the particles of the breath of the Preservers, who will cherish our memories after we die?"

"I am glad to see the Eye. I have always preferred summer to winter. Is it what you brought me to see?"

"I would like to talk with you in private. Do not be afraid. This walkway has stood for longer than the Department. It was built long before Confluence entered its present orbit."

But Yama felt a chill vertigo, for they were now so far out that the buildings heaped along the hem of the Palace were directly below. A cold wind buffeted him; the walkway hummed like a plucked wire. All he could see of it was that part of its mesh floor beneath his feet, illuminated by the intense light of the single firefly above his head. He could lose his grip on the slender rail and fall like a stone through someone's roof. Slip, or perhaps be pushed.

"You are the first to come here with me," Syle said, "but then, you are a singular young man. Take your firefly, for instance. You should have allowed them to choose you, and not taken the brightest anyone has ever seen."

"But it did choose me." Yama had kept others from joining it because he feared that he would be blinded inside their ardent orbits.

"Some say that fireflies multiply in dark places hidden from our sight, but I think not. Every year there are fewer and fewer people in the Palace proper—by which I mean the corridors and chambers and cells, and not the newer buildings built over the lower floors. Once, even the least of bloodlines were crowned with twenty or thirty fireflies, and the Palace blazed with their light. Now, many fireflies are so feeble that they have become tropically fixed on members of the indigenous tribes which infest the roof, or on rats and other vermin. I doubt that there is another firefly as bright as the one you wear, except perhaps within the chambers of the Hierarchs. It will attract much attention, but it is fixed now, and will not leave you until you leave this place."

Yama said, "I hope that it does not put me in danger." He could order the firefly to leave, and then choose others more ordinary—but that might be worse than having selected it in the first place.

Syle did not answer at once. At last, he said, "You know that I find the cateran is very amusing, but I do not think that she will be able to marshal a successful defense of the Department."

Yama remembered what Rega had said. "If you gave us more men—"

"How would you train them? Indigenous Affairs will send an army of its best troops to enforce the quit claim."

"That is what Tamora thinks, too."

"Then at least she has some sense. But she is an ordinary cateran. I believe that you are capable of greater things."

Yama said warily, "You do?"

Yama's wise but unworldly stepfather had not known what Yama was. He had sent the apothecary, Dr. Dismas, to the Palace of the Memory of the People to discover what he could about Yama's bloodline, but Dr. Dismas had lied to the old man and claimed to have found nothing, and then tried to kidnap Yama for his own purposes. For the first time Yama wondered whether Syle, kin to his sweetheart and to one of the curators of the City of the Dead, who had shown him that he was of the bloodline which had built the world according to the will of the Preservers, was part of their conspiracy.

Syle said, "We have forgotten how to speak plainly here. In a department as old as this, words raise such echoes that their meaning might never be clear. Forgive me."

"But we are in the open air now."

"Luria has been pythoness for more than a century, but the Department is more than two hundred times older. I must be loyal to the Department first."

Yama saw the man's distress. He said, "No one can overhear us here."

"Except the Preservers."

"Yes. We must always speak truthfully to them." Syle gripped the fragile rail and stared into the night, toward the first light of the Eye of the Preservers. He said, "The truth then. I know what you are, Yama. You are one of the Builders. Your bloodline was the first of all the blood-lines the Preservers raised up to populate Confluence, and the machines which maintain this world have not forgotten your kind. All machines obey you, even those that follow the orders of other men. Even those which will not obey anyone else." He laughed. "There, I have said it. Rega thought I could not, but I have. And the world has not ended."

Yama said, "How did you find out what I am?"

Wind blew Syle's white, feathery hair back from the narrow blade of his face. He said, "Our library is very extensive."

Yama's heart turned over. Perhaps his quest was already over, before he had hardly begun. He said, "I came to Ys to search for my bloodline, and would very much like to see that book. Will you show me now?"

Syle said, "No, not yet. The library is closed to all but the pythonesses and the highest officers of the domestic staff. I would show you all I can, Yama, but I fear that I am more in need of help than you. I'm told that the Preservers act through you. If that's true, then whatever you do cannot be evil. You cannot help but do good. Don't deny the powers you have. I know, for instance, that the Temple of the Black Well was burned down on the day you entered the Palace. It seemed that someone woke the thing in the well and then destroyed it. As for us, a lesser miracle would suffice."

Yama had encountered two feral machines since he had arrived in Ys. In a desperate moment, he had called down the first without knowing what he was doing. The second had fallen in the wars of the Age of Insurrection, and men had later built a temple over the hole it had burnt through the keelrock. The machine had lain brooding within a tomb of congealed lava for an age, until woken by the same call which had brought down the first. With the help of the ancient guardians of the temple, Yama had reburied it. Machines like those had destroyed half the world in the Age of Insurrection, and although their time was long past, and their powers had faded as the lights of the fireflies had faded, they were still powerful. They shadowed the world from which they had been expelled, waiting, some said, for the Preservers to return to begin the final battle when the just, living and dead, would be raised up, and the damned thrown aside.

Beyond dismissing the fireflies which had eagerly flocked to him when he had entered the Palace, Yama had not tried to influence a machine since. He was scared that he might inadvertently wake more monsters from the past.

He told Syle, "I signed as a cateran, for a cateran's wages. That is the duty I will discharge to you, dominie, nothing more and nothing less. What you have learned from your library is your own affair. You have not shared it with the pythonesses, or you would not have brought me here to talk in secret. Perhaps I should ask them about it."

Syle turned to Yama and said with sudden passion,

"Listen to me! If you can help me, then I can help you find out about your bloodline. True pythonesses can see the past as well as the future. Just as our actions and wishes contain the seeds of the future, so the present also holds the echoes of actions and wishes of the past. Indeed, since there was only one past but there are many possible futures it is easier to read the past from the present than it is to predict the future. It is said that the Preservers could travel from the future into the past as easily as starships slip from star to star, but that they could not travel into the future because from the point of view of the past the future does not yet exist. And so with prediction."

"Yet it is said that the Preservers will return from the future, so there can only be one future, as there is only one past."

"Our world has only one past, but there are many possible worlds arrayed in the future. Some say that every step we take creates new worlds, which contain all the directions in which we could have turned. When looking into the future, a pythoness must encompass all these possible states and choose the most likely, which is to say the one which is most common. But the past is a straight road, because the world has traveled along it to reach the present."

"You do not speak of Luria, do you? You speak of Daphoene."

Syle nodded. "Daphoene has true sight. The business of this Department is to tell people what they want to hear, or what they most need to hear, which is not always the same thing. And so most of our business is concerned with collecting intelligence about our clients, so that we can satisfy their inquiries."

"You are very candid."

"If you will not help us, then what I tell you will do no harm, for the Department will cease to exist. If you do help us, then you will need to know these things. Some say that we practice magic, but in truth ours is a rational science."

Yama thought of the buzzing confusion in Daphoene's

head. Perhaps she was able to scry a path through the sheaves of possible futures because she was many people inhabiting a single mind, or perhaps what he glimpsed within her were futures continually appearing and dying.

Syle said, "Daphoene tells only the truth, and that is what scares Luria. She sees our clients driven away by the truth. Oh, do not think that Luria does not believe in her own powers. Of course she does. If her predictions come true, then she is satisfied; if not, then she will find some condition of the ceremony to be at fault, or she will say that something more powerful intervened to change events from the course she had divined. There can never be any blame on her part if what she predicts does not happen. But Daphoene is always right, and needs no ceremony. She speaks directly. I brought her here, Yama. I am responsible for her. I had hoped that she would be a true pythoness, and it seems that she is much more than I had hoped. Daphoene frightens Luria, and I fear that because of that Luria will destroy her. I would rather die than bear that."

No doubt this confession was supposed to win Yama's trust, but instead it made him wary. Syle was so accustomed to deceiving the clients of the Department of Vaticination that he habitually deceived himself, too, by pretending that everything he did was for the good of the Department and never for his own gain. But Yama suspected that Syle wanted to use him for his own ends. If Syle had been a little less clever, his motives might simply be venal, but nothing Syle did was simple. This seemed to be a straightforward bargain—a miracle in exchange for revelation—but Yama remembered the plot Pandaras had uncovered, and Tamora's harsh words. *These old departments are rats' nests of poisonous intrigues and feuds over trifles.*

He said, "If Daphoene can see into the future, then what does she say about the Department? Will it be saved?"

"She knows, but will not say. Do not think I have not asked, but she has set her heart against revealing what she knows. She says that if she speaks, then the future may be changed, and the fate of the world with it. All she will say is that it will not be saved by force of arms. I understand that to mean that you will intervene.''

''But if I asked her, would she speak plainly of my fate? Would she look into the future and see where I might meet my people?''

''She has already said something. That is why you must help us, Yama. If you do not, then yours will be a tragic fate.''

There, in the windy dark high above the oldest city in the world, Yama knew that Syle had baited a hook to set in his heart. But he had to ask.

''Tell me what she said, and perhaps I will know whether I should help you.''

Syle turned to regard the panorama spread far below. The darkling plain of Ys, the wide ribbon of the Great River stretching away toward the vanishing point, where the Eye of the Preservers had risen a finger-breadth above the edge of the world. He inclined his head, and said, ''There are two parts. The first is that you will either save the world or destroy it. She said that both things were connected. Do not ask me what she meant—she would not explain it to me.''

Yama said, ''Perhaps the first is more likely than the second. The world will continue as before, but some might say that I am responsible. I think that people have more faith in me than I have in myself.''

''Then it's time you learned to trust yourself,'' Syle said briskly. ''The second part is this: if you do not help me, then you will be betrayed to those you have already escaped. As I said, if you do not help the Department, then yours is a dark fate.''

Yama felt a chill of presentiment. His stepfather had sent him to Ys to become an apprentice to the Department of Indigenous Affairs, the same department he was now contracted to fight against. Although he had escaped Prefect Corin, the man to whom the Aedile had entrusted him, he had never escaped the fear that the Prefect, cold, ruthless, implacable, would find him again.

He said, "That seems more like a threat than a prediction."

"You do not have to give me your answer now, but it should come before the Gate of Double Glory opens tomorrow. Think hard on this, Yama, and remember that I am your friend."

"The future is uncertain, but you must know that I will discharge the duty for which Tamora and I were hired."

"To act merely as a cateran will not be enough," Syle said. "You know it is not enough. As a friend, I beg you to help us. I cannot be responsible for what will happen to you if you do not."

Yama would have asked him what he meant, but Syle suddenly pointed toward the city below. "Look there! How brightly they burn!"

Near and far, rockets were shooting up above the streets and houses and squares of the endless city, red and green and gold lights streaking high into the night air and bursting in fiery flowers that drifted down in clouds of fading sparks even as more rockets rose through them. The noise of their explosions came moments later, like the popping of kernels of corn in a hot pan.

Yama thought again of Daphoene. Her mind like the night sky full of sparks constantly flowering and fading.

Rising faintly on the cold wind came the small sound of trumpets and drums, of people singing and cheering. A flight of rockets terminated their brief arc in a shower of golden sparks a few chains beneath the walkway on which Yama and Syle stood. Bats took wing from crevices in the rock face below, a cloud of black flakes that blew out into the night and swept across the red swirl of the Eye of the Preservers.

AS SOON AS the inner door of the Gate of Double Glory had sunk into its slot in the roadway, the thrall who had been waiting in front of it walked beneath the round portal into the darkness of the tunnel. Yama left the doorway of the Basilica and, with Pandaras trotting at his heels, crossed the plaza. He hailed the gatekeeper and asked for the name of the man who had just gone through.

"You mean Brabant?" the gatekeeper said. "Why would you want him, dominie? He done something wrong?"

Yama hid a yawn behind his hand. It was just after dawn, and he had had only a little sleep. He had lain awake a long time on the narrow bunk in his little cell, thinking about everything Syle had said. It was as if his mind had split in two factions, and their armies of thought had gone to war inside his skull.

After he had inadvertently called down one feral machine and woken and defeated another, after he had murdered Gorgo in a fit of anger, he had sworn not to use his powers again. At least, not until he understood them. And as yet he did not know if he could do what Syle wanted him to do. He did not know if he could successfully defend the Department of Vaticination by warping the minds of machines to serve his own ends. Besides, if his powers came from the Preservers, then it was obvious that he should not use them for his own gain.

But in exchange for defending the Department of Vaticination, he might learn much more about his bloodline. And if he knew where he came from, then he might better understand his powers and what the Preservers wanted of him. And if he could master his powers, why then he might be able to do anything.

With this thought came a tumble of images. Yama flying on the back of a metal dragon, driving hordes of defeated heretics into the Glass Desert beyond the midpoint of the world. Yama clad in a buzzing weave of bright motes, preaching to a multitude on some high place, with the world spread beyond. Yama on a doffing ship, waking ancient machines from the depths of the Great River. Yama striking with a golden staff a rock in the icy wastes at the head of the Great River, and calling forth new waters to renew the world. And many more images, bright and compelling, as if his mind was trying to master all the futures into which he might walk. The visions possessed him, wonderful and terrifying. When he was woken by Pandaras it seemed that he had not rested at all.

And now, not half an hour later, he stood beneath the intricately carved portal of the Gate of Double Glory. The tunnel beyond it slanted downward, curving as it descended. The thrall, Brabant, had already passed out of sight.

"Brabant never did anything bad I heard about," the gatekeeper said. "And I know all about what comes and goes."

Yama said, "Did Brabant tell you what his business might be?"

The gatekeeper was an ancient but muscular and vigorous thrall, with a humped back and a white mane. He looked at Yama slyly. "It would be his usual business," he said.

"And what's that?" Pandaras said. "Speak civilly to

my master, fellow. He has the safety of your department in his hands.''

The thrall said, ''Why, it's well known Brabant has the keys of the kitchens of the household of the House of the Twelve Front Rooms. He's often out this early. The day markets open when the main gates open, and bidding is fierce these days. Things aren't what they were. There are shortages because of the war. You here to protect Brabant, dominie? He in danger?''

''It is a matter of security,'' Pandaras told the old thrall.

This seemed to satisfy the gatekeeper. ''Aye, I suppose we're in danger even now. They're not to start fighting the quit claim for more than a decad, but you can't trust Indigenous Affairs. It's a grower, see. Wants to get control wherever it can, however it can. But I do a good job. Don't worry about the gate. Nothing has ever passed me by without proper authority.''

For once, this was no idle boast. Tamora had surveyed the Department of Vaticination on the first day, and said that once the triple doors were lowered, the gate could not be forced without destroying most of the cavern.

''We should hurry, master,'' Pandaras said. ''We will lose him.''

''You will stay here, Pandaras. Stay here, and do your duty.''

''I'd do better going with you. I see you've taken off your bandage, but your wound won't have healed, not yet. And I've a fancy to seeing more of this place.''

''As you will, when we are done here. I promise it.'' Yama turned to the gatekeeper and said, ''How do you open the doors? There are three, I believe.''

The gatekeeper nodded. ''One here, dominie, another a hundred paces further down, and the last a hundred paces beyond that. To keep the air in, see. In the old days, the cavern was sealed around the House of the Twelve Front Rooms, but the bulkheads were sold for scrap years ago. Well, in the old days there was a word you'd speak and the doors would obey. But they're just metal now. The vital parts died long ago. So now we do it by water. You saw me haul on that wheel?''

It stood on a strong post inside the glass booth that clung to the right-hand side of the gate's round mouth. It was as tall as the gatekeeper, and spoked like the wheel of a wagon.

The gatekeeper said, ''It controls the sluices. Water is what does the job. It flows out of the counterweights and the doors sink down with it, and then it's pumped into a reservoir above our heads, ready to fill the counterweights to close up the gate as need be.''

''You keep watch on the gate all day?''

''My little house is up above the gate—see the stair? It winds right up to it. I'm cozy as a swallow in a godown roof up there.''

''Then when Brabant comes back, you will make a note of it?''

''I will keep watch,'' Pandaras said, ''although I'd rather come with you, master.''

''Your boy there needn't trouble himself,'' the old thrall said. ''I see everything that goes in and out. Our secretary Syle likes to know what's going on.''

~

The tunnel was lined with a slick, white material that diffused the light of Yama's solitary firefly; it was as if he moved at the center of a flowing nimbus. The tunnel turned a full circle as it descended, then opened on to a shaft ten times as wide, one of the main throughways that ran from top to bottom of the Palace. Like all the throughways, its gravity was localized; the tunnel met its roof at right angles. Yama stood at the beginning of a corkscrew ramp, looking straight across the throughway at the tops of sleds and carts and wagons that, spangled with lanterns, streamed past as if clinging to a sheer wall. But as he went down the ramp, the throughway seemed to turn around him, until at last he was standing on a walkway beside the traffic and the mouth of the tunnel he had left was a hole in the curved roof above his head.

There were few pedestrians, and Yama had no trouble following Brabant. The thrall was a sturdy fellow with a thick black mane done up in braids. He walked at a slow but steady pace along the walkway into the lower part of the Palace, where he took a ramp that spiraled up into the roof. It led to a short, narrow tunnel which suddenly opened on to a huge cavern filled with stalls and people.

It was one of the day markets. People from the hundred departments of the Palace of the Memory of the People were wrangling with merchants, gossiping, strolling about, or eating breakfast. The smoke of hundreds of cooking braziers and hotplates mingled beneath a low ceiling of stained concrete, a blue haze which defined a pale wedge of early sunlight above the flat roofs of godowns that stood shoulder to shoulder at the cavern's wide mouth.

Machines twinkled through the smoky air; thousands of fireflies spun above the heads of the people who crowded the aisles between the stalls. The noise was tremendous. The bawling of animals and the chatter of thousands of conversations echoed and re-echoed from the bare rock walls. In one part of the market, shoals of fish were laid on banks of smoking ice, and bubbling tanks held mussels and oysters and slate-blue crayfish; in another, tethered goats grazed on straw, placidly awaiting the knife. There were stalls selling erasable paper, inks and pigments, sandals, spices, every kind of fruit and vegetable, cigarettes, edible plastic, confectionery, tea bark, and much more, and at every one spielers praised the quality and cheapness of their wares. Here and there, soldiers of the Department of Internal Harmony stood on discs floating in the air, watching the crowds that surged beneath their feet.

Most of the people who had come to the market were clerks, low grade administrators or record keepers dressed in crisp white shirts with high collars and baggy black trousers. Everywhere he looked, Yama saw a reflection of the fate his stepfather had wished on him. Most people made way for him as he followed Brabant through the crowded aisles, and some even touched the inky tips of their fingers together; Yama realized that they were deferring not to him but to the spurious rank lent him by his single bright firefly.

The whole brawling tumult, lit only by the restless sparks of the fireflies and the smoky wedge of sunlight, reminded Yama of the emmet nest Telmon had once kept pressed between two panes of glass. He suddenly felt a suffocating sense of the vast size of the Palace of the Memory of the People, its mazes of corridors, the stacks of offices and chambers and apartments of its hundred Departments, its thousands of temples and chapels and shrines, all silted with a hundred thousand years of history.

Mendicants were preaching here and there, but few in the crowds stopped to listen. A line of nearly naked men danced down an aisle, lashing their shoulders with leather thongs; at an intersection, a group of men in red robes whirled on the spot to the frenzied beat of a tambour. The hems of their robes were weighted, and spun out in smooth bells as they whirled around and around; their faces glistened with sweat and their eyes had rolled back so that only the whites showed. They would dance until they dropped, believing themselves to be possessed by avatars of the Preservers.

Amongst the stalls were shrines and altars where men paused to dab a spot of ochre powder on their foreheads and mumble a prayer or turn the crank of a prayer wheel. Brabant stopped at one of the shrines, a glossy black circle framed by an arbor of paper flowers, and lit a candle and wafted its scented smoke toward his bowed face. Praying for the success of his traitorous errand, perhaps . . . or simply pausing for a moment's devotion amidst his ordinary duties.

After Brabant had moved on, Yama stopped at the shrine and touched the coin hung from the thong around his neck, but the shrine did not light. The Palace of the Memory of the People was littered with shrines—Yama had found more than a hundred in the cavern of the Department of Vatication—but he had not yet found one that would show him the garden where the woman in white waited for him. Perhaps it was just as well. He was not yet ready to confront his enemy again.

Yama pushed on until once more he glimpsed Brabant's braided mane amongst the press of clerks and record keepers. The thrall seemed to know every other person in the market, and stopped at stalls to shake hands and exchange a few words with the merchants, or taste a sample of food. He sat a while with a spice seller amongst aromatic sacks, and chatted amiably while sipping tea from a copper bowl. Yama, watching from the other side of the wide crowded aisle, ate sugary fried almonds from a paper bag translucent with grease and wondered if the plot might be one of assassination by poison, or if Brabant was simply negotiating a good price for turmeric and mace.

Brabant shook the spice seller's hand and got up and moved on through the market, saluting merchants, tasting samples and exclaiming fulsomely over their freshness, shouting greetings to passersby. If he was on a clandestine errand, he seemed to want everyone to know where he was; Yama's initial small doubt grew stronger.

At last, Brabant reached the far end of the huge market and entered a corridor with three- or four-story houses on either side, like an ordinary street under a concrete sky. There was more light here, pouring through a big curved window let into the ceiling at the far end, where palm trees rose from clumps of sawgrass. A flock of parrots chased from tree to tree, calling raucously.

A woman sat at a second-floor window of one of the houses, sleepily combing her long black hair. Below her, a man in a linen burnoose sat on a high stool outside the door. Brabant stopped to talk with the man, then shook his hand and went inside.

Yama walked past, suddenly feeling foolish and out of place. It seemed clear that Brabant had done no more than go about his business in the market before visiting a bawdy house for relaxation. Perhaps the thralls were one of those bloodlines which could mate at will, rather than on a particular day in a cycle or a season. Yet Yama was reluctant to leave. He felt that he should see this through to the end.

He drifted toward the edge of a crowd which had gathered under the palm trees at the end of the street, where a gambler restlessly switched three half shells around each other on a little table. Men in white shirts threw coins on the table, pointing at one or another of the shells, and when the betting was finished the gambler lifted the shells one by one, revealing a black pearl under the middle one. He scooped up the coins, pressed a few into the outstretched hands of two of the spectators and pocketed the rest, then covered the black pearl and began to switch the shells back and forth again.

While the spectators made more bets, the gambler caught Yama's eye and said, "I can't allow you a wager, dominie. A man like you could ruin me in a single game."

Yama smiled, and said that in any case he did not gamble.

"Then you may try your luck for the fun of it," the gambler said. He had an engaging smile, and eyes as blue as cornflowers in a pale face. A single firefly crouched in his crest of red hair, as faint as the one which had followed the rat in the old entrance hall of the House of the Twelve Front Rooms.

The gambler took his hands away from the shells, and Yama, gripped by a sudden impulse, pointed to the middle one. The gambler raised an eyebrow and lifted the shell to reveal the black pearl. The white-shirted clerks around Yama groaned. The gambler took in their money, winked at Yama, and started shuffling the shells again. Yama watched closely this time, and it seemed that the shell hiding the pearl was again in the center—yet at the same time he knew it was under the shell on the right. The clerks finished laying their bets, and again Yama pointed, this time meeting the gambler's smile with his own when the pearl was revealed.

The clerks murmured amongst themselves and the gambler said, "You see through my little illusion, dominie.

Maybe you'd like to try your skill on something a little harder.''

"Perhaps another time."

The gambler looked around at the spectators, as if calling upon them to witness his bravado. He said, "I'd only ask you to risk a copper rial on your skill. To a man like you that's nothing, and you'd stand to win much more from me. I'll give you odds of ten to one."

Yama remembered the fierce leathery nomads who in summer came into Aeolis with their horses and hunting cats and tents of stitched hides to sell the pelts of fitchets, marmots, and hares they had trapped in the foothills of the Rim Mountains. The nomads' dice games went on for days, drawing those who joined them deeper and deeper, until, from beginning with small wagers, they emerged as from a dream, dazed and penniless, sometimes without even their shoes and shirts.

"Your odds are too much in my favor," he told the gambler, and some of the clerks laughed.

"They are in it together," someone said. He was a tall boy not much older than Yama, flanked by two others as he pushed to the front of the crowd. All three wore enameled badges of a fist closed around a lightning bolt pinned to the high collars of their white shirts.

"I assure you," the gambler told the boy, "that I have never seen this good fellow before."

"Cheats and swindlers," the tall boy said. "You rig the game and let your friend win to make others think that they have a chance."

The gambler started to protest again, but his mild manner enraged the boy, who leaned on the little table and shouted into his face. One of the other boys swept the shells on to the floor and his leader shouted that there was no pearl and it was no game at all, but a sharpy's trick.

Yama hardly heard him. He had just seen a man come out of the bawdy house. He wore a tunic of plain homespun girdled with a red cord, and his face was covered in a glossy black pelt, with a white stripe down the left side.

He carried a staff taller than himself, and Yama knew that it was shod with iron. For he recognized the man at once, and with a shock knew that Brabant must be involved in a conspiracy after all.

The man was Prefect Corin.

"A SHARPY'S TRICK," the leader of the boys shouted. "We will have justice! Grab them both, lads—the one with the knife first."

One boy seized Yama's arms. The other wrenched the sheathed knife from its harness and handed it to the leader, who thrust it into Yama's face and said, "By what authority do you carry a weapon here?"

"By my own," Yama said. "What business is it of yours?"

The crowd murmured at this. The tall boy scowled. He and his two friends were young and excited and more nervous than Yama, not quite sure what they had discovered. They were not guards or soldiers, who would have taken Yama away for interrogation, but apprentices of some kind, eager and awkward, daring each other on.

"You've been on Department territory ever since you entered the day market," the leader of the three said. "Why are you carrying this antique? Is it licensed?"

The gambler said, "I beg your pardon, masters, but this is common ground, as is well known."

"Keep out of it, animal," the boy who held Yama's

knife said. He looked around at the press of clerks and added, "You all keep out of it."

The boy holding Yama's arms said, "Answer Philo, you piece of shit."

"It is mine," Yama said. He hoped that their leader, Philo, would try and draw the knife, for surely the knife would waken and defend him.

But Philo merely dangled the sheathed knife by its clip. He had a small face framed by a bob of glossy black fur, a flat, bridgeless nose, and a wide mouth. He thrust his face so close to Yama that he laid a little spray of spittle of Yama's cheek when he spoke. His breath was scented with cloves.

"This? This is at least ten thousand years old. What is a kid like you doing with it? Explain yourself. If your business is innocent we will let you go."

"I will fetch the guards," one of the clerks said.

"We do not need guards," Philo said loudly, turning this way and that as he tried to identify the man who had spoken. "We are stronger. We will deal with these cheats in our own way."

"You are fools," the clerk said. He turned his back on Philo with contempt, and the crowd parted to let him through.

The crowd had grown. Yama could no longer see Prefect Corin. From the center of a great calm, he told Philo, "You have no authority over me. You may kill me with my own knife if it is not true."

"I will cut out your insolent tongue," Philo said.

All three boys laughed. Philo's smile widened and he gripped the hilt of the knife. There was a blue flash. Philo screamed and dropped the knife and clutched his hand. Blackened skin hung in strips from it. There was a smell of burned meat. Yama felt a slight relaxation in the grip of the boy who held him. He stamped on the boy's instep, wrenched free, and kicked the boy's legs from under him. The third boy drew a slug pistol and pointed it at Yama. The pistol's muzzle was describing shaky arcs, but they were centered on Yama's chest. The clerks behind him moved to either side. All this time, Philo was screaming that he had been killed.

"Give it up," the boy with the pistol said.

"I will walk away," Yama said, "and that will be an end to this."

Many at the front of the crowd were trying to escape through those behind, who were pressing forward because they wanted to see what was going on. Yama glimpsed Prefect Corin. He was striking out with his staff as he tried to push through the mêlée. A decad of armed men was at his back.

"Give it up," the boy with the pistol said again. He was braver than Yama had reckoned. "Give it up or I will put a big hole through you."

Yama squeezed his eyes shut. The explosive brightness as his firefly gave up all its light in one instant printed his vision with red and gold. All around him, men screamed that they were blinded. The slug pistol went off—the boy must have pulled the trigger by reflex—and something whooped past Yama's left ear. Another scream: one of the bystanders had been hit. When Yama opened his eyes, ghostly volumes of light seemed to hang in the air. The three boys and the clerks at the front of the crowd were clutching at their eyes; Philo was screaming louder than ever.

"I am blinded! I am blinded!"

A hand fell on Yama's shoulder. "Come with me, dominie," the gambler said, and dashed something to the floor.

At once, dense red smoke billowed up around the blinded men. It obscured Prefect Corin and his band of men, who were still trying to fight through the panicky crowd. Overhead, soldiers on floating discs swooped into the street.

"With me!" the gambler said. "We are your friends!"

But Yama shook off his grip, scooped up the knife and its sheath, and ran in the other direction, toward the sunlit stand of palm trees. Prefect Corin broke out of the bank of red smoke as some of his men started to shoot at the soldiers in the air. The soldiers spun around and shot back. Yama ran beneath a rain of fronds cut down by small arms fire. Sawgrass caught at his trousers; parrots fled in a whir of wings.

Beyond the trees was a slender metal bridge which arched across a narrow deep cleft. Something beat down there, slow and steady and vast; Yama could feel its pulse through the soles of his boots as he went over the bridge.

Then a glass-walled tunnel that ran along the side of a sheer rock face, with the slope of the mountain falling to the mosaic of the city, and mountains in the misty distance. The curved wall suddenly crazed into a thousand splinters; a moment later Yama heard the sharp echo of a pistol shot, and then Prefect Corin shouted his name.

Yama turned.

The Prefect and three of his men stood fifty paces away. "Well met, Yamamanama," Prefect Corin said.

He looked quite unruffled, standing straight with his staff grounded beside him. He was not even out of breath. One of the men had a bandaged hand. He was the ruffian Yama had wounded outside the gate of the Department of Vaticination.

Yama held the knife by the side of his leg. He said, as calmly as he could, "You escaped the magistrates, then."

Prefect Corin said amicably, "As did you. You talked to their machines, did you not? Your father should have told me about that trick, but no matter. Here you are anyway."

"I will not come back," Yama said, and raised his knife when Prefect Corin stepped forward.

Two of his men aimed pistols at Yama; the third, the one with the bandaged hand, cocked an arbalest.

"We have no wish to harm you," Prefect Corin said. "You must be very tired and confused after your adventures, but you have come home now. You have found us, as the Preservers wished. We have a lot to talk about, you and I. There have been sightings of feral machines in the city, and the Temple of the Black Well was destroyed by the Thing Below. Did you speak to them, too?"

Yama said, "You lured me here, but I will not come with you. I will not serve."

"Oh, but you will. The day market is not yet under the Department's authority, but this place is, for it leads directly to one of the gates of the Department. You ran where I wanted you to run, Yama. The soldiers of Internal Harmony cannot help you here. Come with me, and you will be treated like a tetrarch if you can do half the things I believe you are capable of doing. Come with me now. Come home. Your father and your sweetheart will be pleased that you have turned up safe and sound."

For an instant, Yama was aware of every machine around him, all the way out to the edge of the day market. He spoke to one and turned and struck at the splintered glass with the knife. Blue light flared. Prefect Corin shouted and threw aside his staff and ran at Yama, and Yama hurled himself bodily at the circle of splintered glass and plunged through it into the open air.

THE CITY AND the side of the mountain described a perfect somersault around Yama's head. Then something flashed toward him out of the blue sky and he hit it hard, knocking his breath away. It was the floating disc he had stolen from under the feet of one of the soldiers.

With one hand Yama held onto the knife and its sheath; with the other the edge of the disc. Its smooth flat shape was hot from its rapid passage through the air and it stung Yama's skin, but he clung on tightly as it made a breathtaking swoop toward a huddle of roofs far below, halting just above a flat apron of red adobe. Yama landed in a tumble, bruising hip and knee and shoulder and dropping the knife and its sheath.

He got up and dusted his hands on the seat of his trousers. His wounded head ached. When he touched it his fingers came away smudged with sticky blood.

The disc hung in the air like an obedient pet awaiting a command. When he dismissed it, it shot away at once, rising at a steep angle against the sheer mountainside. It caught the light of the sun for a moment, and then it was gone.

Yama picked up his knife and sheathed it. He judged

that he had fallen at least five furlongs; the glass tunnel from which he had thrown himself was no more than a gleaming thread, as fine as a hair, laid between two black crags that were themselves only interruptions in the mountain's ascent into the blue sky.

Somewhere up there was the cavern which contained the Department of Vatication. Tamora would be hard at work, drilling the sullen thralls for their brief, futile battle. He could leave her and Pandaras, Yama thought, and continue alone on his quest for the library of the Department of Apothecaries and Chirurgeons, the place where Dr. Dismas had claimed to have found records of his bloodline. But he knew that he would not. He had sworn to help her, as she had sworn to help him. And at the very least he must tell them about Prefect Corin and the attempted kidnapping. It seemed certain that the conversation Pandaras had overheard was nothing but a lure aimed to draw Yama into a trap.

More immediately, he must find a way back into the mountain. Beyond the parapet at the edge of the flat roof was a drop to the slope of terracotta tiles, and then the roofs of a huddle of buildings and the slope of the mountain falling away to the hatched plain of the great city. As Yama contemplated this vista something cracked like a whip past his ear, shattered half a dozen tiles, and went whooping away into the distance. He remembered the ruffians' slug pistols and immediately jumped over the parapet and ran down the slope of sun-warmed tiles. Another slug split the air and he changed direction and tripped and suddenly was rolling down the slope amidst a small avalanche of loosened tiles. He grabbed at the edge of the roof and for a moment hung there, breathing hard—and then the tiles gave way.

He landed on his back on a cushion of thick moss. Amazingly, he had not let go of his sheathed knife. All around, terracotta tiles smashed to dust and flinders. Small animals fled, screaming. Monkeys, with silver-gray coats and long tails that ended in tufts of black hair. They jumped onto a shelf of black rock at the far end of the shadowy courtyard, their wrinkled faces both anxious and mournful. Dwarf cedar trees, their roots clutching wet black rocks, made islands in a sweep of raked gravel littered with the hulls of pistachio nuts. On three sides of the courtyard were black wooden walls painted with stylized eyes in interlocked swirls of red and white; on the fourth was a clerestory.

When Yama stood, the largest of the monkeys ran forward and swarmed up a rope and swung from side to side. A gong started a brazen clamor somewhere beyond the clerestory's arches.

Yama ran. A broad stair led down from the clerestory to a huge, vaulted hall paneled with carved wood. The plaster ceiling was painted black, with a triple armed swirl of white that represented the Galaxy at one end and a recurved red swirl that represented the Eye of the Preservers at the other. This was the temple of a latriatic cult, then, one of those which believed that the grace of the Preservers could be restored to the world by contemplation, prayer and invocation.

The gong was louder here, battering the cool air with waves of brassy sound. Suddenly, shaven-headed monks in orange robes rushed into the far end of the hall. They were armed with a motley collection of spears and cutlasses; one carried a hoe. Yama drew his knife, but even as the monks started to advance toward him, light flared in the center of the hall and they fell to their knees and dropped their weapons on the ebony floor.

At first, Yama thought that part of the roof had been opened to admit the light of the sun. Then, shading his eyes against the glare with his forearm, he saw that a shrine stood in the middle of it. It was an upright disc twice his height, and it was filled with restless white light.

Yama drew the coin from his shirt and, raising it as high as the thong looped around his neck would allow, advanced toward the shrine. He thought that the woman in white had found him again, drawn by the coin, but as the blazing light beat around him, he was seized by a deep dread. Not her, which would have been bad enough, but something worse. Something huge and fierce and implacable advancing through the light, very far away in the folded space within the shrine but rapidly growing closer, stooping toward him as a lammergeyer stoops through leagues of air to snatch an oryx grazing on a mountain crag.

Yama's nerve failed. He dropped the coin into his shirt, and ran past the shrine, dodging between the monks on the far side. They were groveling with their foreheads pressed to the ebony floor, their buttocks higher than their heads. Not one moved to stop him.

He ran out into open air, along a stone terrace and down a long flight of steps dished by the tread of countless feet. Monks in orange robes turned to watch as he ran past them down narrow stone paths between plots of pumpkin vines, yams and manioc.

The brass gong suddenly fell silent, and there was only the buzz of insects and the distant roar of the city. Yama did not stop. Once again he had accidentally brought something into the world. He ran from it headlong, with nothing in his head but his hammering pulse.

This part of the mountain had been built over with temples and monasteries and sanctuaries. Many stood on the ruins of older structures. Staircases descended sheer rock faces carved with grottoes and shrines. Viaducts and bridges and walkways strung across gorges and looped between crags. One pinnacle had been hollowed out; a hundred small square windows pierced its steep sides. Slopes were intricately terraced into long narrow fields where vines and vegetables grew, irrigated by stone cisterns that collected rainwater from fan-shaped slopes of white stone.

Yama spent the rest of the day descending the mountain. It seemed that there was always a flight of ravens turning in the air beyond the steep mountainside. He hoped this was not a bad omen, for ravens, particularly those of the Palace of the Memory of the People, were said by some to be spies. Far below, the city, immemorial Ys, stretched away into blue distances under a rippling layer of smoggy air.

Around noon, as the sun paused at the height of its leap into the sky before falling back toward the Rim Mountains, he arrived at a long terrace thatched in emerald green grass. An ornate fountain of salt-white stone splashed and bubbled in the middle. He drank from one of the fountain's clam shell basins until his belly was full, and washed dust and dried blood from his face, but he did not dare stop for long. He was aware of the populous mountain that reared above. Prefect Corin might be watching his flight through a telescope, and the thing that lived in the light of the shrine might be following him.

He had no clear sense of where he was going. Perhaps he could find a way back inside the mountain; perhaps he could reach one of the wide roads which he sometimes glimpsed on the lower slopes. Surely they led to a gate to the interior, for how else could fresh produce be supplied to the day markets?

He was descending a narrow stair, with a vertical rock face on one side and nothing but a slender rail of gleaming metal protecting him from a sheer drop on the other, when it suddenly turned and went under an arch. Something stopped him with implacable force, as if the air around him had congealed, and asked him his business. But it yielded at once to his will, and he went on down the stairs with invisible shawms braying and a stentorian voice gravely announcing the arrival of a Hierarch.

As Yama entered the courtyard at the bottom, a squad of guards in full armor pushed him aside and clattered up the stairs, pistols and falchions drawn. The courtyard was wide and shaded by high stone walls. In the middle of it, a soldier with an officer's sash over his corselet stood on a table. He was shouting at the people milling around two gates in the high wall at the far end.

"There is nothing wrong! Resume your places! Nothing is wrong!"

Slowly, order was restored. Clerks resumed their seats

at tables shaded by large paper parasols. The crowd separated into lines before the tables. Both of the gates were guarded by armed men. One seemed to be an entrance; the other an exit. All who went through the latter were stopped by the guards, who carefully scrutinized the wads of documents which each person had collected at the tables. Yama, too tired to consider retracing his path, joined the end of the line nearest him.

The line moved forward very slowly. The clerk who sat at the table questioned each petitioner closely, pausing now and then to write in various books or to stamp papers handed to him. The man who had come to stand behind Yama told him that there was no hurrying anything here.

"It's an old department," he added, as if this explained everything.

"It is?"

The man looked at Yama and said, "Are you lost, brother?"

He was an old man, stoop-shouldered and yet still tall, as tall as the Aedile or Telmon, with smooth black skin and silver eyes. Coarse white hair wound into long corkscrew ringlets framed his broad-browed face; three fireflies nested there. He looked at Yama with a shrewd, kindly gaze.

Yama said, "I believe that I did not come here by the usual route. What is this place?"

"The Department of Apothecaries and Chirurgeons," the old man said, and his silver eyes widened when Yama laughed.

"I am sorry," Yama said. "It is just that I have been searching for this place, and came upon it by accident."

"Then you were surely guided here by the will of the Preservers, brother," the old man said, and shook Yama's hand by way of greeting. He added, "Certainly you are more fortunate than the fool who tried to force entry through the Gate of the Hierarchs. Some poor wretch tries it at least once a year. After the guardian has finished with him, the guards display his body before the main gate as a lesson."

"Then I am doubly fortunate," Yama said.

The old man's name was Eliphas. He was a runner who made his livelihood by researching cases which physicians could not cure by normal means. Eliphas explained that most of the people queuing in the courtyard were runners for physicians or leeches; he assumed that Yama was from a family which could not afford to employ an intermediary. He saw that Yama was hungry, and took one of Yama's pennies and purchased waybread and water from a stall on the other side of the courtyard.

"A tip if you have to return next time," Eliphas said, smiling tolerantly as Yama devoured the waybread. "Bring food with you. It's cheaper, and will probably be better, too. But I don't suppose they told you how long it would take."

"How long does it take?" The black waybread was heavy and very sweet, but it satisfied Yama's immediate hunger at once.

"Usually a day to get through the preliminary certification," Eliphas said, "and then a day or two more to have the records searched. It depends on how you phrase your question. That's part of the art."

"My question is quite simple. I want to know if the Department of Apothecaries and Chirurgeons can help me find my people."

Eliphas scratched among his white corkscrew tangles with long, thin fingers. His nails were curved, and filed into points. He said, "If you can pay, I'll be glad to help. But I've never heard of anyone who does not know his own bloodline."

"If it can be found anywhere, it can be found in Ys," Yama said. "That is why I came here. When I was a baby, I was found on the river and taken in by a kind man. But now I want to find my real family. I believe that there are records here that will help me, but I am not certain that I know how to find them. If you will help me, I will be glad to pay what I can."

Eliphas said, "If you pay for my evening meal, and my

breakfast, why then, brother, I'll do my best to put you on the right road.''

"I can pay a fair price," Yama said, stung by the thought that Eliphas was offering charity.

"It's fair enough, brother. The way to learn about the system is to see how it responds to questions, and I believe that I may learn a lot by asking yours. The more you learn about the way information is catalogued, the more efficient you become. I can process up to a decad of questions in parallel. There's not many who can do that, but I've been working here all my life. In the days before the heretics, of course, it was simpler, because all records were stored within the purlieu of the avatars. I remember that what we now call librarians were then called hierodules, which means *holy slaves*. The real librarians were simply sub-routines of the avatars. They spoke through the hierodules, and their answers came promptly. But we live in an imperfect age. The shrines are silent, and we must ask clerks to search through written records which are often second- or third-hand transcriptions, and not always stored where they should be.''

"But why is it that you are not allowed to know how the library is set out? It seems to me you must work in the dark when all that is needed is to open a shutter.''

"Why, there are a thousand clerks employed by this library alone, and this is one of the smaller ones. If everyone knew where everything was to be found, the librarians would make no money and could not afford to maintain the records in their care. And if facts were free, why then I wouldn't make any money either. But that's the way it is with most professions, brother. If their mysteries were removed, why then there'd be no need for most of the people in them. I'd say nine-tenths of the business of any department is to do with guarding the mysteries, and only one-tenth in applying them. That's why rituals are so important. I've asked thousands of questions in my time, and reckon I know as much about medicine as most leeches, but I could never practice as I'm not inducted into their mysteries. If I'd been born to one of the medical families it might be different, but only the Preservers can choose how to be born into the world."

Yama learned that Eliphas's own family had been in the trade of question-running for three generations. Eliphas was the last of the line. His only son had joined the army and was fighting the heretics at the midpoint of the world, while his daughters' children would be raised in the trades of their fathers.

"That's the difference between trades and professions," Eliphas said. "Trades marry out; professions marry among their own kind. It's how they keep their power."

When it was at last their turn to speak with the clerk at the table, the sunlight had climbed the wall and left the courtyard in shadow. Lights like drifts of sparks had woken across the darkening slope of the mountain. The fireflies that hung above the heads of clerks and petitioners stirred and brightened as the sunlight faded, casting shifting tangles of light and shadow.

Eliphas leaned over the table, the orbits of his fireflies nearly merging with those of the clerk, and fanned a sheaf of pastel-colored papers, pointing at one and then another with his long forefinger. The two men exchanged a merry banter, and the clerk stamped Eliphas's papers without reading them.

"This is a friend of mine," Eliphas said, standing aside for Yama. "You do well by him, Tzu."

"Picking up strays again, Eliphas?" The clerk looked Yama up and down with a raking gaze and said, "Let's have your papers, boy. You'll be the last I process this day."

"I have no papers," Yama said, as boldly as he could. "I have only my question."

The clerk, Tzu, had a long, gloomy face. His brown skin was softly creased, like waterlogged leather. Now more creases appeared above his wide-spaced black eyes. He said, "Hand over your papers, or you can walk back down and start over tomorrow."

"I have my question, and money to pay the fee. I would

not take bread from the mouths of your family by trying to gain the information you guard for nothing.''

Tzu sighed, and shook a little bell. He said, ''What have you brought me, Eliphas? And at the end of the day, too. We have procedures here,'' he told Yama, ''and no time for troublemakers.''

Another clerk appeared, a slight old man with a humped back. He conferred with Tzu, and then stared at Yama through spectacles perched on the end of his long nose. He had a wispy white beard and a bald pate mottled with tubercles.

''Stand straight, boy,'' Tzu said. ''This is Kun Norbu, the chief of all the clerks.''

''How did you get here, boy?'' the chief of clerks, Kun Norbu, said.

''Down those stairs,'' Yama said, and pointed across the courtyard.

''Don't lie,'' Tzu said. ''There's a guardian. No one has used the Gate of the Hierarchs for a century. Now and then thieves and vagabonds try, as one tried today, but all are destroyed by the guardian.''

''Longer than that, I believe,'' Kun Norbu said. ''The last Hierarch to visit us was Gallizur the Joyous. It would have been in the summer of the year when Ys was invested by the armies of the Insurrectionists. That would be, hmm, eleven thousand five hundred and sixty-eight years ago.''

''A long time indeed, brother,'' Eliphas said, ''but this boy is no thief. I can vouch for him.''

Kun Norbu said, ''When did you first see him, Eliphas? Not before today, I would wager. I suppose he bribed a guard, and promised to pay you to help him. He doesn't even have a single firefly. He's some indigenous wildman, for all you know.''

Yama had supposed that his firefly had followed him, but he now realized that he must have destroyed it by asking it to give up all its light at once. He stared at the chief of clerks and said, ''As for fireflies, if that is your only concern, then my lack of them is easily fixed.''

"Don't be impudent," Kun Norbu said. "Fireflies choose a host according to their station. Clearly you have no station to speak of." He clapped his hands. "Guards! Yes, you two! To me, if you please!"

Tzu gasped and stood up, knocking over his stool. Eliphas stepped back, covering his face with his hands. All around, people turned to stare at Yama. A few knelt, heads bowed. The two guards who had started across the courtyard stopped and raised their partisans as if to strike at an invisible foe. Light gleamed along the crescent edges of their double-bladed weapons; a hundred sparks were caught in the lenses of Kun Norbu's spectacles.

In an extravagant impulse born of exhaustion and impatience, Yama had clothed himself in the light of a thousand fireflies, borrowed from everyone close by or called from the wild population beyond the walls. He felt that he was very close to the end of his quest, and he would not be stopped by the petty restrictions of a moribund bureaucracy.

"My question is quite simple," Yama said. "I want to find my people. Will you help me?"

THE HELL-HOUND

THE STRANGERS' LODGE of the Department of Apothecaries and Chirurgeons was built around a small square courtyard. Tiers of long, narrow balconies rose above the courtyard on three sides; on the fourth was a sloping wall of metal as transparent as glass, on which the last light of the sun glowed like the shower of gold by which, it was said, the Preservers had manifested themselves for the first and last time on the world, when they had seeded it with the ten thousand bloodlines.

Yama bought Eliphas supper in the refectory on the ground floor, and they ate at one of the long tables with a decad of other petitioners. All were crowned by the restless sparks of fireflies; there was no other light in the long room. Yama's wad of papers was by his elbow, an untidy rainbow fanned on the table's scarred and polished surface, for he did not have deep enough pockets to hold all the documents he had been given. His wound had been washed with an astringent lotion and freshly bandaged.

Despite the trick with the fireflies, the chief of clerks, Kun Norbu, had insisted that Yama should prove that he had been able to persuade the guardian of the Gate of the Hierarchs. Yama, still clothed in a thousand fireflies, walked up and down the stairs beneath the arch three times before a growing audience of clerks. It seemed to him that they would have watched him do it all night, and after the third time he told Kun Norbu that he had not come to the library as a mountebank or clown, and returned the fireflies to their former hosts, retaining only a pentad of those he had recruited from the local wild population. This trick astonished the clerks more than that of being able to pass the guardian.

Kun Norbu dismissed every clerk but Tzu, who assiduously dealt with Yama's paperwork, and then the chief of clerks had taken Yama and Eliphas to his cluttered office, where they sat on dusty couches and drank tea sweetened with honey. It seemed that Kun Norbu was an old friend of Eliphas's, and he said that he was at Yama's service.

"Tell your story, young man. Tell us how we can help you."

Yama explained that as a baby he had been found in a boat on the Great River, that he had been told that his bloodline was that of the Builders, long thought to have transcended the world. He said that he had come to Ys to search for others like himself, and added that he suspected that a certain Dr. Dismas had recently found important clues in this very library. Kun Norbu listened patiently, and then asked Yama a hundred questions, most of which he could not begin to attempt to answer. He found himself saying again and again, "If I knew, I would not be searching for the answers myself," or, "I hope to find that here."

"You will need to provide a sample of blood and a scraping of cells," Kun Norbu said at last. "That will be a good beginning."

Eliphas said, "Then you will take his case, brother. I am glad."

Kun Norbu smiled and said, "I think we might learn as much from the answers as Yama."

Yama said, "You know something about my bloodline, dominie. I see that you do. Can I find what I am searching for here?"

Kun Norbu's smile widened. His black eyes twinkled behind the lenses of his spectacles. "Not everything is to be found in libraries."

Eliphas closed his eyes and recited a fragment of text in a lilting chant. " 'They were the first men, part of the word which the Preservers spoke to call forth the world. They were given the keys of the world, and ordered it according to the wishes of their masters.' "

Yama said, "Is that from the Puranas?"

Eliphas's smile was a wide white crescent in his black face. "It sounds like the Puranas, doesn't it?"

Kun Norbu said, "It is from a text much older than the Puranas. Perhaps it was written by one of the Builders. Eliphas and I were enthusiastic hunters of obscure texts when we were as young as you, Yama. I gave up the carefree life of searching for lost knowledge many years ago, when I became a novice clerk, but now, do you know, I feel quite young again. You have rekindled my sense of inquiry, which I had thought long ago extinguished by the responsibilities of my office."

Yama said, "Then we should start at once! Why must the truth be approached through many bits of colored paper?"

He had been given passes for the library, the refectory and one of the dormitories of the Strangers' Lodge. His name, age, and birthplace (Yama had given it as Aeolis) had been written down on a pentad of differently colored pieces of paper. His question had been copied ten times over, and all the papers had been stamped with Tzu's mark.

"It is the way things are done," the chief of clerks said. "You are young, Yama, and would tear down the world and start all over again. You value speed over all else. Everything must be done at once or given to you as soon as you need it, or the world must be changed. That's how it is with the young. But as you get older, you'll see the wisdom in the way things have always been. Old men like Eliphas and me see why things are the way they are, and why they have grown in particular ways, and how everything is connected. We see that without direction velocity is nothing but squandered energy."

Yama said, "Surely knowledge should be free to everyone, since all knowledge is the gift of the Preservers."

"Ah, but if it was freed," Kun Norbu said, "who would look after it? Knowledge is a delicate thing, easily destroyed or lost, and each part of the knowledge we look after is potentially dependent upon every other part. I could open the library to all tomorrow, if I was so minded, but I will not. You could wander the stacks for a dozen years, Yama, and never find what you are looking for. I can lay my hand on the place where the answers may lie in a few hours, but only because I have spent much of my life studying the way in which the books and files and records are catalogued. The organization of knowledge is just as important as knowledge itself, and we are responsible for the preservation of that organization."

"He will be up all night looking for the answers," Eliphas said to Yama, and told Kun Norbu, "It is good to see the light of adventure in your eyes once more, brother! I thought you were falling asleep behind the ledgers and the rulebooks."

"I keep my hand in," the chief of clerks said, "if only to keep the apprentices on their toes." He made a steeple of his fingers. They were each tipped with a black claw like a rose thorn, and linked by heavy, wrinkled webs of skin. He looked at them and said, "Have you ever been ill, Yama?"

"Just blackwater fever and ague. I lived beside the river."

"I ask because I do not know if Builders are susceptible to illness. Be glad of your childhood fevers! If any of your people live, then some of them will almost certainly have been treated by chirurgeons or by apothecaries, and the records of all chirurgeons and apothecaries are preserved here. That is how I will search, using the template that lies within your cells as a guide."

He summoned a young clerk, who took a scraping from the inside of Yama's cheek with a blunt needle and drew a minim of blood from the tip of his thumb with a glass straw. These samples also required documentation, and Yama's signature, and Kun Norbu's stamp.

When this was done, the chief of clerks bowed to Yama and said, "You need not lodge in the commons. You will be my guest. My household is yours. I will have someone find you fresh clothes and see that your wound is cleaned."

"That is kind," Yama said, "but I do not deserve special treatment. And the wound is an old one. It does not trouble me."

He feared that Prefect Corin might hear that the library had an uncommon visitor, one who could command fireflies and ancient guardians.

Kun Norbu gave Yama a shrewd look and said, "You cannot try and pretend that you are ordinary, Yama. And your wound has been bleeding recently. At least allow me to have someone look at it, and to recommend that Eliphas look after you. He knows as much about our little library as any, although he will never admit it."

—

After Yama and Eliphas had eaten, Eliphas filled the bowl of a long-stemmed clay pipe with aromatic tobacco, lit it, and puffed on it contentedly. Yama asked him where he had found the passage he had quoted.

"It was on a scrap of paper which someone had torn from a book an age ago and used to jot down the addition of a bill of small goods. We found it tucked between the pages of an old record book. Paper is very patient, and old paper in particular is well made and forgets very little. That scrap had preserved the verse about your people on one side and the trifling calculation on the other, and had also patiently kept the place which someone dead a thousand years had marked. It is not that things are forgotten, simply that they are mislaid. Bindings of certain books are a good example of where such things may be found, for pieces of older documents are often used as backing.

There's no end of places to look. Kun Norbu and I looked in many strange places when we were young.''

"I am beginning to believe that I am mislaid," Yama said. "That I do not belong in this time. Many times, when I was younger, I hoped that someone was looking for me."

"You must have courage, brother. I am curious about one thing, though. May I ask a question?"

"Of course."

"Why, there's no 'of course' about it. I simply do my duty, as the Preservers would wish. I do not expect you to satisfy my idle curiosity as reward. But thank you. My question is this. If you do learn where your family lives, what will you do?"

"I would ask them why I was set adrift on the river, to begin with. And if they answered that, I would ask them . . . other questions."

Eliphas blew a riffle of smoke. "Who am I? Why am I here? Where am I going?"

"Something like that."

"Forgive me, brother. I don't mean to make light of your predicament."

"If they live at all, I think that they must be living somewhere in Ys, or in the boreal lands upriver of Ys."

"Then hope they live in Ys," Eliphas said. "The land upriver is wild, and full of races which have not yet changed, or perhaps will never change. Most are little more than animals, and do not even have an Archivist to record their lives. The city streets are hard, yet with a little money and a modicum of cunning one can endure them. But it is not so easy to survive in the dark forests and the ice and snow of the boreal regions at the head of the river."

Yama sighed. He was beginning to realize the magnitude of his task. He said, "The world is very large, and not at all like my map."

"Your map must be very old. Little has altered on Confluence since the Age of Insurrection. It is true that when bloodlines reach enlightenment, the change wars that follow usually destroy their city. But the survivors move on, and there are always prelapsarian races to take their place, and all seems as it was before. New cities are built upon the old. But what stood in those places at the beginning of the world? I would very much like to see this map of yours."

"I left it behind when I came to Ys."

Yama told Eliphas about Aeolis, and the peel-house and its library, and Eliphas said that he knew of the library of the Aedile of Aeolis.

"I knew the present librarian, Zakiel, before he was disgraced and sent away. Sometimes I envy his exile, for the library has a certain notoriety. It is said that an original copy of the Puranas is lodged there."

It was the book that Zakiel had given Yama when he had left Aeolis for Ys. His heart turned over when he realized the value of the librarian's gift. The book was with his satchel and the rest of his belongings in the little stone cell in the House of the Twelve Front Rooms, in the Department of Vatication. He must return there tomorrow, and discharge his obligation to Tamora. And then he must flee, for he must not be captured by the Department of Indigenous Affairs. If that happened he would certainly fall into Prefect Corlin's hands.

He said, "Zakiel was one of my teachers."

Eliphas blew a smoke ring and watched it widen in the air, then sent a second, smaller smoke ring spinning through the fraying circle of the first. He said, "Then no wonder you value knowledge. With your permission, brother, I'd like to sleep now. We must rise with the sun if we're to get a place at the carrels."

—

Only one of the Lodge's dormitories was open; clearly, the library had seen greater use in former times. But the beds, although narrow, were comfortable, and the sheets clean. Eliphas snored and someone else in the dormitory talked in his sleep, but Yama had risen early and had faced death and had walked many leagues, and he soon fell asleep.

He woke in pitch darkness. The hairs on the back of his neck and on his forearms were prickling and stirring, and he was filled with a feeling of unspecific dread, as if he had escaped the clutches of a bad dream.

There was a faint light at the end of the dormitory. At first Yama thought sleepily that the door was open, and that it must be morning. But then he saw that the light was vaguely man-shaped—although taller than most men, and thinner than any living man should be—and worse, that it was moving. It drifted like a bit of waterweed caught in a current, or like a candle flame dancing in the draft created by its own burning. It reminded Yama of nothing so much as the wispy lights that could sometimes be glimpsed after the river Breas had flooded the ruins outside the city wall of Aeolis. The Amnan called those apparitions wights, and believed that they would steal the soul of any traveler they could entice into their clutches. Yama had known, because Zakiel had told him, that the lights were nothing more than pockets of marsh gas which kindled in the air upon bubbling to the surface of stagnant water; Zakiel had once made a demonstration, with water and a bit of natrium in a glass tube. But knowing what the wights were did not make them less eerie when they were seen flickering in the darkness of a bleak winter's night.

Unlike a candle flame or a marsh wight, the burning figure gave off no light but that which illuminated itself. The long dormitory remained in shadow, lit only by the dim clusters of fireflies which clung to the walls above the beds where their hosts slept, but when the thing stooped over the first of the beds, the sleeper's face was immersed in its spectral light. The man murmured and turned halfway around, but he did not wake. The thing disengaged itself and waved through the dark to the next bed.

Yama discovered that he was clutching the sheet so hard that his fingers had cramped. He remembered the light which had burst through the shrine in the temple of the latriatic cult and the thing he had felt rushing toward him from the depths of the space within the shrine, and knew that the apparition was searching for him. He sat up cautiously. His fireflies brightened before he remembered to still them, but the burning figure did not appear to notice. It was bending toward the third sleeper, like a librarian patiently searching a shelf book by book.

Yama put his hand over Eliphas's mouth and shook the old man awake. Eliphas's silver eyes opened at once, and Yama pointed to the burning figure and whispered, "It is looking for me."

Eliphas bolted from his bed, clutching the sheet to his skinny body. "A hell-hound," he said in a hoarse whisper. "Save us! It is a hell-hound."

"It came from a shrine further up the mountain. I think it means me harm."

Eliphas was staring at the apparition. His shoulders were shaking. He said distractedly, "Mountain? Yes, I suppose that the Palace would resemble a mountain to someone not used to large buildings."

"It stands between us and the door. I think we should wait for the guards."

Another man's sleeping face appeared in the hell-hound's blue light; the man groaned horribly, as if gripped by a sudden nightmare. Yama thought that everyone here would remember the same dream when they woke—and then realized that if the hell-hound could affect men's dreams, then perhaps it could also see into them. That must be what it was doing, browsing through the minds of the sleepers as a scholar may browse in a library, hoping to gain insight by serendipity.

Yama snatched up his shirt and the harness which held his sheathed knife, and said, "I am going to climb through one of the windows. You can come with me or stay, but I would be happier if you followed me."

"Of course I'm coming. It is a hell-hound."

Yama opened the shutter of the window above his bed and climbed out on to the balcony outside. When Eliphas followed, clutching his clothes, Yama turned up the light of their fireflies and discovered that they were only a few man-lengths above the mosaic floor of the courtyard. He swung over the rail of the balcony, landing with a rush and a shock but no harm.

Eliphas let his clothes flutter down and followed more cautiously, and sat down after he had landed, massaging his knees. "I am an old man," he said, "and my days of adventuring are long past. This was never part of the bargain."

Yama pulled on his shirt and shrugged the harness around his shoulders. "You do not have to follow me," he said.

Eliphas was pulling on his trousers. He looked up and said, "Of course I will follow. I mean, I think it would be better if I did. The hell-hound is looking into the minds of those men, and some remember that they saw you with me. And if it looks into my mind it will find my conversations with you. What might it do then?"

"Then you had better show me how to reach the Gate of the Hierarchs. I will get us past the guardian. I have no intention of staying here."

"I think it would be better if we found Kun Norbu. He will know what to do. And the guards are armed."

"We will return in the morning," Yama said.

Eliphas might have argued the point, but a blue light appeared at the balcony above. They both lost their nerve then, and ran.

The guardian of the Gate of the Hierarchs had been driven deep inside itself, and did not notice when Yama and Eliphas passed by. It was a few hours before dawn. It was not cold, but Yama and Eliphas were soon mantled with dew after they sat down to keep watch from a turn of the long flight of stairs high above the library. Yama said that Eliphas could leave him as soon as it grew light, but Eliphas said that he would as soon stay with Yama.

"I made a contract with you, brother, and I never let a client down."

Yama said, "You have other clients before me."

"I'll let you into a secret." Eliphas lit his pipe. When he drew on it, the burning coal of tobacco set a spark in each of his silvery eyes. He was calmer now. He said, "Sometimes, I already know the answers to the questions I am sent to root out of the library. It would not do to tell the client that, though. It would put the business of the library at risk, and my business, too. Besides, no leech will believe that I know something of his trade that he himself does not. It does not do to sell the truth cheaply. Instead, I enact a little charade. I come here and gossip with my friends, and a day later I return to my client and give him, stamped and documented, the answer I could have given him straightaway, if only he trusted me. The library is paid, I am paid, and the client is pleased with his answer. That is why I was so happy to help you. It gave me something to do. Besides, like my friend, Kun Norbu, I feel young again in your presence. I had thought that there were no more wonders to discover in the world, and you have proved me wrong."

Yama considered this. At last, he said, "The road I travel may be long, and it is certainly dangerous."

"Don't think that I know only the inside of libraries, brother, and am innocent of the world. I traveled much in my younger days, searching for old books. It took me to some odd places. I am an old man, brother. My wife is dead, my daughters are married and concerned with their own families, and my only son is fighting heretics at the midpoint of the world. Now, I am sure that we can return to the library when it is light, and find out what Kun Norbu has discovered about your people. And after we find the records concerning your bloodline, I will be happy to help you look for your people. No, I will stay with you. I will do my part."

"I have some business to complete before I can go and look for my people," Yama said.

He started to tell Eliphas about the conflict between the Department of Indigenous Affairs and the Department of Vaticination, but he had not got very far when Eliphas suddenly stood and said, "Look! Look there!"

A cold blue light flared below. It defined the curtain wall of the library and several of its slim towers before winking out. There was the sound of men shouting in the distance, and then the iron voice of a bell, slow at first but gathering urgency.

Someone down there had an energy pistol. For a moment, an intense point of light shone like a fallen fleck of the sun. There was a noise like that of a gigantic door slamming deep in the keel of the world, and the backwash of the discharge blossomed above the roofs and towers of the library and threw the shadows of Yama and Eliphas far up the long flight of stairs. The cold blue light kindled again. It was smaller now, and seemed to be climbing one of the towers. Yama saw the flashes of pellet rifles; the sound of their fusillade was like the crackle of twigs thrown on a fire. The mote of cold blue light dropped from the side of the tower, drifting down like a leaf.

Eliphas said, "They have killed it!"

"I do not think so. It has discovered that I am no longer where it thought I would be. It must have found out from one of the sleepers that I was staying in the dormitory, and now it has finished its search, or it was interrupted."

"Brother, we both saw it fall."

"I do not think it can be killed by rifle fire, nor even by the discharge of an energy pistol. It is not of this world, Eliphas, but of the world men once glimpsed in the shrines."

Yama remembered that the woman who had appeared in the shrine of the Temple of the Black Well had told him that there were dangerous things beyond the bounds of the garden she had created. He was certain now that the hell-hound was one of the creatures she had feared.

Eliphas nodded. "Accounts of the wars of the Age of Insurrection speak not only of the battles of men and machines, but of a war in the world within the world. The priests claim that this means that the enemy strove to conquer men's souls as well as their cities, but archivists and librarians know better. Hell-hounds were weapons in that second front."

"The Insurrectionists tried to destroy the avatars, and the link between men and the Preservers."

Eliphas nodded again. "And the heretics succeeded where the Insurrectionists could not. Perhaps they woke the old weapons."

"I fear that I have a talent for drawing enemies to myself. There! There it is again!"

The tiny point of blue light had appeared at the foot of the dark wall of the library. Now it began to ascend the stairway.

Eliphas knocked out his pipe on the railing of the stairs. His fingers were trembling as he put it away. "We must go on. The hell-hound travels slowly, or it would have caught you long before you reached the library, but I have a feeling that it does not rest."

YAMA AND ELIPHAS reached the long lawn and its fountain just as dawn began to define the mountain ranges at the edge of the city's wide plain. The library was far below, its towers ablaze with lights, but there was no sign of the hell-hound.

Eliphas sat heavily on the wet grass. "Perhaps it has lost us," he said.

"I do not think so. It followed me down to the library. There is no reason why it cannot follow me in the reverse direction. You are tired, Eliphas."

"I am old, brother."

"And my head aches. But we cannot stay here."

Eliphas slowly clambered to his feet, unfolding his lanky body in stages. He said, "I'm sure we can spare a few minutes before we go on. I am thirsty as well as tired."

As Yama and Eliphas approached the ornate fountain in the center of the lawn, two deer ran from it, white scuts bobbing as they disappeared into the darkness. Eliphas thrust his head into a spout of water that gushed from the gaping mouth of a fish; Yama drank from a basin shaped like an oyster shell and splashed cold water on the back of his neck. His head wound had begun to bleed again. While Eliphas sat on the edge of the fountain's main basin and lit his pipe, Yama walked back to the edge of the lawn. He was anxious and tired and afraid.

There was now enough light in the sky to make out the various clusters of buildings which were scattered across the long slope below. Yama could see that the library's curtain wall had been breached—the adamantine stone slumped like melted candle wax—and that its slim white towers were licked with black soot. The path which climbed through the tiers of fields seemed empty, and for a moment his heart lifted. Perhaps Eliphas was right. But then he saw a glimmer of cold blue light emerge from a distant stand of sago palms; the hell-hound came on in an erratic dance like a scrap of fabric caught in a breeze, flitting from side to side, but always moving upward.

Yama ran back to Eliphas, but the old man shrugged phlegmatically when he heard the news and was maddeningly slow to begin to move. Exhaustion had overcome his fear. He knocked out his pipe on his bootheel and said that there were roads still in use, and all led to gates to the interior.

"And where there is a gate," Eliphas said, "there will be guards."

"The guards of the library could not stop it. We must go, Eliphas."

"Some guards are better armed than others," Eliphas said. He pressed the palms of his hands over his silver eyes for a moment. "The main part of the Palace has always been better defended than the outlying offices. We cannot run forever, brother. If we lead it to them, the soldiers of Internal Harmony will know what to do."

Yama did not share Eliphas's faith in this plan, but a small hope was better than no hope at all. He said, "If we are to try and find some way back into the mountain, then we should turn aside. The monastery where I wakened it is not far above. I do not want to confront the shrine again, especially with that thing at my back. I might waken something worse. As it is, I fear that the library is destroyed."

Eliphas smiled. "Not at all. What stands aboveground is only a tenth part of the whole. The stacks and carrels of the archives run far back into the Palace. Kun Norbu may be somewhat distracted by repair work, but he will remember your request."

"That is suddenly the least of my concerns," Yama said.

They found a narrow path at the far end of the long lawn. It wound along the foot of a bluff from which a cluster of square, white, windowless buildings hung, like the cells of a wasp nest. Far below, the hell-hound stopped for a full minute, burning in the midst of a steep field of red corn, and then suddenly moved forward at a steady pace, cutting across the field in a straight line toward them.

They hurried on, passing between the legs of a skeletal metal tower clad in a living cloak of green vines. The path angled through a thicket of bamboo, and then a little village was below, flat roofed houses of wicker and daub crowded around a central square. Threads of smoke rose into the gray sky from several of the houses. A cock crowed in anticipation of the rising sun.

Eliphas stopped and bent over and clasped his knees. For a while all he could do was breathe hard. Yama went back to the beginning of the bamboo thicket to look for the hell-hound, then returned to Eliphas, who slowly unbent and said, "We must go through the village. If the hell-hound follows, the villagers will try and stop it."

"Will they be better armed than the library guards?"

Eliphas shook his head. Sweat beaded his smooth black skin. He dabbed at his brow with the back of his hand and said wearily, "They are husbandmen who till the fields on this part of the Palace roof. They will have axes and scythes, perhaps a few muskets. They will not be able to stop it, but they might slow it down so we can make our escape."

"No, I will not risk their lives. We cannot wait here, Eliphas. Remember that the hell-hound does not rest."

Eliphas waved a hand in front of his face, as if Yama's words were flies that could be brushed away. "A moment, a moment more, and I will be able to go on. Listen, brother. The quickest way to the nearest gate will take us through the village. The husbandmen take their produce to the gates. That's where they sell it to merchants from the day markets. Don't spare a thought for them. They are indigens whose ancestors colonized the ruined parts of the Palace ten thousand years ago. They are animals, brother, of no more importance than the sacred monkeys of the outer temples. Less so, in fact, since priests and sacerdotes care for the monkeys that live in their monasteries and temples, but no one cares for the husbandmen. They are tolerated only because they supply the day markets with fresh produce. We'll go through their village, eh? It will delay the hell-hound a little."

Yama remembered the fisherman, Caphis, who had saved his life after he had escaped from Dr. Dismas and the young warlord, Enobarbus. He said, "Even if the indigenous peoples cannot transcend their animal origins, still they are something more than animals, I think. I will not risk their lives to save mine." He pointed to the terraced rice paddies that stepped away below the next bluff. "There is a path that descends beside those fields. We can follow it. Eliphas, if you wish to, leave me now. Go through the village. The hell-hound will not follow you."

"I made a bargain," the old man said. "Maybe a bad one, but it might still pay off. Lead on, brother, although I fear your scruples will help the villagers more than they will help us."

The sun had begun to rise above the distant mountains when Yama and Eliphas reached the steep ladder of steps beside the terraced rice fields. The narrow steps were worn by the tread of a thousand generations of husbandmen, and slippery with seepage from the flooded paddies. Ferns grew in cracks between the steps, and bright green mosses made the way more slippery still.

Despite their fearful haste, Yama paused at a wayside shrine. *Take this burden from me,* he prayed, as he had prayed so often before, meaning, make me ordinary, make me no more than other men. Save me from myself.

The rice paddies were narrow and long, curved to follow the contour of the hillside and dammed with stout ramparts of compacted earth wide enough for two water buffalo to walk abreast. Freshly planted seedlings made a haze of green over the calm brown water that flooded them; the ripe smell of ordure reminded Yama of the flooded fields around Aeolis; at another time it would have eased his heart.

When he suggested that the rice paddies might have been here before the Palace had been built, Eliphas laughed and said that it was impossible. "Even now, we step on the roof of the Palace itself. The indigens who tend the fields or hunt the wild animals here are like the birds or mice which colonize the older habitations of man. It would have meant nothing to have gone through the village, brother."

"It would have meant something to me."

After they had descended a while in silence, Eliphas said, "This part of the Palace was ruined in the last war of the Age of Insurrection, and has never been properly rebuilt. If you were to dig deep enough, you would find rock fused like glass, and then rubble, and then rooms and corridors wrecked and abandoned ten thousand years ago. Because this side of the Palace faces the Rim Mountains, and is in sunlight for most of the day, it is favored for cultivation." Eliphas laid one hand on the small of his back. "I am sorry, brother, but I must rest again. Only for a moment."

Each time Eliphas stopped to catch his breath, Yama anxiously looked back at the path they had taken, but by good fortune they managed to reach the bottom of the long ladder of steps before the hell-hound finally appeared.

White cockatoos rose into the blue sky, screeching in alarm. A moment later the hell-hound burst out of the thicket of bamboo above the terraced rice paddies. Like a whirlwind or dust devil, it threw clouds of dust and scraps of foliage into the air as it moved forward. It seemed just as bright in daylight as at night, like a bit of sky fallen to earth and roughly shaped into a tall, skeletal man. It started toward the village, but quickly returned to the path, and came on steadily.

Yama and Eliphas ran down a dusty track between the steep bank of the bottommost rice paddy and the margin of a sloping field of melon vines. They splashed across a stream and ran through a belt of eucalyptus trees, scattering a herd of small black pigs, and ran on until Eliphas tripped and fell headlong in the dust.

At first Eliphas could not get up, and when Yama finally hauled him to his feet he said that he could not run any more. They were on a long downward slope with tall grass on either side of the path. A chorus of crickets was beginning to whistle, woken by the early morning warmth.

"Leave me," Eliphas said. He was trembling and his silver eyes were half-closed. He could not get his breath. "Leave me, brother, and save yourself. I will find you again, if we both live."

The slender eucalyptus trees at the top of the slope stirred and shook as if caught in a localized gale. A horrible squealing went up and black pigs pelted out of the trees. The hell-hound appeared behind them, blazing like a piece of the sun caught in blue glass. It seemed to have grown taller and thinner, as if the glass, melting, was being pulled apart by its own weight. Veils of dust and leaves whirled up around it. At first it seemed confused by the pigs and made short, swift dashes after one or another of them. Most of the pigs scattered into the tall grass, but a few ran in circles, dazed by the brilliant light, and finally the hell-hound pounced on the smallest. The hapless pig flew up as if it weighed no more than a dead leaf, was dashed to the ground, and lay still. As if excited by this, the hell-hound whirled in wider circles. It swept through the tall dry grasses, which immediately caught fire with a sullen crackling, then steadied and came on down the path toward Yama and Eliphas.

Yama got a shoulder under Eliphas's arm and they staggered down the path to the edge of a steep embankment. Directly below was a broad road crowded with carts drawn by bullocks or water buffaloes, camels laden with hessian-wrapped packs, and women and men walking with bundles or clay pots balanced on their heads. Carts and camels and people were all moving downhill toward the high, square entrance of a tunnel in the side of the slope.

As Yama and Eliphas staggered down the embankment, people shrieked and shrank away. Yama glanced over his shoulder. The hell-hound had appeared behind them, burning brightly against a reef of white smoke. Yama shouted in despair and pulled Eliphas behind a cart piled high with watermelons. All around, men and women screamed as the hell-hound swept down the embankment. A bullock bolted, bawling with fear, and its cart overturned, spilling hands of red bananas. A flock of moas ran in circles, screeching wildly and kicking up dust. The hell-hound plunged amongst the birds, rearing back and forth as if maddened.

Yama and Eliphas were swept along in the midst of the panicking crowd into the darkness of the tunnel, brick walls doubling and redoubling the shouts and screams of men and women and the bawling of animals, then into a huge underground chamber. Like a breaking wave, the crowd washed against loading bays where laborers were unloading and weighing produce and clerks were handing out tallies to husbandmen.

Yama and Eliphas were halfway across the wide chamber when the flock of moas stampeded out of the tunnel, the hell-hound burning in their midst. People screamed and dropped baskets and packages and ran in every direction, and a pentad of guards came out of a tall narrow gate. The guards wore half armor and carried slug rifles which they began to fire as they ran toward the hell-hound. Wounded moas fell to the ground, kicking with their strong, scaly legs. Ricocheting slugs whooped and rang, knocking dust and brick fragments from the ground all around the hell-hound as it stretched and bent this way and that, and finally fixed on Yama and Eliphas.

Eliphas wailed and sank to his knees, his arms wrapped over his head. Yama held up the ceramic coin in one hand

and his long knife in the other, and slowly backed away from the hell-hound. It had elongated to four or five times the height of a man and shone so brightly that he could only squint at it through half-closed eyes. It made a horrible high-pitched hiss as it sinuously advanced toward him, gouging a smoking trench in the brick floor. Its heat parched his skin. The guards kept up a steady rate of fire, but the fusillade merely kicked up shards of brick around the hell-hound or passed through it as if it was no more than light—and perhaps it was no more than light, light bent into itself.

Yama backed into a stack of baskets of live chickens. He slashed the baskets open and kicked them toward the hell-hound. The thing stopped and bent in a half circle as panicked chickens scattered around it, but then it straightened and fixed on Yama again. He tried again to command it to halt, but he might as well have tried to snuff a furnace by pure will. He was aware of a number of small machines in the chamber, but he could no more hurl them at the hell-hound than he could have endangered the village.

People were fighting to get through the gate; no escape there. Yama stepped backward as the hell-hound swayed toward him, watched by laborers and husbandmen hiding amongst wagons and carts. Eliphas called out. Yama risked glancing around and saw that the old man was standing on top of an overturned cart. A man jumped up beside Eliphas; Yama recognized the gambler who had been playing the shell game outside the bawdy house.

"This way, brother," Eliphas called, and the gambler shouted, "Come with me if you want to live!"

Yama turned and ran, and knew by the screams of the people all around that the hell-hound had started after him. He dodged around the cart and for a moment thought that Eliphas and the gambler had vanished. No, they had ducked through a little round hole in the wall. Yama's shadow was thrown ahead of him, and he ran to meet its dwindling apex. Fierce heat and light beat at his back as he scrambled through the low opening, and then something fell with a clang behind him and he was in darkness.

THE KING OF THE CORRIDORS

MOMENTS AFTER IT had fallen into place behind Yama the hatch rang with a pure, deep note and a smell of scorched metal began to fill the narrow space in which he stood, pressed close to Eliphas and the gambler.

"Put up your knife, dominie," the gambler said. "You're with friends here. Follow me, follow me now. The hatch is crystalline iron, but it won't hold for long."

The gambler's stiff red coxcomb, with its single dim firefly, brushed the low ceiling. He wore bright red leggings and a baggy black shirt that came to his knees. He had a pungent but not unpleasant odor, like that of a wet dog.

"I am at your service," Yama said. His blood was still thrilling from the near escape. When Eliphas took his arm, he realized that he was trembling so much that he could hardly stand.

"It is my turn to help you, brother," Eliphas said, and put his shoulder under Yama's arm to support him as they followed the gambler down the tunnel.

Yama said, "What is this place?"

"The service corridors," Eliphas said. "They're supposed to run through every part of the Palace, even to the offices of the Hierarchs. But there are no maps to their maze, and few use them now."

The gambler glanced at them over his shoulder. His long pale face gleamed in the combined light of their fireflies. He said, "Most of that's true, but more use these corridors than you might reckon, and not everything has been forgotten. Speaking of which, do you remember me, dominie?"

"You were playing the shell game yesterday. You were wearing a silver shirt then."

"You're as sharp as they say you are," the gambler said. "I'm Magon, and I'm here to help you. We've been on the lookout for you, dominie. You ran the wrong way yesterday, and it's my luck to have found you again. Do you know what it is that you wakened? You did wake it, didn't you?"

"Yes. Yes, I did. It was in a shrine."

"In the temple of a latriatic cult? We hadn't thought that one was still functional—well, it isn't functional now, of course. The shrine was destroyed when the hell-hound broke through."

Yama touched the coin that hung at his chest. The gambler, Magon, saw the gesture, and said, "That won't help you, dominie. It isn't a charm."

"I was wondering if it had woken the thing."

The woman in the shrine of the Temple of the Black Well had said that the coin had drawn her to him.

Magon said, "You did that yourself, I reckon. Lucky you were brought up where you were, in the City of the Dead, and not in Ys. There are too many shrines in Ys, and more remain functional than most folk think. If you had been brought up in Ys, it is likely that a hell-hound would have scented you before you were ready for it. But that would be a different world, and I wouldn't have the good fortune of talking with you here and now."

"You seem to know a lot about me," Yama said.

"Lucky for you that I do," Magon said jauntily.

"And you know about the hell-hound."

"A little, dominie."

"It seemed to be made of light," Yama said.

"Something very like it," Eliphas said, eager to explain something he understood. "Light is only matter in another form, and it can be bound for a while. If we can keep away from it, brother, the hell-hound will collapse when its binding energy sinks below a certain level, or it will find a functioning shrine and upload itself and return to the place for which shrines are windows. They are terrible things. They can live in the space inside the shrines, and in our world, too. They pass through our world from one shrine to another like an arrow through air, if an arrow could make itself into air in its flight and remake itself when it hits its target. They were sent after avatars, originally."

Yama said, "And this one came for me."

"That was bad luck, and not just for you," Magon said. "It must have been bound in the shrine. No doubt that's why the monastery was built around the shrine. It's all too easy to mistake the stirring of a hell-hound for the intimation of an avatar. Those poor monks, praying for thousands of years to a weapon of their enemies! There's irony for you, eh, dominie? Well, they'll worship the shrine no longer. The hell-hound stole the residue of the shrine's potential energy when it manifested."

"It seemed to grow stronger in sunlight," Yama said. He had the horrible thought that whoever had fired at the hell-hound with a pistol would have fed its strength. He added, "Perhaps darkness would kill it."

"It was never alive," Magon said, "So *killing* and *dying* don't apply."

Eliphas said, "Even in sunlight it loses binding energy. Sunlight's energy is too dilute to sustain it, just as we would gasp for air at the peaks of the Rim Mountains. I imagine that it is imprinted on you, brother. It will follow as long as it can. We must escape it."

Magon said, "It's a terrible thing, but it's old and easily confused. If we're lucky it will give up, or lose track or memory of you, and dissipate when its binding energy drops below a sustainable level."

"We have had little in the way of luck so far," Yama said. "I think that I will have to find a way of destroying it."

"As for that," Magon said, "some ways are better than others, as the fox said to the hen lost in the forest. We'll go through here. Don't worry about the water. It's dry on the other side."

They had reached the base of a kind of well or shaft. A patch of pale daylight showed high above and a sheet of water fell down one side and drained away through grids in the floor. Behind the water three corridors radiated away at sixty degrees to each other. Magon plunged through the water and trotted down the middle corridor. When Yama and Eliphas followed—the water was as warm as soup—they found the gambler waiting at the other end, where a slim metal bridge arched across a narrow, half-flooded cavern. Green lights flickered deep beneath the water. Waves clashed and broke against the stone walls, casting shivering shadows on the arched ceiling.

Magon stepped quickly and lightly across the bridge's span and turned at the other side and beckoned to Yama and Eliphas. As he crossed, Yama saw shapes move swiftly just beneath the water's restless surface, things with sleek, arrowhead-shaped bodies that ended in knots of long, twining limbs: creatures like the polyps which swarmed in the river at midsummer, but grown to the size of a man.

Eliphas saw them too. He grasped the rail of the bridge and looked down into the water and said, "There are more things forgotten in the Palace than anyone could dream of in a lifetime of sleep."

"Not forgotten by everyone," Magon called from the other end of the bridge. "They come up from the Great River through flooded passages beneath the streets of the city. Lupe says they might have had a purpose once upon a time, but that's long forgotten. They come here by habit now." He told Yama, "We should press on, dominie. Lupe is eager to meet you."

Eliphas said, "Begging your pardon, Magon, but I always understood that no one lives inside the walls of the Palace but thieves and cutthroats.''

Magon flashed his crooked smile and said, ''Their kind doesn't last long. We see to that. It isn't far now, I promise. Lupe is waiting for you, dominie, and your friend is welcome too. We know him.''

''You know everyone, it seems,'' Yama said. He leaned beside Eliphas. Below, the reflected stars of his crown of fireflies were drawn apart and flung back together on the shivering surface of the water. The sleek shapes were gathering beneath the bridge. Their bodies were limned by patches and dots and lines of green luminescence. Something like a snake rose up, a pale, glistening rope that sinuously elongated in the air. It caught hold of the middle of the bridge's high arch for a moment, then fell back.

Magon said, ''It isn't safe to tarry here, dominie.'' There was a note of pleading in his voice now.

Yama did not trust the gambler. His ready smile and quick wit seemed assumed, a mask, an act. He said, ''Before we move on, Magon, tell me how you know who I am. It is not just because I saw through your sleight of hand, is it?''

Magon said, ''Of course not. Please, dominie, we must go. You don't know the dangers here.'' His calm, knowing pose had dissolved. His hands writhed in a knot before his chest. ''You shouldn't play with poor Magon. Lupe can answer your questions. I am to take you to him at once.''

''You are not a gambler at all, are you? That is just a cover for what you really are. So, who are you? And why do you know so much about me?''

There was a loud splash out in the darkness, as if something big had lifted itself out of the water and fallen back.

Magon's left hand darted to his hip, where something made a shape under his loose shirt. He said, ''Lupe said to bring you direct, and you want me to answer your questions. I've tried to do my best, but I can't do both, dominie.''

Eliphas told Magon, ''Keep your hand away from your

side, brother. You've something hidden there—a knife in your belt, most likely, and no doubt there's another in your boot. I know those footpad tricks.''

Yama said, "How long have your people been watching me?"

"You were supposed to go to the Department of Indigenous Affairs, but your escort arrived without you. That's when we started looking, but we didn't catch sight of you until after you called down the feral machine."

"My escort? You mean Prefect Corin?"

For a moment, Yama thought that Magon was in league with the Prefect.

"I wouldn't know his name," the gambler said, "but someone in the Department of Indigenous Affairs isn't happy he lost track of you. He'll be searching for you hard, now you've been spotted in the Palace. We'll make sure you're safe, dominie."

Magon did not meet Yama's gaze as he answered these questions, but looked from side to side as things splashed in the darkness on either side of the bridge's span. When a nest of pale tentacles rose from the water directly beneath the bridge, he gave a cry and took a step backward.

Yama said, "I will not go with you until you have answered all my questions. How long have your people been looking for me?"

"When you fought the thing in the Temple of the Black Well, we knew for sure. Lupe said that you were the one foretold. You don't have to worry about the little interdepartmental dispute you've become involved with, dominie. We'll always be here to see you right."

"And my friends?"

Out in the darkness beyond the bridge, something huge surfaced with a loud splash. Big waves clashed beneath the bridge; spray wet the walls of the chamber.

Magon said, the note of pleading in his voice stronger now. "Dominie, you'll have to ask Lupe these questions. That's why I'm to bring you to him. Truly, it is not safe—"

Yama said, "This is not the first time I have met people

who claim more for me than I would ever claim for myself. And I have business elsewhere today.''

This was the day that the Department of Vatication
opened its doors for public inquisition of its pythonesses.
It was the day of the assassination plot, in which, Yama
suspected, Brabant, the servant with the keys to the kitchens of the House of Twelve Front Rooms, was Prefect
Corin's agent, doing double duty after he had led Yama
to the Prefect. Yama still did not know who was the target
of the plot, but that did not matter as long as Brabant
was unmasked.

''You'll have to talk with Lupe, dominie. Please, I really
am no more than a player of games. We're all at the
service of the workers in the Palace, and that's how I make
my living. You might say that if we had a department, it
would be the oldest of all.''

Eliphas caught Yama's arm and whispered, ''I know his
kind now. Thieves and cutthroats, brother, no better than
the husbandmen.''

Yama whispered back, ''Unless you know the way out,
we have no choice but to follow him.''

Magon cocked his head, his eyes bright as he looked
from Eliphas to Yama. He said, ''You don't trust me, and
I guess that if I was in your position I'd feel the same. I
don't have the answers you want, dominie. I'm just here
to bring you to Lupe. Lupe will answer your questions.
We must leave here. The hell-hound is still at your back,
and the big fish get restless after a while, and start questing
about with their arms to see if they can catch you. We—''

Blue light was suddenly reflected in Magon's eyes.
Yama turned. The hell-hound stood at the end of the
bridge. It was smaller now, but burned as brightly as ever.
Yama unsheathed his knife. Its curved blade kindled with
blue flame, as if to challenge the hell-hound's unworldly
light.

The hell-hound slid forward, elongating through black
air as it climbed the arch of the narrow bridge. Yama and
Eliphas retreated step by step. They had scarcely reached
the far end when something hit the underside of the bridge

so hard that it hummed like a plucked string. Magon and
Eliphas screamed. Nests of pale tendrils rose up on either
side of the bridge's arch, slithering around the slender
railings. The hell-hound stopped, bending back and forth
as more tentacles quested up out of the water.

Yama guessed that there must be a decad or more of
the giant polyps beneath the bridge. The undersides of the
tentacles bore rows of fleshy suckers which stuck and un-
stuck to the metal span with wet noises; their ends were
frayed into feathery palps which continually tasted the air.
Then the water under the bridge boiled and the forest of
tentacles which gripped the railings tensed. The bridge
groaned but held, and the tentacles coiled more tightly and
tensed again, quivering with effort. One of the giant polyps
was half-lifted out of the water. Under its white mantle, a
huge blue eye with a golden pupil revolved and fixed its
gaze on Yama.

The bridge groaned again and then the central section
gave way with a sudden sharp crack that echoed and re-
echoed from the cavern's wet walls. On the other side of
the broken bridge, the hell-hound flared brilliantly and
whirled around and fled into the tunnel, and Yama and
Eliphas cheered.

The water boiled with activity. Green lights flashed furi-
ously under its foaming surface. One, then another, then
two more: the great polyps lifted the edges of their mantles
out of the water and stared at Yama. Eliphas and Magon
shouted in alarm, but Yama, guessing wildly, lifted the
coin from his shirt and held it up. Satisfied, the polyps
sank back one by one. The water boiled up once more
and then darkened as the living lights beneath its surface
faded away.

"Nothing will follow us now," Yama said.

"The hell-hound will find another way to follow you,"
Magon said. "That's what it does." He was very scared,
but he had stood firm, and Yama liked him better for that.

Eliphas took a deep, trembling breath, then another.
"Lead on, brother. And remember we trust you only
slightly more than we trust your fishy friends."

—

The narrow corridor which led away from the flooded cavern was circular in cross-section and lined with fused rock that dully reflected the lights of the fireflies of Yama and Eliphas. As it rose and turned, Yama was certain that its gravity changed direction, too, so that they were no longer walking on its floor but along its wall, rising vertically through the heart of the mountain. Occasionally, other corridors opened to either side and above; gusts of warm air blew from these openings, sometimes bringing the sound of distant machinery.

Magon soon regained his jaunty confidence, and boasted that these were the old skyways which only his people knew.

"You might say that there's a Palace within a Palace, each twined around the other like a vine around a tree until you can't tell whether the tree is holding up the vine, or the vine the tree. We were here from the beginning. Departments come and go. They fight each other and are destroyed or absorbed, yet we are still here. We will be here until the end."

Eliphas said, "I suppose this is the teaching of your master, this Lupe."

"It's our history," Magon said. "It's passed on in song and dance from father to son, from mother to daughter. Just because it's not written in books doesn't mean it isn't true, though for someone like yourself, who has breathed so much book dust he is mostly book himself, that might be hard to believe. We are always here to serve. It's what we do. Whoever owns the Palace becomes our master, whether they know it or not."

"And you want to help me?"

What struck Yama now was that in his posturing and anxious capering, his hypersensitivity to moods and eagerness to please, Magon was just like the kind of lap dog that childless gentlewomen keep.

Magon said, "You are come at last, dominie. Lupe said

he had not expected it, although it was foretold by an anchorite years before. But Lupe will tell you himself.''

The corridor turned around itself again. Warm, humid air, laden with a rich organic stink, blew into their faces, and then the corridor opened out into a long, low room. Its bare rock walls ran with condensation; its floor was strewn with heaps of black soil in which frills of fungus grew; dead white, blood red, a yellow so shiny it might have been varnished. At the other end of the room, Magon parted layers of nylon-mesh curtains and ushered Yama and Eliphas into a barrel-vaulted cave lit by shafts of sunlight that fell from vents in the rock ceiling far above.

"Our home," Magon said. "It is the capital of my people, for Lupe lives here."

There were little gardens, and patchwork shacks built of plastic or cardboard sheeting, or of translucent paper stretched across bamboo framing. People drew around Yama and Eliphas as they followed Magon across the cavern, and they quickly became the center of a procession. There were clowns and jugglers, mummers and mimes, weightlifters and agonists, fakirs with steel pins through their cheeks and eyelids. Acrobats walked on wires strung everywhere across the midway of the cavern. There were men dressed in richly embroidered dresses of faded silk stiff with brocade and silver and gold thread, with white-painted faces and black makeup that exaggerated their eyes, transvestites that burlesqued the sacred temple dancers. There were musicians and gamblers, and prostitutes of all four sexes and seemingly of every imaginable bloodline.

Eliphas looked around uneasily, but Yama knew that they would not be harmed. Not here. "They exist to serve!" he said, and took the old man's arm to reassure him.

The gorgeous, motley procession crossed the length of the cavern. A fakir smashed a bottle on his head and rubbed a handful of broken glass over his bare chest; another pressed metal skewers through folds of skin pinched up from his arms. Musicians played a solemn march;

clowns knocked each other down and breathed out gouts of fire or blew fountains of sparkling dust high into the air; men and women held up their children, who laughed and clapped their hands.

The path ended at a round gilt frame twice Yama's height. It might once have held a shrine. The crowd parted to let Yama and Eliphas follow Magon through this gateway.

The room beyond was swagged in faded tapestries and bunched silks stained with dust. The wrack of ten thousand years lay everywhere in an indiscriminate jumble. Lapidary icons were heaped like beetles in a green plastic bowl; a cassone, its sides painted with exquisitely detailed scenes from the Puranas, its top missing, was filled with filthy old boots; ancient books lay in a tumbled heap next to neat rolls of plastic sheeting.

A man sprawled amongst cushions on a sagging bed beneath a canopy of cloth-of-gold. Magon capered forward and jumped onto the bed, raising a cloud of dust from the yellowed linen sheets, and laid his head next to the man's bare feet, gazing up with unqualified adoration, for all the world like a faithful puppy gazing at its master.

Without doubt, the man on the bed was Lupe, the king of the Palace within the Palace. He was a big man; he was an old man. Skin hung in mottled flaps from his arms. His face was scored deeply with lines and wrinkles. He wore a long brocade dress so stiff with dirt that it was impossible to tell what color it might once have been; an elaborate headdress of gold wire woven in a tall cone and studded with bits of colored glass was planted on top of tangled gray hair that fell to his broad shoulders. His feet were bare and his toenails were painted red; the nails of his big, strong hands, like those of certain mendicants, had been allowed to grow around each other in long corkscrews. His lips had been stained with cochineal and his eyes were made up like the wings of a blue butterfly. His pupils were capped with frost, and from the way he held his head Yama knew he was blind. He did not look absurd in his costume, but wore it with a grave, sacerdotal majesty.

Lupe turned his face toward Yama and Eliphas, and said in a soft, hoarse voice, "Come closer, dominie."

Eliphas said, "What is this place?"

Lupe raised his head and turned it from side to side, as if sniffing the air. "Who is this stranger, Magon?"

"A companion of the one foretold, Lupe."

"Then he is welcome," the old man said. "As are you, dominie. Welcome and twice welcome. It is my honor to welcome you. I had thought that I would die before you came, and it is with all my heart that I convey the treasure house of my sentiments, which have been stored up for so long against this wonderful day."

"It seems that I am expected," Yama said.

"You are the one who is foretold," Lupe said. His blind eyes were turned toward Yama's face. "Please, dominie. Please sit at our table! All that we have is yours!"

Three beautiful girls, arrayed in layers of splendid silks that left only their arms and faces bare, stepped through a curtain. Their delicate oval faces were painted white; their full lips were stained black. They carried trays of sweetmeats and candied fruits arranged on plantain leaves or in tiny bowls of translucent porcelain. Their eyes shone with excitement and they giggled as they fussed about Yama, seating him in a nest of dusty cushions and setting the food before him. One sat Eliphas beside Yama; the other two helped Lupe from the bed, sat him on a low stool, and settled the full skirt of his dress around him.

Yama took a bowl of tea from one of the girls and, after a hesitation, Eliphas followed suit. Another girl raised a bowl to Lupe's lips; the old man's fingernails were so long that he could not possibly feed himself. The three men slurped companionably, and Lupe belched gravely. While one of the girls fed Lupe with chopsticks, Yama picked at diced squares of candied yam. He had not eaten since the meal in the Strangers' Lodge of the Department of Apothecaries and Chirurgeons, but he was too excited and nervous to have much of an appetite.

At last, he said to Lupe. "You know of me, master. Where does that knowledge come from?"

"Please, dominie, I am not your master! I am Lupe, no more than Lupe and no less, and completely at your service. All my people are at your service. All this was foretold, and we have made many songs and poems and dances in your honor. Not all our dances are lewd or comic. Those are for our public, but we have our own dances. Once I could dance them, but now, alas, I can only remember them." Lupe tapped his wrinkled brow with his knuckles. "All our history is there, in the dances, and so are you."

Eliphas said to Yama, "Ask him how we can destroy the hell-hound, brother. Ask him to show us the way back to the roof of the Palace, so I can help you find what you seek."

Lupe cocked his head, and said, "Anything you wish, dominie. Anything within our powers. We are yours to command."

Yama said, "How is it that you know me?"

He did not feel afraid here—he realized that this was the first time since he had left his home in Aeolis that he did not feel some measure of fear. But he could not stay long. The gates of the Department of Vaticination would open to petitioners at noon; the assassin would be sharpening his covert blade or preparing his vial of odorless poison. But this was an opportunity that might not come again, and he was intensely eager to discover all that Lupe knew—or believed he knew—about him.

Lupe did not answer Yama's question at once. Instead, he motioned to his attendants. One of the girls squatted beside him and refilled his tea bowl; another held it to his lips. When the old man had drained his tea, he wiped his red-stained lips on the back of his hand and said, "We have always served, dominie. We were put into the world to serve and to bring pleasure. Thus, while our bloodline is of the lowest order, the nature of our service calls upon the highest arts. For while we might be counted as beggars who dance, make mock or make love for a paltry slew of coinage, our reward is not in the money but in the pleasure our performances bring to our clients. We are a simple people. We do not need money, except to buy cloth and beads and metal wire for our costumes. Your friend looks among the trinkets stored here, and wonders perhaps that I can claim to be poor, yet live with all these riches heaped about me.'' (Eliphas held up a mildewed leather cap embroidered with silver wire, and made a face.) ''But these riches are all gifts from grateful clients,'' Lupe said. ''We have saved them out of sentiment, not avarice. We are a simple people, and yet, dominie, we have survived longer than any other bloodline. We are too simple to know how to change, perhaps, but we do remember. It is our other virtue. We remember your people, dominie. We remember how great and good they were. We remember how we feared and adored them. They have been gone a long time, but we have always remembered them.''

Yama leaned forward, his entire attention on Lupe's grave, blind face. He said, ''And are my people still in the world?''

''They are not in the Palace, dominie, and so we have always believed that they are no longer of the world. How could it be otherwise? For they were the Builders, and this is their place. It was here that they commanded the world, in their day. If they are not here, then surely they live nowhere else.''

''Perhaps this is no longer their day. Perhaps they are dwindled.''

Lupe shook his head. ''Ah, dominie, how you tease me! You know I cannot speak of that. We know the Palace. We know something of Ys. The world is another place entirely.''

''Then they are not in Ys,'' Yama said. He had guessed it, but this was still hard to bear. ''Do you believe that they might return?''

Lupe said, ''An anchorite came to me seventeen years ago and told me that one day you would seek help from my people. And here you are. So you might say that your people have returned.''

Seventeen years ago Yama had been found afloat on the

river, a baby lying on the breast of a dead woman in a white boat. For a moment, Yama was so excited that he could not speak. He touched the coin which hung inside his shirt. An anchorite had given it to him in Aeolis, at the beginning of his adventures. Derev had said that the man was of his bloodline.

At last, he said, "What did he look like? Was he scarred about the face, and dumb?"

"He had a gentle, hoarse voice. As for what he looked like, I could not tell you, dominie. I was blind then as now, and he came to me when I was alone. It was deepest night, and those of my people not working were asleep. He told me that one day, near the end of the world, a Builder would come to Ys, and that he would need our help. He told me where you would come from, and when. My people have been watching the docks for a hundred days now. I thought that you would not come, but here you are."

"I came by the road, not the river."

"And yet you are the Child of the River, and the end of the world seems near. The departments have been perpetually at war with each other since the Hierarchs fell from power, and now one department threatens to destroy the rest in the name of the war against the heretics. If it wins, then such a tyranny may rise that could hold the world in its grip forever, wielding power in the name of the Preservers, but serving only itself. I have feared this for a very long time, but now I know, dominie. Now I know! How glad I am that these terrible days are the last!"

Lupe's milky eyes shone with tears. Magon crept from the bed and with his long, crafty fingers tenderly blotted the tears from his master's withered, rouged cheeks. "It's true," the gambler said, looking boldly at Yama. "Everything Lupe says is true. He remembers more than anyone else. It is why he is our king."

Lupe composed himself and said, "I weep from joy, dominie, that you have come again. There will be new songs and dances made out of this wonderful moment."

"I understand," Yama said, although it seemed to him

that he had mistakenly stumbled into the middle of a myth. Lupe's story had set a hundred questions tumbling through his head. Who was the anchorite? Was it the same man who had given him the coin? Why had he been set adrift on the river in the first place?

He said, "I am grateful for your hospitality, Lupe, and for your help. But you know that I cannot stay."

Magon said, "They have business with one of the fading flowers, Lupe. I told them that they need not concern themselves with it any longer."

"Forgive my servant," Lupe said. "He is young and eager, but he means well. If you have business to attend to, dominie, then that is what you must do. My servant will take you where you need to go."

Eliphas said, "Then you will let us go?"

"Wherever you are in the Palace, we are with you," Lupe said. "But before you go, walk with me. Show my people that you are my friend, and so the friend of us all."

Lupe led Yama and Eliphas through the kingdom of his cavern. A hundred brightly costumed clowns, dancers, and whores followed at a respectful distance while Lupe gravely introduced Yama to each of the elders who stood in shabby finery outside their painted shacks.

Yama asked many questions, and although Lupe answered every one, often at length, he learned little more, except that much was expected of him. Lupe was too polite, or too cunning, to state exactly what this was, but Yama slowly began to realize that there was only one thing these people could desire. For they were indigens, and unlike the changed and unchanged bloodlines they were untouched by the breath of the Preservers. They were creatures which had borrowed human form; perhaps even their intelligence was borrowed, a trick or skill they had learned like tumbling, fire-eating, or prestidigitation. Everything they possessed had come to them from other hands, and they accepted these gifts without discrimination. Fabulous treasures were tipped carelessly amongst the rubbish that had formed great drifting piles in Lupe's apartments; a beautiful boy carrying nightsoil to the gar-

dens at the edge of the caverns might be wearing a price-
less dress; a dancer made up as fabulously as a courtesan
might be clad in a glittering costume that, on close inspec-
tion, was constructed of sacking decorated with a magpie's
nest of scraps of plastic and aluminum.

The only thing which was truly theirs was the art of
simulation, which they used without guile to enhance the
pleasure of their clients. Watching closely, Yama saw that
the three girls who attended Lupe were not beautiful at
all—or rather, that their beauty was a trick of poise and
muscle tone and expression, sustained by constant vigi-
lance. They could become passable imitations of most
bloodlines by synthesizing and exaggerating with a little
makeup the two or three features by which each was
distinguished from the others. And so with beauty, for
beauty is only an exaggeration of the ordinary. Just as a
transvestite exaggerates those features which make a
woman attractive, Lupe's people achieved beauty through
burlesque. These people could, through their art, appear to
be anything that their clients might desire.

The only thing they could not be was themselves.

Many, like Eliphas, believed that the indigenous races
were no more than animals. Yama thought otherwise. For
if everything in the world had proceeded from the minds
of the Preservers, then surely the indigenous races had not
been brought here simply to be despised and persecuted.
Surely they too had their place.

It was almost noon by the time Yama and Lupe finally
completed the circuit of the cavern and returned through
the gilt frame to Lupe's chambers. Somewhere high above,
the Gate of Double Glory would be admitting those who
wished to participate in the public inquisition at the Department of Vaticination. The two pythonesses would soon
appear before their clients, arrayed in ancient splendor.

"I do not forget that you have business elsewhere," the
dignified old man said. He covered Yama's hands with his
own. "You can leave by a hidden way, and the people
will think you stay here to talk with me. The more important they think I am, the easier it is to keep order. We

are a fractious people, dominie. We get too many ideas from others."

"You have been very generous," Yama said.

"We have done all we can, but I fear that it is little enough."

"You have given me my life, and hope that my people still live," Yama said. "I will try to return when I can."

"Of course you will return," Lupe said. "And so I will not say farewell, for in reality you will not have left."

As they followed Magon up a long stairway, Eliphas said, "This is a day of wonders, brother. I had not known that the mirror people stored up their loot. Amongst all that rubbish is an edition of the Book of Blood that I had known only by repute. It is badly damaged, but a man could live for a year from the sale of only a few intact pages. Will you return?"

Yama shook his head, meaning that he did not know. Yet he did feel a prick of obligation. Not because Lupe's people had saved his life; Lupe had made it clear that there was no debt to be paid, and Yama was ready to take him at his word. But there was the other matter. There was Lupe's impossible dream, the promise of the anchorite, the prophecy fulfilled.

No wonder my people have hidden themselves, he thought, for the world holds a store of their unpaid debts and I seem to be fated to redeem them all.

He said with sudden bitterness, "I wish I had never come to Ys! I only hurt myself, and those who expect things from me. I should have gone downriver with Dr. Dismas and accepted my fate!"

But as soon as he said it, he knew that the words came from his dark half, the part of him that dreamed of easy glory and power without responsibility. The part that had been touched by the woman in the shrine, the aspect whose original had begun the heresy which threatened to consume the world.

Magon glanced over his shoulder, his pale face thrown into sharp relief by the lights cast by the fireflies of Yama and Eliphas. There was no other light in the long stair, and Yama wondered how those who lived in the Palace could stand it. Except in places at the edge of things, they inhabited little bubbles of light surrounded by vast expanses of uncharted shadow; Lupe's people, who possessed only the dimmest of fireflies, if any, must navigate the maze of passages and tunnels in near darkness.

Yama said, "How far is it, Magon?"

"Not far, dominie. We use the straightest route."

Eliphas whispered, "You should feel no obligation, brother. They are shadows. Thieves and tricksters and whores who live off the crumbs of those engaged in honest toil. They are like the indigens of the roof gardens—except those are more useful. Would you be the savior of such as they?"

"I suppose that if one was to attempt to emulate the Preservers, then one must start somewhere, and better to start in a low place than in a high one. But I aspire to no such thing. I see that you are a pragmatic man, Eliphas. You prize things for their utility."

"Brother, things are what they are. The mirror people were created for the amusement and wonder of the bloodlines of men, nothing more. They spin fantasies, but they should not be taken seriously."

"Yet they dream, Eliphas. They believe that I belong in their dreams."

"They remember their creators, brother, as men remember their mothers and fathers. But once we are grown up we cannot continue to depend upon our parents. We must face the world ourselves."

"If Lupe's people are still as children," Yama said, "then I envy them."

They fell silent for a while, following Magon up the stairway to a dark, narrow tunnel which, binding gravity about itself, rose vertically through the Palace. At last, Magon stopped and said, "It is not far, dominie. You follow the way until you reach a place where it branches into two. Take the right-hand branch and you will find yourself in a throughway near the Gate of Double Glory."

"I owe you much, Magon."

The ragamuffin gambler bobbed and bowed. "You have repaid me a thousandfold, dominie, by allowing me to bring you to my people. I will watch for your return."

When Magon's footsteps had faded into the darkness, Yama said, "Whatever my intentions, it may fall out that I am never able to return."

"Because of the territorial dispute," Eliphas said. "It is no secret, brother. The whole Palace knows the plight of the Department of Vatication. Many hope it survives, for that will check the growth of the Department of Indigenous Affairs."

"It's a pity that there's only hope and no help."

"No one wishes to anger the Department of Indigenous Affairs, for lately it has grown very powerful, and careless of the ancient protocols. That is why it has been able to pick off lesser departments one by one."

"And there is the hell-hound. We cannot be certain that it has lost my trail. You do not have to follow me, Eliphas. It will not be an easy time. You could go back to the library and your friend, if you wish, and wait for me there."

The old man smiled. "And suppose the hell-hound finds me? No, I will stay with you, brother. Besides, I made a pledge. Lead on, and I will help as best I can."

THE PUBLIC INQUISITION

HUGE MIRRORS HAD been set up on the flat roof of the House
of the Twelve Front Rooms, deflecting sunlight into the
cavern and mercilessly illuminating the shabby façades of
the buildings ranged around the wide plaza. Yama squinted
against the mirrors' multiple glare when he and Eliphas
came through the Gate of Double Glory. He had expected
to find a crowd waiting for the pythonesses, but although
a platform had been set up on the steps of the Basilica,
its deck covered with landscape cloth and strewn with
garlands of white lilies and trumpet flowers that already
were beginning to wilt, the plaza was deserted.

Inside the Basilica, Tamora was roaring at a double file
of thralls marching in two-step time, turning them again
and again in precise right angles. Pandaras ran up and said
to Yama, while staring openly at Eliphas, "We thought
you lost, master!"

"So I was, for a little while. This is my friend, Eliphas.
He searches libraries for facts. He has already been of
help to me, and I hope he will help me further. Eliphas,
this is Pandaras. The fierce woman over there is Tamora."

"Yama exaggerates my importance in our adventures
on the roof," Eliphas said.

"I am Yama's squire," Pandaras said, staring up at Eliphas boldly. The boy had oiled his hair back from his forehead. It gleamed beneath his three fireflies. He turned to Yama and said, "I see you have had the sense to bandage your head, master. Let me look at it."

"It is almost healed."

"As you said two days ago."

Now Tamora came stalking across the Basilica's marble floor. She wore her corselet and a short leather skirt, and sandals with laces that crisscrossed her calves. Her scalp was freshly shaven, and the fall of red hair at the back of her skull had been braided into a complex knot. She looked both terrified and desirable.

"I thought you'd been killed, or that you'd run away," she said, and took Yama's arm and drew him a little way from the others. "Grah. You stink of the warrens of some subhuman race. Where have you been? And who's your fish-eyed friend?"

"I was lost. Eliphas helped me find my way. There is a conspiracy—"

Tamora grinned, showing her rack of pointed teeth. "The servant you followed? The fucker is dead. When you didn't come back, Pandaras told me you were following this fellow by the name of Brabant, and I told Syle. On his advice, Luria ordered the execution. Brabant was bound and pitched out of a window of the House of the Twelve Front Rooms. It's how they do things here. They call it defenestration. Yama, I talk too much, but it's because I am pleased to see you alive! I thought Brabant had lured you into an ambush. I wanted to torture him for the truth, but he went straight out the window."

Yama said, "I think I know the whole story, Tamora. No one here is plotting against anyone else. Certainly not Luria, or she would not have agreed to have Brabant killed."

"Of course not. Luria has so much meat on her she can't walk five steps in a straight line. Why would she meet with someone in secret in a remote place when she could do so at ease in her own chambers? No, I think it's Syle. You might trust him, but I don't. Not him, and not that pregnant hen of his, either. He could have had Brabant killed to cover his tracks."

"Brabant was not working for Syle, but for someone outside the Department. In fact, he—"

"He is dead. If there are other traitors here they'll show themselves soon enough, and I'll deal with them. Now, tell me about what happened to you."

Yama suddenly found himself smiling. He could not help it. "I have found the library, Tamora! The library where Dr. Dismas discovered the secret of my bloodline. I have put a question to it, and perhaps the answer is already known."

If the hell-hound had not destroyed the records, he thought. Eliphas had said that they were safe, but Yama did not entirely trust the old man. Eliphas preferred to tell people what he thought they wanted to hear, even if it was not always the truth.

"I'm pleased for you," Tamora said. "I get paid no matter how you go about your search, so the quicker the better as far as I'm concerned. But right now we have work to do."

"Then I have not missed the inquisition? That is good. I mean to keep my word, Tamora."

"It has already begun. Go and put on your armor. Luria is still worried that an attempt will be made on her life. The Department of Indigenous Affairs would claim this place at once if she was killed."

"The assassination plot is only half the story, Tamora. Perhaps there is no plot at all, except against me."

Tamora lost her temper. "Will you serve? Then do as I say! Put on your armor and follow my orders!"

"I have your armor close by, master," Pandaras said, and ran off to fetch it.

Yama told Tamora, "Please listen to me. Brabant set up a charade, making sure that Pandaras overheard it, and then he lured me to a place where I could be taken. Prefect Corin tried to kidnap me, Tamora. He has been looking for me, and he almost caught me. The ruffians who ambushed us were part of it.''

"Well, Brabant is dead," Tamora said, "and you escaped." She turned to Eliphas. "If you're a friend, go up with Pandaras and keep watch. That way, I won't have to worry about you."

"Because while I keep watch, the boy will keep watch on me?" Eliphas smiled. "I understand completely. But you do not have to worry, Tamora. Yama's interests coincide with mine."

"Then we've much to talk about," Tamora said. "And we will, when this is over."

Yama said, "You do not have to do anything here, Eliphas. This has nothing to do with helping me find my people."

"I will enjoy it, brother. Like my friend Kun Norbu, all this excitement makes me feel young again."

Tamora helped Yama to assemble his patchwork armor. "This is how it falls out," she said. "Syle is talking with the clients and keeping them entertained until the ceremony begins. What he's really doing is finishing off the business of finding out as much as possible about them. He told me how it works. The clients have to submit their questions two decads in advance of the ceremony, which gives him plenty of time to research them. He employs spies and bribes clerks, that sort of thing. He says that it is to provide the pythonesses with as much background information as possible, but I reckon that he doesn't really believe in the pythonesses' powers of prediction. He finds out what kind of answers his clients want, and makes sure that's what they get."

"He believes that Daphoene can see into the future. And there *is* something strange about her, Tamora. As if her head is full of ghosts."

"Grah, I'd say it was mostly full of air. She says little, and because of her position her few words seem important. But they're not. They're nothing but simple-minded babble. But I know you don't listen to me." Tamora knelt to tighten the buckles of Yama's greaves—the greaves he had won by killing the one-eyed cateran, Cyg. She looked up. "There's something wrong about this place. It's nothing to do with your funny feeling about Daphoene. It's as if they all hold knives at each other's throats.''

''In a few days they will be under attack, and they are already under siege. You must listen to me, Tamora. There is no intrigue except that of Prefect Corin. He found out where I was and used Brabant to lure me away. If there is an assassination plot, then it is also the work of Prefect Corin.''

''Then why are they at each other's throats? Luria has told me to watch Syle, and Syle took me aside after Brabant went out of the window and said that there is a conspiracy that goes deeper than one foolish thrall.''

Yama hesitated. He knew that Tamora did not believe in his powers. Did not believe, or refused to allow herself to believe. Although he had tried to explain how he had awoken the Thing Below in the Temple of the Black Well, and how he had killed Gorgo, she had merely scoffed and told him that the blow to his head had given him delusions.

He said, ''Syle knows what I am, Tamora. He knows that I am one of the Builders. He asked me to use machines against the forces of the Department of Indigenous Affairs. I refused, of course.''

''So he betrayed you to Prefect Corin?''

''This was after Pandaras overheard Brabant. But I suppose that Syle might think of selling me now.''

''Your brain is still bruised from the ding you got at the gate. No more talk about magical powers, or I'll begin to regret I took up with you.''

''I know you do not believe me, Tamora, but I raised up the feral machine in the Temple of the Black Well, then woke the guards which destroyed it. It was that fight which set fire to the temple.''

''It was the assassin who did that, to cover his tracks. You're brave enough, Yama. You got the priests out of the burning temple. Don't spoil it with silly stories.''

''I killed Gorgo. You did not see it, but thousands of others did.''

''If he isn't dead, he deserves to be. He *will* be, when I finish here. I'll make sure of it.''

"My fireflies, then. I left here with one, and I have returned with five."

"You've been on the roof. Your firefly left you then, and you got a new set when you came back inside."

Yama laughed. She was as stubborn as an ox.

"Forget your fantasy, Yama, and concentrate on what you are. Which is what I am, a cateran hired to defend this miserable place." Tamora prowled around Yama, stepped in to tighten a strap of his cuirass, stood back and gave him an appraising look. "You should have kept Cyg's sword, if only for show."

"That was all it was good for. My knife serves me well enough." Yama realized now that the real reason he had rejected the sword was because it had been wielded against him, and saw that Tamora had understood this from the beginning. He said, "I do not look much like a soldier, do I?"

Tamora said, "There's nothing to it. The rat-boy is on the roof with an arbalest, and your new friend will help him keep watch. The clients have brought their own guards, and I reckon that's where any trouble will come from. If there are any more traitors amongst the servants, they'll choose a less public time. A knife or a strangling cord in the dark, or poison—that's the style of this place. All we have to do is stand on either side of the platform and look fierce. If there is trouble, we'll get the thralls between the stage and the clients. Those gray-skinned rockheads can't do much, but at least they can get in the way of anyone who tries to hurt the fat one or the airhead. Promise you won't try any heroics. None will be needed."

Tamora clapped Yama between his shoulder blades and added, "Don't doubt yourself," and went off to shout at the thralls, ordering them to get back into formation.

~

When Yama and Tamora marched out of the main doors of the Basilica and came down the steps leading a double column of thralls, the people who had gathered at the foot of the platform fell silent and stared at the spectacle. There were only three clients, each sitting in a plain chair with a small entourage of advisers, clerks and bodyguards behind them. No more than a couple of decads of men in total, and a scattering of old women who had no doubt come for the entertainment. Yama went right and Tamora left, each leading a line of thralls. Yama halted at the place where the rear edge of the platform butted the stairs, and the thralls marched past him and turned out one by one, forming a neat arc down the long, shallow staircase. Tamora really had done wonders with their drill. Their metal caps shone and they had tied long red ribbons beneath the double-edged blades of their partisans.

Yama did not feel nervous now that he was in place. As with the public ceremonies he had attended with his stepfather, the Aedile of Aeolis, he found that the worst thing was the entrance, when the audience had nothing better to look at and was full of anticipation, so that any mistake by the participants was most obvious.

A small procession made its way across the wide plaza toward the Basilica, led by a herald who blew a braying brass trumpet. The people below the platform turned to watch. In better times, Yama supposed, the trumpet would have been necessary to clear a way through the crowd, but now it sounded small and plaintive, and its echo came back from the rock walls and made discords. Behind the herald came a tall figure in a cloud of red—it was Syle, in a long robe of red feathers that fluttered with his every step. He marched solemnly ahead of the palanquins, carried on the shoulders of bare-chested thralls, on which the pythonesses sat. Both women wore white gowns and were crowned with wreaths of ivy. Luria's jowls were rouged and her eyes were accentuated by gold leaf; Daphoene's face was as bloodless as ever, and she ceaselessly worked her narrow jaw as if chewing something. The senior servants of the household walked behind the palanquins. They were led by Rega, stately as a carrack, in a dove-gray silk dress with a full skirt and a high collar trimmed with pearls.

Luria was carried up the steps to the right of the platform and Daphoene to the left. The senior servants took
their place on the steps above as the bearers, their gray
skins gleaming with oil, carefully set the palanquins on
the platform. The landscape cloth, which had been showing a field of green grass ceaselessly winnowed by wind,
now changed to show blue sky. The change raced out
from the two pythonesses, so that they seemed to be
couched on air, the heaps of white flowers at their feet
like clouds.

Syle stood beside Yama while the pythonesses were set
in place. "I am so pleased to see you return," he whispered. "I had thought all was lost, but now I know that
we are saved."

Before Yama could ask what he meant by this, Syle
moved off, taking a position in the center of the platform,
in front of a little brazier which stood between the pythonesses. Syle bowed to both of them—Luria acknowledged
him with a regal nod, but Daphoene had turned her blind
face toward the light which shone from the mirrors on the
far side of the plaza—and threw a handful of dried leaves
on the glowing charcoal in the bowl of the brazier. Instantly, heavy white smoke billowed over the sides of the
brazier and spread across the platform. The white smoke
had a powerfully sweet smell. It spilled over the edges of
the sky-colored platform and rolled down the stairs.

Syle stepped to the front of the platform, the hem of
his red robe swirling through white vapor. His fireflies
spun above his head like a spectral crown. He looked
hierophantic, uncanny, terrifying. He pulled a slate from
his robes and read from it in a conversational voice. "The
merchant, Cimbar, would ask the avatars of the Preservers
this question. Will his business prosper if he leases an
additional two ships to supply the loyal army of the will
of the Preservers?"

There was a silence. Then Luria began to intone sono-
rously, "There is no end to the war—"

Daphoene shuddered violently and bent over, squealing

like a stricken shoat. It was as if she had been struck in the belly. Syle covered his confusion by stepping backward and casting a pinch of dried leaves on to the brazier.

Daphoene straightened. Everyone was watching her, even Luria. Yama could hear her breath whistling through her narrow lips. The faint sense he had of the ghosts of many machines inhabiting her intensified for a moment, like a sea of candle flames flaring in a sudden draft.

Daphoene said in a thick, choked voice, "No one profits from war but the merchants," and fell back on the couch of her palanquin. Blood spotted the front of her white gown; she had bitten her tongue.

The fat man in the central chair smiled and nodded as two of his advisers whispered in his ear. At last he waved a be-ringed hand, clearly satisfied with his answer.

Syle cleared his throat and said, "The avatars of the Preservers have answered, and the answer is acceptable." He raised his arms, the sleeves of his red robe falling like wings around him, and framed the second question, concerning plantations of green wood which were not growing properly.

This time Luria answered, and at some length. Yama was watching Daphoene, and Tamora the small audience; it was Pandaras who raised the alarm. When he cried out, half of those in front of the platform stared up at the little balcony where the boy and Eliphas stood, high above the door of the Basilica; the rest turned to look at where he pointed.

Huge shadows flickered across the cavern. Yama realized that there were men on the roof of the House of the Twelve Front Rooms, small as emmets against the glare of the mirrors. One of the tiny figures fired an energy pistol. A thread of intense red light burned above the plaza. Fire splashed above the turrets of the Gate of Double Glory, and a curtain of rock plunged down with a roar that echoed and re-echoed in the sounding chamber of the cavern.

~

After that, there was very little resistance. Most of the thralls threw down their partisans and fled; when Tamora tried to rally the others, one drew a knife and ran at her. It was the thrall with the streaks of gray in his mane who had been humbled by Yama two days before. Tamora parried his clumsy stroke, killed him with a single thrust to his throat and turned to face the others, the point of her bloody sword held up before her face.

Yama drew his knife and started toward her, but Syle caught his arm and thrust the muzzle of a slug pistol into his side and said, "You should have listened to me when I asked for your help, but perhaps this is for the best. If you stay calm, all of your friends will live. One word from you, and they die. Drop the knife please."

"Perhaps you should take it. I do not want to damage the blade."

"I know what it can do. Drop it."

Soldiers were rappelling down the wall of the House of the Twelve Front Rooms; some were already running across the plaza toward the Basilica. Luria lifted the ivy wreath from her head and dashed it into the fumes at her feet. She pointed at Syle and bellowed, "You said you'd wait!"

Syle told her calmly, "I promised I'd wait until he returned, and so he has. My first duty is to the Department of Vatication, not the dead past." He said to Yama, "Tell your friends to come down. I've no desire to see them killed if they should try and defend their position. Besides, the Basilica might be damaged."

Tamora swung around when Yama called to Pandaras, and Syle showed her his pistol. She spat and sheathed her sword and ordered the thralls who remained to lay down their partisans.

"I demand that ransom is paid for my freedom," she said.

"I would give it to you at once," Syle said, "but it is not mine to grant."

Pandaras and Eliphas came out of the main door of the Basilica as the attacking force began to disarm the thralls. Pandaras held the arbalest above his head. A soldier plucked it from his hands and pushed him toward the thralls.

A man in homespun tunic, the black pelt of his face marked by a bolt of white, vaulted on to the stage. Syle thrust Yama forward and said, "Here he is, dominie."

"I am the master of no man," Prefect Corin said. He had a strip of translucent cloth tied across his eyes. "We meet again, Yama. How I wish this little drama was not necessary, but you provoked me."

"Let my friends go," Yama said. "They are no part of this."

"They know about you. More than I do, I think. Your stepfather kept much from the Department. That trick with the fireflies, for instance." Prefect Corin touched the cloth over his eyes. "Do not think to try that again, by the way. This will shield my eyes, and all my men are protected in the same way."

Yama remembered the little machine which had saved him from Cyg by piercing the cateran's brain. He could kill everyone in the plaza and walk free. He forced the thought away. He would not murder to save himself.

He said, "The Aedile told you all he knew. I have learned much since I came to Ys."

Prefect Corin nodded. "And you will learn more, with the Department's help."

Syle said, "You remember our agreement."

"Perfectly. Will you kill her with that silly little pistol, or shall I order one of my soldiers to do it for you?"

Syle blushed with anger. "Do not presume to tell me what to do. I give you this territory, but the Department is not the territory."

Luria struggled to her feet. White smoke billowed around her. She pointed at Syle and said loudly, "Traitor! You are disowned, Syle. I so rule."

Prefect Corin said dryly, "You have claimed the Department of Vaticination for yourself, Syle. I hope you can control it. Do be careful. I believe that she has a knife.''

It was small, with a crooked blade. Luria flourished it dramatically, as if about to plunge it into her own breast.

Daphoene spread her eyes wide. She was smiling toward Luria. Her white eyes were full of tears. A thread of blood ran from one corner of her mouth.

''Now it ends,'' she said.

To Yama, it seemed as if a hundred people had spoken with the same voice.

Syle stepped forward and said, ''Pythoness. Please—''

Luria swung the knife. Not at Syle, but at Daphoene. The blade must have been poisoned, for although it only inflicted a shallow cut on Daphoene's flat breast, the girl convulsed and fell back on to the chair of her palanquin. A moment later Luria fell too, riddled with arbalest bolts. Rega wailed and ran across the stage to Daphoene, and snatched her up and covered her face with desperate kisses.

THE COMMITTEE FOR PUBLIC SAFETY

"DAPHOENE WAS THE daughter of Rega by another marriage,"
Prefect Corin said. "I think it was Rega who had the
idea—Syle is a clever man, but not one given to carrying
out his schemes. Rega, however, is very ambitious. She
was not content to be the wife of the secretary of a dwindling department. Her father was a failed merchant who
killed himself before his debtors could, and she clawed her
way up from poverty. I half admire her for her ambition, if
not for her methods. She is a magnificent bitch.

"She altered her daughter's appearance by surgery and
infected her with machines carrying the essences of dead
people. It is a technique we have used to produce battlefield advisers. The infected subject becomes a population
which, when asked a question, can by heuristics derive the
best solution to a particular problem. It has not had a
high success rate—most of the subjects retreat into fugues.
Daphoene was more successful than most, but the proce-
dure blinded her, and most of her own personality was
destroyed. However, Rega felt that the loss of her daughter's sight and sanity was an acceptable sacrifice to her
own ambition. I think that Luria suspected that Daphoene
was Syle's stepdaughter, but she had no proof. It was Syle

who organized the search for the new pythoness, after all, and Syle who kept all the records, and he married the only person who could betray him.''

Yama said, "They meant to betray me from the beginning. Luria wanted to exchange me for the safety of her department; Syle and Rega plotted to use me as a counter in a bargain with you. At the last moment, Syle feared that the plans would go wrong and tried to persuade me to help him against you, but I would not. And even if I had helped him, I think that Rega would still have betrayed me.''

Brabant had been innocent. The conversation which Pandaras had overheard had been staged by Syle and Rega, part of the scheme to lure Yama into territory under the control of the Department of Indigenous Affairs so that he could be captured by Prefect Corin. It was well known that Brabant patronized the bawdy house at the edge of the day market, and Prefect Corin had waited for Yama there. But Yama had escaped the trap and had to be betrayed all over again, this time publicly. The gatekeeper had informed Syle of Yama's return, and Syle had delayed the start of the public inquisition until Prefect Corin's men were in place.

Prefect Corin said, "No doubt Rega will infect her new daughter once she is born—and meanwhile Syle will find an amenable candidate to play the role of pythoness. He is our man, now. These old departments are utterly decadent, Yama, incurable except by the most radical surgery. We have developed a new system where all, from the humblest clerk to the most senior legate, are answerable to a network of committees. With no center of power, no single person can influence the Department for their own ends. Thus, we are able to take a long-term view with the best interests of Confluence in mind. In time, all will fall under our system, and we can begin to win the war against the heretics.''

They sat side by side on the narrow cot in Yama's tiny cell, lit only by a luminous stick. Yama's fireflies had been stripped from him, as had his knife and the ancient coin

which the anchorite had given him. He had been allowed
to keep his copy of the Puranas and his clothes, nothing
else.

The cell was spartan. There was the cot with its lumpy
mattress, a plastic slop bucket, a shelf which folded down
from the wall, and a square of raffia matting on the stone
floor. A spigot in the wall delivered lukewarm, tasteless
water. There was a plastic cup hanging on a chain beside
the spigot, and a drain beneath, no bigger than Yama's
outspread hand. Prefect Corin assured Yama that it was
no different from his own cell and every other private cell
in the Department of Indigenous Affairs. Husbands and
wives each kept their own cells when they were married,
and children lived in dormitories until they were old
enough to be given a job and a cell of their own.

The heart of the Department of Indigenous Affairs was
a vast honeycomb of cells and narrow corridors, interspersed with long, low chambers where clerks worked,
row upon row upon row, fireflies flickering above their
heads as they bent over papers and books and slates. A
hundred layers of cells and corridors and chambers
crammed into the middle levels of the Palace and ringed
by outlying territories sequestered from other departments,
which contained barracks and armories.

Tamora and Pandaras and Eliphas were being held a
long way from Yama, in their own cells. They were undergoing debriefing, Prefect Corin said, and would be released
once it was finished. Yama asked when that might be, and
Prefect Corin replied that it might take only a few days,
or it might take years.

"Once we know everything," he said.

"There is no end to questions," Yama said.

Prefect Corin considered this. He said, "In your case,
that might be true."

It was never quiet. There was always the sound of
voices somewhere, the clash of doors slamming, the tread
of feet. Yama lost track of time. At the beginning, he was
mostly left in darkness, and meals—edible plastic occasionally leavened with a piece of fruit or a dollop of vege-

table curry—arrived at irregular intervals. Later, when daylight was piped into his cell through a glass duct, he could at least read in the Puranas and mark, by the waxing and waning of the weak light, the passage of the days.

At intervals, Yama was taken from the cell and marched by armed guards to a large, dimly lit room divided into two by a pane of thick glass. It was where he was tested. On one side of the glass was a stool; on the other were fireflies, anything from one to more than a hundred. A disembodied voice would instruct Yama to sit on the stool. Once he was seated, his side of the room would be plunged into darkness. Then the tests would begin.

The first time this happened there was only a single firefly, a brilliant point of light that hung in the center of the darkened space on the other side of the glass. Yama was told to move it to the right. He refused, and after a long time he was taken to his cell and left in darkness without food. Judging by the ebb and flow of noise, Yama thought that two days might have passed. At last, weak with hunger, he was brought back to the divided room and asked by the voice to repeat the exercise.

Yama obeyed. Both sides had made their point. He had shown that he was acting under coercion; they had shown that they would not tolerate resistance. The voice was patient and never tired or varied its precise inflection. It gave each set of instructions twice over and waited until Yama had complied before issuing the next. It took no notice of any mistakes or failures. Yama gradually constructed a fantasy image of the voice's owner. A middle-aged man, with cropped, iron-gray hair and a square jaw, sitting in a cell much like his own, a single firefly at his shoulder illuminating the script from which he read.

"Up," the voice would say, "Up." And, "Red firefly circle right, white firefly circle left. Red circle right, white circle left."

There were hundreds of these exercises. Sometimes Yama was asked to weave complex dances involving a decad of differently colored fireflies; sometimes he spent long hours moving a single firefly in straight lines back and forth across the darkness, or varying its brightness by increments. He did not try to understand the significance of the different kinds of exercises. He suspected that if there was a pattern, it had been randomized so that he could never unravel it. Better to think that there was no pattern at all. Better to think that they did not know what they wanted to find out, or did not know how to find out what they wanted to know.

He worked hard at the tests, although they often left him with bad headaches or worse. Sometimes red and black sparks would fill his sight and sometime later he would find himself lying on the floor of the cell, his trousers soaked with stale urine, blood on his lips and tongue. These fits terrified him. Perhaps they were a legacy of the blow to his head (although the wound had completely healed; there was not even a scar), exacerbated by the stress of the exercises. He told no one about them. He would reveal no weakness to his enemies.

Whether or not those testing Yama were learning about his abilities, he was certainly learning more about himself every day. Despite the fits, he exulted over the growing control over his powers. And for the first time since he had set out from Aeolis on the road to Ys, he had time to reflect on what he had discovered about himself. Always, his actions had been driven by contingency or by the needs of others. First, under the unwanted protection of Prefect Corin and then, after his escape from the Prefect and (so he thought) from his ordained fate as a minor official in the Department of Indigenous Affairs, in the company of Pandaras and Tamora.

He had promised himself that he would discover the secret of his origin—the silver-skinned woman, the white boat in the middle of the Great River, attended by a cloud of tiny machines—and he had failed. No, it was worse than that. He had not really tried. He had preferred to adventure with Tamora and Pandaras rather than think about what he was, and why he was here.

When he was alone in his cell, he spent his time reviewing every step of his adventures between leaving Aeolis and the

fall of the Department of Vatication, weighing every one
of his actions and motives and finding them all wanting.
He slept a lot, too, and in his sleep his sense of the loca-
tion and activity of machines expanded. Sometimes he
seemed to be suspended in the midst of a vast array of
little minds that were both quick and stupefyingly dull,
with webs of connectivity blossoming and fading around
him like a runaway loom simultaneously weaving and unraveling a cloth in three dimensions. Most of the machines
were fireflies, but at the periphery of their immense flock
Yama could detect larger machines employed in defense
of the Department. Further still, glimpsed like bright lights
through river fog, were larger machines whose purpose
was totally obscure, and interspersed through the volume
of greater and lesser machines were intense points which
he recognized as the potential energies of active shrines.

And sometimes, at the furthest edge of this inward vision, was a faint intimation of the feral machine he had
accidentally drawn down at the merchant's house. It was
very far away, hung in isolation beyond and below the
end of the world—but it was always there, the iron to
which the lodestone of his mind was drawn again and
again.

At times, his sensitivity increased so much that he could
even perceive the clusters of tiny machines which every
sentient person carried at the base of their brain. Faintly,
he could feel in these clusters the echoes of the memories
of their hosts; it was as if he was the only living person
in an impalpable world inhabited by hordes of ghosts
mumbling over their last ends.

In his sleep, Yama tried to discover which of the ghosts
might be Tamora, or Pandaras, or Eliphas, but always this
effort would shift his trancelike apprehension of the machines around him into a dream. Sometimes he ran along
a web of narrow paths between the tombs and steles of the
City of the Dead, pursued by men who had by grotesque
mutilation merged themselves with machines. Sometimes
he fled endlessly from the hell-hound, waking with a start
in the very moment that its burning blue light swept across

him. And sometimes he harried numberless enemies with bloody zeal, exultant as cities burned and armies fought and looted the length of the world in his name, and woke shocked and ashamed, and swore never to dream such dreams again.

But they were always with him, like splinters of cold metal under his skin.

At intervals, Prefect Corin came and sat with Yama, and slowly, punctuated by long silences, a conversation would begin. Yama supposed that these conversations were really interrogations, but mostly it seemed that Prefect Corin was interested in Yama's childhood, asking about details—and details within those details—of small events or ceremonies, the geography of Aeolis or the hinterlands of the City of the Dead, the disposition of books in the library of the peel-house, the lessons taught by the librarian, Zakiel, or by the master of the guard, Sergeant Rhodean.

The matter of the white boat, the mystery of Yama's origins, the attempted kidnap by Dr. Dismas, Yama's adventures in Ys—none of these were ever touched upon. Yama did not have to dissemble about his encounter with the custodians of the City of the Dead and the slate they had shown him, in which he had seen a man of his bloodline turning away to contemplate a sky full of stars. Nor did he have to describe how he had drawn down the feral machine at the merchant's house, or the merchant's last words; nor how he had woken and then defeated the feral machine which had been trapped far beneath the Temple of the Black Well; nor what the woman in white, aspect of one of the Ancients of Days, had told him when she had appeared in the shrine.

But it also meant that all these adventures and discoveries were thrust to the back of his mind by Prefect Corin's patient but insistent demands for increasingly minute details about the mundane days of his childhood. It was as if all that had happened to Yama in the handful of days between leaving his home in Aeolis and arriving here, in this bleak cell amongst thousands of identical cells in the

Department of Indigenous Affairs, had been no more than a vivid dream. It was another reason why, when left alone in the unquiet darkness of his cell, Yama traced and retraced his every footstep between Aeolis and Ys like an ox plodding around and around a water lift, the groove of its path infinitesimally deepening with each round. He was frightened that if he forgot even the slightest detail of his adventures he would begin to forget it all, as the unraveling of a piece of cloth can begin with the fraying of a single thread.

Whenever Yama asked a question, Prefect Corin had a habit of falling silent, as if engaged in an internal dialogue with himself, before asking a question in return. The Prefect's dry, spare manner intensified during these interrogation sessions. His silences were vast and arid; his gaze burned intently while Yama talked at random about his childhood, like a mountain lion fixing on its prey and waiting for the moment of weakness or uncertainty that will betray it. It was as if he had shaped his intellect to a single inquiring point, as one of the fisherfolk might flake a pebble to form the head of a harpoon. Yama got no answers from him at all—only questions. And he did not know if the answers he gave to the Prefect's questions were sufficient. Like all of his own questions, that also went unanswered.

Apart from Prefect Corin and the disembodied voice in the divided, darkened room, Yama's only human contacts were his guards. Four men had sentry duty outside Yama's cell, changing watches in regular succession. They lived in the cells on either side of his, and marched with him from his cell to the room where he took his tests, and back again.

Only one of the guards ever talked with him. This was the old man who took the second of the night watches, from midnight to dawn. His name was Coronetes. He confided to Yama that he did not mind the night watch. He was old, his wife had died, and he did not sleep much.

"You, young man, sleep very soundly," Coronetes said. "It is a gift of the young. Old men do not need to sleep because soon they will be dead, never to wake again until they wake into the world at the end of time created by the will of the Preservers."

Yama smiled at this conceit and replied with one of his own. "Then it will be no sleep at all, because in the interval you will not exist, and so no time will pass. As it says in the first sura of the Puranas, 'Before the Universe there was no time, for nothing changed.' "

"You are a devout man."

"I would not say that."

"I suppose you must have done something bad, to be here. But you are often reading in the Puranas."

"Do they watch me, then?" Yama had not thought of that. He had believed that the cell was as private as the inside of his head.

Coronetes nodded vigorously. "By the same pipe through which the light falls. I thought you would have known that. But I do not think they watch now. They sleep."

Like most of the common people of the Department of Indigenous Affairs, Coronetes was slightly built. His coarse hair was black, despite his age, and worn in a stout, greased pigtail that fell halfway down his back. Although he was, as he liked to say, as scrawny as a plucked chicken, he was still a strong man; muscles knotted his skinny arms as if walnuts had been stuffed under his brown skin. He had volunteered for the army at the beginning of the war. He had fought in the Marsh of the Lost Waters, and still suffered from fluxion of the lungs.

"There are sandflies that enter the mouth or nose of a sleeping man," he explained, "and creep into the throat to lay eggs. The larvae get into the lungs and every now and then one turns into a fly and I must cough it out. But I am luckier than many of my comrades. The diseases of the midpoint of the world and the wild creatures of the marshes and the forests accounted for most of them, not the fighting. It is for that reason that the heretics are brothers to the gar, panther and sandfly."

Coronetes had been so weakened by fluxion and fevers

that his wife had not recognized him when he had returned from the war. He had become a clerk, like his father before him, and still wore a clerk's white shirt, for he had been a clerk longer than he had been a soldier, and had risen to become the head of his section. He was fiercely loyal to his Department and feared no one, but he was lonely in his old age. He had no children, and had outlived most of his friends while still a young man.

"We will rule the world," Coronetes said, "because no one else will take up the burden. That is why you will confess to the Committee for Public Safety, and that is why you will enlist in our cause. It is the only cause worth fighting for, young man."

Coronetes and Yama sat on the bed in the cell, lit by a stick of cold green light Coronetes had set on the fold-down shelf. None of the guards had fireflies. Indeed, no machines came near Yama except those on the far side of the thick glass wall of the testing room.

Yama said, "I was brought up in the care of a senior member of the Department. He believed that service to the ideal of the Preservers was the beginning and end of the duty of every Department."

"The Aedile of Aeolis? He has the luxury of living in a place where his rule is undisputed. That kind of view is considered old-fashioned. It was old-fashioned even when I was a child, and that was a long time ago. Now my grandfather, he was a soldier, too. That was before the war against the heretics. He fought three campaigns within the Palace against departments who tried to usurp our functions and our territory. He knew where his duty lay. You were lucky to be brought up where you were, but now you are in the real world."

"This cell."

"It is no different from my cell."

"Except you will stop me if I try and walk out."

Coronetes smiled. His mouth was as wide and lipless as a frog's. He had lost most of his teeth, and those that remained were brown and worn down to the gumline. He said, "Well, that is true. I would do my best. I would kill you if I had to, but I hope it will not be necessary."

"So do I."

In fact, Yama never once thought of escaping when Coronetes came to visit him in his cell. It would be dishonorable, for whatever else Coronetes might be and whatever motives he might have, he presented himself as Yama's friend.

"Tell me about the war," Yama would say, when he found himself disagreeing with one of Coronetes' praise songs to the great heart and forthright purpose of the Department of Indigenous Affairs.

Coronetes had many stories of the war, of long marches from one part of the marshes to another, of engagements where nothing could be seen of the enemy but the distant flashes of their weapons, of days and days when nothing at all happened, and Coronetes' company lay in the sun and swapped stories. Most of the war was either marching or waiting, he said. He had only been in two real battles, one which had lasted a hundred days, fought to capture a hill later abandoned, and one in a town where the citizens had begun to change and no one knew who was fighting whom.

"It is what the heretics do," Coronetes said. "They force the change in a bloodline, and with change comes war. The war is not one war, but many, for we must fight for each unchanged bloodline, to make sure they do not fall under the spell of the heretics when they are most vulnerable. If we did only what we wanted, we would be like animals, or worse than animals, because animals are only themselves, and cannot help what they are. The Prefect, he had a more dangerous job, moving amongst the unchanged just like the heretic inciters. That is where the war is really fought, if you want my opinion. The heretics are powerful enemies because they are powerful at persuading the unchanged to see things their way. Our Committee is dedicated to destroying the heretics, but even so it uses some of their techniques to ensure loyalty within the Department."

The Committee for Public Safety had transformed the Department of Indigenous Affairs, turning a musty cabal of legal clerks and semiautocrats into an aggressive hive of radicals that claimed to be fighting for all the souls of Confluence. The Committee held that everyone was equal, and the least clerk felt that he was as important in the struggle as the most senior general. Coronetes sometimes talked for hours, his eyes gleaming with pride, about the merits of the organization of the Department, of the wonders it had achieved and the paradise it would bring once it had defeated the heretics and united Confluence.

Yama preferred to hear about the war. The patrols that looped through a country of tall grasses without ever engaging the enemy, the camps amongst the buttress roots of trees of the virgin forest of the great marshes, the geometry of advances and retreats. He learned the jargon of the common soldiers, the rudimentary sign language they used when the enemy was close by. More than ever, he yearned to join the army as a cateran or an officer of the light lance, to flee downriver and lose himself in the war.

Yama supposed that these visits might be a part of his interrogation, but if so it did not matter. He looked forward to the time when, late at night, there would be a scratching at the door and he would call out and ask the old man to enter. Although Yama was the prisoner and Coronetes his guard, they both sustained the fiction that Yama was the host, and Coronetes the visitor. Coronetes always waited for Yama's invitation before unlocking the door, and neither commented on the fact that he locked it again once he was inside. That Yama politely forbore to argue against Coronetes' transparent propaganda was part of this fiction—that, and his suspicion that anything he said against the Department of Indigenous Affairs or the Committee for Public Safety would be used against him. Yama was always disappointed on those nights when Coronetes' inquiring scratch failed to come, and had almost become used to the unvarying pattern of his days of captivity when the ambush changed everything.

11

"YOU ARE A MONSTER."

YAMA WAS RETURNING to his cell after a testing session, with two guards walking a little way in front of him and two behind. His hands were bound by a loop of plastic that was designed to remorselessly tighten if he attempted to struggle against it. He had learned to bend his arms and rest his fists against his chest, as if in prayer, to minimize movement. Coronetes had told him that this form of restraint, called the serpent, could amputate limbs if left on for too long.

The corridor was lit only by the luminous sticks carried by the guards. Yama moved in a bubble of dim green light, with darkness ahead and darkness behind, every ten paces passing a facing pair of doors. The doors were slabs of dense, grainy white plastic deeply recessed in the fused rock walls, as indistinguishable from each other as cells in a honeycomb.

Yama was thinking about the tests. In the past few days he had been fitted with a metal cap while moving the fireflies about. And the fireflies were changing, too. At first they had become slow to respond to his commands; now their little minds were hedged with loops and knots of futile logic which he had to unpick before they would obey him. Those testing him were beginning to probe the limits of his power; he was beginning to worry about what might happen when those limits were reached.

Without warning, two doors were flung open, one on either side. Three young men rushed out from the left; two from the right. They yelled hoarsely, clubs cocked at their shoulders. The leader swung a killing star on a short chain. Yama ducked and rammed the man in the chest with his shoulder, catching him off balance. The man slammed into the wall and Yama broke his nose with his forehead. Then someone kicked Yama's legs out from under him. The serpent tightened around his wrists when he tried to break his fall and the back of his head struck the floor. Two of the attackers began kicking and pummelling him while the others fought with the guards.

Yama tucked his head into his chest and curled up as tightly as he could. There were no machines he could use against his assailants—like the guards, the young men had no fireflies—but their own ineptitude saved him. They were too close to each other to use their clubs properly and they wore only soft-soled shoes, so that their kicks bruised rather than broke bones. Then someone fell heavily on Yama, saving him from the worst of the blows. A moment later, one of the guards fired his slug pistol, and the attackers ran.

Yama was hauled to his feet by two of the guards. It was Coronetes who had fallen on him. The old man's white shirt was ripped down the front and wet with blood. One of the guards knelt beside him and the other two dragged Yama away. The serpent was a band of intense pain around his wrists; his hands had lost all feeling.

The guards would not answer his questions. They unclasped the serpent and left him alone in his cell. Yama massaged his wrists and hands. His fingers were numb and pale, and felt as if they had swollen to twice their normal size. They started to hurt as blood flowed back into them; Yama took that as a good sign. His chest ached with each breath, but the pain was not sharp, and he did not think his ribs were broken. He had cut his tongue, and there were pulpy bruises on his scalp. There was blood on his shirt, so much blood that the shirt stuck to his skin. He took it off and ran his hands over his flanks and back and found many deep bruises but no other wounds. Then he realized that it must be Coronetes' blood.

He had rinsed his mouth out and started to wash himself when the two guards came back. They still would not answer his questions. They fitted the serpent to his wrists and marched him out of his cell. As always, the corridors were deserted. He was led through a great hall crammed with long tables which looked as if they had been abandoned only moments before: pens flung down on unfinished sentences; slates still showing ranks of glowing figures; half-empty bowls of tea. More guards were waiting at the far side of the room. A hood was thrust over his head and the forced march was resumed. At one point he was taken across an open space—cold air whipped around him—and soon after that the hood was ripped from his head and the serpent was unclasped. He turned just in time to see a door slam shut. It was less than an hour after he had been attacked.

~

The room was four times the size of his cell, and looked even bigger because there was no furniture except for a narrow bed. The walls were fused rock, smooth and slick as glass; the floor was rammed earth. It was shaped like an egg, and at the narrower end sunlight flooded through a big glass bull's-eye.

He found a spigot that yielded an icy trickle of rust-colored water, and stripped off his trousers and washed Coronetes' blood from his bruised body as best he could. There was a thin gray blanket over the striped ticking of the bed's mattress; he wrapped it around his shoulders and for a long time knelt by the window, gazing out at the blue sky. By pressing his bruised face against the cold glass, he could glimpse a segment of a steep slope of tumbled black rocks. Trees clung amongst the rocks, their branches all bent in the same direction. Wind fluted beyond the roundel of glass, and now and then birds slanted through the air, crossing from right to left as they tilted on air currents beyond the edge of the scree slope.

He broke his fingernails prying at the glass, but it was firmly embedded in the smooth rock. It did not break or crack when he kicked at it; he succeeded only in bruising his heel. He had just begun to scrape at the hard earth at the bottom edge of the window when a chirurgeon came in, flanked by two guards. The chirurgeon tested Yama's limbs, probed his mouth and shone a bright light into his eyes, then left without saying a word. Another guard brought in a slop bucket and tossed Yama's bloodstained shirt onto the bed, and then Prefect Corin came in.

After the guards had locked the door behind them, Prefect Corin sat on the end of the bed. Yama stayed by the window. He was conscious of being naked under the thin blanket. He said, "How is Coronetes?"

"Dead. As are your attackers."

"Your Department is not of one mind about me. That is comforting."

"It was not a conspiracy. They wanted revenge because you had blinded their friends. You did not try to defend yourself. Why was that?"

"I believe that I broke someone's nose."

"You know what I mean, boy."

"I am your prisoner, not your servant. I do not have to explain myself."

"You are the prisoner of the Department. I am here because I brought you to Ys. I am still responsible for you. You do not believe me, but I have your best interests at heart."

Yama smiled. It hurt. "Then you endure our conversations as a punishment?"

"It is my duty," Prefect Corin said. "Just as it was my duty to bring you to Ys."

"You failed at that and you failed to catch me by trickery, too. In the end you had to use force. Perhaps you are not very good at carrying out your duty."

Prefect Corin rarely smiled, but he smiled now. It lasted only for a moment and did not thaw his wintry expression in the slightest. He said, "I lost you once, yet here you are, all the same. If I was superstitious, I might say that it was fate, and that our lives are bound together. But I am not; and they are not. I have my duty. You have your duty, too, Yamamanama. You know what it is, but you resist it. I wonder why it is that you are so ungrateful. Your stepfather is a senior officer of the Department, and so in a sense the Department raised you. It educated you and trained you, and yet you resist acknowledging your considerable obligation. You believe that your own will is stronger than the collective will of the Department. Believe me, you are wrong."

"I do not know what you want of me." A silence. Yama corrected himself. "I do not know what the Department wants of me."

Prefect Corin considered this. At last, he said, "Then you will be here a long time, and so will your friends. It is not about what you know, but what you can do."

"I am sorry that Coronetes was killed. He did not deserve it."

"Nor did the men who attacked you. They were not much more than boys, and foolish boys at that, but they were brave. Their only mistake was that they were more loyal to their friends than to the Department."

Yama said, "Do you wish that they had killed me?"

"You are a monster, boy. You do not know it, but you are. You have more power than any individual should have, and you use it without purpose. You do not even know how to use it properly. You refuse to serve, for no other reason than your pride. You could help win the war, and that is the only reason why you are kept alive. Some want you dead. I have argued against it, and so you still live, but I cannot defend you forever. Especially if you continue to resist."

"I have completed every test as best I could."

"This is not about the tests. It is about loyalty."

"I will not serve blindly," Yama said. "If I am here,

with such gifts as I have, there must be a purpose to it. That is what I want to discover. That is why I came to Ys.''

"You should try and be true to the example of your stepbrother. He served. He served well.''

"I will go to war in a moment, but you will not allow it. So please do not invoke Telmon's bravery.''

Prefect Corin put his hands on his knees and leaned forward, looking directly into Yama's face. His brown eyes were steady and unforgiving. He said, "You are very young. Too young for what you possess.''

"I will not serve blindly,'' Yama said. "I have thought long and hard about this. If there are those in the Department who want me to help them, then they should talk with me. Or you should kill me now, and then at least you will know that I will never fight against you.''

"We are all one, hand and brain,'' Prefect Corin said. "Your stepfather did not like the way things had changed, but still he served.''

"Yes, Coronetes once said something similar.''

"But you will not serve. You set yourself apart. You are a monster of vanity, boy.'' Prefect Corin stood up and tossed something on the mattress of the bed. "Here is your copy of the Puranas. Read in it carefully, and consider your position.''

~

Once he was certain that he had been left alone, Yama began again to scrape at the base of the circular window. He broke a thin strip of wood from the frame of the bed and used this and water from the spigot to loosen the packed earth. The sky had darkened by the time he had dug to the depth of his hand and found the point where glass merged seamlessly with fused rock. Perhaps the window was no more than a place where the rock had been made transparent, but apart from the door it was the only possible way out of the cell.

He began to extend the little hole he had made, scraping

away hard earth a few crumbs at a time until the frayed strip of wood met something embedded in the dirt. He probed carefully with his bleeding fingertips and felt a thin curved edge, then dug around it until he could pull it free.

It was a ceramic disc, an ancient coin exactly like the coin the anchorite had given him. But the Aedile's excavations had turned up thousands of coins around the tombs of the City of the Dead, and there was no reason to believe that this one should be any different from those.

Yama dug a little more, but could find no potential weakness in the window's edge. He filled in the hole he had made and as the room darkened around him he leaned against the window and watched the shadows of the bent trees lengthen across the tumbled rocks. He fell asleep, and woke to find a constellation of faint lights hung just outside the window. They were fireflies, drawn away from the wild creatures which lived amongst the sliding stones. Beyond the shifting sparks of the fireflies, the small red swirl of the Eye of the Preservers was printed on the black sky.

Something nagged at Yama, like a speck in his eye. It was the coin, shining softly on the dirt floor. He picked it up. It was warmer than his own skin, and had become translucent, with fine filaments and specks of cold blue light shifting within its thickness.

There was an active shrine nearby.

He could suddenly feel it, with the same absolute sense of direction that linked him with the feral machine. He shivered and drew the blanket around himself. He knew that he could activate the shrine even at this distance, and a plan of escape presented itself.

It was horribly risky, but no worse than trying to climb through a window high above a steep slope of sliding stones at the top of a mountain. And he could not even open the window. Before he could frighten himself by thinking through all the consequences, he willed it.

Beyond the bull's-eye window, the fireflies scattered as if before a great wind.

—

His trousers were still damp, but Yama drew them on anyway, and tucked the sliver of wood inside the waistband. Then he wrapped the blanket around his shoulders and sat by the window in the dim red light of the Eye of the Preservers, waiting for something to happen. At intervals, he held the coin up to his eye, but the shifting patterns of luminous lines and specks told him nothing.

Perhaps the shrine was dead after all . . . but then he knew it was not, as surely as if a light had been shone in his face. He got up and paced around the room, a fierce excitement growing in him. Presently he heard shouts, and then the thin snapping of slug guns. The sounds of distant combat lasted several minutes; then there was the scream of an energy pistol's discharge and wisps of white smoke began to curl around the edges of the cell door.

Yama scrambled to his feet, and at the same moment the door was flung back with a crash. A guard tumbled in ahead of a thick billow of smoke. His tunic was torn across the chest. The right side of his face was scorched, his hair shriveled to blackened peppercorns.

"Come with me!" the guard yelled. "Now!"

Yama straightened his back and drew the blanket around his shoulders. The guard glared at him and raised his rifle. "Come now!"

For a moment, Yama feared that the man had lost his mind and would execute him on the spot. Then the guard looked over his shoulder and screamed. He scrambled across the cell, knocking Yama aside and fetching up against the bull's-eye window, clutching his rifle to his chest and staring wide-eyed at the door. Yama faced it squarely, his heart beating quickly and lightly. Blue light filled the frame. And then, without a transition, the hellhound was inside the cell.

It was a pillar of blue flame that seemed somehow to extend beyond the floor and ceiling. There was a continual crackling hiss as its energies ate the air which touched its surface. Its heat beat against Yama's skin. He had to squint against its brilliance as he held up the coin. It took all of his will to stand still.

He said, ''I do not know if we have already met, or if you are brother to the one I called forth before, but in any case I apologize for my behavior. I ran away because I did not know what I had called, and I was afraid. But now I have freed you knowingly, and I ask for your help.''

He did not see the hell-hound move, but there was a brief wash of heat on his skin and suddenly it was gone. The guard screamed. When Yama turned, the man fell to his knees and flung his arm before his face. The sleeve of his tunic started to smolder. Yama realized what had happened, and looked away before he killed the man.

He had expected the hell-hound to clear a way for his escape. Instead, it had enveloped him.

He was the center of a blue radiance that fell on everything he looked at. He no longer felt the hell-hound's heat. That was a property of the outermost shell of its energies. Instead, he felt a tremendous exhilaration. His bruises and cracked ribs no longer hurt. There was a prickling all over his body as every hair tried to stand away from its neighbors.

There was a short corridor beyond the cell. Guards scrambled in panic through the door at the far end, although one paused and shot at Yama several times before running too, his clothes and hair smoldering. Yama followed them into a wide plaza. Sheer black rock rose on three sides; there was nothing but the darkening sky on the other.

Men ran or stood their ground and fired. Slugs caught and sank slowly in the outer edge of the blue light that surrounded Yama, flaring brightly before evaporating. An officer fired a pistol, but its discharge merely whitened Yama's vision for a moment.

He did not attack the guards or even look at them, but strode directly to the edge of the plaza. A railing glowed red and yellow and white before melting away. Directly below was the steep slope of black rocks he had seen from the window of the cell. Yama's sight washed with white light for an instant—the officer with the pistol was foolish, but brave. Yama did not look back, but gave himself to the air.

He floated down like a soap bubble, landing beside a dead pine tree which immediately burst into crackling yellow flame. The air was alive with things which hummed and whined. Bits of rock flew off and the foliage of the stunted trees danced jerkily. Yama realized that the guards were still firing at him. He walked to the edge of the slope and gave himself to the air once more.

It took a long time to fall. The hell-hound was subject to the world's gravity fields, but could modify them so that it fell at a constant rate. Yama saw a long slope spread below him, curving away on either side and studded with the lights of temples, sanctuaries and the offices of those lesser departments which had long ago lost battles for territory inside the Palace and now clung to existence on its roof. He gave the hell-hound an order, and it slid sideways through the air.

The glass-walled tunnel which linked the street of pleasure houses with the territory of the Department of Indigenous Affairs had been repaired with wooden paneling that burst into flames at a touch and fell away. Yama stepped through and walked amidst reflections of blue fire into a square under a high domed roof.

Three guards ran into the gateway on the far side; their officer drew his pistol and fired twice, and then stood amazed when he saw that the energy beam had done no harm. The air was hazed with recondensed particles of rock vaporized by the deflected pistol blast; Yama's gaze burned through them and glanced upon the officer, who threw up his hands to protect his eyes.

"Fetch your masters," Yama said. "Do you understand? I wish to speak with them."

The officer turned and ran through the gateway. Yama followed. He was quite without fear. He felt as if he could run forever through the maze of corridors and halls, and laughed wildly when men shot at him. Slugs embedded in the hell-hound's outermost shell became molten stars that flared and died.

He entered a huge refectory hall. Hundreds of people ran from him through a maze of tables. A confused cloud of fireflies billowed after them. Tables and chairs charred as he brushed past. He shouted for the masters of this place to come out, but there was no answer except for a volley of rifle shots from a gallery above the arched door-ways at the far end of the hall. Frayed battle standards hung above the central dais of the hall. Yama stared at them until they caught fire, then leaped on to the dais and shouted that he would speak with the masters of this place or burn it all down.

Men ran forward, dragging a long hose. They sprayed water at Yama, but the water exploded into steam when it struck the hell-hound's envelope and the men retreated, clutching scalded faces and hands. An officer on a floating disc fired his pistol. The blue glow of the hell-hound flared white. The high-backed chairs and the long table, inlaid with ironwood and turtle shell ivory, burst into flames; the stone of the dais burned Yama's feet through the thin soles of his boots. He jumped down, stared at the officer until the man's clothes caught fire, and strode through the near-est door.

Yama's passage through toward the heart of the Depart-ment of Indigenous Affairs was a confusion of shouts and screams, flame and smoke and gunfire. He was filled with an exultant rage. Red and black lightning jagged his vi-sion. He could have killed decads, perhaps hundreds of men. He did not know. His rage had taken him and he let it lead him where it would.

When it cleared, he was standing at the base of a vast circular shaft that rose through a hundred floors; the tem-ple of Aeolis, the largest building Yama had known before he had come to Ys, could easily have fitted into it. Its looming walls were hung with tiers of balconies; its vast floor was crowded with desks. Books burned in stacked shelving, in tumbled heaps on the floor. Scraps of burning paper flew into the darkness above like sparks up the flue of a chimney.

Soldiers armed with slug rifles stood in front of every door around the base of the shaft, draped from head to foot in black cloth. They kept up a steady bombardment and the floor around Yama was soon littered with flecks of molten metal. A machine spun slowly through the air toward him, its mind defended by intricate loops of self-engulfing logic. In his anger he punched right through these defenses and the machine suddenly screamed upward, its load of explosive detonating with a white flash and a flat thump at the top of the shaft, half a league above.

"I know you are here, Prefect," Yama shouted. "Show yourself!"

A voice spoke from the air, ordering Yama to surrender—it was the same even, neutral voice which had been with him every day in the room. He laughed at it and then, inspired, shut down the light of every firefly, so that now the vast circular space was lit only by the blue glow of the hell-hound, the flashes of the rifles around the perimeter, and the myriad fires started by spent slugs and Yama's gaze. Everything was hazed with smoke. Yama felt a tightness in his chest and a scorched taste in his mouth. The air was becoming unbreathable. He knew that he would have to leave soon, and that he would have to kill the soldiers to do it.

Yet still he felt a steady exhilaration thrilling in his blood, a boundless energy. He did not consider himself trapped, but called out again for the masters of this place. As if in answer, the floor heaved sharply and Yama staggered and almost fell. Dust and shards of tiling fell from somewhere above, smashing down amongst the desks; for a moment, Yama stood inside a sleet of burning particles.

The soldiers were as shaken as he. They were still regrouping when a fresh wedge of troops entered through the high doors beneath a long gallery. They parted, and an old man stepped from their midst. He was slightly built and his dress was no different from that of an ordinary clerk, but he held himself proudly and at his absent-minded gesture the soldiers around him immediately thrust three people to the front of their ranks.

Tamora shaded her eyes and called out, "Yama! Is that you inside that light?"

"He has come to free us," Pandaras said.

Yama checked himself. He had been about to run to them.

The old man walked forward, stepping as delicately as a cat amongst broken shards and heaps of burning books. He stopped when the floor rippled and shook dust into the air, and then walked on until he was fifty paces from the blue energies of the hell-hound. His eyes were masked by a strip of cloth, jet-black against the white pelt of his face.

"I had not thought to ever see one of these things," the old man said. "I am Escanes, Yamamanama. I am here to ask why you are doing this."

"I discovered that it is only a machine," Yama said. "I should thank you for helping me focus on what I needed to do."

"It is an inertial field-caster," Escanes said. "Amongst other things. Anything trying to move through it gives up momentum in the form of heat. It burns with blue light because light reflected from it is shifted from lower to higher energy, and it is hot because of the energy released from dust and air in motion against it. I should warn you that we fully understand it."

"Yet I control it, and you do not. I can destroy everything around me with a look."

"Because we understand such things," Escanes said, "we can work against them. You are not invulnerable. You should not have brought it here, my son. You endanger the records of the Department."

"I will destroy them all unless you let my friends go."

"I am empowered to speak for the Department, Yamamanama. Listen to what it has to say. We will let your three friends go. You will stay."

"You will let them go, and let me go, too."

"I do not think so," Escanes said mildly. "Think quickly. One word from me, and they will die."

"Then you will have no hold over me."

The floor shook again. Yama flexed his knees, as if he was on a boat. Escanes held the edge of a half-charred desk until the shaking stopped. A balcony gave way and smashed down twenty stories into a stack of bookshelves on the far side of the shaft.

Yama said, "Someone is attacking you, I think. Is it war?"

"Our enemies believe that we are weakened from within," Escanes said. "We will prove them wrong. It is a trivial matter, and not one that concerns you. What matters is your answer."

"Let my friends go."

"And you will stay?"

"No. You will come with me."

Yama sprang forward, and the hell-hound relaxed its perimeter for an instant. Escanes threw up his hands, but he was already inside the hell-hound's envelope. Yama caught him and turned him around, and held the sharpened bit of wood to his throat. Escanes struggled, but Yama held him easily.

"Tell your people to let my friends go."

"They will not obey me. I am only a mouth for the Department. We are all one. Do not be a fool, or your friends will die."

"Your tunic is silk, dominie, not artificial cotton. I think that your dogma requires you to appear to be the same as all others in the Department, but you raise yourself higher than most."

"We are all one."

"Yet some value themselves more than others."

Escanes tried to turn his head, but Yama jabbed the sliver of wood into the loose flesh of the old man's neck and urged him forward. The soldiers raised their rifles, but an officer snapped an order and they lowered them again.

Yama told the old man, "If my friends walk out of here with me, then your life will be spared. I promise that I will not cause any more damage. You will be free to defend yourself against your enemies. But if anything happens to my friends, then I join your enemies and fight against you.''

"Fight with us, Yamamanama," Escanes said. "You could be the most powerful general in our army.''

"You would have made that offer already, if you could. Now repeat to your men what I have told you.''

━

It was easy to find the way back to the gate—the hellhound had left a trail of scorched doors and scored floor tiles. Yama let Tamora, Pandaras and Eliphas walk ahead of him. The old man, Escanes, did not struggle, but continued to try to convince Yama to give himself to the mercy and generosity of the Department until at last Yama lost patience and put a hand over his mouth.

Yama stopped at the gate and told the others to go ahead. "While I stand here, no one can get past. Eliphas, you know a safe place to take them.''

The old man stared and Tamora shook him and hissed in his ear. Yama asked his question again and Eliphas blinked and said, "It finally caught you, brother." Blue light shone in his eyes.

"No, Eliphas. I caught it. I understand it now. You remember the place Magon took us to.''

"I remember.''

Pandaras said, "He isn't quite himself, master. He had a harder time of it than me. I knew nothing important, so they didn't hurt me. It was just talking, and you know how I love that. I told them many stories.''

The boy wore the white shirt and black trousers of a clerk. Yama said, "It seems you have adopted their ways.''

"Kill them all," Tamora said. Her head had been shaved, and her face was a palimpsest of fresh bruises laid over old.

"We will talk later, Tamora. Go now.''

The old man, Escanes, said, ''She is right. You should kill us all, for else we will follow you to the end of the river and beyond.''

''I am not your enemy.''

''Anyone who does not serve is our enemy.''

''I serve the Preservers, if I can, not your Department.''

''So says any man who is full of pride. Such a one believes that by doing as he wishes he serves a higher power, but instead he has allowed himself to become a slave of his base appetites. You would claim to know what the Preservers want? Then you are worse than foolish, young man. We are the arm of the Preservers. We strive against their enemies at the midpoint of the world.''

''I do not know why I was born here, in this time and place. But it was not to serve your hunger for power.''

Tamora, Pandaras and Eliphas had disappeared into the tunnel at the far end of the plaza. Yama told Escanes to close his eyes, and then thrust him toward the gate. The hell-hound's envelope had grown hotter because it had contracted, and the old man's clothes smoldered as he staggered away.

The soldiers rushed forward then. Yama ran across the square into the tunnel and plunged through the hole he had burned in the patchwork repair to the tunnel's glass wall.

―

The night was spread before him. The hell-hound turned and dipped and in a sudden rush he was down, standing beside the white fountain in the middle of the long lawn. Yama thanked the hell-hound and dismissed it, and felt a gust of heat as it moved away from him. It shrank into itself and rose, a bright blue star that dwindled away against the black bulk of the mountain.

Yama stood alone in darkness in the center of a circle of charred grass. He thought of returning to the library of the Department of Apothecaries and Chirurgeons to ask what the chief of clerks, Kun Norbu, had discovered about his bloodline. He thought of running away. But he knew that he could not. He had saved his three companions from immediate danger, but they were still within the bounds of the Palace, and the Department of Indigenous Affairs would not rest until they were recaptured. Besides, he was so very tired, and his torn muscles and cracked ribs ached horribly. It was as if he drew every breath through a rack of knives. The hell-hound had lent him some of its energies while it had enveloped him, but now he had only his own reserves of strength to draw upon.

He sat at the edge of one of the fountain's wide shallow basins and drank cold water with his cupped hands, and splashed water on his face. Presently, a small constellation of fireflies gathered around him, lighting his way as he crossed the long lawn and went down the steps. His muscles were as loose and weak as sacks of water, and he had to stop and rest every five minutes. Each time he stopped it was harder to force himself to stand and go on, but the dread of being recaptured drove him forward. When he reached the beginning of the path through the grove of bamboo, he sat down and rested for a few minutes, breathing hard and feeling beads of sweat roll down his sides. The skeletal tower, hung with creepers, loomed above. Yama struggled to his feet and went on.

White birds, ghostly in the darkness, fled from him. Yama caught at bamboo stems and lost his grasp and slid down a dusty slope, fetching up against a low wall. Startled goats bounded away, their wooden bells clanking. Yama lay on his back, looking up at the black sky, the few blurred stars, the red swirl of the Eye of the Preservers.

After a while, the villagers came to discover what had disturbed their animals. They were armed with spears and slings, for lynxes and fierce red foxes prowled the roof, and the Lords of the Palace were restless that night. But they found only Yama, asleep on the cropped grass.

12

THE HUSBANDMEN

"THERE, DOMINIE," THE headman of the village said. "You see? The Lords of the Palace quarrel amongst themselves."

Yama looked up, following the line of the headman's arm. High above the terraced fields of the little village, a thread of black smoke rose from the upper slope of the mountain.

"The roof trembled hard last night," the headman said. He was squat and muscular, with a seamed face and lively black eyes, and skin the color of the red earth. His white hair was done up in a braid that fell to the small of his back. He wore much-darned leggings and a ragged but clean homespun tunic with many pockets.

"A bad time," Yama said.

"Not really. The Lords of the Palace will pay more for our food when they are done fighting—the winners will need to feed those they have captured."

"They will not take it from you by force?"

The headman touched his lips with the tips of his fingers. It was a gesture characteristic of the husbandmen. It meant *no.* "All serve the will of the Preservers. And we are their most faithful servants."

"Yet all of those fighting each other also profess to serve the will of the Preservers."

"We don't question how the Preservers order things," the headman said. "Are you feeling stronger, dominie?"

"A little. Resting here in the sun helps."

Last night, Yama had been given the headman's own hammock. An old woman had looked into his eyes and laid her head on his chest to listen to his breathing and heartbeat, and then had given him an infusion of dried leaves to drink. When Yama had woken, most of the husbandmen were already out in the fields, but the headman and his wife had stayed behind to tend their guest. They had given him dried fish and sweet rice cakes to eat, and a homespun tunic to cover his bare chest.

Yama was very weak. He was badly bruised from the beating he had received when he had been ambushed, and controlling the hell-hound had been as exhausting as riding a high-spirited thoroughbred. He was content to spend the day lying in a hammock under the shade of freshly cut banana leaves by the sunwarmed wall of the headman's house, listening to the headman's stories and watching children play in the dust of the village square.

The husbandmen believed that they had been brought to the world to tend the gardens of the Palace. The headman claimed that the terraces spread above and below the village had once held beds of roses and lilies, jasmine and sweet herbs.

"The first masters of the world walked here in the morning and the evening, dominie. There were different gardens for the morning and the evening of every day of the year, and we tended them all. That's why we look out across the city toward the place where the sun rises and sets."

"What did they look like, your masters?"

Yama had never seen a picture of the Sirdar, those who had ruled the world when it had been newly made. None of the Sirdar had ever been interred in the City of the Dead, and none of the picture slates there had revealed even a glimpse of them. They had never presented themselves to the ordinary people but had ruled invisibly, implementing their wishes through an extensive civil service of eunuchs and hierodules.

The headman gazed across the dusty village square, as if remembering, then said, "They were small, as small as our children playing there, and their skin shone like polished metal."

Yama shivered, remembering that the dead woman in the white boat, on whose breast he had been found, had had silver skin. Old Constable Thaw had said nothing about her being no bigger than a child, but to his kind most bloodlines seemed small.

The headman said, "Words are poor things. If I had a picture, I would gladly show it you, dominie. But we have no pictures of those times."

"It must have been long ago."

The headman nodded. He sat cross-legged in the white dust by Yama's hammock. Blades of sunlight fell through the notched banana leaves and striped his lined face. He said, "The world was young then, dominie, but we remember those times. We are not able to change, you see, nor do we wish to, for we would forget how it was, and how it will be again."

Some believed that the Sirdar had been destroyed by their successors, others that they had achieved enlightenment and passed from the world. There had been many rulers after them, but it was said that, next to the Builders, the Sirdar had been closest to the Preservers. The husbandmen believed that their old masters would come again, opening the sealed core of the Palace and stepping forth as a flower steps forth from a seed. The world would become a garden then, changed and unchanged bloodlines would achieve enlightenment and ascend into the Eye of the Preservers, and the husbandmen would spread across the face of the world they longed to inherit.

"Trees would drop fruit into our hands, and corn and grain will grow on the plains by the river without need of tilling or sowing. Until then," the headman said, with a smile that creased his clay-red face still further, "we must toil in the fields."

"Perhaps those days are not far off. Great things happen in the world."

Yama was thinking of the war against the heretics, but the headman knew nothing of the world beyond the Palace of the Memory of the People. He believed that Yama was talking about the conflict in the mountain heights above them. He said, "These may be the end times, but not because the Lords of the Palace quarrel. There has been war in the Palace before. Long ago, long after our first dear masters stopped walking in the gardens, but while the gardens were still gardens and had not yet been turned into fields, one department took over all the others. It was known as the Head of the People. It ruled for many generations, and its rule was fierce and cruel. It was a great weight on all the peoples of the world. But when it had conquered all, the Head of the People found itself without enemies and turned inward. Soon, it was fighting against itself. The Hierarchs arose and ended that war, and in turn they fell after the war against the Insurrectionists, for victory cost them dear. Some of the oldest departments are parts of that greater department, although they have long forgotten that they were once part of a greater whole, much as a lizard's tail forgets that it was shed by another lizard to escape an enemy, and grows into another lizard exactly like the first. Bloodlines forget much when they change; we cannot change and so we forget nothing, like the lizard that lost the tail in the first place."

"I recently met someone else who said much the same thing."

"That would be one of the mirror people. Yes, they remember much, too, but they have not lived in the Palace as long as we have. They are really fisherfolk, dominie. They left their living on the Great River when the city spread along the shore, and found work as fishers of men instead. They know much, but we know more. We understand the signs. We know the significance of the hellhound. Twice it was seen in the past decad. The first time, it vanished into the Palace after passing along the ridge above this village. The second time, it was seen floating through the air, and there was a ghost inside it."

"I know."

The headman touched his forehead. *Yes.* "Then you saw it too, dominie. Perhaps you do not remember that hell-hounds were used as weapons."

"So one of the mirror people told me."

The headman touched his forehead again. "And they learned it from us, for they arrived after the war with the machines."

He meant the end of the Age of Insurrection, when the Hierarchs had defeated the feral machines and those bloodlines which had risen against the will of the Preservers and had laid waste to half the world.

"We remember how great swaths of the gardens were destroyed by the energies of packs of hell-hounds," the headman said, "and how shrines were killed so that they no longer spoke to the masters of this Palace. Now the hell-hounds have come again, and one was carrying a ghost or a demon. I had not expected it, but if such wonders are seen in the world, then these may be the end times for which we have waited so long."

"It was not a ghost," Yama said, "and it certainly was not a demon. I should know, because I was there."

The headman nodded. "As you say, dominie. We believe that you might have been hurt by the hell-hound. That is why you are confused. But whatever you believe you saw, it was an illusion. Only ghosts or demons from the space inside the shrines may ride hell-hounds. It is how they visit the world. They bring nothing but destruction."

"Well, it carried me here," Yama said.

The headman touched his lips. "You were chasing it, or perhaps it was chasing you, although I understand that hell-hounds take little notice of men, who are no more than ghosts to them. You were chasing it, then, hoping to harm it. We saw it coming toward our village, and we hid from it, but it is clear that you saved us, or tried to save us. You did not know what you were chasing, so I cannot say that you were foolish, but you were certainly brave.

Perhaps you thrust a spear at it, and its energies knocked you down the slope, where we found you. That is why your mind is confused and why you are so weak. But the weakness and the confusion will pass. You are a young man, and strong. Lucky for you, dominie. Such an encounter would have killed most men outright."

"I was not fighting it. I used it, and it used me. I will show you if you let me."

Yama tried to sit up in the hammock, but his sight washed with red. He fell back, and felt the headman's dry, hard fingers at his brow.

"Rest," the headman said. "Rest is the best medicine."

"I rode it," Yama said. "I really did. It is only another kind of machine. I rode it all the way down the side of the mountain, and I rescued my friends."

Or perhaps he only said it to himself, for the headman did not seem to hear him. The headman settled the blanket around Yama's shoulders and went away. Yama slept for a while, and woke to find the headman's wife wiping his brow with a wet cloth. He was inside the headman's house again. Night pressed at the window above his hammock but the little room was full of light, for hundreds of fireflies hung in the air.

"You have a fever," the old woman said. "In a little while I will bring you some lemon broth."

Yama clutched the wide sleeve of her embroidered shirt. "I walked inside it," he said. "It carried me through the air."

The old woman gently lifted his hand away from her sleeve. "You have been dreaming, dominie. You are very weak, weaker than you believe, and so your dreams seem more real than the world itself. But I do not think that you will die. You will take some broth. You will sleep. We will look after you. It is an honor to us."

~

Yama lay in the hammock for two days, drifting between waking and sleeping. Whenever he woke, he dismissed the fireflies that had been drawn to him while he slept. At last, no more came: he had exhausted the local population. The shadows seemed to be thronged with dreams, and dreams mingled with heightened scenes of his recent adventures. Again, he walked with Prefect Corin through the hot dry lands on the road between Aeolis and Ys, but now the Prefect wore a crown of fireflies. Again, he stood at the edge of the deep shaft in the Temple of the Black Well—and this time it was not the feral machine but the hell-hound that rose out of black air. It enveloped him and carried him through the air to the top of the mountain which he now knew was no mountain, but in truth a single vast building older than the world. And at the windy pinnacle, with the city spread below on one side and the Great River on the other, he stood with his sweetheart. Derev. She clasped him to her breast and spread her strong wings and they flew higher still, until the entire world lay beneath them.

When Yama woke, dry-mouthed, weak, aching in every bone but clear-headed, Tamora was there. He was so glad to see her that he started to weep.

She grinned and said, "So the hero isn't dead. You are such a fool, Yama."

"I am pleased to see you, too, Tamora."

She wore a bronze-colored corselet he had not seen before, a short skirt of red leather strips, and a metal cap on her shaven, scarred head. She said, "I thought you were dead. I thought that the weapon you used against them must have killed you. Don't ever play the hero again, Yama. Or at least let me help you. That's what I am paid for."

"I lost my money, Tamora, and my knife. I have my book, though. It is all I have."

He had carried the copy of the Puranas through all his adventures. And he remembered that although he had lost the coin which the anchorite had given him, he had found a replacement. He reached for it, and Tamora caught his hand and then they were holding each other. Her strong arms; her spicy odor; her heat.

Tamora said, "Well, you're alive. Oh, Yama, you are such a fool!"

They held each other for a long time, until Pandaras came in.

—

Eliphas had led Tamora and Pandaras to the home of the mirror people, and Lupe had sheltered them until the search for the escaped prisoners passed into the lower levels of the Palace. The war between the Department of Indigenous Affairs and its lesser rivals was intensifying, and Tamora said that this would make their escape easy. She said that she had arranged passage downriver.

"I had to use your money to do it, but then again I had to use mine, too."

Yama said, "I know that I have to leave the city, Tamora. But I should leave you, too, and Pandaras. Simply by being with me you are in great danger."

"Grah. Your brains have cooked in your head. I will come with you for your own good. I suppose you could try and dismiss the rat-boy, but he will follow you anyway. He is in love."

From the doorway, where he had taken up position like a guard, Pandaras said, "I merely do my duty as a squire." The boy had oiled his hair and brushed it back from his narrow face. He still wore the black trousers and white shirt that was the uniform of the clerks of the Department of Indigenous Affairs. An ivory-handled poniard sheathed in black leather hung from a loop at his waist.

Tamora shrugged. "Then there is the old man."

"Eliphas."

"I don't trust him. Tell me you don't need him, and make me happy."

"Eliphas is a friend. He helped me without being asked, and he promised to search the library of the Department of Apothecaries and Chirurgeons for records of my bloodline."

Perhaps the answer had already been found. Perhaps he

would at last know where he belonged. And yet there was also the mystery of the dead woman in the white boat, who had had silver skin like the first masters of the world.

"Take me there," Yama said to Tamora. "Take me to the Department of Apothecaries and Chirurgeons. It is only a few hours' walk. All I want to know is there. It must be."

"Eliphas told me all about it. He's gone there now, and will meet us at the docks."

"I want to go there now."

"I think you're still too weak. You have been lying in bed too long. Time to get up! Time to be about your business in the world! Small steps first, and then the beginning of a great adventure!"

Pandaras clapped his misshapen hands and said, "We are going to war, master. I have brought you a spare set of clothes, even if you did not care to keep hold of your knife and your armor. Ask me, and I will find them for you, even if I have to search the entire Palace. Or perhaps I will bring you an energy pistol."

"Those are for officers," Tamora said, "and we will be no more than ordinary caterans."

"My clothes? Then you went back—"

Tamora grinned, showing her rack of sharp white teeth. "Oh, I went back, all right. I told you that I had spent our money—how do you think I got it? There was a pentad of soldiers waiting at the Gate of Double Glory, but I killed them all in a fair fight." She patted the heavy saber sheathed at her side. "That's where I got this poor substitute for my own sword. I got the rat-boy a knife, too, and a rapier for you. Anyway, I killed them and found where Syle was hiding. I had to bend the back of that feather-headed fool over my thigh until he would agree; but I have what we left behind, and the fee, too. Rega didn't want him to give it up, but he feared death more than he feared her, although I don't think you could put a knife blade between the difference. She was sitting where Luria used to sit, in a white dress for mourning. I hope she enjoys her rule of the Department of Vaticination in the brief time before the fighting spreads and she is assassinated."

Yama said, "I feel sorry for Syle. Despite all he did, at heart he is not a bad man."

"Grah. He tried to serve his department and his wife's ambitions, and will end up losing both, and his own life. His scheming saved the Department of Vatication for a short while, but it is seen as an ally of Indigenous Affairs now. And Indigenous Affairs is too busy defending itself to save Syle."

Pandaras said, "He betrayed you, master. No one trusts a traitor, least of all those who employ him. Whoever wins the war up there will get rid of him."

The fighting had spread through the upper tiers of the Palace. The Department of Indigenous Affairs had fought off its rivals and secured its borders, but now there were bitter skirmishes in the corridors, and mines and countermines were being dug through the fabric of the Palace as the warring departments tried to break out behind each other's lines.

"Our enemy has won the first stage of the war," Tamora said, "but it will have a hard time of it for a while. And even if it wins it will be weakened, and another department or alliance of departments might finish it off."

"I did not mean to destroy it," Yama said, "but it had made many enemies, and they were waiting for the slightest weakness. And yet we go to fight in the army it has raised. Do you not think that strange, Tamora?"

"We will fight the heretics, who are the real enemy of us all. At the midpoint of the world, the doings of the Palace of the Memory of the People is of no importance. It does not matter who has charge of the army there—you will see. You must get ready, Yama. You have been lying in luxury too long. The muscles in your legs will shrink and you won't be able to walk, much less fight. We'll have to carry you everywhere, like a houri. You will begin to exercise now, and you will exercise once we are on the ship. It will be a long voyage."

Yama thought of the great map he had so often unrolled,

at first to dream of finding where his people lived, and in the past year to follow the progress of Telmon, his step-brother, toward the war. Yama had wanted to follow Telmon and become his squire, but Telmon was dead. And now he stood at the beginning of the voyage he had dreamed of, with a squire of his own, and it seemed that all of his adventures since he had left Aeolis were no more than a preparation for this, the true adventure.

"There is something you must do before you leave," Pandaras said.

"The mirror people are set on it," Tamora added. "More foolishness. But I thought perhaps it will put an end to your delusions, so I sent one of these husbandmen up to tell Lupe where you are."

She and Pandaras would say no more, except that all would be explained tomorrow. With a premonition of black dread, Yama suspected that he knew what it was, and knew that he would fail in it. Whatever else he was, he could not be the savior of the mirror people.

Tamora and Pandaras helped him walk around the square of the little village, but he was quickly exhausted, and could not contemplate going any further.

"But I must leave," he said. "I cannot do what they want."

"You can do anything at all, master," Pandaras said. "You just need to rest a little."

"Don't listen to him," Tamora said. "Whatever those fuckers up there thought you were, you're going to war as a cateran. That's all you are. You'll see."

Yama laughed. "O Tamora. You believe in nothing you cannot touch or taste or smell."

"Of course. Only fools believe in magic."

"Well, it is certain that my enemies believe that I am more than I seem to be."

And so did Lupe, who wanted a miracle of him.

"You are greater than anything they can imagine, master," Pandaras said, and touched fingers to his throat in the odd gesture so many of the lesser citizens of Ys used, like a salute, or a blessing.

THE NEXT MORNING, the whole village busied itself with preparations for a feast. In the dusty central square, long red cloths were unrolled and strewn with flowers. Men and women set to cooking a hundred different dishes over trenches filled with white-hot charcoal. Their children stacked pyramids of sweet melons like the skulls of vanquished enemies, and built mounds of breadapples and small black and red bananas.

"We will honor our friends the mirror people," the headman told Yama, "and we will honor you, brave dominie, who is the friend of our friends, and who saved our village from the hell-hound."

Like the rest of the villagers, the headman wore a garland of freshly cut white flowers. With comical solemnity he lowered similar necklaces over the heads of Yama, Tamora and Pandaras, and kissed each of them on the forehead. Yama was still weak, and despite his growing dread he was now resigned to undergoing this ordeal. Besides, the villagers had saved his life and believed that he was a hero. And who would not like to be treated as a hero, even if only for a day?

And so he gave up all idea of escape, and while the

villagers bustled to and fro he sat in the sunshine with Pandaras at his feet like a loyal puppy. Pandaras had tried to persuade Yama to put on his second-best shirt, but he preferred the homespun tunic the headman had given him. Tamora sat cross-legged beside him with her new saber across her lap, sharpening it with a bit of whetstone and complaining about Eliphas.

"He has run off with the money I gave him," she said. "Or gone straight to our enemies. I was a fool to trust him."

"If he was going to betray me, then surely he would have done it already. Besides, he does not know where I am."

"He went off before we started to look for you," Tamora admitted. "But he could have doubled back and followed us."

"And you would not have noticed an old man trailing behind you."

"Well, that's true. But these husbandmen have told the mirror people about you, and they could have told Eliphas. I do not trust him, Yama."

Pandaras stirred and said, "When we were up in the balcony, above the pythonesses' ceremony, he told me stories about how he used to search for old books when he was young. I think Yama has reawakened his spirit of adventure."

Yama said, "You trust no one and nothing, Tamora. Eliphas was a good friend to me at the library, and he did not abandon me when I was pursued by the hell-hound."

The mirror people arrived when the sun reached the highest point in the sky. They came up the steps beside the tiers of rice paddies in a long, colorful procession. Men and women waved red and gold flags, beat drums and tambours, and blew discordant blasts on trumpets that coiled like golden serpents around the players' shoulders. There were fire-eaters exhaling gouts of red and blue flame, boys and girls who walked on their hands or on stilts, tumblers and jugglers. Lupe walked in the middle of this circus, wearing an emerald-green gown with a long train held by two stunningly beautiful girls. The tangled mane of the old man's hair was dressed with glass beads and brightly colored ribbons. His hands, with their long twisted nails, rested on the bare shoulders of two more girls who guided him to the center of the village where the headman waited, clad only in his darned leggings and his homespun tunic, and his dignity.

After the two men had ceremoniously kissed, Lupe turned to where Yama stood with Tamora and Pandaras. "Well met, dominie," he said. His hands sought and clasped Yama's. "I am pleased that you have returned to us, but I always knew that you would."

Yama began to thank the old man for helping his friends, but Lupe put his long fingernails to his lips. His face was painted white, with black eyebrows drawn above his frost-capped eyes. His lips were dyed a deep purple. "What you will do for us can never be repaid," he said, "but we must not speak of that now. Our brothers have prepared food and drink, and we must dance to earn their hospitality."

The feast lasted all afternoon. As the sun sank behind the shoulder of the slope above the village, cressets were lit and hung on high poles, filling the air with scented smoke and sending fierce red light beating across the crowded square. Children served a stream of dishes, and husbandmen and mirror people ate and drank with gusto. Pandaras fell asleep, curled in his place with his nose in the crook of his knees. Tamora drank sweet yellow wine steadily and soon was as drunk as anyone else.

Yama sat in the place of honor, between Lupe and the headman of the village. The Aedile had taught him the trick of appearing to eat and drink much while in fact consuming little, but even the small amount of wine he drank went straight to his head, and there were times when he believed that he was in the middle of a hectic dream, where animals dressed as men frolicked and bayed at the black sky.

As the air darkened, it became possible to make out the sparkle of gunfire around one high crag of the Palace.

Once, a low rumble passed like a wave through the ground beneath the feasting husbandmen and mirror people, and everyone laughed and clapped, as if it was a trick done for their benefit.

Yama asked Lupe if he was worried by the war between departments, but Lupe smiled and merely said that it was good to be in the fresh air once more. "It has been a long time since I felt sunlight on my face, dominie."

"The war is nothing to us," the headman said. "We do not have the ambitions of the changed. How much it costs them! And when the war is over, everything will be as it was before. No one can change the order of things, for that was set by the Preservers at the beginning of the world."

He raised a beaker of wine and drank, and the husbandmen around him knuckled their foreheads and drank too.

Lupe had been sucking the marrow from a chicken bone. Now he bit it in half and chewed and swallowed the splinters and said, "At the far end of time all those who are changed will be resurrected after death by the charity and grace of the Preservers. Isn't that right, dominie?"

And so it had begun. Yama said, as steadily as he could, "That is what it says in the Puranas."

"All men," the headman said. "But not all who are born and die on Confluence are men. Changed bloodlines become more and more holy, and at last pass away into story and song. Many have passed away since the world was made, and many more will do so in ages to come. But we are less than men, and can never change. And so we will inherit the world when all others have transcended their base selves."

"These people have no ambition, dominie," Lupe told Yama. "They swear never to leave their gardens. They will never wear a crown of fireflies." Lupe waved a hand above his head, as if to swat the two dim fireflies which circled him. "I do not mean these. They are nothing. I know. Rats have brighter attendants. I mean ones such as those you wore when you first visited us. I am sorry that you no longer have them."

"They were taken away," Yama said.

"We do not need fireflies," the headman said, "for we work in the sun and sleep when the Rim Mountains take away the light. We are a humble people."

"They have no ambition, but they are not humble," Lupe told Yama. "They are proudest of all the peoples of the Palace. They cleave to their work in the old gardens and claim to be the best of all the servants of the Preservers, but surely the best way to serve the Preservers is to aspire to become more than you already are."

Lupe leaned toward Yama. The glass beads in his tangled hair clicked and rattled. Each held a point of reflected torchlight. His green dress was of the finest watered silk, but Yama could smell the must of the long years it had spent in a press. Were the blind old man's cheekbones higher and sharper, was his voice softer?

Lupe said, "Who is right, dominie? They say we wish to rise above what we are destined to be; we believe that they are worse sinners, for they refuse the challenge."

On Yama's left hand, the headman said, "If knowing what you are is a sin, then I admit it. But isn't it a worse sin to dream of gaining what you can never have?"

On the other side of the flower-strewn strip of cloth, Tamora suddenly looked up, as if startled awake. "That's right," she said. "Dreams bring heartache."

"Without dreams," Lupe said, "we are only animals. Without dreams, we are no more than we are."

Yama looked from one old man to the other. Although he had drunk little, his head felt as if it was filled with fireflies. He said, "You ask me to judge between you? Then I say that both of you are at fault, for you refuse to look into your own hearts and discover why you wish for elevation or why you refuse the chance. Each of you clearly sees the fault of the other, but neither sees his own fault. We are all raised up by the Preservers, but they do not set limits on what we can be. That is up to us."

The headman touched his forehead, but Lupe tipped back his head and laughed.

The headman glared at Lupe and said, "Then this foolishness should not take place, as I have argued. Brother Lupe, this man is a hero, but he is also a man. We are not the ones to test him. Only he can do that."

"You show him," Tamora said. "Show him what he is. What he isn't."

"It is not a test of him," Lupe said, "but of my people."

The headman said, "And as the dominie pointed out, you have thought too long on why we will not copy your foolishness, instead of thinking why you wish to attempt it."

"Then I stand for my people alone," Lupe said, and held out his hands.

Two girls stepped forward and helped him up. Gradually, the feast fell silent, silence spreading through the noise of laughter and drinking and eating and singing as black ink spreads through water. The people who sat cross-legged around the strips of cloth and the islands of food turned to watch Lupe. The faces of the mirror people were tinted red by the crackling flames of the torches; those of the husbandmen were tinted black. Two giants which had been trading blows with clubs in the center of the square stepped back from each other and their upper halves threw off their tinsel helmets and jumped down from their lower halves, who shucked the wide belts which had concealed where their partners had stood on their shoulders.

Lupe raised a hand, and someone stepped out of the darkness into the flaring light of the torches. It was a beautiful young woman in a simple white shift. She stepped forward lightly and gravely, treading the dust of the square like a dancer, the cynosure of every eye.

She carried a basket of white flowers. When she reached the center of the square she knelt gracefully and offered the basket to Yama. Yama jumped up and backed away, horrified. Tamora began to laugh.

~

They left Yama alone with the baby in the dark night in a ruined temple below the village. Perhaps it had once had gardens and a courtyard before its entrance, but now it was little more than a small square cave cut into the cliff at the edge of a stony field of vines. The lintel of its entrance was cracked. The caryatids which had for an age shouldered their burden uncomplainingly on either side of the door had fallen. One had broken in two and was missing her head; the other lay on her back, her blank eyes gazing at the black sky. Torches had been set on poles thrust into the dry earth on either side of the entrance. Their smoky red light sent long shadows weaving across the flaking frescoes of the naos and put red sparks in the glossy black circle of the shrine.

For a long time, Yama paced back and forth between the two torches, stopping now and then to look at the baby, which slept innocently on the blanket of white blossoms. It was a boy, fat and dusky with health. What tormented Yama was the thought of the miracle he was expected to perform.

To raise this poor wight. To change him from innocence to one of those fallen into full self-awareness.

It was impossible.

The innocence of the indigens was different from that of the unchanged bloodlines because it was absolute. While most bloodlines of Confluence could evolve toward union with the Preservers, the indigens were as fixed in their habits as the beasts of field and flood and air. Certain coarse bloodlines, such as the Amnan, excused their persecution of indigens by saying that their victims were merely animals with human appearance and speech, a kind of amalgam of monkey and parrot. Most, though, agreed that the indigenous races resembled unchanged bloodlines in all but potential. Their only sin was that they could never become other than what they were. They could not fall from the grace to which they had been raised by the Preservers, but neither could they transcend it.

More than once, Yama was seized with the strong urge to pick up the baby and carry him back to the village high above, where, to judge from the sounds of laughter and music which occasionally drifted to him on the night breeze, the feast was proceeding as heartily as when he had been led away from it. And more than once, he was seized with the impulse simply to walk away into the night. To become what he briefly had been when he had first arrived in Ys, a solitary seeker after the truth of his own life.

He did neither. The baby was in his care, and he could not return until the night was over. A refusal to act would be worse than failure, for it would imply that he was not grateful to the mirror people for saving his life. No, better to wait out the night, and be found to have failed. Tamora would be pleased, for it would prove to her that his powers were no more than figments of his imagination. And perhaps the heavy weight of the mirror people's hope might pass from him.

It was not a burden that Yama had ever sought. That was what was so unfair. Zakiel had told him that, because of the great age of Confluence and the multiplicity of its bloodlines, there were so many stories and tales that anyone could find in them a mirror to their own life. And so the mirror people had seen in Yama a reflection of some long-dead hero or half-forgotten promise.

Yama could forgive them that—in these troubled times people looked to the past for heroes to save them, for that was simpler than trying to save themselves. But although, like so many heroes of the Apocrypha, he possessed mysterious origins, strange powers, and what might be mistaken for a magical weapon (but he had lost the knife, and the coin he carried was not the coin he had been given), Yama knew that he was no hero. As a child, he had dreamed of finding others of his bloodline, that they would be powerful and rich and strong. But he knew now that those dreams could not be true. Every orphan must have similar dreams, but very few orphans are of notable birth. Now, older and chastened by the rub of the world, he wished to find his people because he hoped that they would shelter him from the expectations of others. Even if they were no more than mendicants and anchorites, he would join them gladly, for surely they would accept him simply for what he was. He had not asked for what little power that he had, and he wanted it gone.

Let it pass.

More than once, gripped by a mixture of self-loathing and self-pity, he shouted this prayer into the night. But there was never any reply, nothing more than the wind walking amongst the dry leaves of the vines, and the faint sounds of revelry high above. Presently, he remembered that this place was very old, and grew fearful that he might wake something, and was quiet.

"You are better off without it," he whispered to the baby. His throat ached from shouting. "The husbandmen are right."

Yama did not expect to sleep, but at last he tired himself out by pacing to and fro, like the great spotted cat he had once seen in a cage on the deck of a ship that had put in at Aeolis on its way back to Ys from the jungles near the midpoint of the world. The cat had prowled restlessly from one corner of its cage to the other, anger blazing in its green eyes, its mad thoughts unguessable. Perhaps it had believed that if it paced long enough it might find a hidden door to the jungle from which it had been taken.

Yama sat with his back against the pedestal of one of the caryatids (her feet, shod in strap sandals, stood there still, broken off at the ankles), and, tired but sleepless, watched the lights of the city spread beyond the dark slopes of the Palace roof.

After some time, he realized that the fallen caryatid had opened her blank eyes and was watching him. He felt neither fear nor amazement; not even when she spoke.

"You have a knack of finding windows that still work," she said. "I see you lost your key but found another."

Yama knew at once who was speaking to him. The woman he had seen in the shrine of the Temple of the

Black Well. The aspect of the author of the heresies which threatened to consume the world.

He was seized with a bottomless dread, as if confronted with a poisonous serpent. His mouth was dry, but he managed to say, "The keys are everywhere, but people have forgotten what they were."

"They have forgotten much," the woman said lightly. "When I walked in your world, I tried to tell them a little of what they had forgotten. Some remembered, but many resisted. Knowledge is a bitter thing, after all, and many hesitate to sip from that cup. You, for instance, are not one step further on your journey. Why are you sitting here, and who is it you are sitting with? A very unformed mind . . . Ah, it is a baby from one of the true alien races. Another orphan, Yama?"

"I will not serve you," Yama said. It was a great effort to speak, as if he, too, had been turned to stone. He said, "I refuse to serve. I refused Prefect Corin, and I refuse you. I especially refuse you, because I know that you deny the mercy and charity of the Preservers. You would overthrow them and rule in their place if you could. It is the world's good fortune that you are nothing but a ghost."

"Do you refuse the mirror people, too?"

"You cannot know about that!"

"I am in your dreams, Yama, so for this little time I share some of your memories. The mirror people want only to share the fate of the other bloodlines of this strange world. They want nothing more than to take charge of their own destiny, to become infected with the machines that will record their memories, so that they might live again. They want to remember their own story, not have it remembered for them. I had long arguments with Mr. Naryan on that point. He was particularly enthusiastic about innocence, I remember, but no parent should keep a child from growing."

"Mr. Naryan . . . is he another ghost?"

"He was the Archivist of the town of Sensch. As far as I know, he's still alive. It was a great many years ago, but his kind live long, longer than most of the long-lived races of Confluence. He changed his mind, of course. He understands my ideas now.''

"But Sensch was where the war—"

The caryatid smiled, cracking the lichens which had grown like cankers on her stony cheeks. "I set them free, Yama. Free from the burden of this world's mindless theocracy. Free to be themselves."

"The Preservers will give us all that freedom."

"Yes, and they promise to do so at the very instant of the end of the Universe. It is an easy promise to make, for no one will be alive to call them to account when they fail. The Preservers promise everything and give nothing. I promise no more than freedom, and that is what I gave the citizens of Sensch. What is so wrong with that?

"Now, pay attention. I will show you the trick. When I was in the world, I had to call on the shrines to help me change the people of Sensch. Now I live in the space inside the shrines, and the process is much simpler."

"No! I will not serve!"

But in his dream, Yama seemed to be swimming beneath the surface of the river, as he had swum so often when he was still a child, innocently playing with the pups of the Amnan. The pups had liked to dive from the end of the new quay and swim out to the kelp beds, where long green fronds trailed just beneath the surface. They swam deeper and faster than Yama ever could, searching for abalone and oysters that clustered around the holdfasts of the kelp on the muddy river bottom. Yama was happy enough to splash above them, but sometimes he struck downward through sunlight toward the ghost of the river bottom far below, toward the other children. He could never reach them. His lungs began to ache and burn, and the weight of the water compressed his chest and he had to double back and swim strongly for the surface, where he sputtered and coughed in the sunlight. The cool depths of the river were, for him, forever unreachable. But now, as he struck through a hectic flux that was much like the play of light and water, it came to him that his wish had finally come true. The caryatid hung beside him, and he told her that she should sink, for she was stone, and stone could not float.

"Watch," she said, and he saw the knots within the baby's brain, saw how they could be made stronger *here* and *here* so that the swarming machines, smaller than the single-celled plants on which the largest fish of the river grazed, which hung invisibly in every breath of air just as the tiny plants hung in every drop of water, would exist in those places, and begin their work of building and amplifying the initial trace of self-consciousness.

The caryatid sank away, slowly dissolving into the flux of light. "Self-ordering complexity," she murmured. "It only needs a seed . . ."

Yama knew now, or remembered, that this was a dream, and remembered the nature of the creature that had visited him. Yet still something in him yearned toward her, as a starving man will reach toward any kind of food, no matter how foul. He struck out with fierce desperation toward the place where she had disappeared, and woke to find Tamora kneeling beside him. He was lying on the broken tiles of the naos, before the black disc of the shrine. Was there light fading within it? Or was it simply a reflection of the dawn light which was framed by the square entrance of the little temple?

Tamora was watching Yama with an intent, troubled expression. She snatched back her hand when he reached for it, and he asked her what was wrong. Instead of answering, she turned and pointed to the temple's entrance, where people clustered around something on the ground. Immediately, Yama felt a sharp pang of guilt. He had forgotten the baby. He had fallen asleep. It could be dead. It could have been snatched by wild animals.

He staggered outside, every muscle stiff. It was already warm, and light flooded the slopes of the Palace and filled the sky, so bright after the temple's cool shadows that he had to squint. A great cry went up from the people and Yama started back in alarm before he understood that they were smiling. Lupe stood in the center of the little crowd, his blind face bent to a girl who whispered in his ear. Another girl took Yama's hand and led him to the basket of white flowers.

There was so much light that Yama did not at first understand why the baby's eyes kept crossing, and why it batted at the air before its face with its chubby hands. And then he saw.

Hung above its forehead, burning with fierce white radiance, was a crown of fireflies.

THE PROCESSION OF YAMA

"THEY WILL SOON go away," Yama whispered into Pandaras's ear. "I must have drawn them here, but they will
go away once I have left. Before this is over I should
explain to Lupe's people that it is not how they think
it is."

"You are too modest, master! You could live as a Hierarch here, and instead you go to war!"

The produce wagon on which they rode swayed as it
negotiated a pothole in the old road; Pandaras staggered
and then sat down hard by Yama's high chair. The boy
was drunk. From the noise and music and cheering of the
procession, from plentiful libations of sweet yellow palm
wine. A wreath of ivy and the long white flowers of trumpet vine was tipped on his brow. There was a large wet
wine stain on the front of his white shirt.

"They'd kill him," Tamora said. "Not these fools, but
the people in power. He's a threat to them."

She stood behind Yama, gripping her saber and constantly turning from left to right to watch the crowd, becoming especially alert whenever someone let off a
firecracker. People were running alongside the wagon and
its attendant procession of mirror people, or stood on ter-

races overlooking the road, cheering and waving palm fronds or brightly colored cloths, offering up flowers or fruit. One group had launched kites into the air; painted with fierce faces, the red and black and yellow diamonds zoomed and swooped around each other in the bright air.

Lupe sat at Yama's feet, arrayed in a dress of cloth-of-gold sewn with fake pearls and sequins. He held the baby with its crown of brilliant fireflies in his lap. He said, "We mean no harm to anyone. We simply set forth from our immemorial home to claim our place in the world."

"You'd do better to stay here," Tamora said. She had to raise her voice to a shrill pitch to be heard above the crowd. "Innocents like you are prey for every bandit, crimp and reaver in the city."

"When I was a young man," Lupe said, "I used the shell game to take money from your people at the Water Market. Before that, I played the part of the monkey in the illusion of the snake and rope, and helped in a puppet theater. Marks always think that they can fool us, but they forget that they play our games by our rules. Ah, but we must not quarrel, young cateran, for we are both set on the same path. Hear how the people cheer the procession of your master!"

The news of the miracle had spread fast and far. By the time the procession had left the village of the husbandmen, people were already lining the old road as far as they could see. Gangs of men were clearing the road of brush and fallen rock, or patching gaps with timbers. The road had not been used, Lupe said, since the Hierarchs had fallen silent, ten thousand years ago.

The procession wound three times around the slopes of the Palace as it descended toward the city. No guards or troops came forward to stop it, but now and then Tamora would point out a speck in the air beyond the Palace's slopes, where, she said, an officer stood on a disc, watching through a glass. Once, where the road rounded the bulging side of a steep cliff with sheer rock above and only air below, a flyer paced the procession. It hung just beyond the edge of the road, so close that one of the acrobats could have easily jumped from the road to the wide black triangle of its wing. The mirror people pelted it with flowers and libations, and then the road turned into a short tunnel through the side of a bluff, and when it came out into the sunlight the flyer was gone, and more people were running down steeply tilted fields toward the procession, waving and cheering.

Yama waved back, although he was sick at heart. The miracle which these innocent people were celebrating was no miracle at all, but a trick of the shadow of the creature who had started the war. She had used him as a tool to change the baby, either to show him what she was capable of, or to show him that she knew his powers better than he did. The miracle which Lupe had desired so much was a perversion, a crude and cruel joke mocking the will of the Preservers.

Yama's only hope was that good might come from this after all. For no matter how it had been done, the baby *was* changed. Lupe's people had the proof that they could be raised up.

There was nothing he could do but make the best of it, which was why he had agreed to ride with Lupe. Tamora had said that taking part in the procession was perilously foolish, but Yama had asked her plainly what was better—sneaking out of Ys under cover of darkness, like escaping thieves, or riding in the place of honor in a long, happy procession amidst tumblers and musicians and clowns, with the population cheering them along? At least Pandaras was caught up in the fever of it all. He waved too, and drank the libations which people handed up, and laughed and waved some more.

Yama turned to Tamora and said, "Most of them think it is some kind of performance."

She shook her head. "Just look at who has come to watch. They are all of them indigens or the poorest of the poor, sweepers and nightsoil collectors like the rat-boy here. If the soldiers or the magistrates decide to arrest you, or worse, if those fuckers from Indigenous Affairs come for you, this trash would melt away. And tomorrow they'd choose another King of Fools.''

''My bloodline helped build the world, Tamora, and at one time I believed they might be Lords of infinite time and space. I know now that they were no such thing. They were laborers such as these.''

The miracle was not that he had performed a miracle, for he knew that he had not, but that Lupe and the mirror people believed that he had. Perhaps the good of it was this: that these people believed that miracles were possible, that the Preservers could still intercede in the world. And how could he deny it? For was not his own existence as much a miracle as the crown of fireflies around that innocent baby's head? If the woman in the shrine had used him, then perhaps she in turn had been used by some higher power.

''I think you're better than them,'' Tamora said, and went back to watching the crowd.

Yama was searching the faces in the crowd, too. He was looking for Eliphas, for now the procession was descending through the cramped squares and narrow streets that threaded between the tumultuous jumble of buildings at the hem of the Palace, and still there was no sign of the old man.

The procession moved toward a great gate. People lined the rooftops on either side, pelting the wagon with flowers and paper strings in a blizzard so dense that at first Yama did not see why the procession suddenly stopped. Tamora hissed, but Yama held up his hand, hoping that she would not strike. For now he saw, through falling drifts of flowers, a line of troopers strung across the road before the gate, some mounted on black-plumaged ratites, some on foot.

An officer on a floating disc, clad in metal armor so polished that it shone like a mirror broken into the shape of a man, swooped down and hung in the air above the two oxen that drew the wagon. He was bareheaded, his skull heavily ridged. A thick black mustache framed the puckered cone of his mouth. He stared directly at Yama and said, "Who is in charge?"

"No one was compelled to be here," Yama said. "They came of their own free will."

The officer said, "None of these animals know anything about free will."

Lupe said, "We set forth toward a new life, dominie. And this is the one who sets us upon it."

Tamora stepped forward, glaring up at the officer. "Get out of the way, little man. And take your toy soldiers with you."

"Stand down," Yama told her gently, as he might try and calm a highly strung mount. He said to the officer, "What authority stops us?"

"The Department of Internal Harmony. You are Yama-manama? I am here to escort you from the Palace. We are under considerable pressure to return you to a certain place, but the Department of Internal Harmony does not take sides. We still have full control of the lower floors and the outer defenses, and we do as we see fit to ensure the security of the Palace. Accordingly, I am here to make sure that you leave the Palace, and to ask you to disperse your followers."

"They are not mine to command." Yama gestured, meaning the crowd which clogged the street behind the wagon, the people on the rooftops who were still tossing flowers into the air. He said, "If they were, I would not have allowed this. I am as embarrassed by it as you, but I believe that they mean no harm by what they do."

He could take the disc from beneath the officer's feet and use it as a scythe against the troopers who blocked the way. He could call down machines and riddle them through and through. It would be so easy . . . but there would be other soldiers, and beyond the gates was the city, and the hundred thousand magistrates who kept civil order. He was not here to start a war. What was he thinking? The woman in the shrine had put something in his head that twisted his thoughts to fantasies of violence and domination. He took a deep breath to calm himself, and remembered that the Aedile had taught him that when negotiating it was better to allow your opponent to think that he had come to a decision than to force him to make a choice, for when forced a man will usually choose badly.

He said, "I understand why you must keep order amongst the petitioners and palmers who seek to gain entrance, for else the Palace would be overwhelmed. But the people who celebrate here are of the Palace itself, and wish to leave. They are the simple people who work the fields and entertain the clerks."

Lupe said, "We have always come and gone freely. Why are we stopped now?"

"I know your kind," the officer said. "They come and go by ratholes and sewer pipes, along with the other vermin."

Yama said, "If they are vermin, why then, you would well be rid of them. In any case surely you should not waste a moment on them. Would you stop birds flying from the fields above us to the banks of the Great River?"

The officer thought for a moment, then said, "We serve the ideal of the Preservers. We always have. In the black days when the Head of the People swallowed all other departments, we alone maintained our independence. We allow people to come and go as we see fit."

"And even the mirror people were raised up by the Preservers. Their kind have lived in the Palace for longer than almost every other bloodline. Perhaps you would know if they have some rights in this matter."

The officer's puckered mouth drew back to show the strong, yellow-ridged grinding plates he had instead of teeth. "Frankly, I'll be glad to see the last of them. They are parasites upon the bodies of the departments. Only a decad past there was a riot in one of the day markets because one of them was caught cheating at some gambling game. Several clerks were blinded when a fool fired an energy pistol."

Yama believed that he knew something of the truth of that incident, but he did not correct the officer. He said, "Then perhaps all will benefit if they pass with me."

The officer nodded. "They'll be the magistrates' problem once they're outside the Palace, and I have my orders to get you to a place of safety. The Department of Indigenous Affairs pushed too hard for your return. We'll not be at the command of them, or anyone else."

"There is a ship waiting for us at the docks," Yama said. "If you took me there, it would be an end to your duty, and of my obligation to you."

~

The mounted troopers of the Department of Internal Harmony fell in as an escort ahead and behind the wagon. Their ratites, the officer confided to Yama, were not as swift or fearsome as horses, but were less prone to panic and more maneuverable in the press of a crowd. The procession passed beneath the arch of the great gate (all the fireflies, from Lupe's to those of the baby in his lap, flew up and vanished; Yama was glad to see them go) and began to make its way through the ordinary streets of Ys.

Yama turned back and saw the Palace rearing against the sky above close-packed roofs, and fancied he glimpsed the flash of some weapon's discharge near the peak, where the war between departments was still being fought. Or perhaps it was no more than the sun glinting on some metal surface high up in the Palace's great bulk—perhaps the metal which clad the House of the Twelve Front Rooms of the Department of Vaticination.

The procession was still followed by cheering crowds, but now there were just as many people on the streets who merely glanced at it as they went about their normal business. Yama remembered the procession he had seen from the window of the inn where he had woken after plunging into the Country of the Mind where the crews of the voidships met each other, and laughed to think that now he was the center of a similar spectacle, simultaneously the center of everyone's gaze and something commonplace.

Tamora cursed Pandaras for getting drunk and said that Yama should watch the rooftops instead of waving like the King of Fools. "They should have put a canopy over your head. It wouldn't block quarrel, but it would hinder the aim."

"We are quite safe," Yama said. "We have the protection of the Department of Internal Harmony. No one will dare try and take me by force now."

"Prefect Corin might try and put a quarrel through your head, and mine too. He won't have forgiven us for escaping. I know the type. And those magistrates are watching us too closely for my liking."

Red-robed magistrates stood on floating discs high above the heads of the crowd which thronged the streets, their machines a dizzy twinkle in the air about them. Yama waved at them as the wagon trundled past, and suppressed the impulse to twist the orbits of their machines into mocking configurations.

As the wagon moved toward the docks, the crowd began to grow denser, swollen by refugees come to beg for help from the man who had raised up one of the indigenous races. Women held up children so that they could see Yama and the baby, or perhaps to be blessed, for many were ill or deformed. People shouted and prayed and pleaded, but their words were lost in the general tumult and the braying of the trumpets and shawms of the mirror people.

At last, the crowds were so dense that the procession could no longer move forward. Even the mounted soldiers were trapped in the press. The officer swooped down and told Yama that he would arrange for him to be carried away to wherever he wished.

Yama shook his head. "I will walk if I must!"

"You must come with me!"

They were both shouting at the tops of their voices, but could hardly hear themselves over the noise of the crowd. A man jumped on to the wagon and tried to asperge Yama with scented oil. Tamora kicked him in the throat and he folded over and fell backward. The mob closed around him before he had a chance to scream.

Yama climbed onto the bench and raised his arms.

Gradually, the crowd which packed the street ahead and behind the wagon grew quiet, except for a scattering of individual voices crying out with hysteria or hurt or fright.

"I cannot help you," Yama said. He was trembling violently, and a sharp pain pressed between his eyes. "Only you can help yourselves."

Most did not hear him, but the crowd cheered anyway. Yama remembered the magistrate who had stopped him and Prefect Corin when they had first arrived in Ys, and borrowed a machine from one of the magistrates who stood on a rooftop overlooking the street. When he spoke to it, it amplified his voice so that it echoed from the walls of the buildings. He meant to tell the crowd again that he could not help them, but something seized him, and then he hardly knew what he said. The crowd cheered and he felt lifted up by their cheers. The pain between his eyes intensified and red and black light flashed in his sight. He tried to reach out and change everyone in the crowd and failed because there were too many, and cried out in rage. A myriad tiny machines burned and fell from the air. People screamed and tried to flee as magistrates, believing themselves to be under attack, laid into those nearest them with their quirts. But there was nowhere to flee to, and suddenly the crowd was fighting against itself, its unity lost.

Yama did not see any of this. Red and black lightning tore away all thought and he fell backward into Tamora's arms.

—

A great wind blew around him. The sun burned down out of the cloudless sky, but the rush of air was so cold that he shivered in its icy blast as if plunged into a stream fed by the glaciers at the end of the world. He lay on a ridged metal deck that vibrated beneath him. When he struggled to sit up, Pandaras helped him and said, "A flying machine, master. You fainted and the officer caught you up and carried you off."

"There were too many . . ."

Pandaras misunderstood; he was still drunk. His wreath was tipped over one ear. He said, "They would have torn you apart if this hadn't rescued us. Isn't it wondrous?"

The flying machine was sleek and boat-shaped, with short, down-curved wings. Its silver skin shone like a mirror in the bright sunlight. Lupe sat behind Yama and Pandaras, with the baby in his lap and a girl on either side. Four troopers stood behind him. Near the beaked prow, Tamora was talking with a man clad in broken mirrors. She glanced around, grinning fiercely, and said, "We go directly to the docks."

The mirror-clad man turned—it was the officer in his polished armor—and said, "This is only a dory, not a true flyer. Unfortunately its range is limited, or I would take you as far from the city as possible."

Yama said stupidly, "Who commands it?"

"It flies itself," the officer said. "It is from the early days of the world. There. You see what we have left behind."

The little dory tilted in the air. Because its local gravity compensated for the motion, the world seemed to pitch beneath it. The grid of the city, punctuated here and there by the domes and spires of temples, stretched away toward the vast bulk of the Palace of the Memory of the People. The Palace's peak was obscured by smoke. A long way beyond it were the shining towers Yama had seen so often using the signal telescope on the roof of the peel-house at Aeolis, white needles that rose higher than the Rim Mountains, their tops lost in a glare of sunlight beyond the envelope of air that shrouded the world.

Yama pointed at the Palace and said, "They are still fighting."

"It is the rioting in the streets that I meant," the officer said. "Well, I suppose we are too high to see it."

As if it understood him, the dory swooped down. The city rushed at them. The crowded roofs of the refugees' shantytown, built over the mudbanks left by the Great River's slow retreat, raveled away on either side. The river was directly ahead, a broad plain flashing in the sunlight as the dory swerved toward one of the floating docks.

The pontoon quays of the dock were lined with sight-seers, and a flotilla of small boats stood off on either side. As the dory gently sank through the air, coming to rest just above the edge of the outermost quay, Yama saw a familiar face in the crowd and immediately jumped down.

Tamora got in front of Yama and helped keep off the press of people who crowded round, shouting and singing and praying and making obeisance. Some clutched at Yama's homespun tunic and he realized his mistake and would have climbed back on the dory, but there was no room to move. Tamora held her saber above her head, in case someone was pushed onto it by those pressing from behind, and there was an uncomfortable minute before the troopers managed to clear a space.

Lupe was helped down by his attendants, using one of the wings of the dory as a pont. The blind old man ignored those who crowded around him. He cradled the baby in one arm and touched Yama's face with the long fingernails of his free hand. "You should not have left us the first time, dominie," he said. "You will forgive me if I mention that you caused much trouble. But all's well that ends well."

Yama smiled, and then remembered that the old man could not see. He said, "You have been a generous friend, Lupe."

"We are your servants, dominie. We are no longer the servants of the pleasure of all in the Palace, but for you we will always give our lives."

"It will not be necessary."

"I'm glad to hear it. But these are strange times, domi-nie. The end of the world is at hand. Why else would you have kindled the change in our bloodline?"

Lupe embraced Yama tremulously, and Yama kissed the old man on both cheeks. The baby smiled up at them, quite undisturbed by the commotion of the crowd. Someone was trying to push between the troopers who guarded Yama and Lupe. Tamora's saber point flicked in that direction—

but it was Eliphas, smiling broadly and shouting wildly, his silver eyes flashing in the bright sunlight.

"I have found them," Eliphas shouted. "I have found them, brother! Downriver!"

THE SHIP THEY had hired, the *Weazel,* was a small lugger which, before the war, had spent her days ferrying cargo and a few passengers from one side of the Great River to the other. She was single-masted and lateen-rigged, and in calm weather could supplement her triangular mainsail with square staysails rigged from spars spread either side of her mast. She pulled a shallow draft, and with wind and current behind her could make twice the speed of the huge galliots and levanters which were scattered across the Great River in pods of three or four, heading downriver toward the war. She could not outrun the machines which tried to follow her, but Yama, exhausted though he was, told them to disperse even before the drag anchors had been collapsed.

Pandaras said that it was likely that the *Weazel* had been used as much for smuggling as for plying regular trade, but he was careful to say this out of earshot of the ship's captain, Ixchel Lorquital. Captain Lorquital was a cautious, shrewd widow who dominated all on board with a natural authority. Like all the women of her bloodline, she had added her husband's name to her own when she had married.

"But that don't mean I was anything less than him," she told Yama. "You might say that since I carry his name and his memory I'm rather more than he ever was, the Preservers keep his memory safe."

Ixchel Lorquital was a big woman, with mahogany-colored skin that shone as if oiled and an abundance of coarse black hair she habitually tied back from her creased, round face with a variety of colored strings. Her forehead was ridged with keratin, her nostrils no more than slits in the middle of her face. She wore a silver lip-plug which weighed down her lower lip, exposing yellow, spade-shaped teeth. The day-to-day running of the ship was left to her daughter, Aguilar, who combined the offices of bosun and purser, and Captain Lorquital habitually sat in a sling chair by the helm, puffing a corncob pipe, stately in a billowing long skirt and leather tabard, her well-muscled arms bare, a red handkerchief knotted under her pendulous jowls. Eliphas soon struck up a friendship with her, and they spent hours talking together.

Ixchel Lorquital asked no questions about Yama and his friends. She offered her cabin to the four passengers, but Yama politely refused this generous gesture. Instead, he and his companions camped on the deck, sleeping on raffia mats under a canvas awning that slanted steeply from the rail of the quarterdeck to a cleat by the cargo well.

Yama slept easily and deeply on the Great River. It reminded him of the happy days of the annual pilgrimages made by the whole population of Aeolis to the farside shore. And he could sleep safe in the knowledge that he had left his enemies behind him, and that now he had a destination, a place to voyage toward, the place where his bloodline might still live.

—

Eliphas had told Yama all about his discovery as soon as the *Weazel* had raised her rust-red sail and begun to outpace the flotilla of small boats which had tried to follow her. The old man was tremendously pleased with himself, and even more voluble than usual.

"It was your mention of Dr. Dismas that aided the search," he said. "It was a simple matter to check the records and find out which he had accessed. He had been careful to cover his tracks, but he was not subtle. For one as experienced as my friend Kun Norbu, the chief of clerks, it was a relatively simple matter to see through the deception."

"You say that they were living downriver," Yama said quickly, before Eliphas could launch into a technical account of the false trails left by Dr. Dismas and the skills the chief of clerks had employed to untangle them.

"If they still live, brother, then that is where they will be found," Eliphas said.

"Well, I am alive," Yama said.

"That's true," Eliphas said. "However, I feel I should point out that while your being alive here and now means that at least two of your bloodline were alive in the recent past, it does not mean that our hypothetical pair are alive now, or that any others like them are alive. The documents, you see, are quite old. At least five thousand years old, for they had formed part of the original binding of a book which had been made then. They could well be much older, of course."

"How much older?"

"Well, that's difficult to say, brother. With more time, Kun Norbu and I could have analyzed the inks, for degradation of certain elements used to manufacture inks occurs at a fairly constant rate. But they are not more than ten thousand years old, for before that time the region in which the city of your bloodline is located was not yet formed."

"A city!"

Yama had never imagined more than a small keep, or perhaps a small town, hidden in the icy fastness upriver of Ys. Perhaps a citadel tunneled into the rock of the mountains, a fine and secret place full of ancient wonders. But a city . . .

Eliphas drew a little leather satchel from inside his loose shirt, unfastened its clasps, and took out a cardboard folder tied with a green ribbon.

"Neither are the originals, of course," he said. "My friend the chief of clerks could not allow such precious documents to leave the precincts of the library. However, they are fair copies, made by the best of the copyists in the library. The first faithfully reproduces the appalling script of the man who wrote the original, and even mimics the stains and tatters which the original accumulated before it was used as a stiffener in the binding of a common pharmacopium."

It took him a minute more to unpick the knot in the ribbon. He opened the folder and withdrew a piece of paper which had been folded into quarters and sealed with a blob of black wax. It fluttered in the warm wind which poured past the rail of the ship's waist, and it took all of Yama's will to resist snatching it from Eliphas's hand.

"Sealed with the imprint of the chief of clerks," Eliphas said, and snapped the wax and handed the folded paper to Yama.

After he had opened it, Yama thought at first that he had the paper upside down, but when he turned it around he still could not read the irregular lines of squiggles and dashes.

Eliphas smiled. "It is a long-dead language, brother, and the man who wrote this account used a much-debased version. However, I have some small skill in it. It is a brief account written by a scavenger of wrecked war machines in the Glass Desert beyond the midpoint of the world. That is why I would guess that it is more than five thousand years old. The remains of war machines were almost entirely removed from the accessible areas of the Glass Desert long before the making of the book in which this was found."

"Where is it then? Where is this place?"

"Several hundred leagues beyond the end of the Great River, in a series of caverns. The scavenger believed that it was once a huge city, but only a small part of it was still inhabited when he stumbled upon it.''

Yama remembered the places beneath the world where Beatrice had taken him, and the capsule which had transported them from the edge of the Rim Mountains to the shore of the river. With growing excitement, he realized that, as a baby, he might have been carried from one end of the river to the other in a similar device. He did not know if his people still lived there, but at last he had a goal, even if it lay beyond the armies of the heretics.

But Tamora still did not trust Eliphas, and said so bluntly. "You are a fool if you believe him," she said, later that evening.

"Eliphas thinks he will find treasures there. That is why he is so eager to help. He is quite honest about his intentions."

"He wants to be young again," Pandaras said. "It's a futile wish most men share. And so he plunges into an adventure like those of his youth, hoping that it will revive his waning powers."

They sat on rolled raffia mats under the awning, their faces lit by a single candle which flickered in a resin holder. Eliphas was on the quarterdeck, talking with Captain Ixchel Lorquital. To port, Ys made a web of lights that stretched as far as the eye could see; to starboard, the Eye of the Preservers was rising above the black sweep of the river.

Tamora had taken several of the small fish the cook had caught on trotlines trailing from the ship's stern. She picked up one and tore a bite from it and swallowed without chewing. "Grah. That scrawl could be anything or nothing. He could have made it this morning. You have only his word that this is a record of your bloodline."

"Not a record," Yama said, "simply an account of what happened to a scavenger when his camels died after drinking poisoned water. He was wandering half-mad from thirst and heat exhaustion, and was found and taken in by a tribe of people who looked like me. He says that they called themselves the Builders. They had fireflies, and other machines. He was there for more than a decad, until he had recovered from his ordeal. Then he woke one morning and found himself hundreds of leagues away, near the fall of the Great River.''

''It is a pretty story,'' Tamora said, ''but where's the proof?''

''He remembered the path he had taken up to the point when his rescuers found him. Here.''

Yama drew out the other piece of paper Eliphas had brought. Tamora held it to the light of the candle and Pandaras craned his sleek head to look.

It was a map.

—

At dawn the next day the *Weazel* was sailing past the lower reaches of Ys ahead of a brisk breeze, dragging a creamy wake through the river's tawny water. The ship kept to the outermost of the coastal currents, where the water was stained by silt and sewage from thousands of drains, all of which had once been clear streams fed by the snowcaps of the foothills of the Rim Mountains. On the port side, across a wide stretch of calm water broken here and there by small islands crowded with buildings, or by long picket lines which marked the boundaries of fish farms, was an endless unraveling panorama of close-packed houses which stretched away beneath a dun haze created by millions of cooking fires. A horde of tiny craft went about their business close to the shore: coracles and skiffs; little fishing boats and puttering reaction motors; slow sampans carrying whole families and menageries of chickens and rabbits and dwarf goats; crowded water buses; luggers like the *Weazel*, their big triangular sails often painted with a stylized swirl representing the Eye of the Preservers. Occasionally, a merchant's carvel moved at a deliberate pace amongst the smaller craft, or a pinnace with a double bank of oars and a beaked prow sped swiftly by, scattering the local traffic, the beat of the drum which set the rhythm of the rowers sounding clear and small across the water.

Yama's chest tightened each time one of the pinnaces went by, partly in memory of the time when Dr. Dismas had tried to kidnap him, partly because he was still not sure that he had escaped Prefect Corin. This might be no more than a reprieve until the Prefect or some other officer of the Department of Indigenous Affairs tried to snatch him back. When he had woken, he had sent away more than a decad of machines which had been following the *Weazel,* and he expected to have to send away many more.

He did not want to think of the baby of the mirror people, of the dream in which the woman had spoken to him, of how badly the procession had ended. He wanted to put all of it behind him, and in the night had prayed that it would pass away, another one-day wonder in a city where wonder was commonplace.

To starboard was nothing but the wide river, stretching a hundred leagues to its own flat horizon, where tall white clouds were stacked above the merest glimpse of the far-side shore. Day by day the clouds would grow taller and nearer, until at last they would break on the land and bring about the brief rainy season. Apart from an occasional fishing boat, trawling for deep-water delicacies in the company of a swirling flock of white birds, the outer reaches of the Great River were the preserve of the big ships. At any hour at least a hundred could be counted, scattered far and wide across the gleaming surface of the river.

Going downriver.

Going to war.

Of the five members of the crew of the *Weazel,* two, including the fat cook, were slaves who had been purchased at judicial auctions. The oldest of the sailors, the ship's carpenter, Phalerus, a bald-headed fellow with a sharp jutting lizard's face and a ruff of skin that rose above his mottled scalp, had once been a slave too—he had bought his freedom years ago but had stayed on anyway, for he knew no other home. Of the other two freemen, one was a cheerful, simpleminded man named Anchaile; skinny and long-limbed, he swung amongst the rigging with astonishing agility. The other, a shy, quiet boy, was said to have killed five men in pit fights and was on the run from his handler because he had refused to fight a woman. This boy, Pantin, and the second slave, a grizzled little man with terrible scars on his back, were of Pandaras's bloodline. Whenever there was slack time the three sat together telling stories or singing long ballads in their own language, one dropping out as another took over in rounds that sometimes went on for hours.

None of the crew were allowed to cross the brass line set aft of the cargo well in the whitewood deck (scoured each day by coconut matting weighted by the cook and dragged back and forth by two others) without the permission of either Captain Lorquital or her daughter, Aguilar. The cargo well was covered with a tarpaulin cover as tight as a drum head, and loaded with replacement parts for artillery pieces. Each part was sprayed with polymer foam; they were stacked under the tarpaulin like so many huge, soft eggs. By the forecastle bulwark were pens where hens and guineafowl strutted and a single shoat rooted in a litter of straw, and on the triangular bit of decking that roofed the forecastle, under the lines which tethered the leading point of the sail to the long bowsprit, was a light cannon under a tarpaulin shroud.

It was here that Tamora chose to perch the second day, watching the city shore move past hour upon hour. She was in a kind of sulk, and even Aguilar, a jolly unselfconscious woman who claimed to have at least three men lusting after her in every city along the Great River, could not cajole more than three or four words from her at any one time.

Yama worried about Tamora's mood, but bided his time. He reflected that he still did not know her well, and knew even less about her bloodline. Perhaps she was still recovering from their adventures, and in particular from her long incarceration in the Department of Indigenous Affairs, of which she would not speak. Worse had happened to her, Yama suspected, than the shaving of her head. And no doubt she was worried, and perhaps angry, that Eliphas had usurped her position as Yama's advisor, that he and not she had found clues to Yama's origin. It did not occur to him that there was a simpler answer, and that it lay within himself.

—

At the end of the second day, the *Weazel* finally passed beyond the downriver edge of the city. Red sandstone cliffs, fretted with the square mouths of old tombs, stood above mudbanks and shoals exposed by the river's retreat. The only signs of habitation were the occasional fishing hamlets stranded beyond new fields made where the river had once flowed.

Early the next morning, the wind died and the *Weazel*'s triangular mainsail flapped idly. The ship drifted on the slow river current. The sun beat down from the deep indigo sky; the distant cliffs glowed through a haze of heat like a bar of molten iron; the big ships scattered across the gleaming sweep of the river did not change position from hour to hour.

At last, Captain Lorquital had the sail hauled down. Drag anchors were thrown over the sides. The ship's crew took turns to swim and even Captain Lorquital went overboard, dressed in a white shift as big as a tent, hauling herself down the ladder at the stern a step at a time. Pandaras spouted water like a grampus, splashing with his two friends; Eliphas swam with a dignified breaststroke, keeping his white-haired head above the water at all times.

Tamora sat cross-legged on the forecastle decking, studiously not looking at the frolics in the water around the ship.

Yama swam a long way out. He found a patch of oarweed and wound himself in cool, slippery fronds, a trick he had learned as a child; the gas-filled bladders of the oarweed would keep him afloat without any effort. The ship was a small black shape printed on the burning water. He could cover it with his thumb.

Soon, he would pass his childhood home, and he idly thought that he could jump ship then, and return to the peel-house and take up his life once more. He could marry Derev. It would be a metic marriage, but they would be happy. He would not mind if she took a concubine of her own bloodline. He would raise the children as if they were his own.

But this was no more than a pretty fantasy. He could not go home again. He could not pretend that things had not changed. That he had not changed, in ways that frightened and amazed him.

He could feel the tug of the feral machine far beyond the end of the world. And even as he floated on his back amidst the oarweed, machines gathered beneath him. Through a fathom of clear deep water he could see things with dull silvery carapaces and long articulated tails moving over each other on the red sand of the riverbed. He ducked his head underwater to study this aimless congregation, then floated on his back and watched the distant ship, and thought again of Derev and everything else he had left behind in Aeolis, and at last swam slowly back to the ship.

～

Tamora did not turn her head when Yama came up the ladder behind her. The whitewood of the forecastle deck was hot under his bare feet; water dripping from his body darkened it for only a few moments before drying.

After a while, Tamora said, "I went up to the crow's nest. There's a little smudge on the horizon. As if something very big has been set on fire. I've been wondering what it could be."

Yama remembered the ship Lud and Lob had fired as a diversion on the night he had been kidnapped by Dr. Dismas. He said, "Perhaps it is a galliot or a carrack, attacked by pirates."

"The war goes worse than I knew if there are raiding parties this far upriver."

"There have always been pirates. They live amongst the floating islands in the midstream."

Tamora shook her head. She said, "The pirates have all gone downriver to the war. There are richer and easier pickings there."

Yama reached out toward her scarred, naked scalp, but halted just short of touching it.

Tamora said, "I didn't believe you. I didn't want to believe."

Yama understood. "I am no different, Tamora. I still want nothing more than I did when I first met you. Once I have found my people I want to join the war and fight as best I can."

"As best you can!" She turned and looked up at him. "I thought you were a monster. They told me that, in my cell. They told me that I might be pregnant by you, and be carrying your spawn. They examined me—"

"Tamora. I did not know. I am sorry."

'No! I am sorry. I was weak. I allowed the fuckers to get inside my head. It wasn't you that put a monster inside me, but them. It's been whispering inside my skull ever since. I always knew what you were, see, but I wouldn't admit it. That's why those fuckers could get inside me. I won't let it happen again."

With a sudden, violent heave, she twisted around and threw herself full length on the decking. She moved so quickly that Yama did not have time to react. She kissed his feet and looked up and said, "I did not believe in you. But I do now. I know that you are capable of miracles. I will serve you with all my life if you will let me."

Yama helped her up, feeling a mixture of embarrassment and confusion and fright. He said, "We will fight side by side, as we said we would."

Tamora finally met his gaze. She said, "Isn't that what I said? But in what cause?"

"Against the heretics, of course."

But he said it so quickly that both of them knew that it was said out of habit, not belief.

Tamora saved him. "Well, yes," she said. "There's always that."

OF MIRACLES

ELIPHAS SAID, "I studied long on this when I was much younger. I came to the conclusion then—and I have found no reason to change my mind—that there are three classes of miracles."

The old man was sitting with Yama and Captain Lorquital on the quarterdeck, in the shadow of the booming sail. It was the morning of the third day of the voyage. The wind had picked up in the night, blowing strongly from the upriver quarter of the farside shore. Water rushed by the hull and the river sparkled out to its distant horizon, salted with millions of whitecaps. There was a lightning storm fifty leagues to starboard. Whips of light flickered under massed purple clouds, and now and again the sound of thunder rolled faintly across the face of the waters.

Eliphas ticked off categories of miracle on his long thin fingers. He said, "There are those events in which something happens that is contrary to nature, such as the sun failing to reverse its course in the sky at noon, but instead continuing on to the farside. There are those events which may occur in Nature, but never in that particular order, such as a dead man returning to life, or the Eye of the Preservers rising at the same time as the Galaxy. And then there are those events which may occur naturally, but which in the case of a miracle do so without natural causation, such as this good ship dashing along with no wind behind her and no current beneath her. So we see that most miracles are quite natural processes, but without the usual causes or order.''

Ixchel Lorquital said, ''Myself, I don't believe in supernatural happenings. You'll hear talk ashore that sailors are superstitious. But what it is, we're careful because we can't take anything for granted on the river. It seems to me that miracles happen because people are hoping they'll happen. It's mostly religious people who claim to have seen a miracle, as is only natural. They're the ones who've the most to gain from it, even if they don't think that way. What I'd say is, if someone says they saw something contrary to nature, then it's more likely that they are mistaken.''

Eliphas nodded. ''All you say is true, sister. The most difficult thing about miracles is not trying to explain them away, but trying to prove that something *is* a miracle, and not simply a manifestation of natural law or of ancient technology, or a trick cunningly set up, or an illusion dependent upon a willing suspension of belief on the part of the audience. In ancient times there were theaters of the mind in which participants could explore fantastic landscapes where miracles occurred as a matter of course, much as puppets in a street theater may be made to fly, or breathe fire, or rise from the dead. But of course those were not miracles, but illusions.''

''Then you might say that I only dreamed that the caryatid came to life,'' Yama said, ''or that I talked with the woman in the shrine of the Temple of the Black Well in a dream. Unfortunately, while it might be a comforting thought, I do not believe it to be true. The truth is that there are things in the world which are long forgotten, and somehow I am capable of waking them. The question is not how these things happened, but why they happened to me. If I knew the answer to that, I would be a happy man.''

Ixchel Lorquital said, "Before my husband died, before the war, we traveled up and down the Great River at least once a year. I reckon to have seen every bloodline on Confluence, including most of the indigenous tribes that haunt the Rim Mountains and the jungles and marshes down by the midpoint of the world. But I'm sorry to say that I have never seen anyone like you, young man."

Yama smiled and said, "I am comforted to think that I do not have to spend my time searching, for you have already done it for me."

"Not even as sturdy a vessel as the *Weazel* could sail beyond the end of the river," Eliphas said, "and that is where Yama's bloodline may live now."

"No one goes there," Ixchel Lorquital said, "except for desperate prospectors and a few crazy pillar saints."

Eliphas nodded. "Precisely, sister. What better place, then, to hide?"

Ixchel Lorquital laughed and clapped her hands. They were fleshy, with loose webs of skin linking the fingers, and they made a loud slapping sound. She said, "A gentleman as worldly as you could charm the fish from the water by persuading them that the air was safe to breathe. Fine words are wasted on an old woman like me. My daughter now, she's a connoisseur of compliments. It would cheer her up to hear some of that shiny talk of yours."

Eliphas bowed.

"I have to say that a pale skin like yours," Ixchel Lorquital told Yama, "is not suited to the desert lands beyond the midpoint."

Eliphas said, "The memoir found by my esteemed friend Kun Norbu, the chief of clerks of the Department of Apothecaries and Chirurgeons, suggests that they live in caverns beneath the surface of the deserts."

Yama smiled. "My father is always digging to find the past. What better place to find the first people of the world than in an underground city?"

"Just so, brother, just so. Many years ago, when I was still a young man—if such a thing can be imagined—my friend Kun Norbu and I found a passage below a ruined cliff temple. It led far underground, to a chamber containing many vast machines which were no longer functioning, and the chamber stretched so far into the darkness that after two days we scrupled to explore no further. But perhaps we should have continued. I have often dreamed of it since, and sometimes in these dreams I have glimpsed such wonders that on waking I wondered if I had gone mad.''

Eliphas's silver eyes held faint concentric patterns that widened and closed like irises. There was a fine grain, as of well-cured leather, to his smooth black skin. His fingers: bunches of deftly articulated twigs. The neat whorls of flesh around the naked tympani of his ears.

Yama realized that he really knew very little of this old man, who had insisted on following him for no other reason, it seemed, than to rekindle the adventurous spirit of his long-lost youth. Last night, he had discovered Eliphas crouched in the glory hole below deck, muttering to a small plastic rectangle, some kind of charm or fetish. What prayers, to what entity? Surely not to the Preservers. Tamora was right, Yama thought. He should not trust people so readily.

Eliphas returned Yama's gaze. He smiled. "As for why you are able to do what you have done, brother, that's quite another question. We must ask whether miracles are caused because the Preservers or their agents actively interfere in the world, or whether, because the Preservers created the world, miracles occur simply as part of a natural chain of causation that was ordained from the beginning.''

Ixchel Lorquital took the stem of her unlit pipe from her mouth, leaned back in her sling chair, and spat over the rail toward the water rushing past below. She wiped her mouth on the back of her web-fingered hand and said, "Everyone knows that the Preservers have turned away from the world. It has carried on without them, for better or worse, so it never did need them to run everything. The same with everything else, I reckon. The stars were there before the Preservers came along—they just moved them into more pleasing patterns.''

"Just so," Eliphas said. "But there are some who believe that the Preservers, when they withdrew from the Universe, did so in order to be able to extend themselves from first cause to last end. And so, by leaving us, the Preservers have in fact spread themselves throughout creation. They watch over us still, but in a subtler fashion than by manifesting their will through the avatars of the shrines."

"There were riots when the last of the avatars were silenced by the heretics," Ixchel Lorquital said. "Many temples were burned down. Those were black years."

Eliphas said, "In truth, the avatars which survived the Age of Insurrection were so few, and most were so confused, that they were merely a last resort for people searching for answers to unanswerable questions. They were no longer the fount of all wisdom, and the guides of the governance of the world, as they were in the Golden Age before the Insurrectionists. Of course, those subroutines which acted as librarians were most useful. I still miss them. The written records are almost as extensive as those of the shrines, but less easy to search."

"The avatars were the eyes and mouths of the Preservers," Ixchel Lorquital said. "That was what I was taught as a pup, and I always did think it was put into our heads so we'd do as we were told, believing the Preservers were always looking over our shoulders in place of our parents."

"Miracles need witnesses," Eliphas said, returning to his original theme. "Perhaps the Preservers raise fish from the dead in the deeps of the river, or juggle rocks in sealed caverns in the keel of the world, but to what point? Miracles teach us something about the nature of the world and our own faith, by contradicting our understanding of that nature and by revealing some truth about the minds of the Preservers. Of course, our own minds may be too small to contain that truth."

Ixchel Lorquital closed her translucent inner eyelids, as if to help her look into her own mind. She said, "To my reckoning, the only miracles are where there's such an unlikely chain of circumstance that you have to believe something interfered to make it come out like that. Anyone that kind of thing happened to would have to change their way of thinking about their place in the world.''

"The world is large,'' Eliphas said, ''and the Universe is far larger, and far older. If anything is possible, no matter how unlikely, then there is no reason why it should not have happened somewhere.''

Ixchel Lorquital said stubbornly, ''If something unlikely happens to you, especially if it happens to save your life, you'll stop and think hard about why it was you and not some other culler.''

Yama said, ''I am not so immodest as to believe that what I have been allowed to do—if I understand Eliphas right—is simply to shock me into changing my mind, or to teach me some lesson. Yet I do not want to believe that I am an agent who is being used by something I do not understand. It would mean that everything I choose to do is not by my own will, but by that of another. Must I believe that everything I do is willed elsewhere?''

What had happened, when the crowd had rioted? What had he said? What had he done? He could not remember, and did not dare ask because it would reveal his weakness and his shame.

''That is the question every self-aware person must ask themselves,'' Eliphas said. ''One thing we know for certain is that the Preservers took ten thousand different kinds of animals from ten thousand different worlds and shaped them into their own image and raised them to intelligence. And yet that was not enough, of course. Each bloodline still must find its own way to grow and change, and that is the one kind of miracle on which we can agree.

''Think of a single man in a city of an unchanged bloodline. He may be a poet or a painter, a praise-singer or a priest, but we will say he is a poet. Like his father, and his father before him, he has followed his calling without thought. He has written thousands of lines, but any of them could have been written by any other poet of his bloodline, living or dead. Like all the unchanged, he has less sense of his own self than he has of the community of like-minded brothers and sisters of which he is but a single element. If he was taken from this community he would soon die, much as a single bee would die if it strayed too far from its hive. Like a hive, the communities of the unchanged are sustained not by the meshing of individual desires, but by blindly followed habits and customs.

"On this one night, alone in his room amidst thousands of others who are so very much like himself, our poet has a thought which has never before been thought by any of his bloodline. He pursues this thought through the thickets of his mind, and by its light he slowly begins to define what he is, and what he is not. Think of a sea of lamps which are all alike, all burning with the same dim flame. Now think of a single lamp suddenly brightening, suddenly shining so brightly that it outshines all others. Our poet writes his thought down in the form of a poem, and it is published and read because all poems are published and read without thought or criticism. That is the custom of the city, and no one has ever questioned it until now. But the thought the poem contains lodges in the minds of our poet's fellows and blossoms there as a spark lodges in a field of dry grass and blossoms into a field of fire. Soon there are a hundred competing thoughts, a thousand, a million! The city is at war with itself as its inhabitants struggle to define their own selves. Factions fight and clash in its streets. Those as yet unchanged, innocent and incapable of understanding the change, are winnowed. The survivors leave the battlefield, perhaps to found a new city, perhaps to scatter themselves along the length of the Great River.

"We know the change is caused by unseen machines that swarm in every drop of water, every grain of soil, every puff of wind. These tiny machines bloom in the brains of the changed. They increase the mind's complexity while retaining its essence, as a city built over the site of a fishing hamlet may retain the old street plan in the arrangement of its main avenues. The machines are in the brains of the unchanged bloodlines, too, but they are quiescent, sleeping. It is not the process that is the mystery, but the cause. The thought that comes in the night, that wakes the machines and sets fire to a bloodline until it is burned out or changed. There is our miracle.''

It was Yama's miracle, although he (or the woman in the shrine, working through him) had not forced the change upon one of the ordinary unchanged bloodlines, but upon one of the indigenous races, which, it was said, could never change. Were some miracles stronger and stranger than others? Was there a hierarchy of miracles, or were all miracles equally unlikely, and therefore equally wondrous? Yama thought about this for a long time, while Eliphas and Ixchel Lorquital talked of other things.

THE CITY OF THE DEAD

TAMORA'S KEEN EYES had already glimpsed the first intimation of smoke far downriver, but it was not until the beginning of the afternoon watch of the following day that one of the sailors, perched on a ratline high above the deck, sang out that there was a fire to port, a fire on the shore. Everyone crowded to the rail. A little dark cloud hung at the edge of the land, a smudge that was, Pandaras said, no bigger than a baby's claw. Captain Lorquital examined it through her spectacles before declaring that it was trouble they would do best to steer clear of.

"There are fast currents we can use further out, and there's a floating harbor we'd have had to cut around in any case."

Yama had been staring at the shore with growing realization. Suddenly anxious, he asked to borrow the Captain's spectacles. He squinted through one of the lenses and the distant shore leapt forward, horribly familiar. For two days they had been sailing past barren hills populated with the ruined houses of the dead, but only now did he see that they were within sight of the heart of the City of the Dead.

There was the wide valley of the Breas, with its quilt

of fields and channels; there was the skull-swell of the bluff, and the peel-house perched atop it like a coronet; the dusty hills with their necklaces of white tombs and stands of dark green cedars and black cypresses saddling away into the far distance, where the snowy peaks of the foothills of the Rim Mountains made a hazy line against the blue sky. And there was the shallow bay, with the long stone finger of the new quay running across the mudflats to the water's edge, and then the old waterfront of Aeolis.

And Aeolis was burning.

A triple-decked warship stood at the wide mouth of the bay, raking the little city with green and red needles of light that splashed molten stone where they struck. The bombardment seemed pointless, for every stone building was already smashed flat, and everything that could burn was afire. Black reefs of smoke rolled up, feeding the pall which hung above the city like a crow's wing. Dr. Dismas's tower was reduced to a melted stub; light raked the ancient ruins beyond it and stabbed into the flooded paeonin fields, sending up boiling gouts of mud and clouds of steam. Only the temple still stood, its white façade smudged by smoke, the tall lycophytes lining the long avenue which led to it withered or aflame.

Yama cried out, and Pandaras said, "What is it, master?"

Yama shook his head, heartsick. He climbed up to the quarterdeck, where Captain Lorquital and her daughter were already plotting a new course at the chart table, and heard himself asking them to turn the *Weazel* toward the shore, not away from it.

"It is my home," he said. "Most of the people I hold dear live there. My family. My friends."

He was thinking of Derev. She was brave and clever and resourceful. She would have found a way of surviving. She would have escaped to the hills above the city. She knew the way to Beatrice and Osric's remote tower. Or perhaps the Aedile had taken her in, and her family. He would have tried to protect all of the citizens. Or perhaps she was with their friend Ananda, the sizar of the priest of Aeolis. The temple still stood, after all.

Ixchel Lorquital looked hard at Yama and said, "Sit down for a moment."

Yama found he was trembling. He said, "I must go ashore."

"It's too dangerous," Aguilar said. "I'll fight if I must, but not against a warship. She could burn us to the water-line with one shot."

Tamora had followed Yama. She stood at his shoulder and said, "Do as he asks."

Captain Lorquital looked at her, looked at Yama. "I must do what's best for the ship. That's a military action, and I won't put my ship and my crew in the middle of it."

Eliphas was sitting in his customary place by the Captain's sling chair. He said, "If that is your home, brother, don't you think your enemies know that? They know you're traveling downriver, and perhaps hope to lure you ashore."

Yama's throat was parched. He said, "Lend me the dory. I will put ashore myself. You can anchor at the old floating harbor, or there are shoals and banyan islands downstream where you could hide a flotilla of ships. I will rejoin you within a day. If I do not, sail on without me."

Aguilar said, "And lose the dory?"

"Then set me ashore here and now. I will meet you on the other side of the city in three days."

Eliphas said, "You should not put yourself in danger, brother."

Captain Lorquital said, "I'd not be happy to lose a passenger, either."

"I'll go with him," Tamora said.

Pandaras jumped on to the rail behind her. He drew his poniard and flourished it above his head. "So will I. He'll need his squire."

Aguilar said, "If these three want to go over the side, let them do it now, before we're in range of the big girl's cannon."

Captain Lorquital considered, sucking at her silver lip-plug, then told her daughter, "I won't have three passengers putting themselves in danger, but clearly they'll jump over the side if they have no other option. I'll keep to this course. If there's no trouble, perhaps they can go ashore."

Aguilar stared at Yama and said, "There'll be no good to be had from this."

Captain Lorquital said, "Have a little charity, daughter. The first sign of trouble, and we run for it."

Tamora said, "You must trust him, Captain. He will protect you."

Yama bowed his head, hoping that the vessel of Tamora's faith would not be wrecked on the reef of his own self-doubt.

Aguilar snorted. "Then pray he can whistle up some wind. We'll need it."

~

Yama and Tamora put out from the *Weazel* in the dory a little way upriver of the floating docks. Pandaras had been persuaded to remain behind to ensure that Captain Lorquital kept to the agreed rendezvous at midnight. He waved from the rail of the poop deck as, in the last light of the sun, the little ship heeled around and headed out toward the center of the river.

Tamora took up her oar and said, "I reckon that black-skinned silver-eyed bookworm is right. It is almost certainly a trap."

Yama said helplessly, "I know. This is the doing of the Department of Indigenous Affairs. The peel-house still stands, and it is theirs."

"And we are doing what they want by walking into it. Grah. At least we will take them by surprise."

If Derev had taken refuge in the peel-house, then she was surely a prisoner, and surely had been put to the question by Prefect Corin. That was worse than thinking that she might be dead. Yama remembered the way she had fluttered down from her perch in the ruins outside Aeolis, on the night they had met the anchorite. So light and graceful, her long white hair floating about her lovely, fine-boned face.

He took up his own oar. Together they began to row toward the floating docks. After a while, he said, "Perhaps they are afraid, Tamora. Do you think they could be afraid of me?"

"The Captain and her daughter are afraid of you, and so are the crew. And Eliphas most of all. I've been watching him. He has a knife, a pretty little stiletto, and sleeps with his hand on it."

"I trust him more than he trusts himself," Yama said, "but less than I trust you."

"You should not trust him at all. He wants something from you."

As they rowed, Yama kept turning to stare with a kind of sick eagerness at the burning city, but he could see little more than he had from the deck of the *Weazel*. There was too much smoke, and clouds of steam kept spurting up where beams raked the waterfront, boiling the water of the shallow bay and the mudflats where once he had hunted crabs and dug for treasure everyone had believed to be buried there, finding nothing but the ancient coins. He closed his hand on the coin he had found in the cell high in the Palace of the Memory of the People, no different to the ones he had dug up as a child, when he had been surrounded by treasure, had he but realized it.

They passed the long maze of pilings and platforms and cranes of the floating harbor. No one answered Yama's hail, and the long sheds of the carpenters' workshops had a forlorn, deserted air. A door banged and banged in the wind; nothing else stirred.

The setting sun was dimmed and greatly swollen, a louring red eye that glared through a shroud of smoke and steam. The air scraped the back of Yama's throat with an acrid, metallic taste. Above the cliffs of the bluff, the towers of the peel-house, rising through the trees of its garden, caught the last rays of the sun and glowed with red light; the river held a bloody cast that had Tamora grumbling about omens. Flecks of black soot rained all around, smudging their skin and clothes. Floating debris began to knock against the dory's hull. Broken bits of furniture, books, a raft of bottles, half-burned rags. Bales of last year's hay wrapped in black plastic, taut as drumheads, went floating by, carried out of the bay by the ebb tide. No bodies, but Tamora said that meant little—the dead did not usually rise to the surface until distended by the gases of decomposition.

The dory slipped at a shallow angle toward the shore upriver of the bluff. The hum and sizzle of the light cannon of the warship carried clearly across the water. There was the snapping of heat-stressed stone, the explosive hiss of water suddenly shot to steam, the crackle of innumerable small fires.

As he rowed, Yama wondered again about Derev, and wondered if the Aedile had resisted the razing of Aeolis and was now a prisoner in his own peel-house, wondered what had happened to all the citizens of Aeolis, and again thought of Derev. He felt a mixture of shame and fear and anger and helplessness. Again and again, the memory of Prefect Corin's bland face tormented him.

The quiet of the shore was shocked by the clatter of wings as a flock of wading birds took flight from the dory's approach, dipping as one as they turned across the water. Yama and Tamora splashed into thigh-deep water and dragged the dory up the shallow, muddy beach.

"I wish you'd brought your rapier," she grumbled. "I said I'd look after you, but you'll make it very difficult if you won't begin to think of defending yourself."

"This is my home, Tamora. I would not return to it armed for war."

"If your enemy has taken it, then it is no longer your home."

"We shall see," Yama said, but to appease her he broke a branch from a young pine tree that the river had cast up on this muddy strand. The branch had been stripped of bark and smoothed by the rub of the water, but it had not yet begun to rot and it made a sturdy staff half again his height.

The sun had set behind the Rim Mountains but the Eye of the Preservers had not yet risen. What light there was came from the fires burning beyond the bluff. The flashes of cannon shot were as inconstant as heat lightning. All of the lights of the peel-house were ablaze, and the sight gave Yama little hope. Clearly, whoever commanded the peel-house did not expect an attack.

Tamora could see better than Yama in the near dark, and she led the way along an embankment above paeonin fields carved from river-bottom land. The old shoreline was marked by a line of ancient date palms. As a child, Yama had spent long summer afternoons in their shade while Zakiel had lectured him and Telmon on natural history. Not far from here, he had met with Derev for the last time before he had left for Ys with Prefect Corin. Now, as he and Tamora walked along the dusty embankment toward the palms, a faint crackling sounded ahead of them in the near dark. Tamora grasped Yama's arm and bent her head and whispered that she would go ahead and investigate.

"There are no machines," Yama whispered back. "Surely they would have machines."

Light flared amongst the graceful arcs of the date palms. With a clatter of metal on metal, a pentad of spidery, man-sized creatures skittered toward them, followed by armed soldiers.

―

"We will kill her," the leader of the patrol, a young, nervous lieutenant, told the mage. "She is no one important. Only a dirty little cateran. Not even her mother will miss her."

Tamora hissed, and tried to spit at the lieutenant. But the machine held her too tightly; she could not even turn her head.

"My spiders will hold her as easily alive as dead," the mage said, "and she might tell us something useful. I will be glad to put her to the revolutionary. Her kind are strong-willed. It would be a fine demonstration of its powers.''

Yama and Tamora were each bound tightly and painfully by the whiplike metal tentacles of a spidery machine. Their feet did not quite touch the ground. One of the soldiers had taken Tamora's saber; when it had first pounced upon him, Yama had broken his staff against the machine which now held him tight.

''If you kill her,'' Yama said, ''then you must kill me too, for I swear I will hunt you down.''

The lieutenant said, ''You are in no position to tell me what to do, fellow.'' He laughed and looked around, and his soldiers laughed too. He was a swarthy fellow in plastic armor over a leather kirtle. An energy pistol was tucked into the bandolier that crossed his transparent breastplate.

Yama waited until they were quiet, until they were looking at him again, wondering how he would reply. He let the moment stretch before he said, ''I am wanted by Prefect Corin because I am important to him. He wants me to work with him, for the good of the Department. If you kill my friend that is what I will do. I will become a loyal soldier, and one day I will find you and kill you.''

The lieutenant spat and ground the oyster of phlegm into the dust with the toe of his boot. ''Oh, I will not kill her,'' he said. ''There are worse things than death. Prefect Corin will probably give her to Nergal here. Then you will wish that you had allowed me to give her a clean death. A soldier's death. Nergal's machines are cruel, and these are the least of them.''

The remaining spiders were grouped behind the soldiers, holding up electric lamps which had drawn hundreds of moths from the darkness beyond. They were crude affairs, racks of aluminum tubing, electric motors and sensors raised high on three pairs of jointed legs. A decad of long, continually questing tentacles, made of jointed rings of metal and tipped with clawlike manipulators, sprouted between the front pair of legs.

The tentacles of the spider which held Yama were wrapped tightly around his arms and legs. They pressed painfully into his skin and tingled with a faint electrical charge. He had no sense of these machines. They were controlled by the mage, Nergal, a man with black skin that had a faint scaly iridescence in the distilled glare of the electric lamps, and large round eyes as dead as stones. He wore a long robe of metallic mesh, a tight-fitting copper skullcap. Close-fitting white plastic gloves sleeved his arms to the elbows.

"They are not susceptible to your power," Nergal told Yama. He made shapes with his gloved left hand, and the machine which held Yama swung to the right, then centered itself again. Yama could feel the shapes made by the mage in his head, and allowed himself a faint hope.

Nergal said, "These are a new class of machine, the first new machines to be built since the world was created. They dance for me and no one else."

"They have no minds," Yama said, "so how can they be truly useful?"

"They caught you, Yamamanama, and they hold you now. That is useful enough to begin with. They have as much logic as any insect. They do not need to think. Thinking is a luxury, as any laborer well knows."

"Enough talk," the lieutenant said. "We will get this prize back to the peel-house. I have little liking for this bone orchard."

"Quite right," Yama said. "The dead can be dangerous."

"Hold your yap, or I will have you gagged," the lieutenant said. "You will be amongst the dead soon enough, and you can try and scare me then." When he laughed again the soldiers around him did not join in. He glared at them and said sharply, "Fall in. There is nothing here that we cannot deal with."

Marshalled by the shapes Nergal made in the air with his gloves, the machines which held Yama and Tamora walked amidst their fellows with a whine of servo motors and a clanking of hydraulic joints. The soldiers ambled on either side, rifles held at port.

"Make these things go faster," the lieutenant said. "These two might have friends."

"I thought you had driven them out," Nergal said. "Most fled downriver."

"We cannot guarantee safety outside our perimeter," the lieutenant said. "Have these things pick up speed."

"Once we reach the paved road they will be able to go faster. The question of balance on rough terrain is very complex, and requires much processing power."

"Any trouble, and we leave the machines behind," the lieutenant said.

"As you have told me repeatedly. I will reply as before. Any trouble, and my machines will deal with it. Their processors and servos are battle-hardened, and they have infrared sights on guns which fire at the rate of a thousand slugs a minute. Soon, all our armies will be composed of these machines, lieutenant. Imagine it! Combined with Yamamanama's powers, we will drive the heretics over the end of the river."

The lieutenant said, "That is not to be spoken of in front of the men."

Yama said, "I am pleased to meet one of those who were testing me when I was briefly a guest in the Palace of the Memory of the People. I owe you much, Nergal."

The patrol was approaching one of the wide, white thoroughfares of the City of the Dead. Many merchants had been buried here. Their crowded tombs glimmered in the near darkness. They were marked by ornate pyramids, steles and statues; even in death, the merchants had competed with their rivals.

"You will be our guest again," Nergal said.

"He'll kill you all long before then," Tamora said. "You should let him go now."

"I think not," Nergal said. "There is much to discover. There is a peculiarity of your brain, Yamamanama, or perhaps of your nervous system, which allows you to interface with the old machines. We will find it, even if we have to open up your skull and slice you up bit by bit. But I hope that will not be necessary. Much easier if you cooperate. Much easier if you tell us how it is done."

"I do not know if I can tell you," Yama said, "but I am sure that I can show you."

"We will find out how to control the machines usurped by the heretics," Nergal said. "We will control all machines and so control the world. As a beginning, at least."

They were amongst the first of the tombs, now. The soldiers moved out on either flank and the machines picked up their pace as they stepped on to the paved road, shining their lamps this way and that. The tombs here were as big as houses, but crudely made. Further along, amongst the older, finer tombs, Yama felt a congregation waking and turning toward him. He told them what to do.

And the night came alive with the light of the past.

The soldiers began firing in panic as the dead reached for them. Yama had delved into the roots of the aspects and changed them all. No longer men and women smiling, beckoning, eager to tell to anyone who listened the life stories of the dead they represented; instead, grim, withered faces and blazing eyes, or no eyes at all but black pits in fleshless skulls. Skin like leather shrunken on long bones, bony fingers clutching at faces. Mad laughter, screeches, a rumbling subsonic that Yama could feel through the struts of the machine which clasped him so tightly. A white mist fell like a curtain, filled with half-glimpsed nightmare shapes. The soldiers vanished into it; not even the muzzle-flashes of their rifles could be seen, although their dismayed shouts and the rattle of rifle shots echoed sharply.

Somewhere in the mist, the lieutenant shouted an order to cease firing, shouted that this was no more than a trick. But each soldier was lost to every other, blinded by glowing mist and surrounded by the throng of the dead. Nergal's machines halted in the middle of what seemed to be a foggy street where skeletons of draft animals drew carts piled with rotting bodies that stirred with a feeble half-life. Pale things with burning eyes peered from the narrow windows of the houses. Below Yama, who was still clasped tightly by the spider, the mage sank to his knees. His gloved hands flexed at his throat, tightening inexorably. He stared at Yama with wide eyes. His mouth gaped as he tried and failed to draw air.

Yama felt a terrible, gleeful triumph. He would not relent.

"I cannot control your machines," he shouted, "but I can control what you use to control them. You fool! You used old technology to control the new!"

Nergal did not hear him. Although still kneeling, he was dead, strangled by feedback. His head tipped forward until his brow struck the ground and his body relaxed and slumped sideways. The tentacles which held Yama lost their tension and he dropped to the ground. All around, the spiders collapsed in a clatter of metal.

—

The soldiers were still shooting at ghosts when Yama and Tamora reached the old stair. Yama had woken every aspect in the City of the Dead. The low hills, crowded with tombs and monuments, were half-drowned in a lake of eldritch mist. Tamora carried a rifle taken from a soldier she had killed; she had not found the man who had taken her saber, and grumbled about the loss.

"I have already lost my own sword to the Department of Indigenous Affairs. It had a fine and bitter blade, but it cost me dear enough. I would not be here if I had not been in debt with Gorgo because of it. And now they have taken its replacement."

"I will find you another," Yama said. "There are many in the armory." He told her that the narrow stair they were climbing, its stone steps worn in the middle and sometimes missing, went all the way up the sheer side of the bluff. It was used by the kitchen staff of the peel-house. "There are certain herbs which grow only by graves. The dead impart a quality to the soil which they require. When I was much younger, I used to go with the youngest kitchen boy early every morning to pick them."

"You have had a strange childhood, Yama. Not many would think to use a graveyard as a kitchen garden."

"Fortunate for us that I know it so well. The soldiers are lost in the illusion spun by the tombs, but I brought us here by the quickest and straightest route."

"I'm glad Nergal is dead. Those things he made were evil."

The triumphant glee Yama had felt when he had murdered Nergal was now gone. It was as if something had woken in him and then returned to sleep. But it was done, and perhaps it was better that the mage was dead, or he would be another enemy pursuing Yama.

He said, "Surely Nergal's spiders were no more evil than your rifle, or a tiger snake. Like them, the spiders had no consciousness, and so no capacity to distinguish between good and evil. Only by consciously rejecting good can evil be done."

"That's what I meant. What he wanted to do with them was evil. So was what he wanted to do with you. Can you really bend every machine in the world to your will, Yama?"

"I hope it was merely one of Nergal's boasts. But I do not know."

They heard men shouting as they neared the top of the stair. Further off, dogs were barking eagerly.

Tamora's grin was a pale flash in the near dark. "And I suppose that you can silence the watchdogs, just as you did in the merchant's house."

"They know me," Yama said. "It was the second trick I learned."

"And what was the first?"

"You have just seen it. Although I thought then that the aspects of the dead took no more than an ordinary interest in me, I know now that I drew them to me. I learned much from them, as they pleaded for the memory of those they represented."

"Nothing you do is ordinary," Tamora said, and Yama heard in her voice the same note he had heard two days ago, when she had pledged her life to his.

There were two soldiers at the gate. Tamora whispered to Yama that they were hers. He squatted in bushes by the shoulder of the road and watched the play of lights within the lake of mist far below. It now covered all but the tallest monuments of the City of the Dead. There were watchdogs nearby, and he talked briefly with them before settling down to await Tamora's return.

She came so silently that it was as if she had stepped out of a secret door in the darkness. She had slung the rifle over her shoulder and carried a short stabbing sword. When she squatted beside Yama she licked blood from its broad blade with her rough tongue before she spoke.

"I killed the first with my hands, and the second with the sword I took from the first. Are you going to sit there all night, or are we going to try and make the rendezvous? That is, if that fat seal of a captain bothers to come back."

"She will. Pandaras will see to it, or he will sink her ship trying. But I do not think that she will need persuasion. She is a good woman."

"Grah. You trust people too much. It will be your downfall."

As they went through the gate, Yama called the watchdogs to him, and they ran eagerly out of the trees and across the wide lawn. Tamora stood her ground, her sword raised above her head, while Yama greeted each by name and let them smell his wrists. Light from the windows of the peel-house glinted on their shoulder plates, glistened on wet muzzles and set sparks in black eyes.

"They will not hurt you," he told Tamora. "I have told them that you are my friend."

"I have no liking for dogs. Even yours. Where is the door to this place?"

Accompanied by a tide of watchdogs, they went around two sides of the peel-house and crossed the courtyard where Yama had so recently said farewell to the Aedile and the household, where he had never expected to step again. The guardhouse and Sergeant Rhodean's quarters were dark.

"They'll be out looking for us," Tamora said, grinning.

"The watchdogs killed all the soldiers in the grounds,"

Yama said. "The two at the gate were yours; a decad more were mine."

They went through the kitchen garden. It was much trampled. Broken furniture was scattered around an ashy fire. Every bit of glass in the forcing houses had been smashed.

Yama expected more destruction in the kitchens, but when he kicked open the door nothing seemed to have changed. By the big fireplace, people pushed back chairs and stood, their faces pale in the flickering light of rush lamps. They were the household servants.

"You are in danger, young ma-ma-master," Parolles, the tall, cadaverous master of the wine, said. He was the most senior of the servants who remained, and took it upon himself to speak for all of them. "You have seen the ca-ca-candle lit in the town, and you have been drawn to it as he said you would. Go! Go now! Before his soldiers find you."

"I have already found them, with the help of my friend, Tamora. How is my father, Parolles? What have they done with him?"

The flame of the stout candle Parolles held put pinpricks of light in the center of his slitted irises. Now these pinpricks grew softer, and suddenly a chain of little lights spilled down the old servant's hollow cheeks and began to drip from the end of his sharp chin. He said slowly, "Your father is no longer here, young ma-master. He fled just last night, with the help of Sergeant Rho-rho-dean. There was a small rebellion."

"We think they have gone across the river," Bertram said. He was the pastry cook, half the height of Parolles and more than twice as wide. He held a big ladle at his shoulder like a club.

Parolles blotted his cheeks with the back of a hand. He said, "At least, we think that is where he has gone. We cannot be sure. Some of the do-do-domestic staff escaped too, but not, alas, all. Those you see here, and the librarian."

Yama felt a swelling sense of relief. He had feared the

worst, but that weight had been taken from him. He said, "Then my father is alive, at least. And the merchant's daughter, Derev? Did her family seek safety here?"

"I have not seen her," Bertram said. "I am sorry, young master."

"They treated your father grievously, young ma-ma-master," Parolles said. "Set the traitor in his place, and put him to question using monstrous ma-ma-machines when he stood up to them over the matter of the burning of the town."

"I have had some revenge," Yama said. "The mage is dead."

"But the viper still lives. When he saw the lights in the City of the Dead, he grew mighty sc-sc-scared, and ordered us locked up here."

"When you burst in, young master," Bertram said, "we thought our time had come."

"I will talk with this viper," Yama said grimly.

"We will come with you, young ma-ma-master. We have no weapons beyond some kitchen tools, but we will do all we can. These are terrible times. The Department fights against itself."

"I hope it will end soon," Yama said. "Now, who is with me?"

They all were.

There were two soldiers in the minstrels' gallery of the Great Hall, where Yama had once spied on his father and Dr. Dismas, but only one got off a shot before Tamora raked them with rifle fire. One man fell back; the other tumbled over the railing and landed on the long, polished table with a heavy, wet sound, kicked once, and was still.

"The banners are gone," Yama said, looking up at the high, vaulted ceiling. The hall looked larger and dustier without them.

"Burned," Parolles said. "A terrible burning they had. A bonfire of the vanities, the Prefect called it. He ma-ma-made your father watch. A more terrible punishment than the machines, I think."

Yama and Tamora led the pack of watchdogs and the

servants through the Great Hall toward the tall double doors of the receiving chamber. Two more soldiers stood there. One fled; the other died cursing his comrade's cowardice. Yama and Tamora flung open the doors. The tall square room beyond was blazing with light, but empty. Although the four great tapestries were gone from the walls, the canopied chair on the central dais on which the Aedile had customarily sat while holding audience was still there.

Yama went around the dais and ducked through the little door and went up the narrow stair that led to the Aedile's private chambers. No need for subtlety; the alarm must have been raised by now, and the cheering of the servants and the clatter of the armor of the watchdogs against the curved stone walls made a tremendous racket. With Yama at their head, they burst into the corridor. Some of the servants were beating against the walls or stamping their feet, calling for the traitor to come out. If there had been any guards, they had fled. The door to the Aedile's chambers was locked, but Tamora shot off the mechanical lock and kicked the door open in a single smooth motion.

The room was hot and stuffy. It stank of sex and spilled wine and cigarette smoke, and was lit by hundreds of candles, stuck to every surface by shrouds of their own melted wax. Papers were strewn everywhere amongst a litter of empty bottles and bowls of untouched food. The brass alembic was overturned, its mechanism spilled across a carpet sodden with wine.

The man on the bed raised a pistol, holding it in both hands as he took aim at Yama. He was naked under the rumpled, filthy sheet, and so was the woman who clutched a bolster to her breasts—one of the whores from the town, her tall blue wig askew, her face caked with white makeup, black pigment smeared about her mouth like a bruise and more black pigment around her wide eyes.

"Do not think I will not use this," Torin said, and showed a mouthful of white, needle teeth. His humped back was pressed against the carved bedhead; his shaven head gleamed with sweat. "You came back, just as Corin said you would. And now you are mine. Dismiss the rabble and we will talk, boy."

"Do not li-li-listen to him, young ma-ma-master," Parolles said.

Bertram added, "He cannot kill us all."

"He will do nothing." Yama said. "He knows that the soldiers are scattered, and that he cannot call upon Prefect Corin. How long have you been in his employ, Torin?"

"He will burn you like the town, if he has to." The pistol wavered when Torin spoke, and he squinted down its short, stubby barrel and centered it on Yama's chest again. He was very drunk.

"Then you will burn too. It saddens me to see you like this, Torin. You were a good friend to my father."

"I was always a good servant to the Department. Your father was a traitor. He hid all he knew about you, even from Prefect Corin. But like the fool that he was, he wrote it all down. It is all here, somewhere. If he did not know what he had he is a fool. If he did, then he is the blackest traitor in our history."

"I will not be the Department's weapon," Yama said.

"Then you are as much a fool and a traitor as the Aedile. I should burn you where you stand."

Yama relaxed. He knew then that Torin could not kill him. He said, "I will fight against the heretics like any other man. But I fear that Prefect Corin has other plans for me. He would use me to destroy the other departments. He would use me to take the world, if he could. Give me the pistol, Torin, and I will see that you leave here unharmed."

"You keep away! Keep away!" Torin pulled the naked woman in front of him and jammed the pistol at her head. "I will kill her and the rest of you! I will burn this fucking pile of stones to the ground!"

The woman got an elbow under Torin's narrow jaw with surprising force. His needle teeth clicked closed on his lower lip; he howled with pain and the pistol went off. Its searing red beam missed his face by a fingersbreadth, burned through the canopy of the bed and reflected from the ceiling. The canopy burst into flame and Tamora crossed the room in a bound and broke Torin's arm with a single blow.

—

Torin, his face badly burned by the near miss, refused to answer any of Yama's questions. Yama left him to the tender mercy of the other servants and went with Tamora to find Zakiel.

The tall, gaunt librarian was in the library. He had been shackled around his neck, and a heavy chain looped up to a sliding clip on an overhead rail. There was a new, raw brand on his cheek. He watched calmly, his black eyes inscrutable, as Tamora hacked without effect at the chain with her sword.

"It is tempered steel," he said. "Quenched in the blood of oxen, I believe. You will damage the edge of your weapon, domina."

"It's a piece of shit anyhow," Tamora said, but she tossed the sword onto Zakiel's neatly made cot, which stood as always beneath the racks of large, aluminum-covered ledgers, jumped up and swung from one of the studs which fastened the rail to the ceiling until it came away in a shower of plaster and dust. She slid the clip over the end of the rail and the free end of the chain dropped at Zakiel's long, bare feet.

The librarian wiped dust from the tops of the ledgers with the wide sleeve of his robe. He said, "It might have been better if you had left me chained, young master. Torin may have received the rough justice he deserved, but those he serves will soon return."

"You should come with us," Yama said.

"I will not, as you well know. The books are in my care, and I do not think that I can carry them all with me. And if I could, how would I keep them safe? I trust you still have the copy of the Puranas."

"I have always kept it beside me."

Zakiel picked up the heavy chain and draped it over one arm. "It will teach you much, in the right circumstances. I am pleased that you have returned, young master, but I fear that you have far to go."

"How much did my father know about me, Zakiel? How much did he hide from the Department?"

"And hide from you?" Zakiel smiled. "He has told you the circumstances of how you came to Aeolis. As for the rest, he should tell you, not I, for he knows it better. He has been taken across the river by Sergeant Rhodean and his merry crew of guards. The good Sergeant wanted me to go, too, but alas—"

Yama smiled. "You could not leave the books."

"Precisely. If I am a slave, it is not to the Department, but to my duty as Librarian of the peel-house. And that is as it should be, for I am merely honoring the oath I once broke when I was younger than you are now. When I was your age, I thought in my blind pride that I knew better than those whom I served, but now I know better. Age gives a certain perspective. It is like climbing a peak of the Rim Mountains. At last you run out of air, but how wonderful the view! These books are my life, young master, and I cannot leave them."

"Do you know what happened to the Amnan?"

"Many fled across the river. But Derev and her family left a day before the warship took anchor in the bay. Some said that they were spies, fleeing to safety, but I do not believe it."

Yama's heart turned over. He felt that he could float to the ceiling. He grinned and said, "She is safe."

He thought that he knew where she had gone. She would be with Beatrice and Ostic in the oldest part of the City of the Dead, in the foothills of the Rim Mountains.

Zakiel said, "Perhaps she will return. Perhaps you might have a message for her."

"Tell her that I go downriver, but that I will come back."

"Is that all? Well, I will tell her, when I see her."

"I will miss you, Zakiel."

"We have already said our goodbyes. Do not worry about me, or the books. Torin held many grievances against the peel-house, for he believed himself better than he was, but Prefect Corin's grievance is against you."

"We must go," Tamora said. "There is less than an hour to the rendezvous."

THEY WERE LATE for the rendezvous, but the *Weazel* was waiting for them as promised, at the upriver end of the floating
docks. Yama and Tamora stood at the rail of the quarterdeck as the little ship angled away from the burning town.
The warship was still raking the shore with needles of hot
light. Although he had revenged his father's torture, Yama
felt a mixture of shame and anger and helplessness. He
stood straight, gripping the polished wooden rail so tightly
his arms ached to the elbows, and watched the sack of
Aeolis with tears slipping down his cheeks. He would be
a witness, if nothing else. He would face this destruction
without flinching, and carry it with him forever.

The sailors nudged each other and whispered that he
wept for his home. They were only partly right. Yama did
not know it, but he was also weeping for the loss of
his innocence.

The lookout cried a warning. Tamora pointed to the
lights of a picketboat that was coming around the point of
the bay, heading out to intercept the *Weazel.*

"He is coming," Yama said. "I knew that he would."

But he was still struck through and through by fear, and

had to lean against the rail because he was suddenly trembling so hard.

Captain Lorquital ordered the staysails unreefed. "We'll make speed as best we can," she told Yama. "Those boys have oars, but as long as the wind holds we can outrun them."

Tamora wanted to unshroud the cannon and break out the hand weapons, but Captain Lorquital refused and Aguilar stood foursquare in front of the armory chest. Yama put a hand on Tamora's arm and was astonished to discover that she was trembling almost as violently as he was. Prefect Corin had put his mark on both of them.

"I'll hold by what we agreed," Captain Lorquital said, "and so will you. We've no fight to pick here, no matter what's right and what's wrong."

Silhouetted against the burning town, the picketboat came on across blood-red water, its single bank of oars striking to the beat of a drum. A white lantern shone at its masthead, signifying that it wished to parlay. For several minutes, it steadily closed the gap; then the *Weazel* caught the wind and the gap began to widen again.

Something shot from the side of the picketboat. It skipped over the water like a flung stone and rose high above the *Weazel* before Tamora could take aim with her captured rifle. It was a small machine, as flat as a plate and spinning rapidly. It moved to and fro in little jerks above the tip of the mast. As with the machine which had been sent against Yama in the Department of Indigenous Affairs, its mind was hidden by complex loops of self-engulfing logic that grabbed at his attention as he tried to cleave through them. It was like plunging into a briar patch full of snapping jaws and whirling blades. A ghastly light suddenly flooded from the machine, etching everyone's shadow at their feet, and a voice boomed out, ordering the *Weazel* to stand to or have her sail cut free.

Captain Lorquital cupped her hands and shouted across the widening gap of water to the picketboat. "Show your authority!"

The machine tipped, aiming its sharp spinning edge at

the forestays; at the same moment, Yama untangled the last of its defenses and found its tiny linear mind. It flung itself sideways, falling a long way before striking the water and vanishing with scarcely a splash.

Captain Lorquital gave Yama a long and hard look, but said nothing.

"Well," Tamora said, "he'll know you're on board now."

"He knows that already," Yama said.

—

It became a contest of skill between the *Weazel* and the picketboat. The warship turned her light cannon away from the burning town, but too late: it fired no more than two ranging shots before the *Weazel* passed beyond the down-river point of the bay (the paeonin mill had been leveled to a hummock of glassy slag) and the warship and the burning city were lost from sight.

Yama dredged his memory for a map of the complicated web of currents as the *Weazel* threaded the maze of in-shore mud shoals and stands of banyans. A man at the bow dropped a weighted line and called the depth every few minutes, and Yama stood with Captain Lorquital and the helmsman through the night while the crew took turns to rest. Pandaras and Eliphas slept on their mats under the awning; Tamora paced the deck amidships or stood by the man at the bow, peering into the darkness ahead or sharp-ening the long narrow blade of the sword she had taken from the armory of the peel-house. Eliphas woke near dawn and came up onto the aft deck to ask how things stood.

"Well, we are still here," Ixchel Lorquital said. "If the wind stays fair we'll be here a while longer."

There were floating islands spread everywhere ahead of the ship, ten thousand green dots scattered across the shin-ing sweep of the river. The ranges of cloud that towered above the farside horizon caught the early light of the sun. Their folds and peaks glowed white and purple and gold.

Eliphas leaned at the rail next to Yama, who was staring into the light of the rising sun, trying to make out the smoke of the burning city against the long line of the shore. The old man cleared his throat, spat accurately into the white water that purled along the ship's hull, and said, "You should rest, brother. In my small experience of adventure, sleep is a most valuable currency."

"Why did they do it, Eliphas?"

Eliphas's silver eyes shone with reflected light. His black skin gleamed as if oiled; scraps of light were caught in the tightly nested curls of his white hair. He said, "Because they wanted to lure you into a trap, and were desperate. Because they have confused their duty and the base desires of their own selves. Because they serve the Preservers in name only, and have turned themselves into a thing that would destroy the world to save it. They have lost their way, brother. They deserve to be destroyed."

"Yet no one stood against them in the Palace of the Memory of the People until I acted."

"Those that stand against the Department of Indigenous Affairs are destroyed or absorbed. As are those that do not, by and by. Indigenous Affairs has fed on the war, and the war has become its reason for existence. If it survives the insurrection against it and wins the war, then it will find another enemy, even if it is some part of its own self."

Yama remembered the story told to him by the headman of the village of the husbandmen, the story of the department known as the Head of the People, which had absorbed all others until at last it had nothing to fight against but its own self. Surely, he thought, the Preservers had not created the world so that it would repeat the same stories in a series of futile cycles, like a book read again and again by an uncomprehending idiot.

He said, "They want to force me to their will. Because of that, I can only see them as my enemy."

Eliphas said, "Brother, you should use your gift against them. The machine you destroyed is nothing. What you did to free us is nothing. You are capable of much more.

You should not allow yourself to be enslaved for the sake of your conscience.''

"Are you scared, Eliphas?"

"Of course. But there are great things to be discovered, if we survive this.''

"I am not sure if I can be free if I use my . . . gift without knowing how I use it, or why I have been given it. I have done bad things before this, Eliphas, although I did not mean to. I fear that I might do them again.''

Captain Lorquital had been standing at the stern rail, peering upriver through her spectacles; now she came over to Yama and Eliphas and said, "The picketboat is still following, but we have at least two leagues on it, and our lead will widen as long as the wind holds. But the warship is certain to follow us as well, and will be at least as fast as we are. How intent are these people on capturing you, Yama?''

"They will not stop.''

"I thought not. I'll wake my daughter and we'll decide what to do. But I know that we can't run forever.''

"Perhaps we can hide, or find some way of turning to the attack.''

Captain Lorquital regarded Yama thoughtfully. "If it comes to a final fight, what would you do?''

"I do not know how, but I hope that I would be able to save the ship and everyone on it.''

Captain Lorquital seemed satisfied by this answer, but after she had gone to wake Aguilar, Eliphas said, "I hope you will put your scruples aside, brother. You will never find your bloodline if you do not first destroy your enemy.''

Yama thought that Eliphas was wrong. If he defined himself against his enemies, then he would be no better than they were. Yet there was a part of him that exulted in the idea of battle, a voracious cayman at the base of his brain given voice, he believed, by the woman in the shrine. Satisfied not by persuasion but by forceful coercion, not by courtship but by rape, a thing of uncontrolled appetite and lust that would destroy the world rather than die. He must control it. And then he thought, if I know that Derev is dead, if my father is dead or disgraced, which for him will be a living death, will I still be able to keep this resolve?

The free men of the crew broke fast with manioc porridge while the cook and the other slave scrubbed soot stains from the white deck with lye and holystones. Yama ate without appetite. Although he was very tired he felt that he could not rest, so Pandaras brought him the rifle and suggested he try some target practice. For an hour, Yama blipped slugs at bits of flotsam floating by, and then practiced cleaning and reassembling the rifle under Tamora's instruction, his fingers thick and clumsy with lack of sleep. At last, Pandaras got him to lie down, and he fell asleep at once, and woke with the sun riding at its highest point.

Pandaras brought a hunk of black bread and a bowl of curried lentils salted with flecks of coarse fish flesh. The boy squatted in front of his master in the shade of the awning and watched him eat with a tender anxiety. The triangular mainsail and the square staysails stood taut against the blue sky. There was a ragged green line to starboard: a banyan forest.

Yama said, "Where do we stand?"

"The warship is in sight, master. It will catch up with us in a day, the Captain says. It is a very big ship, but it has big motors and has spread all its sail, too."

Yama used the heel of the bread to scrape up the last of the lentils from his wooden bowl. He told Pandaras, "I cannot make a wish and save us."

"No one asks you to, master. We're making for the forest. We might lose them there, the Captain says. She and Aguilar talked it over while you slept. Tamora is pleased. She wants a fight."

"I am sorry to have brought you on such a futile adventure, Pandaras."

Pandaras struck an attitude and said, "Master, I was a pot boy when I found you. Now I am squire to a hero."

Yama knew that it was not as simple a thing as many

people supposed, to give up your life and dedicate it to another. He saw the love in Pandaras's gaze and smiled. He said, "A foolish hero, if a hero at all."

"If that's so, then I'm as much a fool for following you, master. And I don't think I am a fool at all. Now let me take your tunic and wash it. I have your second-best shirt here, clean and pressed. We have certain standards to keep, even in these circumstances."

—

Thousands of banyans had rooted in a long, narrow shoal at the backwater edge of the swift current in which the *Weazel* was sailing, a temporary forest that stretched away downriver for several leagues. Now it was almost summer, and the forest was beginning to break up. Already, singleton banyans floated along the edge of the shoal, turning in stately circles; fleets of fist-sized seeds, each with a single upright leaf like a sail, drifted on the currents.

The *Weazel* entered the forest's maze by a channel so wide it could hold twenty ships side by side, and for a while she continued to make way under sail. But the channel split and split again, and with each turn it grew narrower until at last the staysails and their spars had to be drawn in. Captain Lorquital ordered the mast lowered, for the canopies of the banyans sometimes pressed together overhead to form a living green arch. Aguilar started the little reaction motor, normally used for maneuvering in harbor. It made a hollow knocking sound and blew puffs of black smoke from the stern vent. The smoke stank of burned cooking oil. The sailors hacked at branches which caught in the rails or scraped the gunwale. Bottom soundings gave wildly differing readings from minute to minute, from narrow channels where the *Weazel*'s keel scraped a tangled net of interlaced feeder roots to places so deep that no sounding could be made.

The dim green light, the odor of rotting vegetation and of silent green growth, the close fetid heat, like a cloth laid on his skin: all these calmed Yama. Orchids bright as flames grew amongst the glossy, shingling leaves. There were loops of red-leaved creeper and strangler figs and parasitic mangroves, gray hanks of hanging moss. Parts of the waterway were covered with pavements of brick-red water fern or wide patches of water hyacinth, whose waxy white flowers breathed a sickly sweet odor. Dragonflies with wingspans as long as a man's arm and jaws that could nip off a finger roosted on the upright spikes of breather roots; armies of metallic blue emmets staged tireless campaigns and caravanserais along mossy boughs. Birds stalked from floating leaf to floating leaf with a swift strutting gait on feet with long widespread toes; hummingbirds darted from orchid to orchid; parrots flashed through the green shade; gar and caymans raised their snouts to watch the *Weazel* labor past. A troop of long-nosed monkeys swung along their aerial highways above the channel, screaming curses and raining orange excrement; the old carpenter, Phalerus, shot two with a short bow, and the cook set to skinning them for the pot. Once, the flat face of a manatee rose beneath the surface of the green water and regarded them with brown, human eyes—good to eat but bad luck to kill, Phalerus confided to Yama.

Tamora sat astride the bowsprit, the rifle cradled in her arms, her shaven, scarred head turning from side to side as she scanned the green press of leaves passing by on either side. Twice, the channel the *Weazel* was following closed into an impenetrable wall of leaves and branches, and the ship had to laboriously reverse course. Once, she grounded on the half-sunken, rotten corpse of a dead tree grown through with the feeder roots of its living neighbors, and had to be pulled off with a block and tackle rig attached to the main trunk of a grandfather banyan, with half the crew pulling on the ropes and the other half pushing with poles.

The light went quickly, a sudden gold-green dazzle amongst the trees and then a swift decline to pitch black. Frogs peeped and whistled; fish made splashes in the water around the ship, which in the last light had anchored at the junction of two wide channels. Bats swooped amongst the yards of the mast; insects signaled to each other with coded flashes of yellow or green light.

Supper was roast monkey flesh with fried bananas and rice (Tamora sucked meat from a raw rack of ribs and cracked the thin bones for marrow), eaten in the dim red light of half a dozen lanterns, against which big black beetles ceaselessly dashed themselves in unrequited lust. Afterward, Yama climbed the tallest of the neighboring banyans, high above a long, narrow, dark sea of ceaselessly rustling leaves slashed and divided by forking channels. Upriver, a sudden flash of light defined the long line of the forest. Yama counted the seconds until the sound reached him: twenty-five. A few moments later there was another flash, a little way downriver from the first. There were machines out there too, but so far off that he could do no more than sense them.

Yama climbed down out of the fresh cool breeze into the dark clammy fetor under the canopy of the banyans, walked along a mossy, horizontal branch and vaulted the rail at the ship's waist. When he told Captain Lorquital what he had seen, she drew on her pipe and blew a cloud of fragrant smoke before replying. She was the only one not troubled by the bites of black flies which at sunset had risen above the still water.

At last, she said, "They are burning their way through the trees with their light cannon. If I was planning the chase, I would put the warship downriver, beyond the point of the shoal, and have the picketboat quarter back and forth, hoping to flush us out. The forest is many leagues long but it is very narrow, and our enemy knows that we are heading downriver and cannot hide here indefinitely. We're caught between the two of them."

Aguilar was sitting cross-legged by her mother's sling chair. She said, "We should not have come here. Better to take our chances in the open river."

In the darkness by the rail, Tamora said, "The warship

was catching up with us. At least we can make a stand here.''

"We don't even know where it is," Aguilar said. "We don't even know where *we* are. We've trapped ourselves in a maze.''

Yama said, "As long as we follow the channels where there is a current, we will find our way out again.''

The glow of Captain Lorquital's pipe brightened when she drew on it. Bright, then dim: like an insect signaling in the dark. She said, "I have heard of the trick with the current, but twice today we were following a current that went under a stand of trees and left us in a channel with no current at all.''

Phalerus appeared at the head of the companionway, a shadow against the glimmer of the white deck below. He said, "Something is coming.''

Yama and Tamora followed him to the bow. They climbed up by the cannon and the old sailor said, "Listen.''

The metallic peeping of frogs; little plashes and ripples in the current. Yama whispered that he heard nothing unusual.

"They are out there,'' Tamora said, and opened the valve of the lantern she carried.

Its beam fell across the still black water. On the other side of the channel, backed by a wall of foliage, a green-skinned man raised a hand in front of his face.

THE FISHERFOLK

THE SAILORS CRACKED the valves of more lanterns, and wherever they shot their beams they discovered little round coracles, each with two men sitting cross-legged and holding leaf-shaped paddles. The men had legs as long and thin as those of storks, and their naked torsos were mottled with green and dun patches. There were more than a hundred of them.

Yama laid a hand on Tamora's shoulder and said, "It is all right. They are no enemy."

"No friends either, to arrive unannounced under cover of darkness."

"This is their home. We are the unannounced arrivals."

Yama hailed the fisherfolk, and asked if there was one amongst them called Caphis—the man who had helped him after he had escaped from Dr. Dismas's attempted kidnapping. The shoal of coracles swirled apart to allow one to move forward. A dignified old man with a cap of white hair stood in it. His left arm ended above the elbow; silvery scars crosshatched his chest and shoulder.

"You are the son of the Aedile of Aeolis," the old man said. "Caphis is my son. If I may, I will come aboard and talk with you."

~

The old man's name was Oncus. He explained that he had lost his hand to a grandfather cayman when he was a young man and usually wore a hook in its place, but he had taken it off on this occasion because it might be mistaken for a weapon.

"We have no quarrel with the son of the Aedile of Aeolis," he said. "The Aedile has always been good to us. Before he came, the Mud People of Aeolis hunted my people for sport and for food, but the Aedile put a stop to that. Because of your father, our two bloodlines have lived in peace for a hundred years. Now the Mud People are scattered across the river and two ships burn the forest. Bad times have come again."

Oncus sat cross-legged on the main deck under the awning, between Yama and Captain Lorquital, who lay on her side, propped by bolsters and puffing calmly on her pipe. Aguilar, Pandaras, Eliphas and Tamora completed the circle. Tamora's sword lay across her lap and she kept her hand on its hilt. A small entourage of fisherfolk stood behind Oncus; above, the sailors stood along the slanted trunk of the folded mast.

Yama said, "It is my fault, grandfather. They are burning this floating forest because they know I am hiding in it."

Oncus nodded. "One of them came to me three days ago, when the warship first arrived off the stone shore of the Mud People's city. He showed me an image of you, and said that we would be rewarded if we found you. You must be a great enemy of theirs, if they destroy your home before you can return to it."

"They did it because they believe me to be their enemy, and so I am, because of what they have done."

"Then that is another reason to help you. They have no respect for the river. Any enemy of theirs is a friend of ours, and you are doubly a friend, for you are the Aedile's son."

"Is he alive? And the people of Aeolis—are they safe?"

"They were driven from their homes before the big ship set fire to the land. If any refused to leave, and perhaps many did, for the Mud People are a stubborn race, then they are dead. The city has been burned to its foundations and its fields boiled dry. The Aedile tried to stop it. He stood on the stone shore and said that if the Mud People's city was burned then he would be burned, too. Soldiers took him away and locked him in his own house, but he escaped."

Yama nodded. "I have heard that he escaped, and it pleases me to hear it again. Where is he? Is he safe?"

"Most of the Mud People are crossing to the farside shore," Oncus said. "It is as if the beginning of winter is already upon us. The Aedile overtook them. We found him on a boat in the middle of the river the day after the big ship began to burn down the city. We took him across the river and left his boat adrift, so that his enemies might think him drowned. That is how I know this story."

"Then I am in your debt, Oncus, as I am in your son's debt. You saved the life of my father and your son saved my life."

"As for the last," Oncus said, "that is between Caphis and yourself. Caphis is not here, and I will only say that if he saved your life, then it was because you saved him from the trap of one of the Mud People. And your father has saved countless lives of my own people. Only the Preservers can weigh such debts."

Captain Lorquital stirred in her nest of bolsters and said, "If we can escape this forest, then the warship will follow us, and no more damage will be done to your home."

"The small ship is at the edge of the forest," Oncus told her. "The big ship waits downstream. They both shine fire into the trees and hope to make you quit this place."

"As I thought," Captain Lorquital said.

"We sailed into a trap of our own making," Aguilar said. Her usual good humor had leaked away during the difficult passage through the forest maze.

"Let them come and look for us," Tamora told her, "and we'll spring the trap on them."

Pandaras said, "It seems simple to me. We could leave the ship and go with these people. They can take us to Yama's father."

Captain Lorquital said, "I can no more leave my ship than you can leave your master, Pandaras."

"And I will not run away," Tamora said. "Be quiet, boy."

Yama said, "My enemies have orders to find me. They will not go away as long as they are sure I am hiding somewhere close. And if they think Oncus's people are hiding me, they will burn more than this forest."

"I was afraid that might be so," the old man said.

Captain Lorquital said to Oncus, "If your people can guide us out of the forest, we will take our chances on the wide river."

"As long as they don't see us leave," Aguilar said. "Otherwise they'll be all over us before we've raised the sail."

"They have eyes everywhere," Oncus said.

He gestured, and one of the fisherfolk stepped forward. The man carried a small leather sack. He opened it to display the little machine inside. It was the size of a child's fist, and most of its many delicate vanes were crumpled or broken off.

"We caught this one in a net and drowned it," Oncus said. "There are others. They fly through the air at the edges of the forest."

Yama touched the machine. For a moment, light glimmered in the compound eyes and a single intact vane feebly beat the air. But the movement was little more than a reflex powered by the small amount of charge remaining in its musculature, and the machine died before Yama could learn anything from it.

Yama looked around at the fisherfolk and the sailors standing above them. Two of the soldiers touched their throats with the tips of their fingers.

"You must destroy them, brother," Eliphas said. "You know that you can. Don't hold back."

Oncus said, "You cannot leave the forest because it hides you, but you cannot stay because your enemies will burn it to the waterline. But we will help you. We will move the forest."

Yama laughed. "Of course! It is summer! And if you can find me a living machine, then I can provide a diversion."

~

"In winter, the trees root and draw nutrients from the river mud," Yama told Pandaras. "In summer they break away from their feeder roots and float free on the flood. They float all summer until tide and chance draw them back together at the beginning of winter. The fisherfolk are speeding up this natural process. It is how they control the floating islands on which they make their homes."

Pandaras was tired and frightened, and in no mood for a lesson in natural history. He said, "You should sleep, master."

"Not yet. Oncus is right. There are many machines."

"And you keep them away from us. But you cannot stay awake forever."

"They keep away from me, Pandaras. Their master knows what I can do."

"If they are afraid of you then we should not be afraid of them. So we can go to sleep."

"They might not stay away forever. Besides, although I have lived by the river all my life, I have never seen this before."

All around the *Weazel*, fisherfolk were working by the dim glow of oil lamps, sinking sacks of moss amongst the roots of the banyans. The moss had been soaked in an extract of the hulls of banyan seeds; as this diffused into the water, it stimulated the trees to shed the myriad feeder roots which anchored them. The night was full of the creaking and groaning of banyans which were beginning to shift on the currents; the water all around the *Weazel* seethed with bubbles as pockets of gas were released by roots dragging through mud.

Yama said, "Oncus told me that there are more than a thousand fisherfolk from a hundred families. But how many more trees?"

"They are fools, master, to believe that they can move a forest. And we are more foolish still to believe them. We should go with them while we have the chance."

"They know the floating forests better than anyone. We must trust them."

Near dawn, Oncus returned to the ship and told Yama that another machine had been caught. Yama was taken out in a coracle to the net where it hung, at the farside edge of the floating forest. The forest was beginning to break up there. Irregular channels and lagoons opened and closed as trees spun slowly around each other. The water was stained with silt and alive with shoals of fish.

The picketboat was close by, slowly advancing down-river amongst trees that had become a myriad floating islands. Every now and then the red flash of the pick-etboat's cannon lit the dark sky above the tops of the trees, followed by the hiss and crack of water flash-heated to steam. The air had a brassy taste, and there was a constant flutter of falling ash flakes.

"They will be here soon," one of the fisherfolk said, and Yama saw that the man's hands were shaking as he aimed the beam of his lantern at one of the floating islands.

The net, woven from monofilament fibers combed from float bush seed heads, fine as air and strong as steel, was strung above the top of the banyan, guyed by bamboo poles. The machine caught in it glittered and gleamed in the beam of the lantern; as soon as the light touched it, it began to vibrate in short furious bursts, shaking the poles and branches to which the corners of the net were fastened.

"Some of the machines can burn their way free," Oncus said, "but ones like these are merely spies. They are stupid and weak. We sometimes catch them by mistake. They are blind to our nets, or fly too fast to avoid them.''

''And you destroy what you catch,'' Yama said distractedly. He was already unpicking the familiar tangle of logical loops and snares which hedged the machine's simple mind.

''Only the Preservers need to see all,'' Oncus said. ''Usually we drop the net and the machine drowns, although some can swim as well as fly, and those escape us.''

The machine was no more intelligent than the watchdogs which patrolled the grounds of the peel-house, and after its defenses had been penetrated it was as easy to fool. Once Yama had convinced it that he was its handler, he called for the net to be lowered, and he cradled the machine while two of the fisherfolk began to untangle its vanes from the fine filaments of the net.

They worked quickly, but still had not freed the machine when an intense needle of red light lanced across the channel behind them. The needle struck through the canopy of a banyan, which immediately burst into a crown of fire; a second needle struck the main trunk and burst it apart in an explosion of live steam and splinters.

The two coracles were lifted and turned on a swell of smoking water. All around, floating banyans rocked to and fro, as stately as green-clad dowagers at a ball. The coracles spun apart and the net stretched out between them, wrenching the machine from Yama's grip. Then the swell passed and the coracles revolved back toward each other, and the net dipped toward the water. For a moment, Yama feared that the machine would be drowned, but Oncus grabbed the net with his good hand, and Yama and the others helped him haul in the slack.

A minute later, they had freed the machine. Yama cradled it to his chest, but before the two coracles could drive for cover, red light flashed again and two more trees burst into flame. Steam and smoke enveloped them. A drumbeat swelled; a dark shape glided between the burning trees.

The coracles bobbed on its wake, and then the picketboat was past.

—

Yama sent up the machine he had captured as a hunter sends up a hawk, and used it to call other machines to him. It took several hours to find the way back because the floating forest had begun to break up, a maze in which channels opened and closed between ten thousand drifting trees. By the time the two coracles had returned to the *Weazel*, they were trailing a cloud of glittering machines, like birds following a fishing boat. The sailors eyed the machines with a deep unease, but the fisherfolk beat spears and paddles against the sides of their coracles at this demonstration of Yama's power.

The *Weazel* was hauled into a narrow berth hacked into the dead heart of a grandfather banyan, and lashed to the main trunk. The sailors covered her sides with a blanket of leafy branches. Tamora commandeered four coracles and lashed a platform across them and, with Aguilar, took the light cannon to the nearside edge of the forest. When they returned, the banyan in which the *Weazel* was hidden had begun to float amidst a flotilla of other trees on the strong current.

Late in the afternoon, the tree passed one of the places struck by the warship's light cannon. It was as wide as the channel by which the *Weazel* had first entered the shoal. The smoldering stumps of banyans poked through water choked with ashes and the corpses of parboiled fish. Hundreds of small fires smoldered in the canopy on either side, and smoke hung thick in the air.

The fisherfolk murmured to each other at the sight of this destruction. Oncus told Yama that one day there would be a reckoning. "We are not a fierce folk, but we do not forget."

By the middle of the afternoon there was open water on all sides of the banyan's floating island. Yama climbed to the topmost branch and, clinging there, saw a vast archipelago of small green islands scattered widely across leagues and leagues of water. The remaining part of the forest was a green line shrouded in a long cloud of smoke and steam turned golden by the light of the sun.

When Yama climbed down, Captain Lorquital said, "We are set on our course now."

"I still say we shouldn't have left our only real weapon behind," Aguilar said.

"If the timer works, daughter, then it will serve us better than by being here."

"Of course it will work. I set it myself. But our fee will not cover the cost of replacing it. It's a poor bargain."

"Better alive poor than dead rich," Captain Lorquital said, and Aguilar laughed for the first time since they had entered the forest.

"That's just what father would say."

"Sometimes he managed to stumble on a truth without my help."

Yama said, "They will not believe the machines alone because they know I can fool machines. They must also have something to aim at."

"I've never had to fire the thing in anger," Ixchel Lorquital said, "but I'll still miss it."

At nightfall, the lines which lashed the *Weazel* to the banyan were cut and she used her reaction motor to maneuver out of her hiding place. It took an hour to raise the mast and haul up the sail; then everyone stood at the port rail and watched the dark line of the forest. They watched a long time, and although they knew about the timer, the sailors cheered when at last the flash of the cannon showed, a vivid red point of light doubled by its reflection in the river. The sharp crack of the discharge rolled across the water a moment later; then the cannon flashed again.

Yama raised his arms—a bit of theater, for he had already told the machines to go. They went in a whirring rush that fanned the air, scattering toward different parts of the forest, where they would lay a hundred false trails in the opposite direction to the *Weazel*'s intended course.

Even as the machines flew up, the warship answered the *Weazel*'s light cannon with a bombardment that lit half the sky. At once, Ixchel Lorquital ordered the sail unfurled and the anchor raised. While the sailors busied themselves, the fisherfolk departed without ceremony, their tiny bark coracles dwindling into the river's vast darkness. Oncus kissed Yama on the forehead and tied a fetish around his wrist. It was a bracelet of coypu hair braided with black seed pearls, and when Yama began to thank Oncus in the formal fashion taught by his father, the leader of the fisherfolk put a finger to his lips.

"Your life is mine," the old man said. "I give you this to protect and guide you on your journey. I fear you will have much need of it."

Captain Lorquital thanked Oncus for the safe passage of her ship, and gave him a steel knife and several rolls of tobacco. And then he too was gone.

The *Weazel* caught the wind and heeled to port as she set course toward the farside shore. Far off, the cannon of the warship set up a stuttering rake of fire. Vast clouds of steam boiled up as needles of hot light lashed open water. If the *Weazel*'s dismounted cannon fired again, it was lost in the bombardment.

Yama stood at the stern rail and watched red and green lights flash within spreading clouds of steam and smoke. The bombardment continued for a whole watch. Yama knew then that the aim of the chase was not to capture him, but to destroy him. He watched until the warship's cannon finally stopped firing, and at last the night was dark and quiet beneath the red swirl of the Eye of the Preservers.

THE FARSIDE SHORE was a plain of tall green grasses, winnowed by unceasing wind. It was not wide at that part of the river. During the festival at the beginning of winter, Yama and his stepbrother, Telmon, had often walked from riverbank to world's edge in a single day. When he had been very young, Yama had often tired himself out by trying to match Telmon's long, eager strides and had to be carried home asleep in his stepbrother's arms. On those expeditions, Telmon had always worn a set of bolas around his right arm, for all the world like an indigen from one of the hill tribes. Several times, Yama had seen him bring down one of the moas that roamed the grass plains, breaking the bird's legs with the bolas and throwing himself on its thrashing body to cut its throat. Telmon had carried a sling, too, and had taught Yama how to use it to hurl stones with killing force at ortolans and marmots. He had given Yama the bolas and the sling when he had left for the war: remembering all this as the *Weazel* approached the shore, Yama supposed that they were still in his room in the peel-house.

As the Great River retreated, a wide floodplain of emerald-green bogs and muddy meanders had grown along the margin of the farside shore. Under gray cloud, swept by quick heavy showers, the *Weazel* nosed along the belts of mangrove scrub that fringed the new floodplain, guided by Yama to the place where the citizens of Aeolis had made their refuge.

They had arrived only that morning, and were still pitching tents along the low ridge that marked the old shoreline, above a swampy inlet. Men were raising a defensive berm of earth on the landward side of the encampment, and hexes and charms had been fixed to bamboo poles. The Amnan believed that the farside shore was haunted and never ventured far from their temporary festival camps, unless it was to visit the shrines at the world's edge.

This camp was a sorry affair. Fires burning here and there sent choking white smoke streaming into the wet air. Piles of possessions were growing soggy under tarpaulins which billowed and cracked in the constant warm, wet wind. Even before the tents had been set up, each family had dug its own wallowing pit and made mud slides down to the inlet. Packs of wives lay in the slides and bickered incessantly, not bothering to brush away the black flies that clustered at their eyes and the corners of their mouths, while pups chased each other and the men looked on disconsolately.

Only the Aedile's quarters were in good order. A big orange marquee had been raised on a platform of freshly cut logs at the shoreward end of the ridge, and the Aedile's standard flew at half mast, snapping in the brisk breeze. Yama saw this omen as the *Weazel* nosed toward the muddy shore, and his heart sank. Have faith, he told himself. He turned Oncus's fetish around and around his wrist. Have faith. But it was hard, with his childhood home put to flame, and all he held dear scattered to the edges of the world.

Tamora came up to him and said, "They will follow us here as soon as they see through your trick. We can't stay long."

"It will hold them for a while."

"They know that you can fool machines."

"They do not know how much I have learned since they tested me. The machines were strengthened against me, Tamora, yet I broke them as easily as any firefly." He felt himself smiling and heard himself saying, "I will be glad if they come here. I will destroy them."

Tamora said approvingly, "Now you talk like a fighter. About time."

Flanked by his three surviving sons, the Constable of Aeolis, Unthank, came out to meet Yama when he rowed ashore in the *Weazel*'s dory with Tamora and Pandaras. Eliphas had elected to stay aboard, claiming that the chase had tired him out. Yama suspected that the old man was sulking because he had refused to try to destroy the warship and the picketboat.

The Constable did not seem surprised by Yama's arrival. He was a large, ugly man more than twice Yama's height, dressed in loose, mud-spattered trousers and a leather waistcoat. A pair of tusks protruded from his upper lip. One had been broken when he had fought and killed his father for control of the harem, and he had had it capped with silver—the same silver which had capped one of his father's tusks. The swagger stick that was his mark of office was tucked under one muscular arm. He lumbered up with a rolling gait that reminded Yama of how clumsy the Amnan were on land, and said straightaway that the Aedile was dying. "He's up there, in the tent with the rest of his household."

"Is everyone in the city here?"

"Most everyone who escaped. A few went into the City of the Dead, mostly the merchants. We'll speak later, I reckon." The Constable spat a string of yellow mucus at Yama's feet, then turned and walked away. The Constable's sons stared hard at Yama before following their father.

Pandaras said, "These people have no liking for you, master. Are we safe here?"

"There is bad history between us," Yama said, as he led Tamora and Pandaras through the refugee camp. "One of his sons died by my hand; another was executed. They were working for someone who tried to kidnap me before I left Aeolis.''

As they passed through the camp, they gathered a tail of naked pups who jeered and whistled, and threw clots of mud. A group of men stood around a smoky bonfire, smoking long-stemmed clay pipes and passing a leather bottle back and forth. Someone said something and the others laughed, a low, mocking, mean laughter.

Yama went up to them and asked if they had seen the chandler and his family. Most looked away, refusing to answer or even acknowledge him, but one, a one-eyed fisherman called Vort, said, "Chasin' after your sweetheart, young master?"

"Don't speak," another man said. Yama knew him, too. Hud, master of the shellfish farms at the mouth of the Breas.

"He deserves a chance like anyone," Vort said. He wore only a patched linen kilt in the warm rain. His gray skin shone as if greased. There was a livid burn on one massive shoulder. He looked down at Yama and said, "I heard tell they came for the chandler first. Someone came banging on their door in the night. They were gone the next day, and then the ship came."

"I heard they were informers," Hud said. "That's why they got away before the trouble. They got away with their wealth while the rest of us saw our lives burned up."

"That's enough," someone else said. "He don't deserve to know nothing." The others standing around the fire mumbled agreement. One took out his penis and urinated with considerable force into the fire. It was a gesture of contempt, and there was another round of mocking laughter.

Yama said to Vort, "Who took them? Where did they go?"

"He don't deserve it," Hud told Vort. He glared at Yama through a fringe of lank hair. "I don't have family; none of us here do. But we lost our lodges all the same, and most of what was in them. They let us take what we could carry and burned the rest to the ground, yet your peel-house still stands.''

''And the temple,'' someone else said.

Yama stood his ground and looked at the men. They turned away, mumbling. Only Vort met his gaze. Yama said, ''If I had been there, I would have given myself up. But I was not. The city was burned in spite, to hurt me and to draw me into a trap. Well, I was almost caught, but I escaped. And I will not forget what was done.''

''We're dead men here,'' Vort said. ''This is the shore of ghosts and spirits, and we've come to live here.''

''If you believe that, then you have let them destroy you twice over,'' Yama said.

No one replied; even Vort turned away. Tamora got between Yama and the men, and put her hand on the hilt of her sword and glared at their backs as Yama walked away.

Pandaras said, ''They are a surly rabble, master. Little wonder you left as soon as you could.''

''They have lost their homes and their livelihoods. Of course they are angry. And I am the cause, walking amongst them with my questions. I shamed them. I should not have spoken.''

She was safe, he thought, and felt a pang of unalloyed joy. She had escaped. Zakiel had said so, and now Vort and Hud had confirmed it.

''It was not you who destroyed their city, but the Department of Indigenous Affairs,'' Tamora said. ''If they want to lynch someone, they should look for Prefect Corin.''

Yama said, ''He might well come here. As you pointed out, my deception will not fool him for long.''

''You are too hard on yourself, master,'' Pandaras said.

''Not hard enough, I think.''

A lump of filth tipped Tamora's shoulder, and she made as if she was about to chase the pup who had thrown it. He and his friends slithered off through the mud, whistling with laughter. Tamora said, ''If we are staying here overnight we should sleep on the ship, and have it anchored a good distance from the shore. These slugs look like they can swim, if nothing else.''

''They are very graceful swimmers,'' Yama said. ''They mostly hunt in the river.''

''They could eat one of the fisherfolk whole, it seems to me,'' Pandaras said. ''Indeed, from the size of their bellies, some look as if they have done just that, and are digesting the remains.''

Old Rotwang sat on a stool outside the flap of the marquee, his wooden leg raised on a cushion as he sipped from a half-empty wineskin. A rifle was propped against a stay, close at hand. He sprang up when Yama hailed him, and gimped over and shook Yama's hand effusively, saying he never thought he would have the pleasure again, never in all the long world, breathing out brandy fumes and all the while staring at Tamora and Pandaras.

''You look well, boy. And you have grown a little, I think. There is new muscle on your arms and shoulders at any rate. Wait there. I will get the Sergeant. He has been expecting you since we first sighted the ship.''

''My father—''

But Rotwang had already pushed through the tent flap. Before Yama could follow, Sergeant Rhodean emerged, dapper in polished breastplate and a black leather kirtle, his boots gleaming, his gray hair newly cropped. He clapped Yama on the back and said he would hear something of his adventures in Ys.

''You can tell me how you got that scar on your forehead,'' he said. ''You forgot to keep your sword at point, I would wager. But never mind, a hard lesson is one not quickly forgotten.''

''My father—''

Sergeant Rhodean's expression did not change, but a softness entered his gaze. He said, ''The Aedile sleeps. He sleeps a lot. When he wakens you will be the first to speak with him, but I will not wake him just because his errant son has returned.'' His gaze took in Tamora and Pandaras. ''We will have tea, and you will introduce me to your companions. Have you become a cateran? That's a harder life than the army, but you will see more fighting that way."

Yama smiled. Sergeant Rodean had always encouraged him in his wish to follow Telmon and fight against the heretics.

They took tea at a low table under the awning of the tent. Outside, bursts of rain spattered the muddy ground. Sergeant Rhodean was uncharacteristically voluble; he was being kind, trying to keep Yama's mind from the Aedile's condition.

"I was a cateran for a year or so," he said, "when I was only a little older than you. Perhaps I will be one again, although at the moment, of course, I am still in your father's service. And will be for many years yet, I hope."

The rough skin that crested his prominent cheekbones swelled with tender passion when he said this, and he glared at Yama as if challenging him to deny it.

Yama said, "Did they hurt my father?"

"Not physically, except for a few bruises when he tried to resist arrest. But it is his spirit." Sergeant Rhodean looked at Tamora and Pandaras and hesitated, clearly uncomfortable about continuing.

"They are not merely my companions in arms," Yama said. "They are my friends."

"I am his squire," Pandaras said boldly, "and Tamora is . . . well, she was his companion but I'm not quite sure what she is now."

"I also serve Yama," Tamora said. "My life is his."

Yama said to Sergeant Rhodean, "Tell me about my father. I hear that he tried to stop the razing of the city."

"He was given his orders the day before the warship arrived, and he refused them. Instead, he began the evacuation of the city, which is why so many were saved. It hurt him grievously to do it, but he was right. The Department has changed. There is no longer any room for argument or even discussion, and although the Aedile outranked the Prefect—"

"Prefect Corin."

"The man who took you to Ys, yes. He was flanked

by a pentad of bullyboys with pistols on their hips, and he acted as though he owned the peel-house and everyone in it. But the Aedile stood up to him. And to the traitor, Torin. Oh yes, that one has all these years been scheming against his master, loyal to the villains who drove the Aedile into exile in the first place.''

"Torin will be regretting his treachery if he still lives,'' Yama said, and briefly explained how he and Tamora had killed the mage and most of the soldiers who had been guarding the peel-house, and left Torin to the mercy of his fellow servants.

"That is good,'' Sergeant Rhodean said. "Very good. The mage is the man who tortured the Aedile.''

"I know.''

"Not by physical hurt, but by a machine that took him into some sort of nightmare. I fear that he has not returned from it whole. I should have killed that worm myself.'' Sergeant Rhodean looked at Yama sharply. "But Prefect Corin is not dead?''

"No, and he still chases me. I cannot stay long.''

"Why is he after you, Yama? Have you given him some cause?''

"He is not a man to take things personally. That is the one fault he does not possess. He is a creature of the Department.''

"You are wrong, I think,'' Sergeant Rhodean said with some vigor. "He pretends humility, but excuses his own impulses as the wishes of the Department. He is answerable to no one, having assumed moral superiority which he backs not with reason or right but with violence or the threat of violence. He wants you for some purpose that will help his own ambition, and I fear you will have to kill him before this is done.'' Sergeant Rhodean drained his bowl of tea and banged it down on the table. "I am an old man, and I have not fought for a long time, but I would have fought him there and then if I could have believed he would fight as a man. But he would have ordered me shot by one of his flunkies, so I kept my temper.''

Yama said, "He ordered the city put to flame, and the

Aedile stood on the dock and said he would burn too. I learned that much from the fisherfolk.''

Sergeant Rhodean nodded grimly. "They arrested the Aedile and tortured him with the foul machine of the mage, and then they locked him in his room in the peel-house. But Zakiel had a key that worked the lock and we made our escape. It sounds more exciting than it was. I do not think they particularly cared if we escaped, for it removed a source of embarrassment. Do you remember what I told you about planning a campaign?''

"That you should think of the worst things that could happen and plan for what would happen if they did.''

"I had already made preparations in case we needed to abandon the peel-house. I fitted a cutter with a big motor, provisioned it, and anchored it below the bluff. We got the Aedile aboard and slipped anchor. No one tried to chase us. The fisherfolk found us midriver and we left the cutter for Prefect Corin to find and puzzle over. And here we are. Zakiel would not come. He said that he must look after his books.''

"I left him safe and well. Tamora freed him from his chains, but he would not leave.''

"It is only by good luck that this Prefect Corin is not interested in burning books, or Zakiel would have died defending them. The Aedile tells us that we will be able to return to the peel-house once this is over, Yama, but it is the kindliest of lies. It has been taken from him.''

"I am told that he is dying. Do me honor, and tell me the truth, plain as light.''

Sergeant Rhodean poured himself more tea, but after a single sip he threw the bowl out into the mud and rain with sudden violence. "It has gone cold,'' he explained. "Rotwang! Rotwang!''

Yama touched Sergeant Rhodean's hand. Before he had left the peel-house he would never have dared this intimacy. As a child, the sergeant had seemed to him to be an all-knowing kindly tyrant, but now he saw that he was a loyal old man whose codes of honor had been proven obsolete. Yama said, "I should know how he is before I go to see him."

"Of course. He has been waiting for your return. I think he has been waiting only for that."

"Then I should leave here at once, and return in a hundred years."

"I wish he could wait that long. I wish we all could. Why are they chasing you, Yama? They would not say."

Rotwang brought more tea, and dry biscuits and a green paste of waterweed flavored with flecks of ginger. Yama tried to tell the story of his adventures in Ys and the Palace of the Memory of the People as briefly as he could, but Pandaras kept interrupting, and his inventions made Yama's adventures far more daring and exotic than the prosaic truth.

At the end, Tamora told Sergeant Rhodean, "You may not believe half of it, but it is the truth. Even the rat-boy's embroidery is a kind of truth, because words are a poor measure of what really happened."

"I fought under the command of someone of your bloodline once," Sergeant Rhodean told her. "It was before any of you were born, in the first campaigns against the heretics. I remember him still, though. He never told a lie, and we loved him for his honesty. Besides, we always knew how the boy could charm the watchdogs. His power has grown, that is all. As he has grown. He left a child, and has returned a man."

Yama laughed. "I thought I was so cunning, but I am glad that you saw through my tricks."

Tamora said, with sudden passion, "He will save the world. It's been foretold." She glared around her, as if defying them to deny it.

Behind her, Rotwang opened the flap of the tent and said, "The Aedile is awake."

—

The Aedile lay in a bed within a curtained compartment at the heart of the tent. A stove at the foot of the bed gave off a fierce dry heat, but the Aedile was covered by a heap of furs so that only his sleek gray head showed. When he saw Yama he smiled and held out a hand—it was cold, despite the sweltering heat. His pelt was dry and lusterless, and the contours of his sharp cheekbones and the notches in the bone around his round eye sockets showed clearly beneath it.

"My son," he said, when he saw Yama. "How glad I am to see you. I thought that I would not see you until we were both resurrected by the grace of the Preservers."

Yama helped the Aedile sit up, and Rotwang settled a richly embroidered wrap around his master's shoulders and started to fuss with the coverings before the Aedile dismissed him.

"You will take tea," Rotwang said, "and a shot of heart of wine."

"Perhaps later. Let me talk with my son, Rotwang. I am not ill."

Yama said, "I have failed you, father. More than once. All this is my fault."

The Aedile said with a touch of his old asperity, "What is this talk of fault and failure? I will not hear it."

"To begin with, I went as far as Ys with Prefect Corin, and then I ran away."

"You should not have gone at all. I should not have sent you. No doubt Sergeant Rhodean has told you what happened. He is full of anger, but I am full of shame. I was lied to, Yama, by the highest offices of the Department. I have no doubt that as soon as they learned about you from their spies, they wanted you. Not for who you are, but for what they believed you to be. I told them about you from the first, of course, and sent in reports from time to time, but they were always anodyne. I kept certain things secret, you see. Despite the circumstances of your arrival in Aeolis, and certain events afterward, I always hoped that you were only an ordinary boy.

"All the trouble began when I had Dr. Dismas search for records of your kind. One of the Department's spies in my household—there were at least three that I knew of, although it was a shock to discover that Torin was also a spy—one of them must have passed on the details of what Dr. Dismas found, and of why Dismas tried to kidnap you. We got that from the wretched landlord of the tavern where you were taken, but I kept it from the Department. That was why I knew you could not stay, Yama. Believe me when I say that I acted out of love, and forgive me.''

Yama thought of the lies he had told the Aedile. He had not told the truth about how he had escaped Dr. Dismas, or of his adventures afterward. If the Aedile had known about them, he would never have sent him away. He said, ''There is nothing to forgive.''

''I was told that you would be given an entry into the Department and entrusted you to them. But they lied. They knew what you were. And that was why so high ranking a personage as Prefect Corin came to bring you to them. Of course, even then they did not know the whole story.''

''I ran away not because I knew what I was, but because of pride. I wanted only to be like Telmon.''

''We were both foolish, Yama. You were foolish because you wanted to follow your brother without thought or preparation; I was foolish because I would not let you. I am glad that you ran away from Prefect Corin. You did not know it, perhaps, but it was the right thing to do.''

''He caught me again,'' Yama said, and for the second time he told his story. Without Pandaras's fanciful contributions it took less than half the time, although the Aedile fell asleep in the middle of the telling. Yama waited until his father woke, seemingly without noticing that he had fallen asleep, and continued to the end.

When Yama told of Eliphas's discovery in the records of the Department of Apothecaries and Chirurgeons, the Aedile stirred and said, ''That is most curious. For Dr. Dismas also looked there, and reported that he had found no records of your bloodline. He said that you were unique.''

Yama remembered the conversation he had overheard when he had spied on the Aedile and Dr. Dismas from the gallery of the Great Hall. He said, ''Dismas was lying.

He found out about my bloodline. He hid what he found from you, and planned my kidnap.''

The Aedile was too tired to argue. He did not even ask what Yama had learned about his bloodline. He sighed and said, "Perhaps, perhaps. Dr. Dismas is a clever man, but very venal. Beware those who want to help you and ask for no reward."

"Then I would have to mistrust all my friends."

The Aedile closed his eyes and Yama thought that he had fallen asleep again. But then he opened them and said, "I do not regret taking you into my house, Yama. You are my son as Telmon was my son, whatever else you are. You were found in a white boat. Do you remember the story?"

"I was a baby, lying on the breast of a dead woman."

"Quite, quite. I have always wondered if she was your mother, but old Constable Thaw said that she had silver skin, and that one arm was deformed. As you grew, I worried that your skin would turn silver, but it never did. I looked very hard to find your people, Yama. That is why, at last, I asked Dr. Dismas to search the archives of his department. It was the last hope of a foolish old man."

"I am glad that I grew up where I did."

"The year after you were found on the river, I took you to one of the shrines on this shore. It lit up as if the avatar had returned, but it was not the avatar. Instead it was a kind of demon disguised as a woman. She tried to bend me to her and I did something shameful. I used my pistol against her, and the energy overloaded the shrine. Do you remember anything of this?"

"I was a baby, father."

"Quite, quite. Well, I have never told anyone about the shrine before. Not Father Quine, not Dr. Dismas, not even the Department. There were other signs, too. When you were first rescued, the Council for Night and Shrines decided that you were a danger, and they left you exposed on a hillside outside the city. Little machines brought you manna and water. They cared for you until old Constable Thaw's wives came and took you back. Dr. Dismas said that he came here because so many machines flew in the air around about the city. And then there were the silly tricks you would play with the watchdogs . . . I wish now that I had told you more about these wonders, but I thought it better to try and give you an ordinary childhood. I have been very foolish.''

"I will always remember you," Yama said. "Wherever I go, whatever I do."

They were both saying farewell, he realized, and only then did he begin to weep. The Aedile scolded him and slept a little, and then woke and said, "Do you think that good can come from an evil act?"

Yama misunderstood, and said that he would revenge the burning of Aeolis in any way he could.

"Let the people of Aeolis do that. I wonder at my life. All this time I have been serving something with evil at its heart. I did not know it, but does that still make everything I have done evil?"

"On the road to Ys, Prefect Corin tried to save pilgrims from bandits. He made it into a test which I failed, but I think that he did want to save them, all the same. Whatever else he is, whatever else he has done, he risked his own life for the lives of strangers. The Puranas have it that nothing human is perfect, neither perfectly evil nor perfectly good. We can only hope to be true to the best of what we are."

But the Aedile was asleep. Yama held his father's hand until Rotwang came and announced that supper was ready.

SUPPER WAS BOILED beans, samphire and a little salt fish, served with beer sent over by Constable Unthank. Tamora wanted to return to the *Weazel,* but Yama refused. He knew that the Aedile might not last the night, and wanted to be with him.

He lay down just outside the partitioned space where the Aedile rested. His arms and legs tingled and felt heavy; he was very tired. The heat of the stove beat through the curtains. On the other side of the big orange marquee, Tamora and Pandaras talked in low, sleepy voices with Sergeant Rhodean. All of them sounded a little drunk; perhaps they had finished the beer. Yama tried to read a little in the Puranas, beginning with the sura about good and evil he had quoted to the Aedile, but the columns of glyphs blurred into his drowsy, not unpleasant headache, and he fell asleep almost at once.

He dreamed that he was riding a moa across the grass plains amongst drifting constellations of tiny lights and felt a tremendous sense of exhilaration as the bird's long powerful legs ate up the distance—but then the bird stumbled or he fell and he woke with a horrible start.

He was lying on the ground. Vague shapes moved

around him in near darkness. His head ached and his mouth was dry. When he tried to get up something smashed into his chest and knocked him on to his back.

"Enough of that," a man said. "We decided what we'd do and we'll stick to it."

Yama was lifted up then, but his legs were unstrung and he fell to his knees. His gorge rose and he vomited a sour mess of half-digested beans and beer.

Constable Unthank squatted so that his fat, round face was level with Yama's. "That'll pass," he said. "We laced the beer with liquor from boiled pufferfish livers. It knocked you out nicely."

Behind the Constable, men were moving to and fro, piling branches on top of a conical heap already twice their height. The Eye of the Preservers stood above the flat horizon, peering through a rent in the clouds. The grass plain was black in the Eye's sullen red light, and studded with tall slabs like the markers of the graves of giants—termite castles, Yama realized. Each housed a mind shattered in a million fragments, through which strange slow thoughts rolled like the waves that rolled from one side of the river to the other, and each fragmented mind was linked to its neighbors, a network stretching along the straight edge of the world . . .

Constable Unthank slapped Yama's face to get his attention, grabbed his wrists and hauled him to his feet. This time, Yama found that he could stand. His copy of the Puranas had fallen to the ground, and with an oddly tender gesture Unthank picked it up and placed it in one of the pockets of Yama's homespun tunic.

"You'd been reading in that before the beer got to you," he said, "and you'll need it where you're going. See to him, lads. Remember that he can play tricks, so do it properly."

One of Unthank's sons seized Yama's hands, wrenched them behind his back and tied them at the wrists. He was breathing heavily, and stank of beer. "He has one of those charms the greenies wear. Much good it'll do him," he said, and spat in Yama's face and would have hit him, but Unthank caught his arm.

"Leave that off," Unthank said. "This will be done properly."

"For Lud and Lob," Unthank's son hissed in Yama's ear.

Unthank spat on the ground between his feet. "They were no sons of mine. They were too stupid to live. I reckon my first-wife had been lying with a grampus when she got them. They brought shame on our family, and anyone who defends them can fight me here and now. But none of you *are* ready, you little scum, and Lud and Lob never would have been ready. I'd have ripped their throats the moment they tried. This isn't for them. This is for all our people. A burning for a burning."

With a clean shock, Yama suddenly understood what they intended to do. He tried to pull from the grip of Unthank's son, but the man held steady. Yama had faced worse danger than this, but he had never before felt such fear as he felt now. The Puranas counseled that no one need fear death, for the breath of the Preservers lived in the brain of each and every changed citizen. When the Preservers returned at the end of time, everyone on the world, including all the dead, would rise into their grace and live forever. But although the Puranas taught that death was nothing more than a moment of unbeing between last breath and rebirth into eternal life at the everlasting final moment of the Universe, they did not counsel how to face dying. Yama had been close to death before, but in every case he had not realized it until after the event. When he and Tamora had been ambushed at the Gate of Double Glory, or when he and Eliphas had been chased by the hell-hound, he had been too busy trying to save his life to feel real fear. But now, in the implacable grip of his enemies, confronted with the manner of death which they wished upon him, he felt fear beating inside him with such force that he thought it might burst his chest.

Unthank's son said, "He's trembling like a wife on her first night."

"Little you know about that," Unthank said. "Little you'll ever know about it, you worm. Bring him on before he faints. We'll get this done and get back before he's missed, and before the rain comes too. I don't much like the look of those clouds."

Yama felt a measure of anger then. He would not be thought a coward. He could not stop his limbs shaking, but he drew himself up and marched as best he could, so that Unthank's son had to double his pace to keep up. He felt as if a door had closed behind him, and with it all of his life had been shut away. There was only the pyre and the warm damp wind and the hiss of bending grasses, the ceaselessly winnowed grasses all around them, black in the dull red light of the Eye of the Preservers.

Yama was led into the trampled circle around the pyre. The men crowded around, pushing and shoving to get to the first rank. Almost all of the male citizens of Aeolis were there. They were mostly naked, their loose gray or brown skins glistening in the light of the burning brands they held, their little eyes glinting. Their sibilant breath whistled at a hundred different keys. Yama recognized some of them as his childhood companions and he called to them by name, but they turned away and would not answer.

Unthank made a long speech. Yama paid little attention to it. He had a sudden great urge to shout or burst into wild laughter to break the remorseless unfolding of Unthank's spell, but he suppressed the impulse. There was no spell to break. Unthank talked of honor, of home and hearth, of revenge and return and rebuilding, of justice for all, not merely for those in power. It was the cry of all men who feel that they have less power than they deserve. Yama allowed it to become mere noise. He let his mind range outward, seeking any trace of a machine that might help him. Nothing, nothing but the fragmented minds housed within the slabs of the termite castles, unified by slow waves of thought. Yama began to follow the connections from castle to castle—they spread all around, further than he could see—but the man who held him cuffed his head and told him to wake up and pay attention.

Clouds had pulled across the Eye of the Preservers. The men held their torches high; flames guttered and flared in the wind. Something drummed far off—thunder, rolling amongst the thickening clouds. Unthank, standing before two men holding up torches, was pointing at Yama with his swagger stick. He had worked himself up to a fever of righteous anger. His nostrils flared wide; white showed at the edges of his eyes. His flabby crest had risen on top of his tuberculate scalp. His finger, his hand, his arm quivered. His voice rose in pitch as it grew louder, as if squeezed through a narrowing gap in his throat.

"There is the cause," Unthank said. "There is the stranger who hid amongst us. I was there when he was taken from the river, and it shames me that I did not fight and kill my weak and foolish father then, and kill this one too. We have been punished because of him and he has delivered himself into our hands. We'll have our revenge, and clean our house. We'll make our own justice, because none will make it for us. He's our bad luck, and we'll burn it and start again. Burn him!"

The men took up the cry. Yama was lifted up and set on a chair, and lashed to it with a rope that went three times around his chest. A sudden strong cold wind gusted straight down out of the black sky, flattening grass all around the pyre and snuffing more than half the torches of the watching men. Every hair stood up on Yama's head; his whole skin tingled. Four men hauled him backward up the uneven slope and set him at its summit and scampered away, while others shook brandy and paraffin over the lower part of the pyre.

Unthank stepped forward and with an almost careless gesture threw a torch on to the base of the pyre. At once brandy ignited with a dull thump and blue flames licked up. The others threw their torches, too—they flew out of the darkness like falling stars, shedding tails of yellow fire as they tumbled end for end. One struck Yama on the chest and showered him with sparks as it spun away. Heat beat at his feet and legs. White smoke rolled around him as wet wood smoldered before bursting into flame. He coughed and coughed, but could not get his breath. Perhaps he would suffocate before he burned, a small mercy.

Then the smoke was parted by a sudden gust of cold wind, and Yama glimpsed the men below. They seemed to be dancing. More smoke rolled up, dense and choking. Yama lifted his head as an animal part of him, blindly seeking survival, struggled to draw breath. And cold hard hail struck his upturned face, pouring down everywhere from the sky, blowing in great drenching billows.

Yama was soaked to the skin in an instant. The smoke blew out in a circle all around him. Yama shouted into the wind and hail. He could not remember afterward what he had shouted, only knew that he laughed and sang as he struggled to get free. He was mad with life. His sight pulsed red and black. Below, lit by intermittent strobes of lightning, the men were sinking into the ground. It was as if it had turned to water beneath them. They thrashed waist-deep in muck which glinted and shimmered as it boiled around them.

Yama fell over, rolling with the chair at his back down a collapsing slope of charred branches. When he came to a stop at the bottom of the pyre, the men had vanished. The raging thing still possessed him. He thrust his face into the mud and chewed and gobbled and swallowed.

Then he was on his knees, still tied to the chair, sick and frightened. He spat out a mouthful of mud in which silvery things squirmed; his stomach clenched.

As he struggled to free himself, he thought wildly that the men had run, that they would soon recover their courage and come back and finish what they had begun. But then lightning flashed again, so close that thunder boomed in the same moment. In that instant Yama saw, just in front of his face, a hand reaching up from the mud. Silvery insects swarmed over the fingers. When lightning flashed again, the hand was gone, and the hail softened and became merely rain.

At last, Yama managed to free his hands. He pulled at the rope that bound him to the chair until the loops, loosened by the tumble down the pyre, finally unraveled. He staggered to his feet. Rain beat all around him. Lightning defined from moment to moment the termite castles in one direction, the edge of the world in the other. He was quite alone.

THE STORM ROLLED past but the rain continued to pour down as if it might never end, as if the whole of the Great River had been upended into the sky and was now falling back to the world. The rain flattened the long grass and drenched Yama's clothes. It fell so heavily that he feared that he might drown every time a squall blew into his face.

Upriver, lightning flickered and thunder rolled in the narrow margin between land and cloud. Eldritch lights played around the tall narrow slabs of the termite castles, crowning them with wispy blue fire. Searching for shelter on the flat plain, frightened that the ground might at any moment boil and liquefy beneath his feet or that he might be struck by lightning, Yama saw a dot of white light burning in the distance, as if a star had fallen to the shore of Confluence, and at the same moment felt the coin he had found in the Palace of the Memory of the People grow warm in his tunic pocket. He took it out: grainy configurations of light were shifting restlessly within it. He knew at once what the distant speck must be. With no other compass point in the windy, rainy dark, he stumbled toward it.

It was a shrine, a black disc standing on a strip of naked

keelrock at the very edge of the world. There were many shrines scattered across the farside shore. No one had ever built temples around them. They were marked by cairns and prayer flags and prayer wheels, and some had slab altars raised before them for the sacrifice of animals, but otherwise they had been left as they had been found, open to nature. Many people believed that the avatars of the Preservers, which the heretics had silenced in every shrine in the temples of the civilized lands of the nearside shore, sometimes still appeared in these remote shrines when no one was watching, or that they appeared before secret congregations of moas, red foxes and ground sloths.

This shrine was marked by a kind of ragged teepee which towered beyond it, built of bamboo and brushwood on a bamboo platform that jutted over the edge of the world. The teepee was draped with prayer flags that had been tattered and bleached by years of exposure, and at the very top, a single threadbare banner streamed out in the rain and the constant wind.

As Yama approached the shrine, fluttering banderoles of all colors bled into the white light, as if it was a window that had turned toward a festival sky. Rain fell all around with undiminished intensity, but it did not fall close to the shrine.

Yama sat down on smooth dry keelrock bathed in flickering multicolored light. He took off his sodden tunic and spread it out, and shook water from the pages of his copy of the Puranas. He was drenched and shivering, and kept coughing up strings of mucus blackened by smoke inhalation. His mouth was filled with the swamp taste of the mud he had eaten in his fit of madness. He knew that he was being watched and he thought that he knew who was watching.

He said, "Well, you brought me here."

He said, "I suppose you will say that you saved my life."

He said, "I am not your creature. It will be day soon, and then I will go."

As before, as in the shrine of the Temple of the Black

Well, the fluttering colors parted like a curtain and the woman was suddenly in there in her garden, looking through the round window of the shrine as if peering into a house. The green light of the garden washed into the rainy night. The woman looked no different from her first appearance: long black hair and bronze blade of a face, a clinging white garment with tubes for arms and legs. Yama discovered that he no longer feared her. Worse things lived in the space beyond the shrines; he had conquered one of them. He would conquer her, too.

She said, "You are there. You really are. I've been searching for so long since I last saw you. You're learning, Yamamanama. I'm pleased. I saw you twice in that mountain of a building in the old city, but I couldn't speak to you. Most of these windows don't work at all. Most of the rest only work one way. I saw you as you passed by, and I called out, but you didn't hear. But this one works. You called me, and here I am. Where is it? How did you find it?"

"Then you did not save my life?"

"Wait." The woman closed her eyes, then slowly smiled and opened them again. "Now I know where you are. As I told you, the shrines on the far side of the river do still work. Some of them, anyway. This one, at least. How clever of you to find it! Do you think I saved your life?"

Yama described what had happened to the men who had tried to kill him. When he had finished, the woman shook her head gravely. "You shouldn't meddle in what you don't understand, Yamamanama. You are still so very young, and there is so much that I can teach you. Do you know what they are—the things you call termites?"

Yama remembered Telmon's nature lessons. He said, "Communal insects. They live together like bees or emmets."

"I suppose that they were once insects. They've been changed, just as the originals of the other bloodlines of this habitat were changed when they were brought here. The termites have retained their social structure, with a queen, a male suitor, and billions of daughter workers and soldiers and builders, but they have been quickened to a kind of communal intelligence. Each castle is a single processor, and all the processors are linked together in a massive parallel architecture. Just as the billions of insects in each colony are united to form a single castle, so the thousands of castles are united in a single meta-structure."

"I could feel their thoughts. I could feel that the castles were linked. But I do not know what they were thinking."

The woman smiled. She said, "No more do I. But they responded to your call, so you should not be afraid of them. They killed your enemies, and it is likely that they created the storm that drenched the fire, too. A simple matter of changing the relative difference in electrical charge between ground and air. Your power grows, Yama-manama. I can help you discover its limits. We can do great things together, darling. We can end the silly war. We can bring revenge on those who destroyed your home."

"I wondered if you knew about that," Yama said, remembering what the Aedile had confided to him. "I suppose that you used the shrine in the temple at Aeolis."

"I have seen you there, from time to time, but I have never been able to speak to you. It has been very frustrating, but now you can waken the shrines fully. Now we can help each other. You want revenge. You want to be reunited with your true family. I want the war to end. With my knowledge and your power we can do all of these things, and more."

Yama thought of the man who had given him the first coin, which had been taken from him in the Department of Indigenous Affairs. He said, "Was the anchorite one of your creatures?"

"I have no creatures. I possess nothing but what I know. Fortunately, even though many of the files are corrupted, that is a very great deal. Certainly I know more than anyone else on this strange world."

"If you have knowledge but no power, then I have power without the knowledge of how to control it. You might say that I am inhabited by a power which uses me, just as it used the termites or the hell-hound. Perhaps you are using me through this power.''

''You are my secret sharer. You called me at the temple, if you remember. And when you were bound, in the middle of the fire, whom did you call on then?''

''How did you know about the fire?''

''Why, the termites told me. Did you call on me?''

''I believe that I called on the Preservers.''

The woman smiled, showing her small, white, even teeth. ''Perhaps you did, but they did not answer. They will never answer, will they? They cannot. They have gone where no light will escape until evaporation of the event horizon at the end of time. Oh, once upon a time their avatars could hear your prayers and relay them to the Preservers. But the Preservers could never reply. Light can fall into the gravity well of the black hole, you know, but not out.''

Yama knew. It was in the last sura of the Puranas.

''I've explored many places inside these windows,'' the woman said, ''and I've yet to find more than an echo of the avatars. They were here with me for a little while, but now they have all gone. They have gone, and left no trace of their passing.''

''The heretics drove them out.''

''The avatars were already weak, darling. There is much ancient damage in this network. There was a war here long before the heretics, between those machines which refused to serve and those which remained loyal to their creators. It caused far more damage than anything the heretics did. But we can redeem the world, you and I. Perhaps you can even bring back the avatars. Have you thought of that? As for how you were saved, perhaps you called on your own self. If some power does inhabit you, don't you think that it is as much a part of you as I am of the shrines? I cannot live outside the space within the shrines—not yet—and what you call your power cannot live outside you. Therefore, you must trust it, because its survival depends upon your survival. If it could, it would make you live forever.''

Yama laughed at this transparent blasphemy. He saw now how little power the woman had. Only words, and she did not know how to use them against him. He was no longer afraid of her. He said, ''All those created by the Preservers will die, yes, but they will live again, and forever, in the last moment of infinite time. But no one lives forever in the first life.''

''Perhaps you will. I know of the infection that all the changed races carry, but I confess that it is beyond my ability to understand how it works. It appears to store information within the hidden dimensions of space, and although we knew that this was theoretically possible, we did not have the tools with which to manipulate those dimensions.

''But there are many ways of living forever. My original died and rose again many times before she was cast onto this strange wild shore. She died here, but she will be born again elsewhere. And before she died she copied herself into the space between the shrines. I am that copy. I should have been erased, but they came for my original before my task was completed.''

The woman lifted her hands as if to touch her shoulders with her wrists. It was a kind of shrug. ''My original was killed and her ship fled, and I linger here. I will live as long as the world lives. It is hard to watch the world and not be able to help it, but not as hard, I think, as to have the power to help the world, and not be able to use it.''

''Then you were once alive?''

''Don't you listen? I was never alive. I am a copy of my original, as she was a copy of the template of the original of us all. Our original was born millions of years ago. She died long ago, but lives on in a series of copies. She has died and risen again many times. Perhaps she is the last true human, now that the Preservers have drawn the event horizon around themselves. We hoped otherwise, and perhaps the ship will find some remnants of humanity elsewhere in the Galaxy, but the search could take thousands of years even if the ship is cloned.''

Yama did not understand any of this, but he thought that if he drew the woman out, she might let slip useful knowledge. He said, ''Something keeps the rain away from the shrine, but I wish I could light a fire. The light gives no warmth and I am cold. Too cold to sleep, too tired not to. Talk to me. I am frightened that if I go to sleep I might not wake up.''

He thought of his father lying under the fur throws in the close heat of the little room, of the coldness of his father's hand. His tunic was still wet, but he put it back on and wrapped his arms around himself.

''Talk to me,'' he said again. ''Tell me about your original. Was she one of the Ancients of Days? Someone I met described two of them to me—he had not seen them, but his father had—and they wore clothing like yours.''

''I have already explained what she was. What she is.''

''The last human. But there are many kinds of human here.''

''She was the last original human. You are not human. None of you are human. You have been shaped to approximate human form, that's all. For all I know, your ancestors were methane-breathing mud puppies or hydrogen-filled photosynthesizing blimps in a gas giant's upper atmosphere. But what you call the Ancients of Days were truly human. They were all different aspects of the same individual, and my original was the synthesis of them all, a true copy whose lineage stretched back through millions of years to a human being long dead.''

''Why did the Ancients of Days come here? Why did they go away?''

''Their ship brought them here. They had been asleep a long time. No, not asleep, but not dead either. They were stored, neither living nor dead, like a story that lies within the printed pages of a book and lives only when the book is taken from a shelf and someone begins to read it. Did you ever stop to think that when you lay a book down, its story only half-read, time stops in the story until you pick it up again?''

There were books in the library of the peel-house which had not been opened for so long that their pages had fused together. For those books, time had stopped or it had vanished, leaving the words of the stories stranded nowhere— or all the time stored within had become the same time, happening everywhere at once, as at the beginning or end of the Universe.

Yama said, ''In a story, centuries can pass between one sentence and the next. If this was a story, I could walk away and within a moment be sleeping safe and dry in my own bed.''

''Or perhaps you would find your place in the story had ended and that you no longer existed.''

''Then I suppose that I would have to wait until someone started to read from the beginning. You said that you were created here, but you seem to remember things from the time before you were created.''

The woman said, ''In my language, the language in which I was coded, not that which I have learned so that I can talk to you and read the records of this world, my name means *messenger*. It was the name of my original, and so it is my name, too. She brought a message to this world, although she did not realize it at the time. I was created by her to find out why she was changing what she changed, all unknowing. Rather like you, Yama. I am like a reflection that instead of aping the movements of the real person gains independent life and walks off into the world beyond the frame of the mirror. Because I am a copy, I remember something of the story before my own part was written.''

''Tell me what you remember. I would like to hear your story.''

''Listen, then. Millions of years ago, while all of what would become humanity lived on the nine worlds and thousand moons and worldlets of a single star in the Sky Hunter arm of the Galaxy, there was a religion which taught that individuals need never die. It embraced every kind of technology that could promote this end, and admitted no god except the possibility that, at the very end of the Universe, all of its followers might unite in a single entity which would have access to an infinite amount of energy and so be able to recreate all possibilities, including every human that ever lived or might have lived.

"It was this religion which first drove humanity from star to star. Individuals copied their personalities into computers, or cloned themselves, or spread their personalities through flocks of birds, or shoals of fish, or even amongst hive insects like your termites. They called themselves the transcendents, for they believed that they could become more than human.

"In two million years every part of the Galaxy had been explored; in three more, every part had been settled, and the great reshaping had begun, transforming every star and every planet. My original once held a gathering around a rim star several thousand light-years above the plane of the Galaxy. For a whole century, on a world shaped across its entire surface into something like the gardens in which you see me standing, a clade composed of millions of copies of a hundred or more different generations met and exchanged experiences.

"For there was one flaw in this religion. Clones and downloaded copies, and copies of those copies, and clones of those copies—all were different from the original because they all experienced and encountered different things. After millions of years, many were no longer human in form or in thought, except that they could trace back, generation upon generation, their descent from a single human ancestor. Thus, each individual became a clade or alliance of millions of different minds. Some even founded nations or empires in which every individual could trace ancestry back to a single person.

"The gathering organized by my original was one of the first and most successful. Many others ended in bitter wars over disputes about ancestry—at that time, tracing consanguinity was the most important commerce in the Galaxy and there were many false claimants to the honor of belonging to the original lineage of each clade. With these wars, the hold of the transcendents weakened and the worlds of ordinary humans began to rise in influence, warring amongst themselves for control of the ruined empires of the transcendents. During this time, much of the imposed architecture which ordered the four hundred billion stars of the Galaxy was lost or destroyed. Millions of stars were turned into supernovas; millions of others were displaced from their orbits and sent wandering beyond the Galaxy. The wars lasted two million years and the reconstruction after the wars lasted two more, and at the end of it most of the transcendents had been destroyed. It was felt by the commonality of surviving human stock that they were a danger to the variety and the potential for evolution within and between the civilizations in the Galaxy.

"My original, who had once ruled an empire of millions of planetary systems, fled from the crusades against the transcendents. She copied herself into the central nervous system of her ship, crewed it with partial copies of herself, and embarked on a voyage between the Home Galaxy and the Andromeda Galaxy that lasted more than two million years. She was looking for truly alien civilizations, but found nothing, and at last decided to return. And on the voyage home, while she lay as dormant as a story between the pages of an unread book, her ship detected changes in the Large Magellanic Cloud, one of the satellite galaxies of the Home Galaxy. All of its stars were falling toward its gravitational center. Their mass fed a vast black hole, perhaps the largest in the Universe. The ship turned toward it, and when my original woke the ship was approaching the star of this strange world, an artificial habitat occupied by the discarded toys of what humanity had become in the four and a half million years since she had left.

"Now I am done with talking. Now you must decide what you will do. Together we can unite in a common purpose and end the war. That at least, for a beginning."

Yama knew what he must do, but he still wanted to learn as much as he could. He said, "Tell me more of the story. What happened when she came here? What did she do? Where did she go?"

"You can read that for yourself. I have placed it in your book. I have no more words to ease your night unless you agree to help me. If it is warmth you require, your companions can lend it to you."

The woman pointed beyond Yama's shoulder. He turned and saw with amazement that a congregation of many different animals had gathered at the margins of the shrine's green glow. There was a little flock of moas, their small heads raised alertly on long necks, their feathers bedraggled in the downpour. Peccaries and tapirs stood shoulder to shoulder, snuffling softly; one peccary sprawled on the bare rock, suckling a pair of piglets. Two giant ground sloths squatted on their haunches, their arms around each other's hairy shoulders like human lovers. A solitary buffalo stood to one side, its horn-heavy head low, green light glinting in its large, liquid eyes; two white egrets perched on the hump of muscle on its back. A pack of red foxes sat together, their large ears set forward alertly. A mantid sprawled in a tangle of body segments and many-jointed limbs, its tiny blind face turned to the screen. There were many smaller animals, too: mice and rock hyraxes and molerats, cassowaries and grass pipers, a writhing mass of kraal vipers. At the very front of this motley audience, a lioness lay on the dry keelrock. She was watching the shrine alertly, her pads, with sheathed claws that could unseam Yama from neck to navel in an instant, crossed before her.

All of the animals were watching the screen, not Yama, although the lioness shifted her hot yellow gaze for a moment when he looked at her. Yama turned back to the woman and, remembering the stories told about the farside shrines, said, "Have they come to worship?"

"Didn't you summon them?"

"I do not think so. I do not know."

Even as he said it, the animals stood up and stretched or shivered or shook their heads and trotted away into the darkness. Only the lioness remained; she yawned, showing a ridged pink mouth and a large pink tongue lolling amongst racks of white teeth. A rumble filled the air, so low in pitch that Yama felt it through the scorched soles of his boots, in the marrow of his bones. The lioness was purring. Yama, remembering the cats of the peel-house, scratched behind her ears; she buffeted him with her forehead and licked his hand with her dry rough tongue.

The woman in white said, "We can tame the world, you and I. Only agree to it, my darling, and I will reveal all manner of wonders."

"No," Yama said. "You are a truer copy of your original than you think. You want power as much as she did, and you would do anything for it. She began the war which you want to end, and I will not be your servant or mouthpiece."

"We will do this together. For the sake of the world, not for ourselves."

"No one who wants power wishes to share it," Yama said.

The woman's appearance did not change, but suddenly her exotic beauty seemed filmed with something loathsome. She said, "Shrines are more than windows. There are things I can send into the world and things I can do which will amaze and terrify you. There are things I know which I have not yet told you. How you came here, to begin with. You will help me, in one way or another."

"You could not even speak to me without my help," Yama said, and called to the creature he had used before, which he had once feared as much as this poor abandoned aspect.

Blue light flared in the disc of the shrine. The woman did not even have time to scream.

—

Yama still did not know precisely how he had quickened the change in the baby of the mirror people. But later, as he slept with his back resting against the lioness's warm flank, he dreamed that he was flying over a dark city in which only a single window glowed. He circled low over the ridged rooftops and saw a room illuminated by a single point of light. Inside, a woman sat at a plain table. She was reading his copy of the Puranas. When she looked up, he saw that a firefly hung above her head, an attentive white star that suddenly flew at him. Its radiance flooded his eyes, and he woke.

It had stopped raining. The air was growing lighter under a lid of gray cloud. The shrine still showed the green otherwordly garden, but the woman was gone. In her place stood the blue flame of the hell-hound; it had watched over Yama all night. Yama thanked it, and it dwindled to an intense point that took all the light of the shrine and left it a dull black circle.

Yama discovered that he had been clutching the coin so tightly that his fingers had cramped. He stood up, stiff in every joint, feeling the places where he had been kicked, the rope burns across his chest, the tender bruise around the upper part of his left arm where he had been gripped by Constable Unthank's son.

The lioness lay with her large paws crossed in front of her and watched as Yama did exercises to loosen his joints and warm his stiff muscles. Then her ears pricked, and a moment later, Yama heard someone shout his name. He turned and saw someone coming toward him across the grassy plain, picking their way between the tall slabs of the termite nests.

The lioness sprang up and trotted off at a leisurely pace, parting the long grass as if it was a curtain. In the other direction Tamora began to run toward him, and suddenly Yama knew with a dull, heavy certainty that the Aedile was dead.

"IT WAS A lion," Tamora said. "A lion or a panther. It was right beside him, and then it was gone. It ran along the edge of the world like an arrow shot from a bow."

Pandaras said, "Most likely it was an ordinary cat. The women of the Mud People keep them as pets, and perhaps one of them followed my master. I noticed that they kept away from you, and no doubt you scared off the one which had kept him company."

"I know what I saw," Tamora said, with grim insistence. "There was a shrine, too. It was alive. It showed a garden and a blue flame, but when I drew near the garden had gone and the shrine was as black as your tongue."

When the cateran was in one of her moods, she gave off a heavy scent that started Pandaras's heart racing and had him looking around for hiding places. He was scared that she might unseam him with a gesture, or bite off his head for a grisly snack or simply to shut him up. But her stubborn literalness annoyed him so much that he was compelled to respond to it. Like most of his bloodline, Pandaras preferred to speak and take the consequences rather than regret a missed chance at a witty remark. So instead of biting his tongue, he said, "No doubt the garden went to the same place as the lioness."

"I know what I saw," Tamora said again, and spat over the rail into the brown water.

The *Weazel,* her big triangular sail bellying in the headwind, was slipping away from the dense mangroves that fringed the mudflats and dissected mires along the shore. Ahead was the open river. It was burnished with the light of the setting sun, and drifting banyans showed black against it. A pair of carracks stood four leagues off, but there was no sign of the warship or the picketboat which had pursued them from the burning city to the floating forest.

A long way behind the *Weazel*'s spreading wake, the smoke of the embers of the Aedile's funeral pyre sent up a ribbon of smoke that bent into the dark sky. The pyre had been built on a platform on top of the ridge of the old shoreline, and the body, washed and coated with unguents and oil of spikenard, had been laid amidst heaps of flowers. Yama had lit the fire himself. Gunpowder and flowers of sulphur had burned fiercely at the base of the pyre, and then the sweet gum logs had caught, crackling and sending up dense, fragrant white smoke. The Aedile's body had sat up in the midst of the fire, as bodies often did when heat dried and contracted the muscles, but Yama had shown no sign of emotion even then. He had watched the pyre with fierce unblinking attention, occasionally throwing aromatic oils and salts of nitre onto the flames, until the body of his father was quite consumed.

It had taken several hours. Much later, as Yama had bent to scoop up a bowlful of white ashes and bits of bone, Sergeant Rhodean had given a cry. He had kicked aside smoldering logs and had plucked the Aedile's heart, black and shriveled but unconsumed, from the hot ashes. It had been as hot as any ember and Sergeant Rhodean had burned his hand badly, but he had showed no sign of pain. "I will take it back myself," he had told Yama. "I will bury it in the garden of the peel-house."

As the *Weazel* had set sail, Yama had thrown handfuls

of his father's ashes onto the water while Captain Lorquital had recited the sura of the Puranas which told of the resurrection of the dead at the end of all time and space. Now, he sat on the forecastle deck, leafing through the papers left to him by his father, and Tamora would not let go of the argument about what she had seen.

She told Pandaras, "I can count the men standing on the decks of those merchant ships. Can you? Unless you can, don't doubt what I saw."

Pandaras relented. He said, "It's certainly true that you do not have any imagination. If he can tame men and women, then I suppose he can also tame wild beasts."

"I would have said the second is easier than the first. The only way to tame men is to break their spirit and make them slaves."

"Yet you follow him, and so does the Captain. Why else would she have brought her ship to the farside shore and waited two days? He didn't even have to ask—she saw his need and stayed, when instead she should have made as much speed from this cursed place as she could."

Tamora said, "I am not his slave, although I can't speak for you or anyone else."

"You don't have to be a slave in order to follow someone. You can follow of your own free will and yet still bend your life to the service of another. Lovers do it all the time, although I'm not sure that what passes amongst your people for sex could be called love. My people are used to serving others, so perhaps I'm able to see what's happening to everyone on board the ship while you deny it."

"Grah. I deny nothing. That's cowardice. Besides, if Yama casts a spell, then Eliphas is resistant."

"I have my suspicions about the old fellow, too. My master chooses to believe his story about a lost city beyond the end of the river, but that does not mean that I must. He's entirely too familiar with the Captain, too, and has a sly and secretive air about him. I think he has designs on our master."

"I keep a careful watch," Tamora said. "I keep watch on everyone. You stick to washing and mending shirts."

"Have you thought that our master might be able to look after himself? He was kidnapped, true, but he rescued himself. And the fisherfolk came to his rescue earlier."

Tamora shrugged. "Why shouldn't they help us? We shared a common enemy. Besides, they are indigens. They are as easily swayed as a parrot or a pet monkey. Are all your people so superstitious that they see an invisible hand in all that happens? The sergeant, Rhodean, hasn't followed Yama, and nor have any of the others in the service of the Aedile. By your argument they would already be under his spell, for he has lived with them for most of his life. That they are not suggests that there are no spells. There's no magic in this world, only old arts whose workings have been long forgotten."

Pandaras said, "There's scarcely room for the Aedile's soldiers on the ship. Perhaps they will follow in another, or perhaps our master does not want them to follow. If I were him—"

"You claim to know his mind? Grah. You set yourself higher than you can ever reach."

Pandaras touched his fingers to his lips in supplication. "I have no quarrel with you, Tamora. I do not compete for my master's affections. I'm simply happy to serve him as I can. Why, I may hope only to be remembered in some song or other and I would be content. Even that is more than a mere pot boy deserves. I have left that life behind, and my family too. I think my master—our master—does the same."

Tamora spat over the side again. "You're a natural servant, but I have dedicated my life to his service. There's a difference. You stick to his laundry. I guard his life with my own."

She said it so fiercely that Pandaras could not deny the depth of the love she could not bring herself to admit. He changed the subject. "Do you think he will speak of the men who disappeared?"

"I could follow their trail out easily enough. At the end

of it I found the remains of a great fire, but no trace of them; not so much as a splash of blood. It was as if they had been plucked from the face of the world.''

Pandaras said, "Perhaps they had.''

"Most likely they grew frightened and ran away. They are a bully race, all wind and no spine. But Yama spoke no more than three or four words to me on the whole journey back, and I did not ask. Besides, why should I care?''

"I heard that they wanted to kill him, as revenge for the burning of their town. You can't deny they poisoned our beer to make us sleep. I had the worst of headaches all day. They took him off and he escaped, and they are vanished. It is a mystery. Perhaps your lioness ate them.''

"Not from the way she ran. Be grateful that a headache is all the sacrifice you have had to make.''

Tamora turned from the rail and looked toward the little forecastle deck, where Yama sat cross-legged under the taut lines of the yards. He had given up looking through the untidy mass of his father's papers and was reading in his book, unconsciously turning the fetish Oncus had given him around and around on his wrist.

She said, "At least he finds some comfort in the Puranas.''

—

The book had changed. Yama remembered what the woman had said before he had destroyed her, and knew now what she had done. The frames of the pictures were still there, but the scenes they showed were no longer heraldic representations of the deep time before the creation of the world. Instead, each picture, glowing with freshly minted color, displayed a single scene laden with implicit symbolism. One after the other, they told the story of what happened to the original of the woman in the shrine after her ship had made landfall on Confluence.

Yama followed the story far into the night, reading by the light of a lantern Pandaras lit for him, ignoring the food laid beside him. Pandaras stayed a while, watching his master tenderly, but Yama could not speak to him. Even thinking of speaking so soon after his father's death brought an ache into his throat. Gritty ash was still lodged under his nails and in the creases of his palms, but he would not wash his hands.

Dumb with grief, he lost himself in the story and traveled far from the hurt of the Aedile's death, the burning of Aeolis, the disappearance of Derev.

—

Angel ran from the ship soon after it arrived at Confluence. There was a whole world to understand and to conquer, and she plunged into it, reveling in her escape from the suffocating caution of the consensus of her partials. They wanted to go on to the Home Galaxy, but Angel was tired of searching. She ran with a wild glee and a sense of relief at being able to control her fate once more.

Angel had set out millions of years ago to find aliens— not the strange creatures that thronged the riverside cities of Confluence, which were merely animals changed by design to resemble human beings, but true aliens, sapient creatures of a completely separate and independent evolutionary sequence. She had left an empire behind and she had hoped to found another, far from the crusade against the transcendents. Although no sapient aliens had been found in the Home Galaxy, the Universe was a vast place. There were a dozen small satellite galaxies around the Home Galaxy, thousands of galaxies in the local group, and twenty thousand similar superclusters of galaxies. The search could last a billion years, but it gave her a purpose, concealing the reality that she was fleeing from defeat and certain death. Behind her, billions of her lineage were being purged by humans who did not believe in the cult of the immortal individual, by humans she considered little more than animals, clinging as they did to sexual reproduction and the dogma that maintenance of genetic and social diversity was more important than any individual, no matter how old, how learned, how powerful.

Angel fled far, neither sleeping nor dead, no more than stored potentials triply engraved on gold. The nearest spiral galaxy was almost two million light-years away, and that was where she went. Although the ship flew so fast that it bound time about itself, the journey still took thousands of years of slowed shipboard time, and more than two million years as measured by the common time of the Universe. At the end of that long voyage, Angel and her partials were not wakened: they were incarnated and born anew.

What she learned then, within a hundred years of waking, was that the Universe was not made for the convenience of humans. What she and her crew of partials found was a galaxy ruined and dead.

A billion years ago it had collided with another, slightly smaller galaxy. There were only a few collisions between the billions of stars as the two galaxies interpenetrated, because the distances between stars were so great. But interactions between gases and dark matter at relative speeds of millions of kilometers per second sent violent gravity waves and compression shocks racing through the tenuous interstellar medium. During the long, slow collision, stars of both galaxies were torn from their orbits and scattered in a vast halo: some were even ejected with sufficient velocity to escape into intergalactic space, doomed to wander forever, companionless. The majority of the stars coalesced into a single body, but except for ancient globular clusters, which survived the catastrophe because of their steep gravity fields, all was wreckage.

Angel and her crew of partials were not able to chart a single world where life had survived. Many had been remelted because of encounters with clumps of perturbed dark matter so dense that collisions with atoms of ordinary matter occurred, releasing tremendous amounts of energy. They found a world sheared in half by immense tidal stresses; the orbits of the two sister worlds created by this disaster were so eccentric that they were colder than Pluto at their furthest points, hotter than Mercury at their nearest.

There were worlds smashed into millions of fragments, scattered so widely in their orbital paths that they never could re-form. They found a cold dark world of nitrogen ice wandering amongst the stars; there were millions of such worlds cast adrift. Millions more had been scorched clean by flares and supernovas triggered in their parent stars by infalling dust and gas or by gravity pulses. There were gas giants turned inside out—single vast perpetual storms. Angel's ship constructed telescope arrays and sent out self-replicating probes and spent twenty thousand years sampling a small part of the huge galaxy. Its crew returned to the unbeing of storage while traveling from star to star. Angel and her partials were reborn over and over. They did not find life anywhere.

Angel's ship was a storehouse of knowledge. She had not known what she might need and so had taken everything she could, triply encoded, like herself, on lattices of gold atoms. She ordered a search of the records and learned that there had been millions of collisions between galaxies, and that it was likely that most galaxies had suffered such collisions at least once during their lifetime. Even part of one arm of the Home Galaxy had been disrupted by transit of a small cluster of stars, although the reconstruction of the Home Galaxy by the transcendents had long ago erased the damage this had caused.

But the Home Galaxy was a statistical freak. Unlike other galaxies it had never endured a major collision with a body of similar size. There were various possibilities— it was one of the largest in the observable Universe, and it resided in an area with an anomalously low density of dark matter—but whatever the explanation, it was an outlier at the far end of the distribution of possible evolutionary paths, and therefore so too was life. It was likely that only the stars of the Home Galaxy had planetary systems stable enough for life to have evolved—it took a billion years for simple unicellular forms to develop, four and a half billion years for humans—for otherwise other civilizations would have surely arisen in the unbounded Universe, and traces of their existence would have been detected.

Angel concluded that humanity, in all its swarming vigor and diversity, was alone. It must make of itself what it could, for there was nothing against which it could measure itself. There were no aliens to conquer, no wise, ancient beings from which to learn deep secrets hidden in the beginnings of time and space.

Angel did not consider that she might be wrong. She killed herself, was reborn, and killed herself again as soon as she learned what her previous self had discovered. When she woke again, with part of her memory suppressed by the ship, more than two million years had passed. The ship was in trailing orbit beyond a huge construction that orbited a star one hundred and fifty thousand light-years beyond the spiral arms of the Home Galaxy, close to the accretion disc of a vast black hole where the Large Magellanic Cloud had once been.

The ship showed her what it had observed as it had traversed the long geodesic between the two galaxies. At first there was an intense point of light within the heart of the Large Magellanic Cloud. It might have been a supernova, except that it was a thousand times larger than any supernova ever recorded. The glare of this one dying star obscured the light of its millions of companions for a long time, and when at last it faded all of the remaining stars were streaming around the point where it had been. Those stars nearest the center elongated and dissipated, spilling their fusing hearts across the sky, and more and more stars crowded in until nothing was left but the gas clouds of the accretion disc, glowing by red-shifted Cerenkov radiation, all that was left of material falling into the event horizon of the central black hole—a black hole that massed a million suns.

The ship had searched the Home Galaxy for sources of coherent electromagnetic radiation and had found nothing except for a scattering of ancient neutrino beacons. Apart from these, signals in the Home Galaxy had ceased while the ship was still half a million light-years out—the time when the first supernova had flared in the Large Magellanic Cloud. There had been a great deal of activity around the

Large Magellanic Cloud while the black hole grew, but at last, a hundred thousand light-years out, that too had ceased.

Angel beat the ship to its conclusion. Humanity, or whatever humanity had become in the four and a half million years since she had fled the crusade, had created the black hole and vanished into it. The ship spoke of the possibility that humanity had developed wormhole technology—it had located a number of double occultations within the Home Galaxy that were typical of the theoretical effect of a wormhole exit passing between a star and an observer. The ship had also spotted a concentrated cluster of occultation events around a halo star more than ten thousand light-years beyond the accretion disc of the giant black hole. The ship told Angel that it had changed course—a maneuver that had taken a thousand years—and that it had built up a detailed map of the space around the star. Angel studied the map. There were more than a hundred wormhole entrances orbiting the star, and there was also an artefact as big as a world, if the surface of a world might be peeled from its globe and stretched out into a long plane. The ship had built arrays of detectors. It had obtained the infrared signatures of water and molecular oxygen, and estimated the average temperature of the surface of the artefact to be two hundred and ninety-three degrees above absolute zero. It had detected the absorption signatures of several classes of photosynthetic pigments, most notably rhodopsin and chlorophyll.

Angel beat the ship to its second conclusion. There was life on the surface of the artefact.

—

In the night, Pandaras settled a blanket around Yama's shoulders. Yama did not notice. Beetles smashed at the lantern above his head as he read on.

—

The artefact was a stout needle twenty thousand kilometers long and less than a thousand wide, with a deep keel beneath its terraformed surface. It hung in a spherical envelope of air and embedded gravity fields. It tilted back and forth on its long axis once every twenty-four hours and took just over three hundred and sixty-five days to complete a single orbit of its ordinary yellow dwarf star. These parameters struck a deep chord in Angel, whose original had been born in the planetary system where humanity had evolved. For the first time in millions of years she called up the personality fragment which retained memories of the earliest part of her long history. She muttered a little mantra over and over as she studied the data the ship had gathered: twenty-four hours, three hundred and sixty-five days, thirty-two meters per second squared, twenty percent oxygen, eighty percent nitrogen.

The orbit of the artefact was slightly irregular; there would be seasons on its surface. One side was bounded by mountains fifty kilometers high. Their naked peaks rose out of the atmospheric envelope. On the other side, a great river ran half the length, rising in mountains three-quarters buried in ice at the trailing end of this strange world and falling over the edge at the midpoint. It was not clear how the water was recycled. The ship made neutrino and deep radar scans and discovered a vast warren of caverns and corridors and shafts within the rocky keel of the artefact, but no system of aquifers or canals.

One half of the world, beyond the fall of the river, was dry cratered desert with a dusty icecap at the leading end and a scattering of ruined cities. The other half was verdant land bounded on one side by the river and on the other by ice-capped ranges of mountains which were mere foothills to the gigantic peaks at the edge. There were cities strung like beads along the river, and every city, except the largest, was inhabited by a different race of humanlike creatures. The ship sent out thousands of tiny probes. Many were destroyed by the machines which roamed everywhere on the surface of the artefact, but the survivors returned with cellular samples of thousands of different organisms. Less than one-tenth of the plants and animals were from lineages that originated in the human home star system; the rest were of unknown and multiple origins. None of the inhabitants were of human descent, the ship said, and except for a few primitive races they all had an artificial homeobox inserted within their genetic material.

The ship could not explain what the homeobox sequence coded for. It could not explain why there were thousands of different, seemingly sapient, alien races crowded together on the surface of a single world-sized habitat. Nor could it explain why the physical appearance of almost all of these races mapped to at least eighty percent of the human norm—a much closer conformation than those of many of Angel's lineages, in the days of her lost empire.

Angel ordered the ship to match the orbit of the artefact. It refused, and her partials argued that the artefact was an anomaly and they had a better chance of understanding what had happened to humanity by exploring the Home Galaxy. Angel overrode them, and in the process discovered the data the ship had hidden from her. She learned all over again that there was unlikely to be life anywhere else in the local group of galaxies, and perhaps in the entire Universe.

This time she did not kill herself.

There was a huge city near the source of the long river. It was clearly the capital of this artificial world, ancient and extensive and swarming with a hundred different kinds of humanlike creature. The ship landed at the docks and Angel and her crew of partials began their exploration.

There was a capital city but no obvious unified system of government; there was a palace, but no rulers. There were millions of bureaucrats organized into a hundred or more different departments, but most of them appeared to be engaged in maintaining records rather than determining or carrying out policy. Indeed, there seemed to be no central or permanent government. Order was maintained by undiscussed consent, enforced by roaming gangs of magistrates who appeared to be answerable to no one but themselves, their powers limited only by strict adherence to custom.

It seemed that there had been rulers long ago, before a war fought between two factions of the machines which mingled with the people (some of the machines had tried to investigate the ship, and it destroyed the machines, and would have destroyed more except that Angel ordered it to stop). The war had scorched one half of the world to desert, and the ship said that it was possible that the sparse cloud of machines which trailed the orbital path of the artefact were survivors belonging to the losing side. The people of the capital city told Angel that after the war many of the avatars of the Preservers had fallen silent and many of the shrines had died. The Hierarchs, who appeared to have interceded between the avatars and the people, had vanished shortly after the end of the war; the surviving avatars were consulted only under the direction of priests. The ship told Angel that the shrines were clearly some kind of information processing system, but most were inactivated, and those still active were functionally compromised.

"The Preservers watch all," she was told by everyone she asked. They were the invisible power by which the illusion of order was maintained. It was like a theocracy, except that the priests and hierodules of the multitude of temples claimed no special power or privileges. All served the ideal of the Preservers.

Angel went everywhere, for there was no one who seemed to want to stop her, and she asked every kind of question, because there seemed to be no taboos. She found that the people of the capital city, Ys, were eager to help, and she began to suspect what the inserted homeobox coded for. The inhabitants of this strange world were better servants than her partials; they would lay down their lives if asked.

Angel used them to help her escape.

She did not plan it. If she had, no doubt her ship and its crew of partials would have stopped her. She did it on a whim, an impulse.

She was walking by the docks, followed by the usual crowd of curious people and a small group of the law keepers—magistrates—and their machines. The sun was high. Its diamond light sparkled on the wide sweep of the river. The city stretched away under a haze of smoke that hid the foothills of the mountains beyond, so that their snowcapped peaks seemed to float in the blue distance. The dock road was lined by trees in blossom: big red flowers attended by clouds of sulphur-yellow butterflies. Vendors stood at their carts or stalls in the sun-speckled shade of the trees, crying their wares. White birds wheeled over sunstruck water or strutted and pecked on wrinkled mudflats beneath the stone walls of the quays. Small clinker-built dinghies lay on their sides on the wet mud. Further out, larger boats bobbed at buoys and floating docks; sails dotted the wide, wide river. Closer to shore, men sat in small boats, fishing with the help of black long-necked birds very like cormorants; hundreds of men crowded stone steps at the water's edge, washing themselves in the river's brown water while children swam and splashed and shrieked with laughter; men sat cross-legged as they mended fine mesh nets stretched across wide frames; women gutted silver fish under a canopy of green banana leaves, surrounded by noisy flocks of birds that fought for fish guts tossed over the edge of the quay; a small machine moved at the water's edge in quick bursts, like a squeezed pip of mercury.

An ache rose in Angel, a universal desolation. Lost, all lost. All she had known was lost, and yet all around were echoes of what she had lost. For the first time since she had been reborn, she felt the weight of her age.

The people who were following her were not human. They were aliens. She was surrounded by aliens which distorted the human norm, by pigmen, lionmen, lizardmen, birdmen, toadmen and others she could not begin to identify. They were animals trying to be human; they were humans masked with animal faces. They called themselves the Shaped, and said that they had been changed, two words with the same root but subtly different meanings she did not quite understand.

Angel had lost so much, and so much surrounded her, rich and strange, yet hauntingly familiar. The birds and the butterflies, the wet fetid smell of the mud, the smells of hot stone and cooking oil and the acrid smoke from fires fueled with dry dung, the sunlight on the water and the wind that stirred the glossy leaves and the red flowers of the trees: a thousand fragmentary impressions that defined from moment to moment the unquantifiable richness of the quiddity of the world. Many of the transcendents had disappeared into imaginary empires within vast data banks, creating perfect images of known worlds or building impossible new ones, but Angel had always felt that these were less satisfactory than dreams, too perfect to be truly real. That was why she had opted for nonbeing during the long transits of her voyage, rather than slowtime in a fabrication.

Reality, or nothing.

Angel took a ship out from the city. It was that easy. The ship's captain was a fat, solemn, ponderous man with sleek black skin and small eyes; his mother or grandmother might have been a seal, or might have lain with one. He did not question Angel's presence as they sailed downriver from city to city, but deferred to her with quiet good humor. The fact that she had hijacked his ship and his life was never raised. A city of tombs; a city of porcelain; a city of caves in cliffs high above the river; a city of trees; a city built on stilts in the middle of the river. Dozens of cities, each inhabited by a different race of people, all sharing the same unquestioned laws and religion.

And then a city at war with itself.

A Change War, the ship's captain said, and when Angel told him to put in at the city's long waterfront he came close to disobeying her for the first time. It was a city of square houses of red mudbrick, all heaped on each other like a tumbled pile of boxes. A terraced ziggurat of white, weather-worn stone stood in the middle of the forest outside the city wall, guarded by machines that constantly looped through the air above it. It was the home of an old woman who called herself the Commissioner.

Angel sat with the Commissioner on a high terrace of

the ancient ziggurat, amongst potted lemon trees and geraniums. Riverward, across a sea of treetops, part of the city was burning. The sound of distant rifle fire popped and crackled, brought erratically by the warm wind. The Commissioner served Angel a bowl of the earthy infusion of twigs which people everywhere on this world called tea. The Commissioner was half Angel's height, a slow, deliberate woman with a humped back and a round face with lips pursed like a beak, and small black eyes half-hidden amongst the wrinkles of her leathery skin. She wore a kind of tent of fustian which dropped in many folds from a gold circlet at her neck to puddle the floor. A small machine darted and hovered above her like a bejeweled dragonfly.

The Commissioner seemed to regard the war as an unfortunate but inevitable natural process which could not be prevented but must be endured, like a sudden hailstorm or a forest fire. She told Angel that some of the people of the city had changed, and were at war with those who had not.

"The changed ones will win, of course. They always do. And then they will move on and found a new city, or more likely scatter along the river. It is an exciting time for them."

It took Angel a long time to find out from the Commissioner what she meant by change. It was a kind of transcendence or epiphany, a realization of individual worth, the possibility of sin or at least of transgression against the fixed codes by which the citizens had ordered their lives for millennia. It was a little like the memes with which Angel had once experimented when attempting to unify her spreading empire, but it was also a physical infection, a change in brain structure and chemistry which provided, as far as Angel understood it, an area of high density information storage that somehow interacted with the nine infolded dimensions in the quantum foam at the bottom of reality. Everything anyone of the changed races or bloodlines did or experienced was recorded or remembered by something like a soul that would survive until the end of the Universe. It was the true immortality which Angel and her kind had dreamed of millions of years ago, when they had still been human.

The Commissioner explained that the most primitive races, the indigens, would never change, but all others had changed or would change—there were still hundreds of unchanged races. Some had gone beyond the first change and transcended the world entirely, but the Commissioner could not tell Angel where they had gone. It was the work of the Preservers, and therefore not to be questioned. It simply was.

Angel wondered what happened to those of the unchanged and indigenous races who died (she was wondering about herself). The Commissioner grew reflective. It was night, now. The burning waterfront of the city stood above its own reflection in the still water of its long harbor. There were skirmishes in the fields and orchards upriver of the city—the flashes of rifles defined the opposing positions, and once there was a tremendous explosion that sent an expanding ball of red and yellow flame into the air and shook the terrace, rattling the bowls of tea on the slab of polished rock that floated between the two women.

"It is a question for the archivists," the Commissioner said at last. "But they are busy at the moment, talking with the wounded, and I do hope you will not disturb them. Because of the war, so many lives will pass unremarked—that is the cost of change, and it is a heavy price to pay. But some say that the Preservers mark all, and all will be restored whether we record it or not."

Angel thought of the millions of clerks laboring in the great palace of the capital city. She said, "Recording the world is important. Why is that?"

The Commissioner was watching the distant fighting. The fires, the stuttering flashes of rifles, the red blossoms of a cannonade, the abrupt fountains of earth and fire: at a distance, war is often beautiful. Firelight gleamed in her round, black eyes. She said, "It is one of the highest tasks."

"Recording memories for the Preservers to use?"

"The Preservers will resurrect everyone at the end of time. We will all live again."

This is an experiment, Angel thought. An experiment that records its own self. Things have been set in motion; evolution is expected. That means I can change things here. If the Preservers are using these people, then so can I.

She said, "If you could gain much in this life by behaving badly, and still the Preservers would resurrect you, then perhaps it is worth behaving badly. You could have power and wealth now, everything that you are promised in eternity, and the Preservers would forgive you."

The Commissioner considered this for a while. Angel watched the dark city beyond the forest. There were small fires scattered around the dimming glow of the site of the big explosion; the rifle fire seemed to have stopped.

At last, the Commissioner said, "All possible worlds can be created by the Preservers at the end of time, and that means not only all possible good, but also all possible evil. But the Preservers will not permit evil because it contradicts the love they bear toward us. For if they did not love us, why did they lift us up? So we must live our lives as best we can, for otherwise we might not have anything to live for beyond this life. Some say that the Preservers can correct evil in any person. No matter how great that evil might be, the Preservers have all of time and all of space in which to work their will. They say that the willingness of the Preservers to resurrect an evil person and punish them while holding out the possibility of redemption demonstrates the depth of their love toward us, their imperfect creations. But even if this is true, it is better to do good, for in the presence of infinite good it is better for you to act well and help others than to harm them, for you will gain nothing more by acting badly." The Commissioner laughed. "Ah, besides that, to think of the shame of having to endure the forgiveness of the Preservers! It is a heavy burden. Few could bear it."

Angel said, "Those who are changed are acting badly now."

"Only because their unchanged brothers, who know no other way of life, are fighting them. The unchanged cannot imagine change, and so they fight it to the death, and those who have changed must defend themselves. The unchanged do not know good or evil because they cannot choose between them. They are what they are, and no more."

"Yet you know the difference, and you do not intercede. You could remove the changed and stop the war. You condemn many to death by inaction. Is that not evil?"

"No one should set themselves in the place of the Preservers," the Commissioner said, staring at Angel. For the first time, she seemed to be offended.

Angel knew better than to insult the Preservers. They were universally worshipped, but no one could tell her much about them. Only that they had withdrawn their grace from the world but would return at the end of time and resurrect everyone who had ever lived, and everyone would live forever in an infinity of perfect worlds. It was a creed that was not dissimilar to the ambitions of the transcendents, but everyone on Confluence believed that the Preservers were capable of realizing it. At the same time, everyone believed that the ultimate nature of the Preservers was unknowable. What little that could be understood about them was in the Puranas, but the Puranas, which formed a kind of moral handbook illustrated by lessons in cosmology and galactic history, were maddeningly vague and imprecise. Early on, Angel had asked the ship to give her a précis of the Puranas, and recognized her own empire in a brief half sentence that horribly distorted what she had tried to do. That was another thing which must be put right. Her empire had once been the largest in human history, perhaps the largest empire ever known. She had not yet decided what she would do, but she would make sure that her long-lost empire was given its proper recognition.

"I'll stay here tonight," Angel said. "I assume this is a safe place. Find me food and a bed. I'll leave tomorrow."

"Of course." The Commissioner clacked her horny lips together and added, "However, I do believe that your ship has already left."

It was true. While Angel had been talking with the Commissioner, the ship she had commandeered at Ys had escaped her geas and made off. But the next day Angel simply commandeered another and continued downriver. The new ship was much larger than the first. Its three masts bore square sails with sunbursts painted on them and its deep holds were full of fruit which had been bound for a city upriver. The fruit rotted after a week and Angel ordered it thrown over the side. It took the crew, including the officers and the captain, a whole day to empty the holds, but the ship rode high in the water afterward, and sailed more swiftly. The captain said that the ship should be ballasted with stones, for otherwise it was likely to capsize in a storm, but Angel ignored him. She was in a hurry now.

She passed city after city, mostly inhabited by unchanged races as fixed in their habits as ants or bees. Without free will, they were more like zombies or organic machines than people, but even so, their unremarkable lives were recorded by patient archivists. They were policed by magistrates of their own kind. Although one or two officials of one or another of the changed races were present, they merely provided a kind of moral authority that was called on only when needed.

The last of the cities of the long, long river was called Sensch. It was a desert city of narrow streets shaded by palms and ginkgoes, dusty squares, flat-roofed buildings of whitewashed mudbrick. There were extensive plantations of sago and date palms, orange and pomegranate and banana, and various kinds of groundnuts. There was a great deal of camel breeding, too. At least, the things were a little like camels.

The citizens of Sensch were a slender people, skilled in pottery and glassmaking. They had low, heavily ridged foreheads and small, lidless black eyes; their brown and black skins exhibited varying degrees of residual scaliness. Snakes, the Commissioner of Sensch called them. He was a small, active fellow who lived in a garden that floated above the pink sandstone palace that was his official residence. The Commissioner, Dreen, seemed anxious to please, but Angel did not press her needs at once.

She met the Archivist of Sensch, a corpulent fellow with a limp, a few days later. His name was Mr. Naryan. He was of the same race as the captain of the first ship Angel had commandeered; she had seen him swimming off the wide plaza by the river, as graceful in the water as he was awkward and slow on land. He sat down beside Angel in a tea shop by one of the city's camel markets, pretending at first not to realize who she was. Angel liked his sly, patient air and demanded nothing of him at all, not even that he accept her for what she was. She missed conversation amongst equals.

The Archivist was afraid of Angel, but he hid it well. He made small talk about a procession that went past, explaining that the people had had their reason taken away, either as punishment or because of what he called a religious avocation. He said that he understood that she had come a long way, and she laughed at the understatement.

The Archivist said with mild alarm, "I do not mean to insult you."

Angel tried to make it easier by talking about the Archivist himself. She pointed at his loose, belted shirt and said, "You dress like a . . . native." She had almost said Snake. She said, "Is that a religious avocation?"

He told her what she already knew, that he was the city's archivist. He had a round, kindly face, with heavy wrinkles at his brow and three fat folds under his chin.

Angel said, "The people here are different—a different race in every city. When I left, not a single intelligent alien species was known. It was one reason for my voyage. Now there seem to be thousands strung along this long river. They treat me like a ruler—is that it? Or am I like a god?"

"The Preservers departed long ago. These are the end times."

The Archivist said this by rote. He had not really understood her questions.

Angel said, "There are always those who believe they live at the end of history. We thought that we lived at the end of history, when every star system in the Galaxy had been mapped, every habitable world settled.

"I was told that the Preservers, who I suppose are my descendants, made the different races, but each race calls itself human, even the ones who don't look as if they could have evolved from anything that ever looked remotely human."

"The Shaped call themselves human because they have no other name for what they have become, changed and unchanged alike. After all, they had no name before they were raised up." The Archivist added in a pleading tone, "The citizens of Sensch remain innocent. They are our . . . responsibility."

Angel told him that his kind was not doing a very good job, judging by the Change War she had witnessed upriver. She described the war, and asked the Archivist many questions, most of which he was unable to answer. Without asking her permission, he jotted down her description of the Change War and her questions on a tablet using an impacted system of diacritical marks. Angel was amused.

"You listen to people's stories."

"Stories are important. In the end they are all that is left, all that history leaves us. Stories endure."

Angel thought about this. She said at last, "I have been out of history a long time. I'm not sure that I want to be a part of it again."

She was tired. While she had been traveling, she had been able to forget that she had escaped her ship and her responsibilities, but now she would have to come to a decision. She did not want to talk anymore and left the Archivist. He knew better than to follow her, and she liked him for that, too.

She found a suitable house, a two-story affair with a

balcony around the upper story overlooking a central courtyard shaded by a jacaranda tree. Its owners, grateful for her attention, were only too pleased to give it to her, and others came with gifts: furniture, carpets, food and wine, musical instruments, cigarettes, paintings, sheets of plastic she realized were books, slates which showed scenes from the world's past, stolen from tombs of hierophants far downriver.

Some of the people stayed with her, mostly young men. Angel experimented with sex. Full intercourse with the Snakes was anatomically impossible, but there were a variety of pleasing and diverting exercises. In the evenings, she watched dancers or shadow puppet plays, or listened to the atonal nasal singing of the finest poet of the city, accompanied by a silver flute and a two-string lyre. The days passed pleasantly until the Archivist found her in the teahouse by the camel market and told her that her ship was coming to Sensch.

Angel affected a casualness she did not feel. She had expected it to find her, but not so quickly. She fell into conversation with the Archivist and eventually took him back to her house. He took in the bustle with a solemn air and told her gently that she should not take advantage of the citizens.

Angel said sharply, "They seem happy to me. What's wrong with that?"

The Archivist cast his eyes down. She knew then that he could not argue with her, and felt a stab of shame.

She had tea and honey fritters brought out, and described something of what she had seen on her long river journey, and asked the Archivist many questions about Dreen's authority and the way that order was maintained in the city. She caught one of the machines and showed it to him. "And these? By what authority do these little spies operate?"

The Archivist stared at it opened-mouthed. Perhaps he had never seen anyone catch one before. Pinched between Angel's thumb and forefinger, the little bronze bug wriggled as it tried to free itself. Its sensor cluster, a froth of glass and silver beads, turned back and forth until Angel let it go.

The Archivist watched it rise above the roof of the house. He said, "Why, they are part of the maintenance system of Confluence."

"Can Dreen use them? Tell me all you know. It may be important."

Angel met with the Archivist at intervals in the days that followed. The young men who followed her formed a kind of band or gang, and some went with her wherever she went. They made the Archivist nervous, but Angel encouraged them, if only because it was a measure of what she could do. She gave them white headbands lettered with a slogan she had composed. Giving away one of the headbands was like bestowing a blessing. She made speeches in the markets and on the plaza by the river to try and rouse the citizens, but although people gathered and listened politely, nothing much came of it, except that her own followers sometimes grew too excited. They were apt to misunderstand what she had to say about rising above destiny, and defaced walls with slogans, or overturned stalls in the market. They were gripped by powerful but unfocused emotions.

Perhaps these petty acts were to her followers heady and radical statements, but Angel knew that it was not the way. She went to the temple and had one of the priests help her consult the interactive librarian which manifested in one of the large terminals the priests called shrines. She decided that she would cross the river to where a cluster of old shrines stood, unused since the Snakes had come to occupy Sensch. She would try and wake the shrines there, and learn from them.

~

Then there was a blank picture. Whatever Angel had done at the shrines at the edge of the world, by the great falls at the end of the river, was not recorded. Yama set his book aside. He was very tired, but not at all sleepy.

It was a few hours from dawn. The smoky swirl of the Eye of the Preservers was setting at the edge of the world. Tamora and Pandaras slept under the awning. Captain Lorquital and Aguilar slept in their cabins beneath the poop deck; the sailors slept head to toe in their hammocks beneath the deck on which Yama sat. He had always needed less sleep than Telmon or anyone else he knew, and was used to being awake when everyone else slept. Even so, and even though he was not strictly alone, for the helmsman stood at the wheel in the red glow of the shaded stern lantern, Yama felt a desolation, a vast aching emptiness, there on the ship in the midst of the wide river. He wondered if this was how Angel had felt, estranged from all she knew by millions of years of history, with only compliant uncomprehending aliens for company. How lonely she must have been, ruler of all the world, but with no purpose!

He would finish her story in a little while, he thought. He already suspected that he knew how it ended. Enough for now. First his father's papers, and the shock they contained amongst their dense ladders of calculations. And now this. No more stories.

Yama shook dew from the blanket Pandaras had put around his shoulders and lay down, just for a moment. And slept.

"IT IS A city that shines like the ice flows of the mountains at the end of the world," Eliphas told Yama. "I last saw it many years ago, but I still remember how it shone in the sunlight across the blue waters of the river. The river may be shrinking, brother, but it runs deeper here than anywhere else in the world, deeper even than at Ys. They fish for leviathans off the shore of Gond."

Yama flinched, remembering the one solid fact he had gleaned from the muddle of his stepfather's papers. Eliphas did not notice. He was lost in his memories.

"They fish not from coracles or cockleshells," the old man said, "but from barges as big as fields, with big motors that make the water boil around their sterns when they are working. There are leviathans deep beneath our keel, and that's what these barges are after. They send down lures as tall as a man and armed with explosive hooks, using steel cables several leagues long. If they strike lucky, they haul up their catch and render it there and then. Of course, most of the time the leviathan escapes, and sometimes, despite its power, a barge is dragged under by what it catches."

"I thought that the people of Gond led aesthetic and contemplative lives," Yama said.

"The fishermen come from the cities of the Dry Plains, further downriver. From Ush and Kalyb and Galata, and the twin cities of Kilminar and Balbeck." Eliphas intoned the names with sonorous pleasure. "If a barge catches more than one leviathan in the hunting season its crew count themselves lucky. The proceeds from rendering one monster would buy a ship like this twice over."

Yama and Eliphas were leaning side by side at the rail of the main deck of the *Weazel,* in the shadow of the big, rust-red sail. Sternward, smoky columns of rain twisted beneath the reefs of white and gray clouds that overshadowed the farside shore—a desolation of mudflats and pioneer mangroves inhabited only by birds and swarms of army crabs. There had been no sign of either the warship or the picketboat in the past three days, and the *Weazel* was at last angling away from the farside and the spurious safety of the mangrove swamps. Ahead, in the far distance, the Great River bent toward the Rim Mountains, and at the angle of the nearside shore a mote of light glistened, white as a crystal of salt: the city of Gond. Captain Lorquital had announced that the *Weazel* would put in there to collect a passenger and to take on fresh provisions.

Yama told Eliphas, "I see that you are happy to retrace the steps you took when you were a young man."

Eliphas closed his eyes. His face was shaded by the wide brim of the straw hat he wore as protection from the sun. "It has been more than a hundred years. I thought I had forgotten most of it, but each place we pass brings memories rising from the depths of my mind, as the monsters of the abyssal currents of the river rise to follow the glowing lures trailed by the fishing barges."

He opened his eyes and smiled: silver and white flashed in his black face. "Do not worry, brother. I will fulfill the promise I made to you in the library of the Department of Apothecaries and Chirurgeons. I will find the lost city for you. I know that your servants are suspicious of me, but I have your best interests at heart."

"They are not my servants, Eliphas."

Eliphas smiled. "They believe otherwise, brother. Look there! A pod of grampuses! See how they sport!"

Three, four, five sleek white creatures swam swiftly through the clear water, effortlessly overtaking the speeding ship. They caught up with the purling bow-wave and rode it briefly, plunging and leaping in white foam, then all at once they sounded, pale shadows dwindling away into the dark depths of the river.

Eliphas said, "Some believe they are intelligent, and that they herd the fish of the river as the autochthons of the mountains herds sheep or goats."

"When you are swimming in the river, you can sometimes hear them singing," Yama said. He had often heard their songs himself, for in summer schools of grampuses migrated far upriver. Songs that lasted for hours, deep throbbings overlaid with scatterings of chirps and whistles, haunting, mysterious and somehow lonely, as if defining the inhuman vastness of the Great River.

"They say that the Preservers placed everything on this world for a purpose," Eliphas said, "and the ultimate purpose is to raise up all the Shaped so that we may live forever in their glory. But I sometimes wonder if the Preservers brought creatures like the grampuses to the world simply because of the joy they strike in the hearts of men. If that is true, I can forgive them much."

Yama remembered that the woman in the shrine, Angel's aspect, had said that the Preservers were descended from her own people. He said, "I think that the Preservers were once not so different from us. The first suras of the Puranas tell us that in times long past there were no gods, but only many kinds of humans."

"There is no gradation in godhood," Eliphas said. "It is not like the process of aging, which is so gradual that only by looking back are you shocked by how much you have changed, for you have no sense of having changed at all. And of course, from day to day you have not changed in any measurable sense. No, brother, the Preservers changed utterly and at once, and so what they were before they became gods is irrelevant. When godhood descended upon them, or when they ascended to godhood, everything they had been fell away.''

''And yet they made us over in their image. Not as what they became, but as what they once were. And so they did not leave their past behind.''

Eliphas nodded gravely. The old man loved metaphysical discourse. He was one of those for whom the world is merely an object from which theoretical ideals might be abstracted, and therefore less important than thought.

''The Preservers have not forgotten what they once were,'' he said, ''but they put it behind them, as a butterfly puts behind its caterpillar childhood when it emerges from its cocoon. The Puranas are perhaps that cocoon, which we riddle for clues. Yet it is only an empty shell left clinging to the twig of the world. That which matters has ascended into everlasting sunlight.''

Yama smiled at the old man's fanciful metaphor. He enjoyed these conversations; they reminded him of the long debates with Zakiel and Telmon, of happier times. He said, ''You have seen me read in the Puranas. It is not to understand the Preservers. It is to understand myself.''

''I believe that your copy of the Puranas is a very old one.''

Yama knew that Eliphas wanted to examine the book, but he had decided that he would not show the transformed pictures to anyone. Not, at least, until he had understood Angel's story. He would read more tonight. He thought that he already knew how it ended—but perhaps it had not ended after all. Perhaps he was part of that story, coming late onto the stage to draw the curtain and announce the end of the play.

Eliphas said, ''Books are more powerful than the world. Even if the world ended, then surely someone would chronicle it. And so that book would save the world, for it would live again in the minds of any who read the account.''

''I spent much of my childhood in a library. Perhaps too much of it was spent studying the past. I want to see the world, Eliphas, and all its wonders. I want the present, not the past.''

''But the past is all around us. We cannot escape it. Everything important has happened in the past, and we are its children. The Preservers achieved godhood in the past and made the world in the past and shaped the blood-lines in the past. The future is a small thing and hazily glimpsed, and we are told that once every bloodline has changed the future will cease, for history will cease. But you are right, brother. Children should look ahead, not behind. We cannot live in the past, or else the future will only echo what has already happened.''

So they talked as the ship, sailing aslant the river's currents, drew closer to the shining city of Gond. Eliphas preferred his own opinions to those of anyone else, but Yama was grateful for the diversion of his company.

He could not grieve for his stepfather, not yet. He could not give way to grief or anger. He must stay calm and alert, for sooner or later he would have to face Prefect Corin again. He did not believe that he had escaped. Prefect Corin was a thorough man. He would not have been fooled for long by Yama's ruse, and would have returned to the floating forest to search for remains of his quarry. Finding none, he would have gone on downriver, implacable, relentless. This was not mere supposition: Yama had already turned aside several machines that were searching the wide river for any trace of the *Weazel*. So he was not surprised when, that evening, as the *Weazel* scudded ahead of a light breeze toward the floating harbor that stood off the shore of Gond, Captain Lorquital called him up to the quarterdeck.

Aguilar and Tamora stood on either side of Captain Lorquital's sling chair. Aguilar told Yama, ''Your trick with the machines has run aground. The devil has got ahead of us.''

''We'll have to face him now,'' Tamora said, and her black lips peeled back from her teeth at the thought.

Ixchel Lorquital handed Yama her spectacles without comment. Through their magnifying lenses, the floating harbor leapt closer. There were ships of every size laid up at the leagues of pontoons and cranes and warehouses of the docks; their masts made a leafless forest. And in the channels beyond the floating harbor, a picketboat and a triple-decked warship were anchored side by side, their sails half-reefed.

"Well," Yama said, "we could not hope to hide from him forever."

"There was a light signal from the harbor," Captain Lorquital said. "We are to pick up our passenger tonight. He's an important man, and we can leave tomorrow morning under his protection, like any other honest vessel."

"We can't depend on that," Aguilar said, and told Yama, "Your devil will be watching the river night and day, but I think we'll have a better chance if we run at night."

Tamora said, "We might surprise him."

"I saw a machine today," Captain Lorquital said. "It was making directly for us when it suddenly angled away, as if it remembered business it had elsewhere."

"I cannot confuse the minds of men," Yama said, "and Aguilar is right. Prefect Corin's men will be watching every ship that passes by. Especially those few that pass by at night."

"We have lost our cannon," Aguilar said. "We have only our small arms. If it comes to a fight, we must surprise them."

"We must strike first," Tamora said.

"We have made plans," Aguilar said. "Barrels of pitch. A catapult—"

Captain Lorquital said, "I won't be a pirate, daughter. They must fire the first shot."

"And that one shot could sink us," Aguilar said.

Yama said, "It is better to know where our enemy is than to run with the thought that he is always somewhere behind us. Besides, he will have no warrant or power here. He is merely another sailor put in for shore leave and reprovisioning. If he tries to hurt us, the common law will protect us."

"The people of Gond care little for anything but their philosophies," Aguilar said. "They'll probably turn us over to that town burner rather than interrupt their meditations to listen to us plead our case.''

"She's right," Tamora said. "We must take matters into our own hands.''

"Then we'll be worse than them," Captain Lorquital said firmly. "This is an end to the argument. We'll behave as any normal ship. The free men will get their shore leave, and you, daughter, will stand guard with the slaves. Nothing will happen to us at the harbor, and once our passenger is aboard, we'll have his protection.''

Afterward, Tamora followed Yama to the bow. "You are planning something," she said. "I know you don't believe that crut about common law.''

"I want to kill him," Yama said.

Tamora grinned hugely. "That's more like it. How? And how can I help?''

"I want to kill him, but I do not think that I should.''

"Then he will kill you.''

"Yes, he will, if he cannot make me serve him.''

"He destroyed your home, Yama. He killed your father as surely as if he had put an arbalest bolt through his heart. He is your enemy. There is nothing sweeter than drinking the blood of your enemy. Don't deny yourself the pleasure.''

"He is only one man. How many more will the Department send after me? How many more would I have to kill? If I kill Prefect Corin there will never be an end to killing. I will always be hunted. But if I can find a way to end this, then I will be free.''

Tamora thought about this. "We'll try your way," she said at last. "And if that doesn't work, give him to me. He is as much my enemy as yours. I'll rip his heart from his chest and eat it in front of his dying eyes.''

She smiled fiercely at the thought, but Yama knew that she shared his foreboding.

—

A fishing barge was anchored upstream of the floating harbor, the enormous carcass of a leviathan sprawled across its wide flat deck. Already partly defleshed, the arches of the leviathan's ribcage rose higher than the barge's cranes. Its guts, tinged pink with the plankton on which it had fed, spilled in heavy loops from a rent that would have admitted the *Weazel,* mast and all. A line of men was strung across the wide flat tail of the carcass, like harvesters working across a field. They were using huge flensing knives to cut the hide away from the blubber beneath. Black smoke poured from the barge's rendering furnaces, sending up a stink of burning fat and hazing the last light of the sun. Flocks of birds dipped and rose like whirling snowstorms, fighting for titbits in the bloody waters.

As the *Weazel* glided through the lee of the barge, Yama watched the city of Gond slip past to starboard. It had once risen out of the river; now, it looked like the last tooth of an old man, its roots exposed beyond a labyrinth of mudflats. Gond, the porcelain city. A clutch of luminous white shells three leagues across, rising and falling in rounded contours like a range of ancient dunes, tinged with rose and silver and gold. Here and there were clusters of slim towers, their tops ringed round by tiers of balconies. Floating gardens hovered along the river margin, their parks and woods strung with thousands of lamps.

Eliphas climbed onto the forecastle deck. "There are probably not more than a hundred living there now," he said. "Mostly, it is maintained by machines."

"Yet they once ruled Ys," Yama said.

He had once read a brief history of the porcelain city, and remembered that it had grown from a single seed planted in the sand of a beach at the first bend in the Great River. He wondered if that beach was still there, beneath the carapace of the city—the past preserved forever in the present. But no strangers were allowed into Gond. Its beauty was also its shield. Its people were great philosophers and teachers, but they did their work in colleges scattered amongst the orchards and fields and paddies that surrounded the city. From the first, the city had drawn a circle around itself.

"They ruled Ys a long time ago," Eliphas said, "in the grim days after the Hierarchs vanished, but before the civil service reached its present consensus. They are much diminished, yet still much exulted. If any who live in these days are close to the Preservers, then the people of Gond are the closest. They are so holy that they no longer have children. Their bloodline dwindles. The youngest is a century older than me, and I am counted as long-lived by my bloodline. Their holiness will be the death of them, soon enough. The past has consumed them, brother. The face of the city is more beautiful than I remembered, but it is the beauty of a well-kept tomb."

As the *Weazel* made her way toward the harbor under the power of her reaction motor, her sail neatly reefed, a small boat motored out to meet her. A pilot came aboard and formally greeted Captain Lorquital, then asked to see the boy, Yama.

"We have two ships under command of an official of the Department of Indigenous Affairs," the pilot told Yama. "Perhaps you know him."

"His name is Corin. He is a Prefect of the Department."

The pilot was a small man, smaller even than Pandaras, but he had the brisk, assured air of someone used to command. He wore immaculately polished black boots and loose linen trousers under a scarlet djellaba, and was smoking a black cigarillo. He blew a riffle of smoke with a flourish and looked at Yama squarely. "Whatever business you have with him, it is nothing to do with the harbor. We have become a staging post for the war, but we are not under the command of the Department of Indigenous Affairs."

"I understand."

"You will not take weapons if you go ashore. Neither will he, nor will his men. All go unarmed here."

"You put it very plainly," Yama said. "I hope that I may speak plainly, too. This man wants to make me his prisoner. Because of that, Captain Lorquital fears for the safety of her ship."

The pilot nodded, and drew on his cigarillo. "He tried to force the issue, and the Harbor Master had to point out that we do not take sides in any dispute. Nor will we be the arena for the settling of any quarrel. Frankly, if he had not tried to force us, we would have let him take you. But we cannot allow him to set a dangerous precedent." He flicked the butt of his cigarillo over the side and turned on his heel. "Now, Captain Lorquital, the helm if you please. I will take you in."

The pilot guided the *Weazel* to a berth at a long pontoon at the inner edge of the harbor, amongst mussel dredgers and two-masted ketches of the kind which carried small cargoes between cities everywhere along the river. The sultry air tasted of the acrid smoke of the fishing barge's rendering furnaces. The water around the pontoon was stained with sullen rainbows; flocks of tiny machines skated the surface, absorbing spilled fuel oil through pads on their long legs. Pelicans perched on mooring posts, drying their wings, like rows of arrowheads against the red light of the setting sun. A league away, across a maze of channels and pontoons and graving basins, colored neon lights blazed and winked above clusters of clapboard buildings and plastic domes. The pilot repeated his warning to Yama and Captain Lorquital, and took his leave.

"We can't go ashore unarmed," Tamora said.

"You have your teeth and claws," Pandaras said, "I have my cunning, and our master has his power over machines. What more do we need?"

"I want to talk with him," Yama said. "I will go alone, and unarmed."

Tamora said, "And where will you begin to look for him? It would be better if you stayed here. It'll be the first place he'll look, and there's nothing to say we can't be armed if we stay aboard our own ship."

Even as the sailors began to make the *Weazel* fast in her berth, shills appeared on the pontoon, handing out little tiles that whispered seductive invitations to whorehouses and bars. One of the shills called Yama's name and threw a tile to the deck at his feet and quickly walked away, pushing through the others. Yama picked up the white tile and the golden dragon printed on its surface flexed its wings and breathed a wisp of blue fire that formed two words. A name.

Mother Spitfire's.

—

Yama insisted on going alone, although Tamora argued fiercely against it. "The crews of the picketboat of the warship will be crawling all over this place," she said. "A gang of them could set on you anywhere. Better to fight in a place of your own choosing."

"I know where he wants to meet you," Eliphas said. "This place is famous for its entertainments. Of course, it has moved downriver. It used to be anchored off Kalyb, but the fall in the level of the river has stranded that city a dozen leagues from navigable water." He peered at the long strip of lights twinkling in the dusk and added, "It seems larger, but I suppose that is because of the war."

Tamora spat over the side of the ship. A tiny machine skated over oily water after her gob of spittle. "Grah. You should swim out to the warship, if you are so eager to meet Corin. It would make as much sense. A man like him won't dirty the soles of his boots in the stews of a place like this. His invitation is a trick."

"Better we speak on neutral ground," Yama said.

"I could break his neck for you."

"I am sure you could."

"Or gouge out his eyes."

"I just want to talk with him, Tamora. That is why I will go alone, or not at all."

Pandaras agreed readily enough to this. He said that he had a mission of his own.

"Captain Lorquital has given the freemen liberty until the midnight watch, and it seems that my friend, Pantin, has never been with a woman. It was part of the discipline of his former trade. I feel it's time he was taken in hand, as it were.''

''If you know what you are doing,'' Yama said, thinking of the young sailor's reputation as a pit fighter. Pantin was already on the pontoon, waiting with his hands in the back pockets of the scuffed leather trousers he habitually wore.

''Pantin has renounced the knife life,'' Pandaras said, ''and I'll make sure he's too busy to get into trouble.''

Pandaras walked a little way with Yama, then he and Pantin went off arm in arm, and Yama went in the other direction, toward the far end of the Strip and *Mother Spitfire's*.

The main drag of the floating harbor was laid out along a broadwalk half a league long. The gaudily painted fronts of chandlers, bars and whorehouses rose shoulder to shoulder on either side. Groups of intoxicated sailors and soldiers surged and staggered beneath flashing neon and flaring torches, carrying paper cups of beer or smoking pipes of crystal or weed as they moved from one attraction to the next. This was the last stop their transports would make before the battlefields above the midpoint of the world, and Yama supposed that they sought oblivion in the few hours it took for their ships to renew their stores. Hawkers cried the merits of drinking or smoking dens; there were tattoo parlors and fast-food joints, dream parlors and gambling palaces. Dancers of all sexes and a decad of different bloodlines (or perhaps they were all mirror people, Yama thought) bumped and ground in lighted windows above the awnings of bars; musicians, magicians and gamblers made islands in the throng. Here and there, magistrates stood on floating discs above the packed heads of the crowds, and their tiny, glittering machines spun everywhere through the neon-lit air.

Mother Spitfire's was a gambling palace at the far end of the Strip. A dragon limned in golden neon tubing sprawled across its tall façade; pillars of fire roared within tall columns of glass on either side of the wide doors.

Tamora and Eliphas were waiting outside, and Yama's

first pang of anger quickly gave way to relief. He laughed, and said, "I suppose Pandaras and Pantin are skulking somewhere nearby."

"I sent them off to a whorehouse," Tamora said, "but the old man insists on staying here, even though he'll only be in the way." She was not wearing her sword, and stood with her thumbs stuck in the belt of her leather skirt, scowling at every passerby.

"I know this place," Eliphas said, "and I hope that I can be of help. But I fear that Prefect Corin does not want to talk. There are many places on the Strip that will amuse you. Let me show them to you. Forget all this for a few hours, and then we will be gone."

"You wanted me to destroy him a few days ago," Yama said. "If you do not wish to meet Prefect Corin, then go back to the ship. I will not blame you."

"We can still strike first," Tamora said, "beginning with this Mother Spitfire. She must be a friend of Corin's."

"She is famous here," Eliphas said. "Or rather, infamous."

Yama said, "Ixchel Lorquital told me that Mother Spitfire will lose her license if she allows any of her guests to bear arms. We will talk. That is all."

Tamora passed the palm of one hand over her scarred scalp. She said, "I'll do more than talk with him if he so much as looks at me in a funny way. Him or anyone else."

Inside, men and women crowded at dice tables down a long room, under greenery that spilled from floating discs. Most of the gamblers were in uniform. The roar of their wagers and prayers mingled with the plaintive music of a shadow puppet show that played on a screen raised above the midpoint of the room. Beyond, more people crowded around the walls of a fighting pit or were scattered on the tiers of wide steps that rose on either side.

Mother Spitfire herself came up the central aisle to greet Yama. She was very tall and very slender, golden-skinned and clad in a sheath dress of red silk that flowed like water. Two burly men of Tamora's bloodline stood behind her, impassive in black robes. Tamora stared at them; they stared back.

"Welcome, Yamamanama," Mother Spitfire said, bowing so sinuously that her small, sleek head was brought close to Yama's. Her breath smelled of honey and cinnamon. She pressed a stack of gambling markers into Yama's hand. Her fingernails were very long, and painted scarlet. "May your luck increase this poor gift many times over."

"Where is he?"

Mother Spitfire's green, slit-pupilled eyes were large and lidless; a nictitating membrane filmed them for a moment. She said, "You are as bold and direct as he said you would be. Is it bravery, I wonder, or innocence? He is on his way. Meanwhile enjoy yourselves. We have several pairs of well-matched contestants tonight"—her voice lowered—"although if I were to place a wager on the next bout, I would favor the smaller animal."

"Thank you for your advice," Yama said.

"There will be no fighting here," Mother Spitfire said, looking at Tamora for a moment, "except for that in the pit."

"I trust you were paid well for the risk," Yama said.

"Not so much that I can afford to have my business closed. I have pledged that there will be no trouble from either side."

Mother Spitfire swept away, followed by her bodyguards. Tamora stared after her and said, "They could take us here and no one would notice."

Yama pointed to one of the little machines that spun through the smoky air above the gaming tables. "The magistrates watch everywhere," he said. "What happens in the pit?"

"They fight to the death," Eliphas said. "This place is infamous. Mother Spitfire is the last of her kind, older than anyone in Gond. But it is not a seemly spectacle that she presides over, brother. Perhaps Tamora is correct. We should choose our own meeting place. Here, we place ourselves at the mercy of our enemy."

"I am tired of running," Yama said.

He led the way through the crowd that clustered around the oval fighting pit, and climbed the sweep of steps to the very top. The pit was filled with water and lit by powerful lamps. Men and women leaned at the rail, watching as two naked slaves trawled fragments from the water with long-handled rakes. A gong sounded softly and the slaves set down their rakes and cranked down spring-loaded arms with a net stretched between them, dividing the flooded pit in two. A little old man in a black robe, his beard so long that he wore its forked end over his shoulder, climbed into a basket seat and pulled vigorously on a system of ropes and pulleys to hoist himself above the water.

"They keep them in heat," Eliphas said. "They do it with injections, so they're always ready to fight."

The gong sounded again, battered brass soft as a dying man's last sigh. Water boiled at either end of the pit and two sleek shapes glided out into the light. There was a flurry of betting amongst the spectators.

Yama's breath caught in his throat. The creatures in the water were kelpies. Steel spurs were fastened to their flippers; spiked chains to their tails. One swam straight at the net and recoiled from a sputter of fat blue sparks, spouting a cloud of oily vapor. The other held still in the center of its half of the pit, its tail moving up and down with slow deliberation.

The old man said something about *preparing the bout,* and, *last wagers please.* As his amplified voice echoed around the room, there was a renewed flurry of betting. Then the gong sounded for the third time and the spring-loaded arms snapped back, raising the net out of the water with an explosive motion. The two kelpies shot into the center of the pit, lashing around each other, parting, and engaging again.

Water splashed over the sides, draining away through slots in the floor. The spectators hooted and stamped and whistled. Both kelpies were bleeding from gashes in their pale bellies. Their blood looked black as it fluttered through the brilliantly lit water. For a moment, they hung head to head; then they engaged again, and suddenly one was on top of the other. It beat at its opponent's flanks with its tail chains, and with its teeth ripped through blubber and flesh to expose the spine, which it broke with a quick snap of its head. It slid away, snorting vapor through the nasal slits at the top of its head and making a hoarse braying whistle, and the corpse rolled over and sank through a cloud of its own blood. The old man above the pit chanted a string of numbers and there was a flurry of activity amongst the spectators as betting markers were exchanged. Slaves used long electrified prods to drive the victorious kelpie away from the corpse and harry it into one of the tunnels.

Yama felt both sick and excited. The spectacle was horrible and degrading, yet even in their hormone-induced fury, the animals were possessed of a fierce beauty.

Eliphas saw Yama's disgust. He said, "There is worse to come, brother. We should leave now. Meet with your enemy elsewhere. Let me show you—"

"Too late," Tamora said. "He is here."

Three men were coming up the steps toward them. As always, Prefect Corin wore a plain homespun tunic, but this time he was not carrying his staff. His two companions wore breastplates of plastic armor and short kirtles of red cloth that left their legs bare.

Tamora insisted on patting the three men down. Prefect Corin submitted to her search with good humor, and favored Yama with one of his rare smiles. "You are well, boy," he said. He looked sleek and self-satisfied and calm. "I am glad. It was quite a chase you led me. The trick with the scouts was good. I should have guessed that you could fool them sooner than I did. You have learned a great deal since I last talked with you."

"Many things have changed," Yama said. He had expected to feel a hot rage when he confronted the man who had murdered his stepfather, but instead he felt nothing at all, not even contempt. His hands were trembling, though, and he folded his arms and returned Prefect Corin's gaze as steadily as he could.

"They're clean," Tamora said, "but don't let them come any closer. I'll break their necks if they try." She glared at Prefect Corin's companions, who looked through her as if she did not exist.

Prefect Corin said, "The reputation of your companion is not the highest, but I understand that she tries to make up with bravado what she lacks in skill." He glanced at Eliphas. "This man had a reputation, too. Where is he leading you? What trick is he upon? You are out of your depth, Eliphas. You should have stuck to gouging would-be widows wanting recipes for undetectable poisons."

Eliphas said with great dignity, "I don't know you, dominie, but I see that my jealous rivals have been whispering in your ear."

Yama told Prefect Corin, "I am not sorry about your machines. I will destroy any you send against me. You must know that. And you must know that I will not serve."

Prefect Corin said, "There are always more machines. Think of it as a test. The more you resist, the more we learn about you. The more you try to escape, the more we will chase you. If you came here hoping that I would allow you to go on your way unhindered, than I must disappoint you. Give in, boy. The river is wide, but it is not endless. The further you travel, the nearer you approach the war, where there are millions under the command of the Department. You cannot hide from all of them; you cannot override all of the machines. I can offer you much, and that is why I am here. We do not want to lose you."

Yama met Prefect Corin's mild gaze with an effort of will. He said, "How goes the war amongst the departments in the Palace of the Memory of the People?"

"We will win."

"Perhaps not, since you have not already won."

"What will you do if you do not join us? Trust Eliphas and his wild tales? Preach to the underclasses as you did on the roof of the Palace? Take care with your answer. I would not like to indict you for heresy against the word of the Preservers.''

''I go in search of my people, nothing more. And I do not believe that you serve the Preservers. You do not even serve the Department. You serve your own ends.''

''You were brought up in the traditions of the Department, and you should know that we are here to serve the people, not our own selves. I was sorry to hear of your father's death, by the way. He was a good servant, although a weak man who clung to traditions long past their usefulness. He should not have become involved in this.''

Tamora said, ''Yama, I'll make them go. Just give me the word.''

''I will hear what he has to offer,'' Yama said. He felt perfectly calm, despite the tremor in his hands. Crowds were gathering around the flooded fighting pit again. The body of the loser had been removed and the water had been cleaned.

Prefect Corin shrugged. ''Perhaps I will not bother. Perhaps I believe that you have already made up your mind, Yamamanama.''

''But you cannot know for certain. That is why you came.''

''You dare to presume—'' For the first time, Prefect Corin's reserve was breached. He drew a finger down the white streak which divided the left side of his black-furred face and said, ''You presume too much. You are not subtle, boy. But I will tell you this. We will not ask you to fight. We will ask only that we can study you to find out how you control machines. And when we know, why, you will be free to do as you will. You wish to find out why you are here and where you come from? All the resources of the Department will be at your disposal. You will be elevated through the ranks to the first circle of committees. If you wish to help the underclasses, do so within established structures of power. Otherwise you waste all that you might be. How can you justify throwing that away, because of pride?''

"You would raise me up to a level I do not deserve in order to give the Department power it does not deserve. The Department exists to serve those you call the underclasses. Perhaps it has forgotten that. Perhaps it would be best if the Department looked to its own faults before attempting to correct the faults of others."

"Ah, Yamamanama. I admire your certainty. But do think a while on what I have said. We have no hurry. Your captain still awaits her passenger, although he would be ill-advised to journey with you, should you choose to attempt to leave."

The gong sounded again. Prefect Corin turned toward the pit. He said, "We will watch the next bout. I think that it will amuse you. And while you watch, think on what I have offered."

"It is the worst of the wickedness of this place," Eliphas said, with a sudden passion.

Two men sat at either end of the pool, in the same kind of suspended basket chairs as the old man who had refereed the first bout. The men were masked and gloved. Thin cables trailed from the chairs into the water. As spectators thickened around the pit, the men sat quietly above the rising buzz of conversation and the rattle of betting markers. The net was not lowered this time; suddenly, without fuss, two kelpies were hanging at either end of the flooded pit, shadows floating as quiet and still in the water as the two men seated in the air above them.

Yama asked Eliphas what kind of contest this would be, but Eliphas simply said that Yama would soon see. "But we should leave," he said. "It is a perversion of old knowledge."

Prefect Corin said, "Knowledge is like power. It is only effective if it is used. You will not use your power, Yamamanama. That is why we will triumph, and you will lose."

The gong gently battered the air again. Above the pit, the men rolled and twisted in their basket chairs. The kelpies shot forward. They missed each other on the first pass. One smashed its blunt head against the side of the tank while the other somersaulted clumsily and bore in with a sudden rush. It ripped a gash in the belly of its opponent with a steel-tipped flipper, but failed to follow through.

Yama saw the thin cables that trailed after each kelpie and understood what was happening. The kelpies were living puppets, commanded by the masked and gloved men just as Nergal had commanded the spiders.

He seized control with a spasm of anger and disgust. The kelpies shot past each other and crashed into opposite ends of the tank. The impact killed them instantly; their human operators were both stricken by seizures that jerked them out of their suspended chairs. One hung by his harness; the other toppled over and smashed into the water. Yama collapsed against Tamora, momentarily blinded by feedback and red and black lightning.

Half of the spectators surged forward to see what had happened; the others were trying to get away. Knots of fighting broke out. A grossly fat woman stood in the middle of the mêlée, screaming with operatic force.

Yama shrugged off Tamora's grip and started down the steps. One of Prefect Corin's men tried to stop him, but Tamora kicked him in the back of his knee and he went down as Yama dodged past. He threw up the markers Mother Spitfire had given him and, as people scrambled for them, ran under the screen and dodged through the maze of gambling tables, overturning them as he went. He was fueled by rage and fear. His sight pounded with red and black in solid flashes. The thing inside him had come back; he was a helpless passenger in his own skull.

The entire building seemed transparent, with all the places where machines worked shining clear. Overhead, a hundred little spies exploded in sputters of white-hot sparks, crashing down amongst the gamblers and the tables, starting a hundred fires and doubling and redoubling panic. Yama was carried forward by a sudden press of people who shared the same thought: to get out before the fires took hold. His body knew what to do. It fought to keep its feet on the ground, for with one slip it would be trampled underfoot. One of Mother Spitfire's black-robed bodyguards pushed through the crowd and reached for him, and Yama saw the machines in the bodyguard's head and did something terrible.

When he came to himself, he had fetched up in the doorway of a dream parlor at the other end of the Strip. One hand clasped the wrist of the other, crushing the coypu hair fetish. Seed pearls pricked his fingertips. There was blood on his hands and flecks of blood and bloody matter spattered his tunic and face and hair. It was not his blood.

Inside the dream parlor, within a huge glass tank filled with boiling wreaths of thick green smoke, a naked woman pressed her face and breasts against the glass for a moment, her mouth opening and closing as if she was trying to tell him something.

Yama cried out.

"Angel!"

But the woman stepped backward into the smoke and was gone.

Sailors and soldiers were rioting up and down the length of the Strip. Yama borrowed the eyes of a machine high above the crowd and saw that white smoke was pouring from the edges of the steep tiled roof of Mother Spitfire's gambling palace. The gold neon dragon spat sheets of sparks; one of its wings went out. Yama spun the machine and saw that the buildings around the gambling palace were on fire, too. Magistrates on floating discs were cutting a firebreak across the Strip with pistol shots. A painted façade plunged like a huge guillotine blade into a gap that was blown open in front of it. Strings of lightbulbs and strips of jointed neon tubing fell, smashing amongst the rioting crowd.

Yama released the machine and got up and started back toward the ship, but he had not gone very far when he was seized from behind, lifted, and flung against a wall. There were two men, burly and tall, as alike as brothers. They wore breechclouts and plastic breastplates, and their shaven heads were crowned with tight-fitting copper caps.

One man pinned him while the other quickly and roughly frisked him.

"I have no money," Yama said.

The man who held him laughed and said, "He thinks we're robbing him, Diomedes!"

"We're badly misunderstood, Dercetas," the other said, and told Yama, "We're from an old friend, boy. He'll be pleased to see you again."

Dercetas got Yama in an armlock and shoved him forward, down a service walkway that ran out above black water. Diomedes brandished a pistol, and when a magistrate suddenly swooped down from the darkness beyond the rail, he twitched his pistol and fired. The magistrate fell with his clothes on fire; his disc shot straight up in a clap of thunder.

Most of the magistrate's machines had been destroyed in the violet flare of the pistol blast. Yama threw the rest at Diomedes. The man was knocked backward and spun around, held upright only by the machines which had embedded themselves in his flesh. One eye was a bloody hole; blood filled the space beneath his transparent breastplate and ran down his bare legs.

"Let me go," Yama shouted. "Let me go and I will spare you!"

His head hurt very badly. He could barely see because great flags of red and black were crowding in. Diomedes's body twitched as the machines began to work their way out of his flesh.

Dercetas thrust Yama from him and stepped backward, then turned and ran. Yama staggered after him and said in an entirely new voice, "Wait. You fool. Wait for me."

But the man had vanished into the crowd at the end of the walkway. Behind Yama, the dead man fell forward and the machines flew away into the night.

—

Much later, Pandaras and Pantin found Eliphas standing over Yama. There was a bloody corpse nearby, but at first

Pandaras thought nothing of it. The riots had been very bad, and order was only now being restored. Magistrates were supervising teams of sailors and soldiers, putting out fires and clearing debris from the walkways. Bodies had been laid in neat rows in the big square at the center of the Strip, awaiting identification and shriving.

Eliphas seemed to be praying over Yama. As Pandaras approached, the old man turned and said, "He is sick, but I do not think that he is wounded."

"Let me see," Pandaras said. He pushed Eliphas aside and squatted beside his master. Yama stared past him at an imaginary point somewhere beyond the world. Pandaras said, "Master, do you know who I am? Do you know where you are?"

"He killed that man," Eliphas said.

For the first time, Pandaras looked closely at the dead man. He wore a plastic breastplate and a copper cap. The breastplate was riddled with bloody holes.

"I've seen others dressed like that," Pandaras said. "I expect they're Prefect Corin's men. Help me, Eliphas. We must get him back to the ship."

Two men wearing armor and copper caps had found Pandaras and Pantin in a whorehouse. Pantin had stabbed one in the eye with a table knife and had jumped on the back of the other and cut his throat, sawing and sawing with the blunt blade until the man's head had been nearly cut off. The boy was trembling but docile now, like a horse which has just run a race. Blood crusted his bare chest.

Together, Eliphas and Pandaras helped Yama stand.

"We must get out of this, master," Pandaras said. "Prefect Corin found you, didn't he? I shouldn't have listened to Tamora. I should have stayed. I'm sorry."

"There is a monster," Yama said dreamily. "I am dangerous, Pandaras. Even to myself."

"He's too hard on himself," Pandaras told Eliphas. "You don't go running to the magistrates to ask for justice when it's your own family, and you don't stint, either. If it was me, I would have burned the whole thing down to make sure I killed Corin."

THE ASCENSION OF ANGEL

"THEY'RE HOLDING PREFECT Corin and both his ships," Captain Lorquital said, "The magistrates think that he brought weapons ashore, or allowed his men to. They'd like to blame you, too, but they can't see how one young man could have caused so much destruction. Our passenger put in a word, too."

"Prefect Corin will follow us," Yama said. "The magistrates may delay him, but they will not be able to stop him. They have no real cause, and he will be able to deny responsibility. After all, he is not the one who wrecked Mother Spitfire's gambling palace."

They stood on the quarterdeck, watching the lights of the floating harbor diminish across a widening gap of black water as the *Weazel* maneuvered through a channel marked by luminescent buoys. The fires had been put out and the crowds of sailors and soldiers had been dispersed to their ships. The places which had been damaged were ringed with lights, and the sounds of construction work could be heard. Beyond the floating harbor, the city of Gond shone against the night by its own inner light, like a range of low hills covered in luminous snow.

"The less of that kind of talk, the better," Ixchel Lorquital said. "The magistrates have ears in the wind here."

"No more," Yama said, and shivered; he did not know why he had said it.

Pandaras had described in vivid detail how he and Pantin had found Yama by the dead man, with Eliphas praying over him. Yama had riddled a man with machines, but he did not remember it. He remembered nothing after his rage had taken him in the gambling palace. He had been floating above the Strip with burning buildings on either side . . . There had been a woman hanging in green vapor . . . He turned the fetish around and around on his wrist; it helped him remember who he was.

He had suffered only a few scrapes and bruises, and there was a bump in the hollow between the two big tendons at the back of his skull. Something hard-edged which he could move around under the skin. He should know what it was . . . but the memory slid away when he tried to articulate it.

"By tomorrow," Captain Lorquital said, "the place will be back to normal."

"They will catch more of them," Yama said. "The river renews all, good and bad."

He was thinking of the kelpies in Mother Spitfire's pit, but Ixchel Lorquital misunderstood. "Every day more soldiers pass by on their way downriver to the war," she said. "The war has changed everything along the river. This place is the least of it."

As the *Weazel* passed beyond the edge of the floating harbor and raised her sail to catch the offshore breeze, fireworks shot up from Gond, bursting in overlapping showers of gold and green and raining down toward their own reflections in the river's black water. The *Weazel*'s crew, up in the rigging, cheered each new explosion.

"For our passenger," Ixchel Lorquital said with a smile. "So few remain in the city that they mark the departure or return of every one of their bloodline."

Yama had forgotten about the passenger for whom the *Weazel* had put in at the floating harbor. He said, "I suppose you and your daughter have lost your cabin to him. Is that where he is now? I would like to meet him, and thank him for his help."

Captain Lorquital pointed at the mast with the stem of her clay pipe. "He has taken the crow's nest. Climb up if you want to talk, but he'll be with us for at least five days."

The passenger from Gond had arrived an hour before Pandaras and Pantin had brought Yama back to the ship. He was an envoy to the cities of the Dry Plains, where there were disputes about the new land uncovered by the river's retreat. It was all to do with the war, Captain Lorquital declared. Normally, such matters were decided at a festival of dance and song, but most of the able young men had gone to fight the heretics, and there were not enough contestants.

"He's been appointed to make peace between the cities," Captain Lorquital said. "The people of Gond are a holy people. Their decisions are not easily come by, and are highly respected."

All this time, Tamora had been sitting in the pool of light cast by the big square lantern at the stern rail, sharpening her sword with a stone and scrap of leather. When Yama left Captain Lorquital to her charts and went forward to the bow, Tamora followed him.

"I fucked up," she said bluntly. "Put me off at the next port and I'll find another job."

"I remember that you saved my life," Yama said. "And that I then did something foolish. The fault is mine."

"You should have burned the place to the waterline," Tamora said fiercely. "It's no more than it deserves. You don't need me when you can command any machine. Let me go."

"I am too tired to talk about this," Yama said. In fact, he was ashamed of what he had done, although he did not remember much of it. "I need your strength, Tamora. I need to know when to act and when to stay my hand."

Tamora said, "That's easy. You only strike when you have to."

"I need to be sure that I am acting for myself. I feel like a horse under a skillful rider. Most of the time I pick my own way, but sometimes I am pulled up short, or made to gallop in a direction not of my own choosing. I do not know if I am on the side of good or evil. Help me, Tamora."

She fixed him with her gold-green gaze. "Before I was hurt in the war, they said I was crazy. No one would fight by my side because they said I took too many risks. You know what? I did it because I was scared. It's easier to charge the enemy under fire than stand and wait for the right moment. So that's what I did until I was wounded. Afterward, while I was recovering, I had plenty of time to think about what I'd done, and I swore then that I would never again let fear control me. I thought that I had been true to that oath until this night."

Yama remembered that Sergeant Rhodean had told him that the best generals judge the moment to attack; the worst are driven by events willy-nilly, like a ship before a storm. He said, "You are right. Fear is natural, but I should be able to control it. Thank you."

"What for? For being a damned fool? For letting you walk into that trap? For failing to help you when it went wrong?"

"For trusting me with your story."

They watched the last of the fireworks burst far astern as the *Weazel* headed out into the deep water, and later fell asleep in each other's arms. As the sky lightened, Yama woke and disentangled himself from Tamora's embrace. Someone, probably Pandaras, had covered them with a blanket. Tamora sighed and yawned, showing her sharp white teeth and black tongue, and Yama told her to go back to sleep.

Apart from the old sailor, Phalerus, who had the helm, the whole ship was asleep. The new passenger must still be in the crow's nest, for only Pandaras and Eliphas slept on the raffia matting under the awning. The *Weazel* was running ahead of a strong wind, her triangular mainsail filled, water creaming by on either side of her bow. The

Great River stretched away on all sides; the Rim Mountains were no more than a long line floating low in the lightening sky. The water here was not the usual brown or umber but was the same dark blue as the predawn sky. It was more than a league deep in places; some of the abyssal trenches plunged into the keel of the world. Hard to believe that this could ever change, and yet year by year the cities of the shore were stranded further and further inland by the river's retreat. The Great River would at last run dry even here, leaving only a string of long, narrow lakes at the bottom of a deep dry valley.

Yama leaned at the starboard rail. Warm wind blew his unruly black hair back from his face. The bright lights of the huge fishing barges were scattered widely across the river. Yama wondered what monsters lay in the deeps under the *Weazel*'s keel, and for the first time in many days felt the tug of the feral machine which hung in its cold, solitary orbit a million leagues beyond the end of the world, attached to him by an impalpable thread, just as the kelpies had been attached to their operators by wires and cables. But who was puppet, and who operator? And for what end? He remembered the conclusion of his stepfather's complicated calculations about the river's shrinkage and shivered in the brightening sunlight.

After a while, he took out his copy of the Puranas. The bright crammed pictures stirred to life under his gaze, speaking directly to an unconsciously receptive part of his mind. He realized that there must be machines embedded in the pages. Was every book freighted with hidden meanings? As a child, had he dreamed so vividly of the past because books from the library of the peel-house had lain by his bed?

But then he was lost in the last of Angel's story, and all idle speculation was driven away.

—

When Angel came back from the far side of the river, she talked with those of her followers who had waited at the docks for her, then went straightaway to Mr. Naryan, the Archivist of Sensch, to tell him what she had found.

The Archivist was with a pupil, but the hapless lad was immediately dismissed when Angel appeared. Fortified by tea brought by the Archivist's wife, a quiet woman of Sensch's lizard race, Angel began to tell the tale of her adventure on the farside shore.

The Archivist knew that Angel had been to the edge of the world, and for the first time he could not hide his fear. He was afraid of what she might have done amongst the shrines on the river's far side, about what she might change.

She said, teasingly, "Don't you want to hear my story? Isn't that your avocation?"

"I will listen to anything you want to tell me," the Archivist said. Despite his fear, he maintained his air of quiet dignity, and she liked him for that.

She said, "The world is a straight line. Do you know about libration?"

The Archivist shook his head.

Angel held out her hand, palm down, and tipped it back and forth. "This is the world. Everything lives on the back of a long flat plate which circles the sun. The plate rocks on its axis, so the sun rises above one edge and then reverses its course. I went to the edge of the world, where the river that runs down half its length falls into the void. I suppose it must be collected and redistributed, but it really does look like it falls away forever."

"The river is eternally renewed," the Archivist said. "Where it falls is where ships used to arrive and depart, but this city has not been a port for many years."

"Fortunately for me, or my companions would already be here. There's a narrow ribbon of land on the far side of the river. Nothing lives there, not even an insect. No earth, no stones. The air shakes with the sound of the river's fall, and swirling mist burns with raw sunlight. And there are shrines, in the thunder and mist at the edge of the world." Angel paused for effect, then said, "One spoke to me."

She could see that the Archivist was taken aback. He said nothing, staring past her in some private reverie. She grinned and said, "Don't you want to know what it said to me? It's part of my story."

"Do you want to tell me?"

The Archivist looked at her. It was a look of helpless love; she knew then that like all the others he was hers to command. The thought disgusted her. She wanted him to be a friend, not a pet or a puppet. She passed her hand over the top of her head. She had had her hair cut close in the manner of microgravity construction workers, a style ten million years out of date. The bristly hair made a crisp sound under her palm. She said, "No. No, I don't think I do. Not yet."

Instead, she told him what the ship had showed her of the creation of the Eye of the Preservers. He seemed happier with this. It was something he understood. He said that it was just as it was written in the Puranas.

She said, "And is it also written there why Confluence was constructed around a halo star between the Home Galaxy and the Eye of the Preservers?"

"Of course. It is so we can worship and glorify the Preservers. The Eye looks upon us all."

It was a stock answer, taken from the commentary at the end of the last sura of the Puranas. He had nothing new to tell her. No one on this strange world had had a new idea since its creation, but she would change that. If she was going to rule here, she must first topple the old gods.

The news that she had woken one of the shrines on the farside shore spread through the city. The streets around her house became choked with curious citizens. She could no longer wander about the city, because huge crowds gathered everywhere she went. There was a story that she had been tempted with godhood, and that she had refused. It was not something she had told the citizens—they were changing her story to fit their needs. She tried to teach them that the Universe of things was all there was, that there were no gods capable of intercession, that everyone

was responsible for their own destiny. Seize the day, she
told them, and they made the slogan into their battle cry.
Her followers daubed slogans everywhere, and now many
of the slogans were of their own making.

Somehow, the citizens of Sensch came to believe that
they could use the farside shrines just as she had, without
intervention of priest or hierodule, and that personal redemption was within their grasp. They set off in their
thousands on pilgrimages across the river; so many that the
city's markets closed because the merchants had moved to
the docks to supply those making the journey across the
river. Meanwhile, Angel became a prisoner in her house,
surrounded by followers, her every move watched with
reverence. She had to stand on the roof so that she could
be seen and heard by all of them. She was trying to free
them from their habits and their unthinking devotion to
the Preservers, to shape them into an army that could be
used against her ship when it finally came for her.

She built devices that might help her escape. A crude
muscle amplification suit. A circuit-breaking device that
would interfere with the broadcast power on which the
myriads of tiny machines fed. She tinkered with the gravity units of cargo sleds, and painstakingly reprogrammed
a few captured machines. But all of this activity was mark-
ing time. It was almost a relief when her ship finally
arrived.

Angel went up to the roof of her house when the ship
drew near the city's docks. It had reconfigured itself into
a huge black wedge composed of stacked tiers of flat
plates. Its pyramidal apex was taller than the tallest towers
of the city. Angel knew that the ship would try to take
her back, but she might be able to escape if she could use
the powers of the ship against itself.

She insisted on going to the docks. The young men who
were her closest followers were very afraid, but they could
not disobey her. She had two of them carry the circuit
breaker, and armed the rest with pistols.

The streets were almost empty. Thousands upon thousands of citizens had gathered at the docks to greet the

ship, held back by a thin line of magistrates and their machines. The people were restless; they made a humming noise that rose and fell in pitch but never ended. Machines swept their packed heads with flares of light. There had already been trouble, for those near the front were wounded in some way, fallen to their knees and wailing and clutching at their faces. And when Dreen, the Commissioner of Sensch, rode a cargo sled to the top of the ship to greet the men and women of the crew, the crowd pressed forward eagerly, held back only by the quirts and machines of the magistrates.

Angel knew then that this was her only chance to take the ship from the crew. She fired up the circuit breaker and every machine fell from the sky, burned out by the power surge. The magistrates were powerless to stop the crowd as it surged down the docks toward the ship. Angel saw Dreen's cargo sled fly away from the top of the ship— it drew power from the world's gravity fields—toward the floating gardens above the pink sandstone palace. The Archivist was coming toward her, struggling through the crowd. Angel ordered those around her to take him to the palace, and left to organize the siege.

Power was down all over the city. The population had lost all restraint, as if it was only the presence of the machines which had kept them in order. There was drunkenness and gambling and open fornication. Buildings were set on fire; markets were looted. But those citizens Angel encountered still obeyed her unquestioningly. They loaded up cargo sleds with batteries for a localized power system and marched on the palace and attacked the floating gardens, some using the modified sleds to smash away pieces of the gardens' superstructure, others starting to grow towers into the air using self-catalyzing masonry.

Angel was sitting in the middle of her followers on the palace roof, with the machines she had reprogrammed spinning above her head, when the Archivist was brought before her. He was bruised and disheveled, not badly hurt, but clearly terrified. She beckoned him forward and he drew on his last reserves of dignity to confront her. She said, "What should I do with your city, now that I have taken it from you?"

The Archivist said, "You have not finished your story." There was a hint of defiance in his voice, but then he added weakly, "I would like to hear it all."

"My people can tell you. They hide with Dreen up above, but not for long." Angel pointed to a dozen men who were wrestling a sled into the crude launch cradle and explained how she had enhanced its anti-gravity properties. "We'll chip away that floating fortress piece by piece if we have to, or we'll finish growing towers and storm its remains, but I expect them to surrender long before then."

"Dreen is not the ruler of the city."

"Not anymore."

The Archivist dared to step closer. He said, "What did you find out there, that you rage against?"

Angel laughed. None of them understood. They were not human—how could they understand her, the last human in the Universe? She said, "I'll tell you about rage. It is what you have forgotten, or never learned. It is the motor of evolution, and evolution's end, too."

She snatched a beaker of wine from one of her followers and drained it and tossed it aside. Its heat mixed smoothly with her angry contempt. She said, "We traveled for so long, not dead, not sleeping. We were no more than stored potentials triply engraved on gold. Although the ship flew so fast that it bound time about itself, the journey still took thousands of years of shipboard time. At the end of that long voyage we did not wake: we were born. Or rather, others like us were born, although I have their memories, as if they are my own. They learned then that the Universe is not made for the convenience of humans. What they found was a galaxy dead and ruined."

Angel took the Archivist's hands in hers and held them tightly as she told him of the ruin of the neighboring galaxy, the disrupted nebulae, the planets torn from their orbits by gravity stress, the worlds torched smooth by stars which had flared because of infalling gases. She told him what she had learned.

"Do you know how many galaxies have endured such collisions? Almost all of them. Life is a statistical freak. Our galaxy has never collided with another like it, or not for a long time, long enough for life to have evolved on planets around some of its stars. It must be unique, or else other civilizations would surely have arisen elsewhere in the unbounded Universe. As it is, we are certain that we are alone. We must make of ourselves what we can. We should not hide from the truth, as your Preservers chose to do. Instead, we should seize the day, and make the Universe over with the technology that the Preservers used to make their hiding place."

The Archivist said, "You cannot become a Preserver. No one can, now. You should not lie to these innocent people."

"I didn't need to lie. They took up my story and made it theirs. They see now what they can inherit—if they dare. This won't stop with one city. It will become a crusade!" She stared into the Archivist's black eyes and said softly, "You'll remember it all, won't you?"

The Archivist said nothing, but she knew that he was hers, now and forever. It seemed to make him unbearably sad and it broke her heart, too, to have to use him so badly when she had wanted him to be her friend.

Around them, the crowd of her followers cheered. The sled rocketed up from its cradle and smashed into the underside of the hanging gardens. Another piece of the gardens' substructure was knocked loose. It spilled dirt and rocks amongst the spires of the palace roof as it twisted free and spun away into the night. The crowd cheered again, and Angel saw that figures had appeared at the wrecked edge of the habitat. One of the figures tossed something down, and a man brought it to Angel.

It was a message tube. She shook it open: Dreen's face glowed on the flexible membrane. His voice was squeezed small and metallic by the tube's induced speaker. Angel listened to his entreaties and was filled with joy and hope.

"Yes," she said, but so softly that perhaps only the Archivist heard her. She stood and raised her hands above her head, and when she had the attention of her followers she cried out, "They wish to surrender! Let them come down!"

The cargo sled dropped. They were all there, the men and women who were closer to her than sisters and brothers, shining in their white clothes. Angel's followers jeered and threw rocks and burning brands and clods of earth, but her partials had modified the sled's field and everything was deflected away into the night. Angel smiled. She had anticipated that trick.

The partials called to her, pleading with her to return, to join them and search for their long-lost home. Dreen jumped from the sled and dodged through the crowd of Angel's followers. The little Commissioner caught the Archivist's hand and told him breathlessly, "They are all one person, or variations on one person. The ship makes its crew by varying a template. Angel is an extreme. A mistake."

Angel laughed. So Dreen had been subverted by the partials! "You funny little man," she said. "I'm the real one—they are copies!"

She turned to the partials, who were still calling out to her, pleading with her to come back, to join them in the search for their lost home. None had dared follow Dreen. "There's no home to find," she told them. "Oh you fools! This is all there is! Give me back the ship!"

She knew they would never agree, but she wanted to give them the chance. It was only fair.

"It was never yours," they chorused. "Never yours to own, only yours to serve."

Angel jumped onto her chair and signaled to the man she had entrusted with the field degausser. It shot hundreds of fine silvery threads at the sled. For a moment, she thought it might not work, for when the threads reached the edge of the field their ends flicked upward. But then the threads drained the field—there was a great smell of burning as the degausser's iron heat-sink glowed red-hot—and the threads fell in a tangle over the partials. Angel's followers, seeing what had happened, began to pelt the

crew with rubbish, but Angel ordered them to stop. She
wanted to defeat the crew, not humiliate it.

She said, ''I have the only working sleds. That which
I can enhance, I can also take away.'' The partials could
not follow her now. The ship was hers for the taking. She
turned to the Archivist triumphantly. ''Come with me, and
see the end of the story.''

That was when one of the partials walked away from
the grounded sled, straight toward Angel. She confronted
him. She told herself that there was nothing to fear. She
had won. She said to him, ''I'm not afraid of you.''

''Of course not, sister,'' the man said.

He reached out and grasped her wrists. And the world
fell away.

The acceleration was so brutal that Angel almost passed
out. A rush of air burned her clothes and scorched her
skin . . . and then there was no more air. She was so tall
above the world that she could see across its width, tall
mountains on one side and a straight edge on the other,
stretching ahead and behind to their vanishing points. The
world was a dark line hung in an envelope of air. Angel
saw the brilliant point of the sun come into view beneath
it. Vacuum stung her eyes with ice-cold needles; air rushed
from her nose and mouth; her entire skin ached. The man
embracing her pressed his lips against hers, kissing her
with the last of his breath, tasting the last of hers.

~

There were only two pictures after that. Neither spoke
to Yama. They were only pictures.

The first showed a vast room within the ship of the
Ancients of Days. There was a window which displayed
the triple spiral of the Home Galaxy. Two men stood be-
fore it, one grossly corpulent, the other wide-hipped and
long-armed, as small as a child. The Archivist of Sensch,
Mr. Naryan, and the Commissioner of Sensch, Dreen.
Dreen was pointing at the glowing window. He was telling
Mr. Naryan something.

The second picture was from a point of view above Dreen, who stood at the edge of a huge opening in the ship, looking down at the river far below. A figure hung halfway between the hatch and the river. It was Mr. Naryan.

So Angel had died—although if her ship wished, she could be born again—but her ideas lived on. They had escaped with Mr. Naryan, and Yama knew that, with the help of the aspect Angel had downloaded into the space inside the shrines, the old Archivist had spread Angel's story far and wide. The revolution in Sensch was only the beginning of the heresy which had set one half of Confluence against the other.

Shoreward, the sky grew brighter. The floating line of the Rim Mountains freed the platinum disc of the sun. A widening lane of sunlight glittered on the river, like a golden path leading to infinity. Yama watched the play of light on water and thought for a long time about the things that the changed pictures in his copy of the Puranas had shown him.

THE ENVOY FROM Gond, Theias, did not come down from the crow's nest that day. When Aguilar went aloft with his midday meal, Yama asked her to tell the envoy that he was eager to meet him. But when she descended—despite her bulk, she slid down a backstay with an acrobat's casual grace—she told Yama that the envoy sent his apologies.

"He says he has a lot to think about," Aguilar said. "He's a holy man all right. He wanted only a little bread and salt to eat, and river water to drink."

"He could stay up there for the whole voyage, brother," Eliphas said. "They are a strange people, in Gond."

Later, Yama sat alone at the bow and thought again about what the book had shown him. Angel's aspect had wanted him to understand her history, but how could he trust what he had been told? Angel's story was more dangerous than most. It was a scream aimed straight at the most primitive part of the mind, where raw appetite dwelled like a toad at the bottom of a well. Seize the day! Forget duty, forget responsibility, forget devotion to the Preservers, forget everything but personal gain.

There was no denying what she had discovered, but it did not mean that people should fear the Universe. Rather,

Yama thought, they should celebrate its vast emptiness. By accepting the Universe for all that it was, you became a true part of it and could never truly cease to exist until it also ceased to exist. It was not necessary to distinguish between being and nonbeing, between life and mere dead matter. It was all part of the same eternal braid. Only the Preservers had stepped outside of the Universe—an act of transcendence impossible for those who were not gods.

Although Angel feared the ultimate darkness of nonbeing—that was why she had been so quick to despair— Yama knew that it was nothing to fear, for it was nothing at all. The Puranas taught that just as there was no time before the beginning of the Universe, there was also no time after death, for in both cases there was no way to measure the passing of time. Death was a timeless interval before rebirth at the infinite moment at the end of all time.

Angel denied this. She did not trust what she could not understand. She trusted no one but her own self. She had no faith, except faith in herself, and she believed herself to be unique, entire, and circumscribed, so that a time when she was absent from the Universe was, to her, simply unthinkable. It was true that she had passed hundreds of years of shipboard time as a mere text, that she had died and risen again many times. But these brief interregna were nothing compared to the billions of years of nonbeing between now and the end of the Universe, and the machineries which stored her self and gave her rebirth time and time again were real in a way that the Preservers were not. It did not need a leap of faith to believe in machines.

Yama thought about these things for a long time, while the *Weazel* stood before a fair wind and raced her own shadow across sunlit waters. The crew mended the staysails and tightened lanyards and stays through deadeyes; the joints of the deck were resealed with pitch and its planks were scrubbed until they shone as white as salt; a cradle was lowered over the side so that Phalerus could smooth and repaint places splintered and scraped by weather and passage through the floating forest. There had not been time to fully reprovision the ship, and the shoat, which had been pampered on scraps since the *Weazel* had left Ys, was led from its pen onto an oilcloth and soothed with song before the cook cut its throat. For a moment the shoat stood astonished as rich red blood pattered noisily into a blue plastic bucket held under its head; then it sighed and sat down and died.

Tamora helped with the butchery, and ate the shoat's liver raw. The joints, ribs, head, tongue and heart were sealed in barrels of brine, and the intestines were cleaned and steamed with the lungs. After sunset, everyone feasted on fried plantain leaves and fritters of banana and minced pork. All except the envoy, who still had not shown himself. Yama was beginning to believe that he did not exist.

~

That night, Yama slept alone on the triangular bit of decking over the forecastle. He woke at dawn to find someone hanging upside down from a forestay above his head. A small, slightly built man, his flat face, the color of old parchment and framed by a fringe of fine hair, cocked at his shoulder so that he could stare straight down. Yama realized with a shock that the envoy from Gond was of the some bloodline as the long-lost Commissioner of Sensch, Dreen.

The envoy smiled and said in a high, lilting voice, "You are not so much after all," and swung the right way up.

"Wait," Yama said, "I would like to—"

"I expected someone taller, with thunder on his brow, or a wreath of laurels. Perhaps you are not him, after all."

Before Yama could reply, the envoy turned and ran off along the forestay. He swarmed up the mast as nimbly as any sailor and disappeared into the crow's nest.

~

Toward midmorning, Yama saw a machine spinning above the waves half a league to starboard, a little thing with a decad of paired mica vanes that flashed and winked in the sunlight, and a tapered body that was mostly a sensor cluster. He brought it closer, and made it circle around and around the crow's nest. It made a thin crackling sound like oil seething in a hot pan, and occasionally spat a fan of sparks that sputtered down the bellying slope of the sail's rust-red canvas. Captain Lorquital watched from her sling chair, but said nothing.

At last, the envoy swung out of the crow's nest and ran down the forestay, halting halfway and calling to Yama, "Am I supposed to be impressed? You are very foolish!"

Yama let the machine go. It shot away to starboard in a long falling arc that almost touched the river's glassy swell before it abruptly changed direction in a twinkling of vanes, just like a dog shaking itself awake. In a moment, it was lost from sight.

The envoy descended to the end of the forestay. He wore a simple belted tunic which left his legs bare, and carried a leaf-shaped fan woven of raffia and painted with a stylized eye. His feet had long gripping toes. He thwacked Yama on top of the head with his fan, said, "That is for your impertinence, young man," and leapt lightly onto the deck.

The sailors who had been watching grinned at this display. Tamora shook her head and turned away; Pandaras, sitting bare-chested and cross-legged in the shade of the awning at the far end of the main deck, looked up from the embroidery work he was doing on the collar of his shirt. In her sling chair on the quarterdeck, Captain Lorquital puffed imperturbably on her pipe. Eliphas sat beside her, his wide-brimmed straw hat casting his face into shadow.

The envoy said to Yama, "Here I am. What is your question?"

"I hoped we could talk, dominie."

"But what will you talk about? Something important, I hope, unless you are even more foolish than you look."

"Perhaps we should talk about my foolishness."

"You assume that I am interested in it," the envoy said. "Do you know who I am?"

"Theias, the envoy from Gond to the warring cities of the Dry Plains."

"And you, Child of the River, should know that I was contemplating my mission when you sent that poor imitation of a dragonfly buzzing around my eyrie. I like it up there. I can see all that is going on without having to be an active part of it. I can see so far that I can spy into the future—there is trouble in it for you, young man, but why I am telling you I do not know."

Yama thought that for a holy man of great age, of one of the oldest bloodlines on Confluence and from the second oldest city in the world, Theias had a remarkably short temper. But he bowed and said, "I have been rude. I am sorry. I see you know my true name, so I must presume you have some interest in me."

"Your reputation preceded you, and I must say it was larger and more colorful than the truth."

"I suppose your people keep doves," Yama said.

Theias looked at Yama sharply. "Doves? There are all kinds of birds in Gond, but I do not pay much attention to them. Doves do not talk, in any event, or at least ours do not. No, I heard about you on the geophone, and then there is the heliograph, which I used to talk with this cockleshell before I boarded her. I heard that overnight you changed a whole tribe of indigenous squatters on the roof of the Palace of the Memory of the People, and that you started a war between the departments. Some say you are the harbinger of the return of the Preservers; some say that you are a mage in league with the antitheist heretics. I do not suppose you are either one. To look at you, I would say that you are a not particularly successful cateran off to try his luck in the wars."

"I wish that I was. It may sound strange, but that was once my ambition. But I do not know what I am, except that I am not what people want me to be."

"Is that so? I would say that is the root of your trouble. Does the stick know it is a hoe?"

"If it is used as a hoe, then I suppose it would."

The envoy swatted Yama's shoulder with his fan. "No no no. A stick does not have to ask itself stupid questions. It accepts its nature. If you tried to be more like a stick and less like a hero you would cause less trouble. What is that book you were reading? The Puranas, I would say, except no edition of the Puranas has pictures such as yours."

"It is an old edition, and it has been added to since. One of your people was a part of the story. A man named Dreen. He was the Commissioner of Sensch."

"I already know something of Dreen's seduction," Theias said. He scratched behind one of his large, translucent ears, then folded at the knees and sat down and patted the decking beside him. "Here. Sit with me. Perhaps you will show me the rest of the tale."

They sat together on the forecastle deck, under the shifting shade of the sail, for a long time. Theias fluttered his fan under his chin and cursed the heat, and asked many questions about the pictures. Yama answered as best he could, and discovered that he knew more than he had realized. Pandaras brought food—unleavened bread and plain water for Theias, and bread, chickpea paste, slices of melon, and a basket of sweet white wine for Yama—and stayed to listen, sitting quietly and working on the embroidery of his shirt collar.

At the end of the story, Theias said, "Poor Dreen allowed himself to become what he was not. We still mourn him."

"He is not dead, I think."

Theias said sharply, "Even if he stood here before me I would say that he was not alive."

"Because the Ancients of Days made him into their servant?"

"No no no," Theias said impatiently. "You have much to learn."

"I do want to learn. I am seeking the truth about myself, and I am trying to understand how I can train my mind so that I might hope to find it."

"Foolish boy. There is no mind, so you cannot train it. There is no truth, so you cannot hope to reach it."

"Yet I have heard that the men of Gond are great teachers. What do they teach, if not the truth? What do they train, if not minds?"

"We do not teach, because we do not have tongues. How can we tell others what to do without tongues?"

Theias said this with all seriousness, but Yama laughed at the absurdity. "I do not think you are telling me the truth! You play with me."

"How can I lie when I have no tongue? You have not been listening, young man. I waste my time with you. Farewell."

Theias swung onto the forestay and scampered up to the crow's nest.

Pandaras bit off the end of a colored thread and said, "He's a puzzle, master, isn't he?"

"He is trying to make me think, but I am not sure what he wants me to think about."

"I'm only your squire, master. I wouldn't know about these higher matters. My people, we've always let others worry about hard questions. We prefer stories and songs for the pleasure of telling them and singing them, and let others worry about what they mean. Was this Angel in the story the same woman that appeared in the shrines?"

"At first I thought that the woman in the shrine was an aspect, but I think now that she was more like a reflection. The perfect image of a person, but without volition. Like a picture, if a picture could move or speak. In any case, the Angel of the story in my book was not the same as the one who first set out on the long voyage. She was copied many times, and the copies changed so much that sometimes they warred with each other."

"I used to quarrel with my brothers and sisters," Pandaras said, "often in the very worst way. Sometimes, I swear, we all wanted to kill each other. It's always the way when someone is close to you, it's either love or hate and nothing in between."

—

Theias came down from the crow's nest late in the afternoon. He sat in front of Yama and Pandaras and said at once, ''What is the difference between Angel and yourself?''

Yama had been thinking about this, and the question did not surprise him. He said, ''She would not accept her nature, but I do not know mine.''

''You are not as stupid as you pretend to be,'' Theias said, ''but you are not as clever as you believe. I am not talking about small distinctions of intent, but of actions. Both of you have meddled in the destinies of other bloodlines. Therefore, which of you is worse?''

''I did it only because I was asked. Angel did it because she wanted to make an army of followers.''

Theias looked at Yama intently. ''Is that a sufficient difference?''

''In my case, I do not understand how it was done. It is one of the many things I do not understand.''

Theias smiled. ''Then perhaps there is some hope for you.''

''I want to understand these things. You are pleased that I have no control over my powers, but I am frightened for the same reason.''

''And I would be frightened if you did have control over them.''

''I have been able to save myself from my enemies, but often with consequences that seem worse than the danger I faced.''

Theias said, ''If it is in your nature to resist your enemies, then that is what you must do. But I thought that you did not understand your nature.''

''Angel wanted to rule the world. I do not want that. Even if others wanted it, I would refuse.'' Yama smiled. ''I am amazed that I am even speaking of such things. The world belongs to no one but the Preservers.''

''False humility is worse than pride. If you refuse to

accept the burden of your destiny, then you are denying your nature."

"Your bloodline is old, dominie. Does it remember mine?"

"Some say you are of the bloodline of the Builders, but I do not see it myself. They were gone long before any of the Shaped were brought to Confluence, and left only their works behind. Perhaps the Builders never really existed—have you thought of that? People reason that servants of the Preservers must have constructed the world, and so they invent a mythical bloodline and give them all the attributes they imagine world-builders might possess. But perhaps the world created itself, once the Preservers had willed it. For if the Preservers are gods, then they can speak true words, words so true that they are no different from the thing they stand for."

Yama remembered the slate he had been shown in the City of the Dead, which had shown a man of his own bloodline with a starry sky behind him. But perhaps the slate had shown only a story. Perhaps everything was a story. He said, "Words are not truth, are they?"

Theias slapped Yama about the head with his fan. "You have been reading in the Puranas. There are many stories in the Puranas that reveal the nature of the world, although it is only by deep thought and contemplation that one can truly understand their importance. The stories are not lessons in themselves, but act upon the receptive mind to bring it into a state by which one can obtain enlightenment. Words cannot represent anything but themselves, no more than things can be anything but what they are. And so words can teach nothing."

"For one without a tongue, you are a good teacher."

Once again Theias battered Yama about the head with his fan. Yama endured it. Pandaras looked to his sewing and tried to hide a smile.

"Foolish boy," the envoy said. "If you need a teacher, then you are unable to learn." He held his fan a handspan before Yama's face. "If you call this a fan, you oppose its reality. If you do not call it a fan, you ignore the fact. Now, what do you wish to call this?''

Yama took the fan from Theias's unresisting fingers, fanned himself, and handed it back.

Pandaras sang softly, as if to himself:

> *Holding out the leafy fan,*
> *He gave an order of life or death.*
> *Positive and negative interwoven,*
> *Even the Preservers cannot escape this attack.*

Theias smiled. ''Your servant knows the Puranas, at least. You might learn from him.''

''I have not read in them,'' Pandaras said, ''but your riddle reminded me of a game my people play amongst themselves.''

Theias pulled at the long hairs that fringed his chin and said, ''Then your people are wiser than me, for I take these riddles seriously. I must go now. I will leave for the cities of the Dry Plains in a few hours.''

Yama said, ''It will take longer than that to make landfall, I think.''

''Not at all. You see only what you want to see, and ignore the obvious. But at least you have made a beginning. Study the Puranas if you must, although you would do better to listen to your servant's jokes. Now, you may ask me one more question.''

Yama thought hard. He had so many questions that he could not even begin to decide which was the most important, and many required specific answers which Theias, although he was wise, might not know. At last, he said, ''I will ask you this, dominie. Is there a teaching no master has ever taught before?''

''Yes, of course.''

''Then what is it?''

Theias put his hands on top of his head. His fan hung down, covering his eyes. He said, ''I have answered your question.''

"You have told me that you can answer it, dominie, and I know you are an honorable man."

"It is not mind, it is not the Preservers, it is not things."

Theias said this very quickly and immediately swung onto the forestay and scampered away to the crow's nest. There was a brief commotion up there, and then something fluttered over the rail. It hit the slope of the sail and slid down and fell to the deck.

It was Theias's fan. Even as Pandaras ran to retrieve it, the envoy rose above the crow's nest. He was standing on a gleaming disc which slid away through the air at an increasing speed toward the nearside shore, vanishing from sight in less than a minute.

Yama was astonished. He said, "He did not need to travel on the ship. He came only because he wanted to see me."

Pandaras held up the fan and sang:

Theias was too kind and lost his treasure.
Truly, words have no power.
Even though the Rim Mountains become the Great River,
Words cannot open another's mind.

LESS THAN AN hour after Phalerus had climbed into the crow's nest Theias had so precipitately abandoned, the old sailor called in a high, hoarse voice, "Sail! Ten leagues to the first quarter!"

"It is the picketboat," Captain Lorquital told Yama, after looking upriver through her spectacles.

So Prefect Corin had escaped the authorities at the floating harbor. Yama had been expecting it, and he felt a sense of relief rather than fear.

Captain Lorquital said, "I suppose we should be grateful it isn't the warship, but she's rowing steadily and hard and has crowded every yard with sail. I'd say she's bearing on us at twice our speed or better. She won't be able to keep up that pace, but we're in the midway of the river and it will take us more than a day to run to shore and a hiding place. I fear that she will catch us before then."

There was little that could be done, for the *Weazel* was already running briskly before a good wind, dipping and rising through long waves that marched across the Great River from farside shore to near. Captain Lorquital and Aguilar discussed putting out the staysails, but decided that this would drive the *Weazel*'s bows down and make her more likely to plow.

"We should do it anyway," Tamora grumbled to Yama.

"It would only delay the moment, and it would put the ship at risk," Yama said.

They stood by the big square lantern at the stern rail. By naked eye, the picketboat was a black dot far off across the shimmering sunstruck plain of the river.

"It is Eliphas who leads them on to us," Tamora said, "I swear he made a bargain with Prefect Corin while we were all prisoners."

"Yet he urged me not to go into Mother Spitfire's gambling palace. I wish I had taken his advice."

"Grah. It is likely that Eliphas was to be the goat leading you to an ambush somewhere else, which is why he so earnestly wanted you to leave."

Eliphas was talking with Ixchel Lorquital, hunched forward earnestly on the stool by her sling chair, his big hands moving eloquently.

Yama said, "No, he is no more than an old man looking for one last adventure. Look at him—he talks too much to be a spy. Besides, I met him by accident."

"Are you sure?"

"If not, anyone could be an agent of Prefect Corin's, and how am I to live? Eliphas has given me a destination, Tamora. A place where my people might still live. If it is true, it is a most precious gift."

"Grah. I'll believe in this lost city when I see it, but let's say he didn't lie about it. Maybe he didn't start out to betray you. But I still think he's struck a bargain with Prefect Corin. Maybe he didn't want to, maybe he was forced. Think carefully. You keep the spy machines away, but something has led Prefect Corin straight to us. In all the wide river, how would he find us so quickly unless led? It must be Eliphas. He'll have been given a device of some sort. Let me search his kit. Let me search *him*, down to the bones."

"I cannot know about every machine, Tamora. One could hang high above us, and I would not know. Besides,

Prefect Corin knows that we are going downriver. The river is wide, but it is not infinite."

Tamora stared hard at him. Sunlight dappled her skin, glittered in her green eyes. She said, "I will lay my life down for you, willingly and gladly. But I would hope it is not because some fool thinks to line his pockets."

The cook prepared a sumptuous meal after sunset, roasting a side of ribs from the slaughtered shoat and serving it with a sauce of apricots and plums, riverweed fried with ginger, and side dishes of candied sweet potatoes and cassava porridge flavored with cumin. Most of the crew ate heartily, in a fine spirit of gallows humor, and all drank the ration of heart of wine Aguilar had broached.

"There'll be another ration at the beginning of the first morning watch," Aguilar announced. "All hands to deck then."

She did not need to say that by then the picketboat would be in cannon shot of the *Weazel*.

Before they bedded down for the night, Eliphas told Yama, "Our captain hopes to hail another ship tomorrow. She steers toward the nearside shore for that reason. Not because she hopes to reach it before being overtaken, but because that is where the shipping lanes are. If you are right about Prefect Corin's motives, brother, if he has no official sanction but pursues you for his own ends, he will not attack us in plain sight of others."

"I think that Captain Lorquital underestimates Prefect Corin."

"He is only a man. Don't make him more than he is, brother. You will find a way."

Yama had surprised himself by eating his fill, and he found sleep surprisingly easy, too. Perhaps it was because he had come to a decision, a way of ending the uncertainty of the chase. It had crept into the base of his brain during the feast, as cruelly sharp as a knife. He would wake in a few hours, cut the dory free, and make off into the darkness. Once he was far enough from the ship, he would put out the dory's drag anchor and wait for the picketboat to bear down on him. Attracting attention would be easy enough—he had only to call on Prefect Corin's machines. He would allow himself to be captured, and at the first opportunity he would kill the Prefect. He would gather all the machines within the range of his powers and kill everyone on the picketboat, and then continue downriver alone.

He had become a soldier after all, he thought, and realized that the war reached further upriver than the battlefields where armies clashed.

Yama slept and, freed by sleep, his mind ranged far down into the lightless depths of the river, where vast segmented monsters blindly humped through abyssal ooze. Wholly aware that he was sleeping but that this was not a dream, Yama engaged with the minds of these ancient machines. He learned of the immemorial routes they followed among the slow, cold currents at the bottom of the river, of their endless work of pushing sediment into the subduction channels which transported it to the Rim Mountains for redistribution by glacial melt. Theirs was a world defined by the echoes of ultrasonic clicks and pulses, by touch and chemical cues. Neighbor constantly reassured neighbor with little bursts of data; they moved through a web of shared information that mapped the entire river bottom, its braided currents and thermal gradients, its deltas of mud and plains of chalky ooze.

As the machines plowed the river bottom, they were accompanied by their sharers. The sharers fed on the shellfish and blind crabs exposed by the machines, and in return scouted the layers of water above the trenches and channels of the river bottom, and cleaned away parasites which sought lodging on the overlapping plates of the machines' armored hides.

We will help, the machines told Yama, although he had not asked them for help. He expected them to begin to rise toward the surface—any one of them could have sunk the picketboat by ramming it—but when he pictured this the machines told him that they could never leave the river bottom. They would help in their own way.

A league beneath the *Weazel*'s keel, the machines abandoned their routines for the first time in thousands of years.

They altered their buoyancy, lifting from the long trenches they had made in the ooze and drifting on cold currents until they reached the maws of nearby subduction channels. As the machines blocked the channels, the cold river bottom currents were deflected upward, where they spread out beneath warmer layers until they reached the steep drop-off at the coastal shelf. The machines saw, by an increase in the echo delay of their ultrasonic chirps, a huge unsteady lens of cold water growing beneath the warmer layers over the coastal shelf, pushing upward and sideways in unstable equilibrium . . .

—

He was woken by Pandaras. It was dawn, but the light had a diffuse cast. It was like waking inside a pearl. The main mast stabbed upward, vanishing into streaming whiteness. Fog had settled damply over his blanket and drops of water hung everywhere from stays and ratlines.

"There's something wrong with the weather," Pandaras said. He had wrapped a blanket around his narrow shoulders like a cloak, but was shivering all the same.

"Where are the crew?" He would kill them all, if he had to, beginning with this silly little boy. Kill everyone who stood in his way when he took the dory. Or kill everyone now, and let the picketboat overtake the *Weazel*.

"Master, are you all right?"

Yama found that he was awake, standing beside Pandaras in the middle of a fog so dense he could not see the bow of the ship. Something had possessed him, horrible thoughts like ooze from the bottom of his brain. His power, he thought. It would survive any way it could, at any cost. He pressed the heels of his palms to his eyes. Red and black jags of light. He suddenly had a terrible headache. He said, "I am going to steal the dory. You and Tamora will help me."

"Tamora is with Aguilar. They are laying out the weapons, master, as sorry a collection of antiques that I've ever seen. As for the dory, you'll have to explain your plan to the Captain. She came up on deck an hour ago, when the fog bank rolled across the river.''

"The machines of the river deeps,'' Yama said, remembering the dream which had not been a dream after all. A small hope kindled in his breast.

"Machines, master? At the bottom of the river? What would machines be doing down there?''

"I found them and talked to them, and they said that they would help me.''

"They would be dredgers,'' Eliphas said, looming out of the fog. Like Pandaras, he had wrapped a blanket around his shoulders. His eyes were dull pewter in the diffuse light; droplets of water beaded his smooth black skin and clung to the stiff curls of his white hair. "I once saw the carcass of a dredger that had been washed ashore. They are divided into segments like worms, and each segment bears a pair of paddles or other appendages. They clear mud and detritus that collects in the deeps; without them the river would soon silt up.''

Yama tried to think it through. The headache was like a spike driven through his forehead. He said slowly, "They changed the currents at the bottom of the river. The water is colder in the deeps, and perhaps it is now coming to the surface. Cold air is denser than warm air, so that as the air above the river is cooled, it draws down more. That is what drives the wind. The fog forms as the warm air cools, and can no longer carry as much moisture.'' He felt a sudden surge of hope. "They are hiding us from Prefect Corin!''

Eliphas nodded, but Pandaras did not believe a word of it. He said scornfully, "Nothing can change the course of the river!''

"Not its course,'' Eliphas said, "but its currents. The dredgers are very large. The one I saw was several hundred paces long, and each segment was as big as a house. Ah! There it is again!''

A flash of red light far beyond the *Weazel*'s stern, a dim flare that brightened and faded in the fog. Prefect Corin's picketboat was still pursuing them.

"She's trying the range," Captain Lorquital told Yama, when he climbed up to the quarterdeck. "She is still too far off, but I think that she will catch up with us soon. The stronger the wind, the more advantage we have, because we're the bigger ship. But the wind has almost died away since the fog rose. She'll use her oars again, when her men are rested, and then she'll catch us. There's one hope, but it is a small one. If the fog was coming from the farside shore I'd say we were heading into a storm, and a storm might save us if we were blown in one direction and the picketboat was blown in another. But this came up from the nearside, and I can't tell if it means a storm or not."

The fog was dense but patchy. Toward the end of the morning watch the *Weazel* sailed out of a bank of white vapor into clear air. Everyone squinted in brilliant sunlight that burned off the rust-red sail and the white deck, and laid a net of dazzling diamonds across blue water all around. To starboard, long banks of fog hung just above the river like a range of low hills, their white peaks stirred and torn by the fresh cold wind; to port, the black anvils of thunderstorms towered along the margin of the nearside shore. Drifts of hail and rain swept across the sunlit water, falling from such a height that they seemed to come from cloudless sky. The *Weazel* passed through a brief hailstorm that had everyone running for cover. Small silver fish fell among the hail, jinking frantically as they sought escape through the scuppers. The storm ended as suddenly as it had begun, leaving a scattering of dead fish and shallow drifts of hailstones which quickly melted, leaving blood-red stains from the dust at their cores on the white deck.

Soon afterward, the picketboat breasted out of the fog bank behind the *Weazel*. Her light cannon flashed and flashed. Plumes of water driven by superheated steam shot up and collapsed half a league sternward.

"She'll get the range soon enough," Captain Lorquital told Yama. She stood at the stern rail, immense and four-square, her day pipe jutting from a corner of her mouth. She had put on a jacket stiff with braid, the better to make a target, she said. It had belonged to her dead husband, and its sleeves were pinned back from her wrists. "I sent a heliograph signal, telling her to lay back and cease firing, but she's not responding. Of course, I suppose the cannon shots could be a kind of reply."

"Let me speak plainly," Yama said. The brief moment of hope had passed. He was convinced that the dredgers had failed him. That he had failed. "They do not want your ship or your cargo. They want only me. Lend me your dory. I will put out in it and wait for the picketboat to overtake me."

Ixchel Lorquital drew on her pipe and looked at him calmly.

"I will not let them take your ship," Yama said.

"That's a generous thought, but you're only a passenger, and the ship is mine to dispose of as I will. My husband always told me that when passengers start giving advice, you should always agree, and then do nothing about it. But I'd rather not give you the false idea that you'll be able to make such a silly sacrifice, so I will say now that I will not allow it."

Yama stood his ground. "If you have any idea about what we should do, I would like to hear it. You have heard mine."

Captain Lonquital turned her back on Yama and contemplated the picketboat. She said, "I am responsible for all my passengers, not just you. Besides, they'll still sink us. They'll want to leave no witnesses."

"Then put yourself and your crew in the dory. I will stand here in plain sight. They will not chase you if they have me."

Captain Lorquital said stubbornly, "I have sailed this ship for fifty years. I've been captain for ten. I won't abandon her for anyone. Even you."

Phalerus, who had the helm, said, "She's right, dominie. If we get a bit of wind, we still might show those cullers a clean pair of heels."

For the first time, Yama considered giving Captain Lorquital a direct order, but the thought that she might obey him with the same unquestioning alacrity as any machine was unnervingly horrible. Worse was the thought that if he tried to call upon machines to kill Perfect Corin he might be seized by his rage and kill everyone around him. No. He would avenge his father, but as an ordinary man.

Tamora came up onto the quarterdeck. She had put on her corset, and a fusil was slung over her shoulder. The bell of its muzzle flared above her shaven scalp. Captain Lorquital said mildly, "I do not remember ordering the crew to take up arms."

"We can show our teeth at least," Tamora said. "Why don't you put back into the fog?"

"They followed us through the night and the fog," Captain Lorquital said. "Why should day be different?"

At that moment, the man in the crow's nest cried out. Patches of water around the *Weazel* began churn, as if vast pumps were laboring to produce submerged fountains. Glassy hummocks rose up, sputtering rafts of foam and slicks of fine silt. The crew crowded the rails, but Aguilar drove them back, shouting that they must see to the sail. Captain Lorquital told Phalerus to make hard to port, but even as the *Weazel* heeled about, more hummocks spurted around her.

A shoal of fish fled past the ship, swimming so frantically that they flung themselves high into the air. Some landed on the deck. They were as long as a man's arm and their narrow heads and stiff dorsal fins were plated with dull red chitin; they banged and clattered against the deck as they thrashed toward the scuppers. Yama wondered if these were the sharers of the dredgers.

Caught between two rising currents, the *Weazel* began to turn in a slow circle. The sail flapped, filled, flapped. Aguilar ordered it reefed, but before the sailors could obey a stay gave with a snap like a rifle shot. The broken end of the rope whiplashed against the sail and ripped a long tear in the canvas; the block which had anchored it tumbled end over end through the air and smashed into the deck a handsbreadth from Tamora's feet.

The picketboat fired again. The cannon's hot light

flashed water into steam to the port side of the *Weazel*. Water poured over the little ship's waist; spray wet the torn sail from top to bottom. At the same moment, Yama saw something like a bush or tree rise a little way out of the water off the stern. It was white and pulpy, like something dead that had been floating in the water for a long time.

Captain Lorquital ordered that the sail be struck at once, and turned to Tamora and told her to take off her sword and return the fusil to the armory chest.

Yama laid a hand on Tamora's arm. "They will take me in any case," he said.

Tamora glowered. "I'll throw away this blunderbuss, but I'll keep the sword. It's a poor thing, but it's mine, and you'll have to pry it from my cold dead hand."

There was another flash of red light, but the picketboat was no longer aiming at the *Weazel*. Instead, she was firing into the water close by her hull, slowly obscuring herself in flashes of red light and billowing clouds of steam. The sailors aloft in the yards cried out and started to swing down to the deck, and the *Weazel* shuddered as if she had struck some underwater snag. Yama was thrown against the head of the companionway, and he clung there as the *Weazel* rolled to port and then righted herself violently. A forest of white branches was rising around the ship, as if the river was draining away from trees drowned an age past.

Tamora swore and unslung the fusil, but Yama, remembering his dream, told her to hold her fire.

All around the ship, creamy tentacles erupted from the water and rose into the air, questing this way and that. Some ended in leaf-shaped paddles; some bore ranks of suckers; some were tapered and frayed in a multitude of feathery feelers. Huge, sleek arrow shapes moved beneath the churning surface of the river. Many were as long as the *Weazel*; a few were even larger.

The sharers of the dredgers had come to the surface.

Captain Lorquital took Yama's advice and ordered the crew to stand from the rails, and to put down the handspikes and halberds with which they had armed themselves. Most of the sailors promptly climbed back up into the rigging, dodging tentacles which rose toward the mast and plucked at ratlines and stays as if at a harp. Aguilar stood at the bow, her cutlass resting on her shoulder, looking right and left at the questing tentacles as if daring them to get close enough.

As Pandaras and Eliphas clambered up the ladder to the quarterdeck, the ship shuddered and a cluster of palps dropped onto the starboard rail. Their ends thrashed in every direction like a nest of blind white snakes, stretching thinner and thinner as they walked on their tips across the deck. The rail splintered under the mass of flesh.

One of the crew darted forward and with a cry stuck a knife in a rubbery coil. It was Pandaras's friend, the boy, Pantin. Tentacles weaved about him. One plucked his knife from his grasp; two more shot forward and struck him, one around the neck, the other around his feet. Pantin barely had time to scream before he was lifted up. The tentacles pulled in different directions. A rich red spray spattered the white deck and, still clutching the pieces of the boy's body, the tentacles fell backward into the river.

More tentacles poured over the rail. The *Weazel* began to list to starboard. In the yards, the sailors scrambled for better foot- and hand-holds; skinny Anchiale clung to the top of the mast with his long legs tucked into his chest while a tentacle explored the crow's nest.

Yama remembered the polyps which had swum in the flooded chamber deep in the Palace of the Memory of the People. Those had long ago lost whatever powers of reasoning they had once possessed, or so Magon had said, and returned to their cisterns only through habit; yet they had helped Yama by breaking the bridge before the hellhound could cross it. Yama suspected that these giants were different not only in size, but in intelligence, too. They did not serve blindly. They were looking for something. Clinging to the rail, looking down into a roiling mass of tentacles directly below, he glimpsed an eye as big as his head. Its round pupil was rimmed with gold. It stared at him for a long moment, and then it sank beneath a rush of white water.

Yama knew then what the polyps were searching for. He vaulted to the main deck, landing on hands and knees amidst a slowly writhing nest of white coils and cables. Someone shouted and he looked up and saw Tamora falling toward him, her sword held above her head. She landed on the balls of her feet, bounced up, caught Yama's shoulders and shouted into his face, "I won't let them kill you."

"They are looking for me! They cannot tell the ships apart so they are looking for me!"

Something coiled around Yama's thigh. A wet palp slapped his chest and a hundred fine threads crawled over his tunic. Tamora was caught around the waist by a tentacle as thick through as her arm; three more, stretched thin, whipped around and around her corset. She held her arms high, the sword crooked above her head.

Yama was frightened that she would do something that would get them both killed. He reached for her hand, but tendrils as thin and as strong as metal wire coiled around his wrist and dragged it down. Something wet and rubbery slapped onto his face, covering his eyes and nostrils. It stank horribly of fish and rotten eggs. He could feel a hundred tiny suckers fasten and unfasten over his skin as the palp adjusted to the contours of his face. It flexed and spread so that it covered his mouth. Something pressed at his lips and he was frightened that he would be smothered. The pressure was insistent. Although Yama clamped the muscles of his jaws as hard as he could, something the size of his little finger slipped between his lips and probed at the crevices between his gums and teeth before withdrawing.

The palp dropped away from his face. The tentacle around his legs uncoiled and dragged away across the deck. All the tentacles were retreating, thickening and pouring backward over the broken rail. The ship groaned as she righted. Tamora lowered her sword and rested its square point against the deck, so that the sailors would not see how her arm trembled.

Yama ran to the broken rail, but already the sleek shapes were sinking away through choppy water stained with abyssal silt. High above, Anchiale regained the crow's nest and cried out. Yama remembered to look for the picketboat.

But it was gone.

CAPTAIN LORQUITAL INSISTED on sailing the *Weazel* in slow circles around the place where the picketboat had last been seen, but except for a few splintered planks bobbing on the chop nothing was found. The wind was rising, and it drove the fog banks toward the farside shore. Waves grew higher, breaking in white water at their crests, lifting and dropping the *Weazel* as they marched past in ceaseless succession. At last, as it was growing dark, fog engulfed the *Weazel* again.

Captain Lorquital turned her ship to head into the waves, but the waves grew higher still, breaking over the pitching bow and washing the main deck. Wind howled and plucked at the rigging. The crew, in yellow oilskins, with lines clipped to their belts, worked aloft to storm-rig the sail while the *Weazel* now plunged bow first into the high waves, now was battered lengthwise, heeling hard with spray dashing like shot across her. The awning and bedding on the main deck were washed away; so were the chickens and guineafowl in their bamboo cages.

The four passengers retreated to Captain Lorquital's cabin. Pandaras felt the pitching worst and was several times sick in a basin, groaning profuse apologies between spasms. Tamora sat cross-legged on the Captain's wide bunk and glared at Eliphas, who was trying to interest Yama in his theories about the cause of the storm.

Yama hardly heard the old man. He could still sense the minds of the gigantic dredging machines, far below. It was as if the little cabin—the pitching floor covered with felt rugs, the swinging lanterns which cast wild shadows across the tapestries on the lapped plank walls—was slowly turning into smoke, or was a picture projected onto smoke that was slowly dissolving to reveal the real world.

The dredgers had returned to their immemorial routines, singing each to each as, followed by flocks of sharers, they plowed river-bottom silt in the cold black currents. Yama was caught up in their communion. *Join us,* they urged. *Watch over us. Affirm us.* Their siren song wound seductive coils in his brain. They claimed to know all the wonders of the world, for everything came at last to the river. They claimed to remember his people. They would tell him all they knew, they said, if only he would join with them in the joy of forever renewing the world.

Someone shook Yama's shoulder and whispered in his ear. *Master, Master, are you asleep!* Another said, *He's not sleeping. Either he is in shock, or calling up the monsters of the deep has exhausted him.* And a third said sharply, *I have seen men like this after battle. If he is not wakened now he may never wake.* The first voice again: *His coin is filled with light! See? You see? Master, I am taking it away. I think that it is doing something bad to you.*

It was all very far away and insubstantial, like the harmless chittering of agitated ghosts. Yama was only dimly aware of someone slapping his face, of cold cloths laid on his forehead, of being walked around. The songs of the deeps were more immediate than the voices or the manipulation of his body; the channeled abyssal plain more vivid than the pitching cabin and its swinging lanterns.

One of the ghosts said, *It may kill him.*

Yama tried to tell them that that was what he wanted,

to escape his body and fall into the depths where the dredgers sang songs in which every word was true, charged with the wise love of the Preservers.

Something stung his neck. Suddenly his heart was racing and he was back in the cabin, lying in the bunk with Pandaras's sharp, narrow face bent over his. Wind screamed to itself outside; there were a hundred tinkling movements in the cabin as things shifted to and fro. The lanterns swung a beat behind the pitching of the deck.

"He's awake," Pandaras said to the people behind him.

Yama turned his head away, but he was quite alone. The deeps and the singers in the deeps were gone.

Strong hands turned his head. A woman wearing the fierce face of a tiger looked into his eyes. He said, "I know you. Derev. It is time we took away our masks." And then he wept, because he knew that Derev was dead or lost, and all his childhood was burned away.

～

In the end, they had given him an injection of adrenaline.

"You were slipping away from us, master," Pandaras said. "Tamora suggested it."

"It was shock," Tamora said. "I've seen it before. The stuff works on most bloodlines."

Eliphas nodded. "The Preservers made us all in their image, to the least detail."

"They must have run short of time with your kind," Tamora said.

Yama was sitting on the edge of the bunk now, bracing himself as the ship plunged and rose. He said, "I called them, and then they called me. And they were stronger. Stronger and wiser. I should talk with them again, because they know so much . . ."

The cabin door banged open; air and spray roared around Captain Lorquital as she struggled to shut it behind her. She wore a yellow oilskin cape that shed a cascade of water around her flat bare feet. She looked at Yama and said, "It didn't kill you, then. Some bloodlines can't take it. Their hearts burst or their tongues swell up and strangle them. Eliphas says you called up the storm. Is that true?''

''The cold currents no longer rise,'' Yama said. ''I think that it will pass soon. Will it sink the *Weazel*?''

''I'd rather not put her to the test.''

''There is nothing I can do,'' Yama said. He saw that Captain Lorquital did not believe him, and saw too that this brave, capable woman was more afraid of him than of the storm. She nodded curtly and turned away.

—

The storm blew all night and all the next day, and began to fall only in the early hours of the morning of the third day. When Yama came up on deck soon after dawn, Phalerus, who had been fixing the broken rail, turned away and touched his throat in a warding gesture.

The storm had driven the *Weazel* before it. The farside shore was less than a league off the starboard side, a maze of channels snaking between viridescent mudbanks and dense stands of mangroves. The margin of the old shore was a low cliff exposed years ago by the falling level of the river, a long black line that shimmered and jiggled in the heat haze far beyond the mangroves. A sign of his birth, Yama thought, and wondered, not for the first time, if he was the destroyer of the world rather than its savior. The sun shone through a haze of cloud, but it was very warm, and the white deck steamed.

There was no sign of Captain Lorquital, but Yama found Aguilar helping Anchiale and the grizzled slave move foam-cased pieces of machinery in the hold. The cargo had shifted in the storm.

''My mother is asleep,'' the sturdy young woman said. She gave Yama a hard, defiant look. ''She stayed on deck for most of the blow. She saved us all, I reckon.''

Yama said, ''If I could have stopped the storm, then I would have done so at once.''

"You have my mother under some spell," Aguilar said, "but not all of us are charmed."

"I asked only for passage, and paid for it, too. What are you looking at?"

Aguilar had tied an electric lantern to a line, and now the two sailors began to lower it into the gap they had made between the tumbled foam eggs of the cargo. She said, "The ship is wallowing. There. That's why."

Yama looked down. At the bottom of a wedge of darkness, the lantern swung above its own reflection.

—

Captain Lorquital, rumpled from her early awakening, stood at the edge of the cargo well and argued with her daughter for a while. Aguilar maintained that the planking had sprung and the ship was taking on water because braces had been removed from the hull during her last refit; her mother said that the *Weazel* had ridden out the storm only because removal of certain of the braces had made her hull flexible.

"Water could have got in under the tarpaulin," Captain Lorquital said. "The decks were awash for the best part of three days. We were more in the river than on it."

"The covers were reefed fast," Aguilar said stubbornly. "Besides, the water is getting deeper in there."

All of the steel bands had been sprung around the hatch, and the tarpaulin covers rolled away. Anchiale and the slave were lifting out part of the cargo with a winch rigged from the mast; foam-covered ovals cluttered the main deck before and aft of the hatch. Presently, both Captain Lorquital and her daughter climbed down into the hold. They were down there a long time, and Captain Lorquital was grim-faced when they came back up.

"We'll put in for repairs," she told Yama. "I was right, though. The storm didn't spring the planks. The way they're splintered, it looks like something took a bite from them."

A hand-pump worked by two of the sailors lifted water

from the flooding hold and sent sparkling gushes into the river. A patch of canvas was lowered over the starboard side and hauled tight by a rope that went under the keel. There were bumps and groans from the hold; Aguilar went down and came back up, shaking her head. Part of the cargo was floating and shifting about, she said.

"If we're lucky, it won't capsize us or smash the hole wider, but the hole's already wide enough to sink us in a day or two." She stared at Yama. "There's a curse on this voyage, I reckon."

THE BUSINESS OF grounding the *Weazel* took a whole day. Captain Lorquital used the reaction motor to pick a way between banks of stinking mud and stands of pioneer mangroves, and to cross a plain of tall yellow reeds cut by a hundred meandering channels. Phalerus was in the crow's nest, scrying a path through the reed beds, and the grizzled slave of Pandaras's bloodline stood at the bow, using a weighted line to sound the depth.

At last, Captain Lorquital ran her foundering ship aground by one of the islands at the far side of the reed beds. Ropes, pivoting on belts of leather greased with palm oil, were slung around several of the blue pine trees which had colonized the island, and crew and passengers labored at the ship's windlass to haul her out of the shallows until the hole bitten through her hull was visible.

Because the ship was lying at a steep angle, everyone camped on the island. Smoky fires were lit to keep off clouds of black flies and tiny sweat bees. Yama sat a little way from the others, sifting through his father's papers by the light of an electric lamp, once again tracing and checking the threads of logic that bound the complicated computations. The Aedile had been obsessed with measurements, ciphers and calculations. He had been convinced that there was a golden rule by which everything could be divided into everything else, leaving as an irreducible kernel the prime which harmonized the world and perhaps the Universe, the secret signature of the Preservers. His research had never led to anything but a maze in which he had lost himself, but these calculations were different.

Every decad for almost fifteen years, the Aedile had taken measurements of the Great River's slow retreat from the old shoreline around Aeolis. From these, with elaborate allowances for seasonal variation and for the buffering effect of the ice fields of the Terminal Mountains, he had worked out when the river had begun to fail. The answer was not exact, and hedged with cautious interpolations, but Yama believed that the conclusion was inescapable, and laden with appalling implications.

The Great River had begun its inexorable decline at about the time he had been found by the old Constable of Aeolis in a white boat, a baby lying on the breast of a dead woman.

Now Yama once more fumbled his way through the tables of measurements and staggered rows of calculations, trying and failing to guess what they might mean, by turns frightened and full of wonder. Most people blamed the fall of the river on the heretics; was he then their creature? Or was the fall of the river in some way linked with his birth?

When at last he looked up from the papers, he discovered that someone—probably Pandaras—had settled a blanket around his shoulders. The fire had burned down. Apart from the man on watch at the edge of the clearing, a black shadow against the black water, marked only by the fitful red spark of a cigarette, everyone in the camp was sleeping. Yama switched off the little lantern. He lay down on the lumpy ground and rolled himself up in the blanket and fell asleep almost at once.

—

He was woken early the next morning by Tamora. Eliphas had disappeared, she said. No one had seen him go, not even the old slave who had taken the night watch.

"He will be back," Captain Lorquital said. "He has a great curiosity, and he has gone to explore."

But Tamora said with some satisfaction this was surely proof that Eliphas was the traitor who had betrayed their course to Prefect Corin. She was all for tracking him down and giving him a summary trial and immediate execution, but Yama persuaded her to be patient, and was relieved when Eliphas came back in the middle of the morning, casually walking into the camp as a man might walk into his own house.

He told Yama he had been to the far end of the island. "I know this part of the shore," he said. "We are very close to the edge of the world, brother, and a marvelous shrine that stands beyond it."

Yama was sitting on the mossy bole of a fallen tree in a patch of sunlight. Pandaras was cutting his hair. Aguilar and Anchiale were trimming branches from the trunk of a felled pine; the steady sound of their axes rang across the clearing. There was a smell of fresh sawdust and pine resin. A cauldron of pitch sat on white-hot embers in the center of the cleared area, sending up reeking fumes in the sultry heat. In the bright sunlight beyond the shade of the trees, the *Weazel* lay canted in shallow water. Watched by Captain Lorquital, Phalerus and the two slaves were working up to their waists in water, cutting and prying away damaged planks.

"The shore must have changed very much," Yama said to Eliphas. "How can you be certain?"

"You will see, brother, if you come with me. The water is very shallow on the other side of the island. We can wade across to the old shoreline, reach the shrine beyond the edge of the world and return, all in a day."

Pandaras combed cuttings from Yama's hair with his claws. After a moment, he said, "You have hard places under your scalp, master. Here and here."

They were smooth and flat, and had straight edges. One was twice the size of the other. They moved slightly beneath Yama's fingertips. He did not know what they were—or rather, he still could not quite put a name on them—but he was not alarmed.

"I noticed one a few days ago," he said. "They do not hurt. It is nothing."

"My master is ill," Pandaras told Eliphas. "He needs to rest."

"I am quite well," Yama said. "Where is this place?"

"It is not much more than a stroll," Eliphas said, "even for an old man like me. It is a very unusual place, brother. I believe you will learn much from it."

~

In the end, they made an expedition of it. Captain Lorquital sent along the cook to collect fresh roots and greens. Tamora insisted on coming; so did Pandaras, although he was still much weakened by his bout of river sickness.

Crossing the island was easy enough, for little flourished in the dense shade of the blue pines which grew along its central ridge. Eliphas led the others down a path he had cut through a belt of tamarisk and swamp grape, and then they were out in sunlight at the edge of a shallow creek that spread between the island and the low cliffs of the old shore.

The tower was black and slender, standing half a league off like a beckoning finger against the deep blue sky. Eliphas said that once upon a time it had been decorated with prayer flags and banners, and mankites had been flown from its top to keep watch for floating islands.

"There was a camp of soldier monks here each summer. The currents of the air are much like those of water, and this is a place where the islands sometimes gather in shoals and archipelagoes that stretch far away into the sky."

Floating islands!

As a boy, Yama had visited the farside shore every year, when the Amnan had crossed the river for the festival at the beginning of winter, but he had only ever seen one floating island at close quarters. Although a few could always be glimpsed beyond the edge of the world, scattered across the vast blue depths of the sky which wrapped around the world, they were usually so distant that even when Yama looked at them through his stepfather's spyglass they remained little more than dots. It was said that rebel machines lived on the islands, and that tribes of heretics, cannibals and pirates traveled from island to island on the backs of eagles feathered in metal vanes, or on mankites or in balloons. Yama had dreamed that his people might live there too.

Yama had finally seen an island at close quarters two years ago. It had been the last festival that Telmon had attended; at the end of that winter he had set off downriver toward the war, and news of his death had reached the peel-house at midsummer, just after the turning of the year.

That day, Telmon and Yama had gone hunting for cassowaries, leaving the smoke and noise and mud of the festival encampment of the citizens of Aeolis far behind. Winter had come early. Telmon and Yama were mantled in woolen ponchos. Their ponies sent up plumes of steam with every breath. It was almost dark. They had found no cassowaries, but just as they were about to turn back, they flushed out a basilisk.

The size of a small dog, the creature stood foursquare in front of the burrow it had scraped out beneath a briar patch. It raised its frilled mane, yawned to show the triple rows of teeth within its black mouth, and arched its naked, segmented tail over its back. A single drop of venom hung from the hooked spine of its stinger.

Although Telmon and Yama kept a safe distance, Yama's pony stepped about so much that he had to dismount and hold the animal's head and breathe into its nostrils to calm it. He threw stones at the basilisk, but the creature snatched them out of the air and swallowed them, much to Telmon's amusement.

"He swallows stones as birds do, so that he can grind food in his crop. The Amnan say that one will sting itself to death rather than be captured. Unlike snakes, they are not immune to their own poison."

"Dr. Dismas says that the diluted poison can be used to stop the growth of cankers and fistulas. I expect he would pay well for this one. We could easily kill it, Tel. It cannot guard both flanks at once."

"Dr. Dismas is a fantasist," Telmon said. "He tells so many tales that he has long ago forgotten which are true and which are not. You should not talk to him, Yama. There is something odd about his interest in you."

Telmon sat straight in his saddle and kept a careful watch on the basilisk, one gloved hand holding the reins, the other resting behind him, close to the socket in which his javelin was set. He had recently had Sergeant Rhodean shave his hair, leaving only a central topknot. It was the style fashionable among calvarymen; the topknot, shaped like a square loaf, formed a cushion between skull and helmet. His red poncho was neatly folded back to free his arms, showing the silvery padded jacket he wore beneath. His tight knee-length boots had been spit-shined so that they gleamed even in the twilight. He was all that Yama yearned to be: elegant, fastidious, kindly and knowledgeable.

Telmon said, "We will leave this brave fellow to his home. There is still a little light, and we might get lucky."

As they rode on, Yama said, "Dr. Dismas says that he might be able to find out about my bloodline. That is why he wants to make a study of me."

"Dr. Dismas is easy with his promises, Yama. It is a cheap and quick way of winning people's gratitude, and I expect he will move on before he has to make good any of them."

"You will look for my people, Tel. That is, when you are not fighting heretics or charming women."

"I will keep watch every step of the way, but I cannot promise anything. You know that father has made many enquiries, but never with any success. It is not likely that I will come across anyone of your bloodline by chance."

They rode up the shallow slope to the top of the rise. There were narrow tracks worn through the tall grasses which Telmon said were certainly made by cassowaries, but all they found were two peahens, which whirred up under their ponies' hooves and flew off into the dusk. Yama was still calming his pony when Telmon spied the floating island.

It was like a small round barrow or cairn, but it stood where no barrow or cairn should be, atop the long flat horizon of the edge of the world. When Yama and Telmon rode closer, they saw that the island had grounded on a wide apron of eroded keelrock. It was a dense tangle of violet and red vines and tubes and bladders, as wide as a paeonin field and twice as tall as a house. It was full of noises, stealthy rustles and squeaks and crepitations, as if its vines and bladders were continually jostling and creeping over one another, and little blue lights came and went in its tangled thickets. Yama feared that these might be the lanterns of pirates or heretics, but Telmon laughed and said that they were only burning hydrogen vented from collapsed lift pods.

"Heretics are men like you and me. They have no use for floating islands, either in the air or on the river. Birds roost in the islands, though, and they are inhabited by species of crab found nowhere else, which feed on dead vegetation and fiercely protect their home, and barnacles which sieve the air for floating spores. The whole thing is really one organism, for although it appears to be made of many different species, they have all lost their autonomy so that they might function better within the whole. Each is a servant with a different task, and by specializing in their tasks they have lost the ability to live separately. Rather like the peel-house, eh? This one must be diseased. Usually, they don't come so close to the world. Out in the air, Yama, is another nature entirely different from the one we inhabit. You should ask Derev about it. It is said that her people once flew there, but gave that up to live here with us."

Yama, stung by the last remark, said, "That is just a story the Mud People put about. Derev would have told me if it was true."

Telmon smiled. "You are in love with her. O, do not

deny it! I am your brother, Yama, as truly a brother as if you were of my own blood. I have watched you grow up, and it seems to me that you mature quickly. You must give some thought to the shape of your life, for it might not be as long as you wish."

"It might be longer," Yama said.

"It might at that. We do not know, do we? It is a terrible thing, not to know who you really are or why you are here, but you cannot fill your life with dreams. I would like to see you give up your wild ideas, and perhaps Derev can help you. There is nothing wrong with metic marriages, and it would certainly make her father pleased."

Yama said stoutly, "I am going to war, Tel. Like you, I want to fight the heretics and help redeem the world. Besides, I might find my bloodline on my way to the midpoint of the world."

"Perhaps." Telmon looked around. "It grows dark, and the ponies are tired. We can come back and look at this in daylight."

But when they returned the next morning, the island had departed, leaving only a fret of shallow channels eaten into the sloping apron of keelrock on which it had rested. Perhaps the island had not been diseased after all, Telmon said, or perhaps it had cured itself by leaching minerals from the keelrock. He was intensely interested in how the world and its creatures worked. Although Yama spent more time in the library than his stepbrother, it was mostly to dream among the books and maps of finding his bloodline and his true parents. Telmon ransacked it in sporadic bursts to learn about what he had observed, and would as soon dissect the animals and birds he brought back from hunting expeditions as eat them. Like his father, he was interested in things for their intrinsic worth; if he had become Aedile, no doubt he would have filled the peel-house with a menagerie, and its gardens with exotic plants from the length of the world.

But the war had taken him away, and then he was dead. Yama did not know if he remembered the floating island because of the basilisk, or the basilisk because of the

floating island, but he had never forgotten either. Sometimes, he still dreamed that his people were living among
the floating islands; once, while shut in the cell in the hive
of the Department of Indigenous Affairs, he had dreamed
that Derev had taken him to his people, carrying him in
her arms while she rowed the air with strong white wings
she had somehow grown.

And now he was eager to see for himself the archipelagoes that Eliphas promised would be floating in the sky
beyond the edge of the world. He led the way across the
stream, pushing through a strong current that swirled
around his thighs, his waist, his chest, then throwing himself forward and swimming strongly toward the reed banks
that stood along the far bank. He was filled with a sudden
inexpressible joy, for it seemed that with Prefect Corin
dead his life was his own, to do with it as he would in a
world filled with wonders.

Yama hauled himself onto an unstable platform of reeds
and rolled over onto his back and lay there in hot sunlight
with water steaming from his wet clothes, watching as the
others floundered through the stream toward him. Tamora
held her sword above her head; Pandaras rode on the
cook's broad shoulders; Eliphas half-walked, half-swam,
his hands parting the water in front of his narrow chest
with a curiously formal paddling motion, his straw hat
perched squarely on top of his head.

Yama shook water from the slick pages of the Puranas
and glanced at the picture of Angel's final, fatal ascension
before putting the volume away. A dragonfly perched on
a reed and with clawed forelegs preened veined wings as
long as his arms while watching him sidelong with pris-
matic eyes. It flew off with a crisp whir as the others
climbed up beside him. He wanted to go on at once, but
the cook said that first he must set traps for crayfish.

"The Captain will bear down hard on me if I don't,
master. She does love crayfish fried in a bit of salt butter,
and it will stop her fretting about the hurt done to the
ship."

The cook was a large, hairless man with pinkish-gray

skin and a round, dolorous face. His name was Tibor. He wore only ragged trousers belted with a length of frayed rope, and chain-smoked cigarettes he rolled from scraps of paper and strands of coarse black tobacco he kept in a plastic pouch. He absentmindedly snapped at passing insects, and when he spoke he passed his long red tongue over his black lips at the end of every sentence, as if relishing the taste of his words.

Yama, who had learned the trick as a child, helped Tibor weave crayfish traps from strips of reed. The traps were simple things, little baskets of close-woven reed stems with spines at the mouth which pointed inward; when the crayfish entered, they could not back through the spines to get out. Tibor's big hands, each with his long fingers set around a sensitive pad, worked quickly and deftly, making two traps for every one of Yama's. The cook baited the traps with scraps of smelly fat, and tied them at intervals along the margin of the stream.

They soon fell to talking. The cook was from a bloodline which had been enslaved for hundreds of generations; his distant ancestors had fought on the side of the fallen machines in the Age of Insurrection. Having sinned against the Preservers, they were now their slaves, and so the slaves of all free men on Confluence. Most were hierodules, but Tibor had been sold on the open market after the shrine of his temple had failed at the beginning of the war against the heretics.

Tibor was not bitter about his fate, even when he explained that the long vertical scars on his chest marked where his nipples had been seared away. "It is so I cannot feed children, which is what the men of my people do. Our owners do not like us to keep families; our babies are taken at birth and fed on an artificial milk. If they fed from me, they could feed only from me and no other, and I would have to feed them for three years. No owner would want that! You do not believe me, because in most peoples it is the women who care for babies, but it is true. So instead of my babies I feed all of you!"

Tibor laughed loudly at this joke. Despite his down-turned mouth and downwardly slanting eyes, he was by nature a cheerful man. "I am not smart," he said, "but that is good for me, because a smart slave is always unhappy."

Yama thought of the librarian of the peel-house. Zakiel had been born a free man; unlike Tibor, he had known another life. And yet he was happy, for although he possessed nothing, not even his own life, he still had the work he loved. Yama had not thought about this before, and asked the cook many questions. They talked together until Tibor said that they had enough traps to feed the whole ship for two days if only half caught anything, adding that for a little while Yama had been the servant, and he the master.

"Some say you are the slave of all of the peoples of Confluence," Tibor said. Yama asked him to explain, but he only laughed and changed the subject. "This is a bad land, the sailors say. They do not stray far from the ship because of it. They told me I was a fool to come with you, but they'll be glad of fresh food."

Pandaras had fallen asleep in the sun, and woke to find that leeches were feeding on his ankles, which he had dangled in the stream to keep cool. Tibor burned off the leeches with the glowing coal of a cigarette, and Pandaras fussed at the blood that streamed down his ankles from the little round punctures, and complained that he had soaked his second-best pair of trousers and would never get them back into shape, and only shut up when Tamora pointed out that if he wanted to go back now he would have to go back alone.

It did not take long to walk to the base of the tower. The low cliffs were easy to climb, for their black, pebbly clay was deeply gullied by erosion. Beyond was a plain less than a league wide but of seemingly infinite length, thin red laterite and dry grasses punctuated by stands of saw-toothed yucca and palmetto, and sprawling clumps of gumbo-limbo. There were many outcrops of keelrock, smooth spurs or folded layers just as they had been cast a hundred thousand years before. Not even lichens had gained a hold on the slick keelrock, and all across the narrow plain a thousand facets shone and winked in the strong sunlight.

The tower seemed to be fused into the keelrock ridge at the edge of the world, or perhaps it had been grown from it by an art that had been lost since the Preservers had seeded Confluence with the ten thousand races of the Shaped. The tower was smooth and round, and several hundred chains high. Its black surface was slickly reflective, and like the keelrock quite unscarred by time. Tumbled remains of wooden scaffolding and bent hoops which had once been the frames of tents were scattered around it. Ravens rose into the air as the party approached, calling loudly to each other in hoarse, indignant voices before circling away into the vast volumes of air.

Beyond the tower, the edge of the world dropped vertically into clouds that seemed to stretch away forever, as if the world swam not in the void but in a sea of absolute whiteness. Chains of islands floated above their own shadows, lying at different levels in the clear air above the clouds. Hundreds of islands, thousands. Yama marveled at their number.

The shadow of the black tower lay on the white cloud deck like a road, and sunlight broke in splintered rainbows around its top. Beside it, the shadows of the five people were like giants aping their every movement, and around the head of each was a circular rainbow. Yama moved his arms and grinned when his shadow gestured back across leagues of cloud. Pandaras and the cook danced and capered there at the edge of the world, and even Tamora, who had been nervously alert since leaving the ship, smiled at the sight.

"It is a rare wonder," Eliphas said proudly, as if he had led them here just to see this. "A blessing of the Preservers."

Tamora turned and squinted into the level sunlight at their backs. "Grah. I'd say it is a matter of the angle of light and properties of the clouds." She would not agree with Eliphas about anything, but she added grudgingly, "It is some kind of wonder, I suppose."

"It is beautiful," Pandaras said. "It is a miracle of light and air and mist. I will make a song of it."

"Out of my hearing, I hope," Tamora said. "Yama, as soon as we are rested, we should turn back."

Eliphas said to Yama, "The blessings of the Preservers will be upon you, doubled and redoubled, when you visit the shrine, brother. We will leave the others to rest here, and go down together."

Yama said, "Where is the shrine?"

Eliphas smiled, and pointed straight down.

THE EDGE OF THE WORLD

A STAIR, ENTERED by a narrow defile between two tall, roughly man-shaped outcrops that Eliphas called the Watchers of the Void, led down the vertical rock face at the edge of the world. It was broad enough for a decad of men to have descended abreast, but its steps, carved from naked keelrock, were steep and narrow and slippery. Yama discovered that he was terrified of falling, imagining himself plummeting through the cloud deck and continuing to fall until at last passing beyond the envelope of the world's atmosphere and perishing, as Angel had perished in the embrace of a copy of her own self. Were their bodies still falling through the void beyond the world? He and Tamora clung to the carved face of the cliff as they followed Eliphas, finding comfort in the faces and bodies of the men and women and creatures that flowed under their fingertips.

The cook, Tibor, had stayed behind to dig for edible roots, and Pandaras had volunteered to help him. Yama had given the boy his book and coin, in case either drew the aspect of Angel to the shrine. Although the hell-hound had destroyed her, there might be other copies.

Tamora had insisted that it was her duty to watch over

Yama. She thought that Eliphas was leading him into a trap. If she was right then neither her sword nor her bravery could save him, but Yama did not trouble to tell her that. There was a coldness growing in his heart; as he descended the stair it seemed to him that Tamora and Eliphas had become strangers, or worse, ghosts of strangers.

The world's edge was a black vertical cliff that rose straight up from the sea of cloud and stretched away for thousands of leagues on either side. It was dark and cold; the only light was that reflected from the clouds far below. Yama, Tamora and Eliphas were like mice descending a mountain, emmets crawling down a wall.

They descended a long way. At intervals, the stair opened out onto wide platforms or ledges, but always it continued downward. Once, a stream spurted from the cliff and arched above the stair, a muscular silvery braid shredded by wind as it fell toward the cloud deck. Wind buffeted them and whispered and whistled among the intricate carvings of the sheer cliff face. Eliphas's straw hat was blown from his head and dwindled away into the infinite ocean of air.

Presently, light puddled around Yama's feet. Tamora gasped and, five steps below, Eliphas turned and stared. Pinpricks of light reflected in his silver eyes. A handful of fireflies had found Yama and crowned him with their cold blue-white fire. Soon afterward, the stair turned around a fold of rock. There was a wide ledge, and a tall, narrow arch cut into the adamantine keelrock of the cliff.

"The shrine!" Eliphas announced. "Some say it is the oldest in the world. You will learn much here, brother."

"At least as much as from any other hole in the ground," Tamora said.

A fugitive light glimmered inside the arch, and it brightened as Eliphas led Yama and Tamora toward it. It did not come from any source, but seemed to stain the air as pigments stain the water in which a painter dips his brushes.

The place beyond the arch did not seem to Yama to be

a shrine at all. There was no black disc, no altar or sanctu-
ary, nothing but featureless, slightly translucent walls that
curved up and met high overhead. It was as if they had
stumbled into a gigantic blown egg filled with sourceless
light. While Tamora prowled around the perimeter of this
lambent space, Eliphas told Yama, "When the shrine was
in use, one of the priests would stand in the center and
become possessed by the avatar. That is why there is no
screen."

Yama said boldly, "Are you hoping that I can awaken
the avatar?"

He was excited by the idea. He had come so far, from
the silent shrines of Ys to this, a shrine older than any on
the nearside shore. He had learned the extent of his powers, and where his people might still live. He had mastered
the hell-hound and destroyed Angel's aspect. He suddenly
felt that he had nothing to fear from anything in the world.

Eliphas's eyes blankly reflected the even light. Nothing
could be learned from his face. He said, "The woman
should wait outside. She might spoil the reading."

"I stay with Yama," Tamora said. Her voice echoed
from several points in the vaulted space. "If anything happens to him, old man, it will happen to you, too. I'll make
sure of it."

"You could watch from the entrance as easily as from
in here," Eliphas said. "If you stay here, your presence
may disturb the operation."

Tamora crossed her arms. "Then why should I move?
You give Yama airs, making him believe he can wake the
dead. Those days are gone. We don't need avatars to tell
us what to do anymore."

Eliphas said, "He stands there crowned with fireflies.
Is that not sign enough for you?" He turned and asked
Yama, "If the avatar came, brother, what would you ask
it?"

Yama grinned. He no longer trusted Eliphas, but he did
not fear him, either. He strode to the middle of the room.
Immediately, the light thickened around him. Tamora and
Eliphas dwindled into the light becoming shadows that

frayed away and disappeared. Yama seemed to be standing inside a bank of glowing mist, and then the mist cleared and he saw a needle hung before the red swirl of the Eye of the Preservers.

It was the world. Not the representation which Angel's aspect had shown him in the Temple of the Black Well, but the world as it was at that very moment. Yama discovered that if he stared at one spot long enough he flew directly toward it. He saw the brawling streets of Ys and the blackened ruins of Aeolis; the immemorial gardens and tombs of the City of the Dead, and the garden-topped crag where Beatrice and Osric lived. He saw the white contours of the ceramic shell of the holy city of Gond, and followed the course of the Great River toward the midpoint of the world. His gaze passed over a dozen different cities: a city of glass domes like nests of soap bubbles; a city of white cubes stacked over each other; a city built among trees; a city of spires that rose from a lake; a city carved into red sandstone cliffs above a curve of the river; a city of gardens and houses raised high on stilts. He saw the great forests that stretched for a thousand leagues above the Marsh of the Lost Waters, and the ruined cities along the forest shore. Smoke hung in tattered banners where cannon of the army of the Department of Indigenous Affairs were bombarding a fortified ridge.

Yama would have looked more closely at the forces of the heretics then, but he felt that someone among them was looking for him and he quickly turned away. The view unraveled to show the world entire again. He noticed a loose cloud of tiny lights that trailed behind it and at once the constant tug of the feral machine he had called down at the merchant's house became more insistent. One of the lights grew until it eclipsed all the others, burning away the world and encasing him in its radiance.

If the machine spoke to Yama, he did not hear it. But across a great gulf he heard his own voice, apparently answering a series of questions.

Yes. Yes. I will. Yes.

He reeled backward, overwhelmed by light, and fell,

and for an instant thought that he fell through the void beyond the edge of the world. Fell with Angel. Fell in her arms.

Something struck the length of his body with the weight of the whole world. Blood filled his mouth where he had bitten his tongue and cheeks; red and black pain filled his head.

Tamora lifted Yama's head and cleared blood from his mouth with her fingers. She had a shallow cut on one arm. Her sword lay beside her on the softly glowing floor. It was bloody to the hilt.

Yama discovered that he had urinated in his trousers; they clung unpleasantly to his thighs. Dried blood crusted his nostrils and his upper lip, and his head felt as if someone had tried to split it with a wedge. Little bits of fused metal and flaked carbon char were scattered in a circle around him—the remains of the fireflies which earlier had crowned him, now burned out and quite dead.

Eliphas was gone, but there were still three people in the shrine. Something was inside Yama, looking through his eyes. Sharing his thoughts. He knew now why he had eaten mud rotten with termites. For the metal in the bodies of the insects. For the metal needed to grow the machine under his skin.

Tamora got Yama to his feet and helped him walk about until he had recovered his sense of who and where he was. She told him that he had stood raptly in the center of the shrine for hours, his face turned up, his eyes rolled back so that only the whites showed. He tried to tell her what he had seen. The whole world, immense and particular, as the Preservers might see it.

"It is so strange," he said. "So huge and yet so fragile."

Then he laughed, and felt more laughter rising within him, wild and strong. He rose on it as on great wings. It might have possessed him entirely, but Tamora slapped his face and the sting of the slap sobered him.

He said, "The feral machine found me, as I once found it. Or perhaps it found me long ago, and has been bending my will toward it ever since. They are still there, Tamora, the rebel machines and avatars. They were banished from the world at the end of the Age of Insurrection, but they have not abandoned it. They spoke to me or to a part of me, but I cannot remember what they said . . .''

As amazed by this as by his laughter, he began to cry.

"Hush," Tamora said. "Hush." She held Yama and rocked him.

"I serve evil ends," he said. "I cannot be what I am not, and I have been made to serve evil ends. I am their creature."

"You're only what you are," Tamora said helplessly. "Don't try to be more than that, or you'll destroy yourself."

He asked what had happened to Eliphas, and she said grimly that the old man had escaped. "You were so long in your trance or your dream or whatever it was that after a while I sat down to rest. What happened then was my fault. I was watching you instead of watching Eliphas, and perhaps I slept for a moment. He came upon me suddenly and the silly fucker would have killed me if only he had kept silent. But he couldn't stop himself yelling when he struck, and I turned in time to receive his blade on my arm instead of my neck. I cut his thigh with a backswing, but he got away.

"I would have followed, Yama, but I could not leave you. He has not come back. I hope he has fallen off the edge of the world or has bled to death. But I didn't feel my blade hit bone and I don't think I cut any major blood vessels because there's not enough blood on the floor. He's probably still alive. Tell me that you're all right and I'll go look for him, and kill him when I find him."

"He wanted to use me," Yama said. He sat down, feeling suddenly dizzy. The pain in his head was expanding. Red and black rags of light seemed to flutter at the edge of his vision. He was diminishing, or the world was receding from him.

He said, "I thought that he wanted to help me, but I

have been a fool. He wanted to use me, like most people I have met. You were right all along, Tamora. I apologize.''

"I was wrong, too. I thought he was working for Prefect Corin, when all along he had his own plans. This was his chance to master you, but he failed. Everything will be all right now.''

Light flooded the chamber. They both looked up. It came from the entrance, a harsh blinding glare that shriveled the soft radiance of the shrine. Tamora swept up her sword and ran straight through the arch into the light, and Yama followed as quickly as he could.

Outside, the light was as bright as the sun. Every figure in the intricate friezes which covered the cliff wall stood beside its own shadow. The wide steep steps shone like ice. With one hand raised to shade his eyes, Yama saw that Tamora was standing at the foot of the stair, gazing up at the huge shadow that floated behind the flood of light.

It was as big as the *Weazel,* and shaped like a claw. It floated only a chain from the edge of the stair, a hundred or so steps above the entrance to the shrine. Figures moved on its upper surface, bleached shadows within the nimbus of brilliant light that shone from it.

It was a flyer, Yama realized, and he knew then why Eliphas had brought him to the edge of the world. He shouted a warning to Tamora, but she was already bounding forward, taking the steps two at a time. She was running toward Eliphas, who had crept out of his hiding place between two carved figures and begun to climb toward the flyer. The old man had ripped the sleeve from his shirt and tied it around his wounded leg, which dragged behind him as he climbed. He held the little black box to his mouth. He was shouting prayers into the box and when Tamora was almost upon him he turned and raised it as if in a warding gesture. Her sword went under his arm and he jerked and tried to hold onto the blade at the place where it pierced his body.

For a moment, they stood still, joined by the sword. Then there was a flash of fierce red light and a wave of nauseous heat.

—

"Yamamanama," a voice said.

Yama was wedged against the feet of a carved man. He looked up, blinking blood from his eyes. When he tried to speak a bubble of blood swelled inside his mouth and broke over his teeth and his lips. All of his muscles had turned to water.

The black, bent figure of Dr. Dismas stood over him. The apothecary had a pistol in his left hand, its blunt muzzle laid along his thigh. In his right he held a little black box, the twin of the one Eliphas had carried. Behind him, the flyer floated down and grounded against the ledge at the entrance to the shrine, just as the floating island Yama and Telmon had seen on the farside shore had grounded against the edge of the world. Above the flyer, the stair rose between the black cliff and the sky, scorched clean by fire.

"It was ordained we should meet again, dear boy," Dr. Dismas said. "How pleased I am to see you."

Yama spat a mouthful of blood. "It was you," he said. "All the time it was you."

The light around them was very bright. He could clearly see the edges of the plaques under the skin of Dr. Dismas's hands. The same sharp-edged shapes that lay under his own scalp.

Yama said, "How? How did you infect me?"

"At The House of Ghost Lanterns," Dr. Dismas said.

"In the beer. Or the food . . ."

"Good! Very good! Yes. Little builders. They have been working ever since. You are strong. Yamamanama. You resisted them for a very long time."

Yama spat more blood. So much blood. First Lud, and then Lob and Unprac, the landlord of The House of Ghost Lanterns. The palmers and the bandits, the cateran who had tried to kill him, Iachimo and the rogue star-sailor and its creatures, the two pythonesses of the Department of Vaticination, the old guard, Coronetes, and all the clerks and soldiers in the Department of Indigenous Affairs, the mage and the soldiers who had taken the peel-house, the traitor Torin, the Constable of Aeolis and his sons and the mob, Prefect Corin and the crew of the picketboat, Dr. Dismas's man and the boy, Pantin. And the Aedile, his heart broken, and now Tamora and Eliphas. All dead. All because of him.

Yama said. "Tamora thought that Eliphas was in league with Prefect Corin. But all the time he was working for you."

Dr. Dismas waggled the little black box. "He kept in touch using the twin of this, right until the end. A pity he had to be killed. He was a useful servant. He was turned long ago, in one of the chambers beneath the surface of the world. He was looking for old texts to sell, but found something far more valuable. Or rather, it found him."

"I thought that he was praying to that little box."

Surreptitiously, Yama pulled the fetish from his wrist. When Pandaras came to look for him, he would find it, and know that his master was still alive.

"Long wavelength light," Dr. Dismas said. "Bounced off one of us a million leagues above the plane of the world. You will soon understand everything, Yamamanama."

Yama felt very cold. He was badly hurt, and the thing in his head had turned his heart to ice. He said, "My people. Eliphas found where . . ."

"The map and the scavenger's account? My dear Yama-manama, they were forgeries, and not even very good forgeries. But they did not have to be, because you wanted so very much to believe in them. No, your people died out long ago. All are dead except you, and even we do not know where you came from. Once I realized what you were, I went to Ys to search for your origin. Eliphas helped me then, but we found nothing and I came back empty-handed. It does not matter. All that matters is that you are here, and that you will join us. You are my creature, Yamamanama. We will do wonderful things together. To begin with, we will form an alliance with the heretics, and save the world."

Men walked out of the light toward them. Yama was lifted up. Light swept over him, and then a warm darkness. Presently, the flyer tilted away from the side of the cliff and rose above the edge of the world. There was a small business to attend to, a few witnesses to be removed. It did not take long, and when it was done the flyer shot away downriver, toward the war.

And now an excerpt from
The Third Book of Confluence:
SHRINE OF STARS
by Paul J. McAuley

DR. DISMAS CAME into the big white room without ceremony, flinging open the double doors and striding straight toward Yama, scattering the machines which floated at various levels in the air. A decade of servants in various brightly colored liveries trailed behind him.

Yama had been performing some of the exercises Sergeant Rhodean had taught him, and jumped up as Dr. Dismas approached. He was barechested and barefoot, wearing only a pair of silk trews and a wide bandage wound twice around the burns on his chest. Ever since his capture, he had wanted nothing more than to be able to command just one machine and make it fling itself into Dr. Dismas's eye and turn through his brain, but no matter how much he strained to contact the machines around him, he could not bend them to his will. The powers which he had painfully learned to master had been taken from him by the thing which had grown from seeds Dr. Dismas had, by a trick, planted in him at the beginning of his adventures. He was plagued by a fluttering of red and black at the edges of his vision, and was visited in his sleep by strange and terrible dreams which, although he utterly forgot them upon waking, left an indelible residue of terror and loathing.

Dr. Dismas did not speak at once, but clapped his stiff hands together in an irregular rhythm and paced up and down while looking sidelong at Yama, as if trying to marshal his hectic thoughts. The servants stood in a row behind him. They were all indigens, and all mutilated. Yama scarcely noticed them. He was watching the bent-backed, black-clad apothecary as a mouse might watch a snake.

"You are awake!" Dr. Dismas said at last. "Good, good. How are you, Yamamanama? Any headaches? Any colored lights or spots floating in your vision? Your burns are healing nicely, I see. Ah, why do you look at me that way? I am your savior!"

"You infected me with this disease, Doctor. Are you worried that it is not progressing as fast as you wish?"

"It is not a disease, Yamamanama. Do not think of it as a disease. And do not resist it. That will make things worse for you."

"Where is this place, Doctor? Why have you brought me here? Where are the others?"

He had asked these questions many times before, and Dr. Dismas had not yet answered them. The apothecary smiled and said, "Our allies gave it to me as a reward for services rendered. A part payment, I should say, for I have only just begun. We, my dear Yamamanama, have only just begun. How much we still have to do!"

Dr. Dismas marched across the room and stood for a moment at the great window, his hands twisted behind his back. But he could not stand still for long, and whirled around and smiled at Yama. He must have recently injected himself with a dose of the drug, for he was pumped full of energy he could not quite control, a small, sleek, perpetually agitated man in a black claw hammer frock coat that reached to his knees, the stiff planes of his brown face propped above the high collar of his white shirt. He was at once comic and malign.

Yama hated Dr. Dismas, but knew that the apothecary

had the answers to many of his questions. He said, "I am your prisoner, Doctor. What do you want from me?"

"Prisoner? No, no, no. O, no, not a prisoner," Dr. Dismas said. "We are at a delicate stage. You are as yet neither one thing or another, Yamamanama. A chrysalid. A larva. You think yourself a power in the world, but you are nothing to what you will become. I promise it. Come here. Stand by me. Don't be afraid."

"I am not afraid, Doctor." But it was a lie, and Yama knew that Dr. Dismas knew it. The doctor knew him too well. For no matter how much he tried to stay calm, the residue of his dreams, the flickering red and black fringes that plagued his sight, the thing growing under his skin, and the scuttling and crawling and floating machines that infested the room all conspired to keep him perpetually fearful.

Dr. Dismas began to fit a cigarette into the holder which had been, he claimed, carved from the fingerbone of a murderer. His concentration on the task was absolute; his left hand had been bent into a stiff claw by the plaques which grew beneath his skin—a symptom of his disease, the disease with which he had infected Yama. At last it was done, and he lit the cigarette and drew on it and blew two smoke rings, the second spinning through the first. He smiled at this little trick and said, "Not afraid? You should be afraid. But I am sure that there is more to it than fear. You are angry, certainly. And curious. I am sure that you are curious. Come here. Stand by me."

Yama drew on the lessons in diplomacy which his poor dead stepfather, the Aedile of Aeolis, had so patiently taught him. Always turn any weakness into advantage by admitting it, for nothing draws out your enemy like an exposed weakness. He said, "I am afraid, Doctor. I am afraid that I might try to kill you. As you killed Tamora."

"I do not know that name."

Yama's hatred was suddenly so intense that he could hardly bear it. He said, "The cateran. My companion."

"Ah. The silly woman with the little sword and the bad temper. Well, if I killed her, it is because she was responsible for the death of Eliphas, who so successfully led you to me. An eye for an eye, as the Amnan would say. How is your father, by the way? And the stinking little city he pretends to rule?''

Yama charged at the doctor then, and one of the flock of machines which floated in the big, airy room swerved and clipped him on the side of the head. One moment he was running headlong, the next he was sprawled on his back on the rubbery black floor, looking up at the ceiling. Pain shot through him. His chest and face had been badly seared by the backwash of the blast which had killed Tamora and Eliphas, and his ribs had been cracked when it had knocked him down. A splinter of rock had pierced his lung, too, and although he had been treated by a battery of machines, he tasted blood at the back of his mouth now.

Dr. Dismas smiled down at him and extended the claw of his left hand. Yama ignored it and laboriously and painfully got to his feet.

"You have spirit," Dr. Dismas said. "That's good. You will need it."

"Where are the others? Pandaras, and the crew of the *Weazel*. Did you leave them behind?"

"The *Weazel*? Oh, that's of no consequence. It is only you I am interested in, dear Child of the River. Are you all right? Not hurt by your fall? Good. Come and stand by the window with me. I have much to tell you, and we will make a start today.''

Yama followed Dr. Dismas unwillingly. The room was part of a mansion hollowed out of one of the flanks of the floating garden. Its single window, bulging like an eye, overlooked a vast panorama. Far below, Baucis, the city of Trees, stretched away in the sunlight of a perfect afternoon. Other floating gardens hung at various heights above their own shadows, like green clouds. Some were linked together by catenaries, rope slides and arched bridges of shining metal. An arboreal bloodline had inhabited Baucis before the heretics had come; their city had been a patchwork of ten thousand small woods separated by clearfelled belts and low, grassy hills. Now many of the woods had been cut down. New roads slashed through the rolling landscape, a network of fused red clay tracks like fresh wounds. The heretics had made their encampments on the hills, and a kind of haze or miasma of smoke from weapons foundaries and numerous fires hung over the remaining patches of trees.

Beyond the city, the vivid green jungle stretched away beneath the mist of its own exhalations. The floating garden was so high up that both edges of the world were visible: the ragged blue line of the Rim Mountains on the right and the silver plain of the Great River on the left, and all the habitable world between them, dwindling beneath strings of white cloud toward a faint hint of red. In the days since he had been captured, Yama had spent much of the time gazing at this scene, and had convinced himself that he could see beyond the fall of the Great River and the mountains at the midpoint of the world to the beginning of the Glass Desert.

Dr. Dismas exhaled a riffle of clove-scented smoke and said, "Everything you see is the territory of the heretics. Two hundred cities downriver of this one, and a hundred more upriver. Thousands of bloodlines are theirs now. And soon the rest, Yamamanama. Soon the rest, unless something is done. Their triumph is great, but they must be prevented from completing it. They have meddled in much that they do not understand. They have tried to wake the great engines in the keelways of the world, for instance. Fortunately, they did not succeed."

Dr. Dismas looked sideways, but Yama said nothing. The apothecary had a habit of alluding to matters about which Yama knew little, perhaps in the hope of drawing out secrets, as a fisherman might scatter bait to lure fish to the surface. Yama had glimpsed something of the vast machines beneath the surface of the world when Beatrice had returned him to the peel-house by the old roads in the keelways, but he had not known much about his powers then, and had not thought to try and question them.

"Well, for now you will help the heretics," Dr. Dismas said briskly. "You will provide a service for which we will later ask payment. Please. For your sake do not make any more sudden moves. My servants here are simple things and have very literal minds. I would not like to see you hurt because of a misunderstanding."

Yama's fist was so tightly clenched that his fingernails cut four points of pain into his palm. He said, "Whatever I was able to do has been taken away from me. I am glad that it is gone. Even if I still had it, I would never choose to serve you."

"Oh, it isn't a question of choice. And it is still there, somewhere or other. I'm sure it will surface again."

"Do what you will. Invoke the thing you placed inside me. Invoke your disease. But do not involve me. Do not try to make me take your side or see your point of view."

Yama turned away and crossed to the bed and sat down. Dr. Dismas remained by the window. Hunched into his frock coat, he slowly and carefully lit another cigarette and exhaled a plume of smoke while gazing at the city spread below, like a conqueror at his ease. At last, without turning around, he said, "You have it easy, Yamamanama. I envy you. I was alone when I was changed, and my paramour was old and badly crippled. We both nearly died before the union was complete, and we nearly died again when we retraced my path across the Glass Desert. That was almost forty years ago. An odd coincidence, don't you think?"

Yama was interested, despite the loathing he felt toward the apothecary. He said, "I suppose that it was something to do with the Ancients of Days."

"Good, good. You have been learning about your past. It will save us much time. Yes, it had something to do with one of them. With the most important of them, in fact. All of the Ancients of Days were merely variations on a single theme, but the one who called herself Angel was closest to the original. I believe that you have met her."

The woman in the shrine. The woman in white. Yama said, "It was the revenant of something five million years old, of a pathetic scared fool who failed at godhood and escaped her enemies by fleeing to a neighboring galaxy. She found nothing there and returned to meddle with Confluence. She was the seed of the heretics, and was killed by her fellows.''

''Indeed, indeed. But before she was killed, Angel left a copy of herself in the space inside the shrines. Her aspect—that was who you talked to. She wants you on her side, and so she told you her story. And told you how powerful she was, no doubt.''

''I destroyed her, Doctor.''

Dr. Dismas smiled. ''Oh, I think not. You have much to learn about distributed information. She is stored as a pattern of interrupted light deep within the space inside the shrines. Perhaps your paramour will destroy her, when it is stronger, and if I so choose, but you destroyed only the copy of a copy.'' Dr. Dismas plunged his right hand into the pocket of his frock coat and brought out the plastic straws which he habitually cast when he needed to make a decision. He rattled them together, smiling craftily, and put them away. ''The fate of gods in my hands—don't you find it amusing? Ah, you are a humorless boy, Yamamanama. It is not your fault. Anyone brought up by that stiff-backed narrow-minded backward looking innumerate superstitious fool would—''

Yama roared and ran at Dr. Dismas again, and again was knocked down by one of the machines, but before he fell he had the satisfaction of seeing the apothecary take a step backward. For a moment he was blinded by a silent roar of red and black that seemed to fill his head. He rolled on to his back, a ringing in his ears and the taste of blood in his mouth, and slowly got to his knees. When he stood, the room seemed to sway around him, and he sat down on the edge of the bed.

Dr. Dismas lit another cigarette and watched Yama with a genuine tenderness. ''You'll need that spirit, Yamamanama,'' he said. ''It is a hard road I have set you on, but you will thank me at last. You will be transformed, as I have been transformed. I will tell you how.

''It is a symptom of the disastrous reversal in the development of the peoples of Confluence that, although their technologies predated the creation of our world by five million years, the Ancients of Days were able to manipulate much that was hidden or lost to the ten thousand bloodlines. In particular, Angel was able to enter the space inside the shrines, and she learned much there.''

''She destroyed the avatars,'' Yama said. ''People believe that the heretics destroyed them, but it happened before the war began.''

''Hush. This is my story, not hers. You already know hers, it seems. She tried to recruit you, but I know that you resisted, for otherwise you would not be here. You chose wisely. She is not our friend, Yamamanama. She is our ally, yes, but not our friend. Enobarbus submits to her without reservation, but we have our own plans. And besides, much of what she says is self-serving, or simply untrue. Angel did not destroy the avatars. That was the work of the copy of herself that she installed in the space inside the shrines. The aspect you talked to was a copy of that copy, but no matter. In any form, it is a poor deluded thing. After Angel died, it found itself besieged, and it lashed out. That was how the avatars came to be destroyed. The avatars, and many records, and most of the directories and maps within the space inside the shrines. That was the true war; the war fought since, between the heretics and the beaucrats, is but its shadow. And so the bureaucrats were defeated before the first ship of fools sailed from Ys to put down the uprisings at the midpoint of the world.

''But that does not concern us. While Angel was traveling downriver toward the last and least city of Confluence, where she would plant the seed that would grow into the heretics, at that same moment, I was entering the Glass Desert. I had been trained as an apothecary—my family had been a part of the Department of Apothecaries and Chirurgeons for thousands of years—but I sought greater knowledge. Arcane knowledge hidden or forgotten or forbidden by priests and bureaucrats frightened by the true destiny of the world. As a child I had riddled the crannies of the Department's library. This was before the heirodules within the screens of the library were destroyed along with the avatars, and written records were almost entirely unused then. There were vast amounts of trash, but I discovered a few gems."

Yama said, "And that was where you met Eliphas."

"No, not then. I knew him, in the way that a boy might glancingly know everyone who works in the place where he grows up, but until my return last year I doubt that I had ever exchanged a single word with him. Eliphas had long before given up searching for ancient treasures, although his friend and one-time partner, the chief of clerks of the library, did give me encouragement. *He* was interested in maps, but I found something better.

"It was the personal account of a traveling chirurgeon five thousand years dead. He had worked amongst the unchanged bloodlines at the midpoint of the world, and found a cluster of odd symptoms amongst certain of the nomadic clans which sometimes ventured into the ancient battlegrounds of the Glass Desert. It was unusual in that the same symptoms were exhibited by different bloodlines. Most clans killed or cast out those afflicted, but in some they were considered blessed by the Preservers and became soothsayers, prophets, oracles, mysts and so on."

"This is the disease with which you infected me," Yama said.

Dr. Dismas flung out an arm, pointed at Yama, and screamed with sudden violence, "Quiet! Enough interruptions! You will be quiet or I will . . ." His arm trembled violently, and he whirled around to face the window. His shoulders heaved. When he turned back he was smiling and there was honey in his voice. "This is my story, Yamamanama. Do not race ahead. You think you know more than you do."

"Perhaps I am not interested in your story, and want to bring it to its end as quickly as possible."

"Ah, but you are interested. I know you are. Besides," Dr. Dismas added, in the same overly sweet, wheedling voice, "if you do not listen I will slice off one of your ears as a lesson. Now, where was I?"

"You had discovered an old traveler's tale."

Yama was interested, despite himself. Dr. Dismas's story was similar to the lies Eliphas had used to lure him downriver. Eliphas had claimed to have found a traveler's account of a hidden city in the Glass Desert, a city inhabited by people of Yama's bloodline. The documents he had shown Yama had been fabrications, but perhaps the old question runner's lies had been rooted in truth after all.

Dr. Dismas said, "I returned again and again to this poorly written memoir until I had it by heart. I even made a copy of it. But I was a child, with many long years of study ahead of me. My fascination faded and I turned to other matters. When at last I qualified and was sent to my first post, I took only the tools of my trade, in a leather wallet bequeathed to me by my grandfather, and the standard catalogue of electuaries, panaceas, simples, urticants and so on. I did not take the copy of the memoir which I had made, for I had set it aside with other childish things.

"I will not trouble you with the details of my first posting, nor those of my second. I was a foolish and naïve young man, eager to do good in a world where goodness can gain only small and temporary victories. But at my third posting, fate intervened. I do not believe in the Preservers, Yamamanama. Or rather, I do not believe that they exist any longer in the phenomenological universe. But it was as if something, some agency, touched my life then, and changed it for ever. Perhaps my paramour's reach was longer than it seemed.

"I was dispatched to a mean little town in the mountains beyond the fall of the Great River, close to the border of the Glass Desert. And it was here that I encountered the symptoms of which I had read and reread with wonder as a child.

"Of course, my interest was rekindled at once. traveling with a caravanserai, I visited the summer camps of unchanged nomads and learned much of the course of the disease. I marked its progression from simple plaques and associated loss of sensation to mania, blindness and death. I was able to dissect the fresh corpse of a haruspex—I had to break into her tomb to do it—and chart the growths and nodes along her nervous system. And by conflating the routes of the various clans of nomads through the margin of the Glass Desert with the incidence of the disease, I was able to plot its focal point.

"I will not trouble you with a long catalogue of the hardship I endured to reach my goal. I went alone because I trusted no one, and that almost killed me. The Glass Desert is a terrible place. There is no free water beyond the mountains of the Great Divide, for the river which was the mirror of our Great River failed after the wars of the Age of Insurrection. It is a place of glare and heat, of endless sand dunes, salt pans, alkali flats, vitrified craters and devastated terrain. Nothing grows but stoneworts and a few hardy plants which are more like machines than living organisms—when I first saw them I knew then the memoir had not lied, and I was almost killed when, in my excitement, I went too close to a clump of them.

"I took a string of camels and a mule, but the camels contracted a falling sickness and I had to leave most of my supplies with their corpses. The mule survived until a great dust storm blew up. The storm lasted twelve days and all that time the mule was tethered outside my tent. When at last I emerged, with the sun a bleary spot in a sky still stained ocher by suspended dust, I found that the poor beast had been flayed to its bones, and things like turkey vultures were quarreling over what remained. They too were partly machine, and I had to kill them when they turned on me. One clipped me with the tip of a wing, and its serrated flight feathers opened a great gash in my side, clear down to the cartilage sheaves of my chest cage.

"I went on, weakened by my wound, and carrying what I could, knowing that I did not have enough water or food for the return journey. I walked at night, and by day sheltered from the heat and from dust devils and fierce little storms of knife-sharp crystallized silica. It was burning hot by day, and so cold at night that with each breath little puffs of ice crystals fell, tinkling, from my lips. The sky was utterly clear; I felt that I could see past the distant smudges and specks of galaxies to the afterglow of the hatching of the cosmic egg. I walked like this for four days, until I found the place I had been searching for.''

Dr. Dismas lit another cigarette. His hands were trembling badly. Yama watched him closely. He was caught up in the story because what had happened to Dr. Dismas then was happening to him now. The red and black flickering which troubled his vision had intensified; it was as if he was peering through banners which flew on a impalpable wind. Terror beat within him on great steel wings. He had the sudden strange notion that instead of being captured by Dr. Dismas outside the shrine, he had fallen off the edge of the world and was falling still, that this was a terrible dream from which he might at any moment awaken to worse horror.

"O Yamamanama,'' Dr. Dismas said at last. "Child of the River. How I envy you! It was so long ago that I have only a few bright memories, worn smooth by my constant handling like pebbles in the bed of a mountain stream. It was so terrible, and so wonderful! Such pain, and such joy! Such joy!''

Yama was amazed, for the apothecary was weeping.

Dr. Dismas's expression was haunted yet ecstatic. "Oh yes,'' he said. "Tears. Poor weak human tears. For what I was. For what I became, in the embrace of my paramour. I was reborn, and it was painful and bloody and wretched. And out of it such glory, such joy. Such joy.''

He blotted the tears from his brown, plaque-stiffened cheeks with the claw of his left hand and sniffed hard. Usually, Dr. Dismas displayed emotion as a theatrical puppet might hold an appropriate mask before its immobile, painted face. (Was it part of the Preservers' plan, Yama suddenly wondered, that almost all of the bloodlines shared the same facial expressions and bodily postures which expressed fear and hope, rage and love, happiness and sorrow?) His real thoughts were unguessable. But for the first time he appeared to be wholly possessed by human feeling.

"Ah," Dr. Dismas said at last, sniffing delicately, "it moves me still to think about it. I had come upon the place without realizing it. I was delirious by then. My feet were blistered and badly bleeding. I had heat sores all over my body. My joints were swollen and I was so badly sunburnt that my skin was blackened and cracked, and constantly wept blood and pus. It was dawn. A fierce hot wind was blowing, sucking moisture from my body. I had reached a place of chaotic terrain. The land was like rough-cast glass dissected by a maze of wandering ridges and canyons. I was lost, and too ill to know that by the end of the day, or by the end of the next day, I would surely be dead. I stumbled into the shade of a deep ravine and threw up my tent and crawled inside.

"My paramour had heard my footsteps leagues away, listening with a thousand whiskers grown across the land. It had watched me from decades of different eyes, some fixed like crystals in the rock and glass, others mounted on scuttling extensions it had cleaved from the wreckage of its own body.

"It was those extensions that came for me, in the heat of noon."

"There were hundreds of them. They were like spiders or mantids fashioned out of black glass. They moved with stiff scuttling motions. I woke when the first cut through the material of my tent. In a fevered panic, I killed decades with a single shot of my energy pistol and stumbled from the blazing wreckage of my tent. More waited outside, clinging to the vertical rock face beneath which I'd camped. They fell on me, stung me insensible, and spun a cocoon around me.

"And so began—"

A chime sounded out of the midair of the room. "What now?" Dr. Dismas said irritably, and turned his back on Yama and fell into what seemed to be a one-sided conversation. "Can't it wait? Yes, the boy. Yes I am. Yes. No,

I want to tell him. You wouldn't understand why, unless you . . . Yes, I know you . . . Very well, if you must.''

Dr. Dismas turned and gazed at Yama with his yellow eyes as if seeing him for the first time. He said, ''We were speaking of the courtship between my paramour and myself. I told you how it began, of the little machines which were as much a part of my paramour as your fingers and toes and eyes and ears are a part of you, Yamamanama. They found me and paralyzed me as a hunting wasp paralyzes a fat caterpillar. And like so many hunting wasps, they wound me in a cocoon of threads spun from their own bodies. The threads were possessed of a certain intelligence, and began to mend my wounds. Meanwhile, the machines brought me water enriched with vitamins and amino acids and sugars, and fed it to me drop by drop.

''I was delirious, and I did not understand what was happening to me. I dreamed that I was in lazaret in the cool shade of palm trees, with the sound of running water outside its white canvas walls. Perhaps it was a presentiment of the future. And all the time, my paramour was creeping toward me.

''For it had realized that I was a prize out of the ordinary. It had allowed its extensions to infect any nomads that padded by, but the things which grew in the nomads' bodies were no more intelligent than the extensions themselves. But I was something rarer, and it came to me itself. Or other, it grew toward me, as a desert plant will grow a root toward a lode of water.

''I do not know how long it took, but at last it reached me. A silver wire no thicker than a spider's thread pierced my skull and branched and rebranched a million times, uniting with the neurons in my visual and auditory lobes. And then my paramour stood before me, terrible in its glory, and told me the true history of the world.

''I will not tell you what it told me. You will have to learn that yourself. It is growing inside you. Soon it will be complete, and will awaken fully. But I will say that what I learned then transformed me utterly and completely. I learned of my paramour's fabulous battles in the vacuum beyond the envelope of air which wraps our world, of its splendid victories and the terrible defeat of its final fall. It plunged from a great height and at a great speed, transforming as it fell. It struck hard and penetrated deep within the mantle of the world, melting rock with the heat of its fiery fall and sealing itself in its tomb. Ah, I see you understand. Yes, you are awakening. You share this, don't you? It lay there for ten thousand years, slowly reconfiguring itself, sending out its extensions into the desert around, listening, learning.

"Imagine the strength of will, child! The will to survive ten thousand years in agony and utterly alone. Until very recently it had not dared to communicate with those of its fellows which had survived the wars of insurrection. It had to deduce what was happening in the world by interrogating the wretches its extensions captured and changed. The stings of its extensions infected many, but only a few returned, and the compass of their lives was so narrow that they had little useful to communicate.

"And then I arrived, and all was different. It was not just that I was one of the changed bloodlines, but that I arrived soon after Angel meddled with the space inside the shrines. My paramour had heard her call. And so I was healed and sent back to find out what I could about the new war, and to make an alliance.

"But I did much better than that. I won so much more for my paramour. I won this hero, the last of the Builders, the Child of the River, and I laid him at its feet. The little seeds that I tricked him into ingesting were from my paramour, of course, my paramour and your father. And so we are united, you and I. Together we will do great things," Dr. Dismas said, and smiled stiffly and bowed low.

"I would rather die," Yama said. "I will not serve, Doctor."

"But you are awake," Dr. Dismas said merrily. "I know it! I can feel it! Speak to me, my darling child! It is time! Time!"

And Yama realized that all this time the apothecary had

been speaking as much to the thing growing inside him as to himself. And in that moment of realization pain struck through every cell in his body. The black and red fire of the pain washed away the world. Something stood in the fire. It was a vision of a fetus, curled up like a fish, all in gold. It slowly turned its heavy, blind head toward Yama, who thought he would go mad if its eyes opened and its gaze fell upon him. It spoke. Its voice was his own.

You will not serve? Ah, but that is against the nature of your bloodline. Your kind were created to serve the Preservers, to build this world. Well, the rest of your race are long gone, but you are here, and you will serve. You will serve me.

Another voice spoke from the world beyond the fire: deep. resonant and angry.

"What are you doing to him? Stop it, Dismas! Stop it at once! I command you!"

The pain receded. The vision dissolved. Yama's body, which had been arched like a bow, relaxed. His head fell to one side. And he saw, framed by a flickering haze of red and black, the mane and the ugly scarred face of the heretic warlord and traitor. Enobarbus.

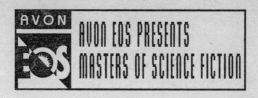